WITHIN THE WALLED CITY

A NOVEL

Virginia Evans

EASTLY
PRESS

ISBN-13: 978-0692435137
ISBN-10: 0692435131

For information contact
Eastly Press
P.O. Box 30663
Winston-Salem, North Carolina
27130

Cover design by Kristen Freeman and Kelly Whitener
Interior layout and e-book by Lisa Parnell, lparnell.com

Printed in the United States of America
Printed by CreateSpace, an Amazon.com Company
Available from Amazon.com, CreateSpace.com, and other retail outlets

22 21 20 19 18 17 16 15   1 2 3 4 5

To Mark,
for every moment of solitude you allowed
and every bit of belief you've always had,

AND TO KAILI,
because to me beloved Siena is you.

"Go not yet away from us.
A noontide have you been in our twilight,
and your youth has given us dreams to dream.
No stranger are you among us,
nor a guest, but our . . . dearly beloved.
Suffer not yet our eyes to hunger for your face."

Kahlil Gibran, *The Prophet*

Siena

It is dusty in August, hot and dry, and as you approach the city gates, the landscape turns to stone. These gates, palatial at one time, stand hunched now, crippled, diminished with the passage of time—unguarded arched entryways into the wide stronghold. The gates, the walls, the arches all tell the tale of a valiant past, a time of battles and royal lines. Now, like Stonehenge, they are a free-standing museum.

Crossing underneath one of these portals is stepping into a dream of a place that existed long ago. At once medieval, the view is stone on stone on sky—rich sky the color of the Mediterranean, often cloudless. Monotone gray streets wind inscrutably around corners, connecting to other avenues, all similarly bent and uneven. The muscles of the city are flayed, an appealing and mysterious maze. Structures, her bones, rise up from the narrow streets, one continuous system of housing, trattorias, markets, churches, hotels, panty shops, wine shops, cigar shops, boutiques, patisseries, tailor shops, butchers, pottery stores, gift shops and hundreds of small cafés.

It is quiet, deserted, until further in, at just the right time of the morning and again just after four, every door swings open simultaneously and the city dwellers bustle in and out like ants on a hill. Small cars move slowly through the streets to avoid the surge of pedestrians, their drivers often honking and shouting *Va!* through the window, pumping frustrated fists at the creeping traffic caused by heedless walkers.

At midday the breezeless city streets are hot, blockaded from sideways airflow, and the sun reflects bright off the stone from directly overhead. Women move from shop to shop, clucking to neighbors they have known since birth as they fill their baskets with bread, spinach, olives, and prosciutto for the day. School children play with balls and sticks around statues seven hundred years old, absorbing the final days of summer, unwatched, careless of the trajectories of their implements.

Roads and piazzas, the movement of the people, all angles and vistas converge in the center of the city as arteries and veins to the heart: the Piazza del Campo, Italy's finest square. Exquisite in its grandiose shell shape, the entire floor, an intricately laid pattern of russet bricks, slopes casually down and inward for a perfectly fashioned drainage system. Though it was built centuries ago, it still functions, collecting water when it rains, funneling it to cisterns below the city.

The outer rim of the shell is a semi-circle of multistory buildings, stores at the ground level, offices and apartments above. From the lowest point, like the stage of an amphitheater, the ancient edifices of government rise up above every other building as in a statement of power. Blackbirds coil and swoop like wisps of smoke, specks in the air at the top of the mighty Torre del Mangia—the three-hundred-foot guard of the city. The bricks of the Campo have endured incessant footfalls since they were first laid. It is never empty.

In the evening, nocturnal old men who have remained hidden during the day at work or leisure, come down to the streets near the center of town to socialize. Posses of caps and slacks stand on corners and against walls, speaking with gross, dramatic animation. They smoke pipes and cigarettes with protuberant bellies and eyes hidden behind creased skin, laughing and buzzing in low, quick tones. Oh, how they laugh with such an easy delight! It is hard to imagine they have ever seen sorrow, that they were ever anything other than deliriously content at the good fortune of having been born Italian. They mingle for a few hours, until maybe ten o'clock in the evening, then mosey away, bidding each other, *Ciao*, in a nonpartisan tone, *until we meet again, tomorrow.* They return home just before the younger generation is unearthed with fresh life for an evening out. They retire into apartments tucked in the folds above a street where Signora is busy cooking a dinner of at least four impeccable courses.

There is a placid appearance to Siena, as if she were only the set of a movie, a place for tourists to slip into the past. This façade masks a potent magnitude of pride, and the honor of generations underlies the rhythm of the Sienese in a way that evades the eyes of visitors. Seventeen *contrade* constitute the acreage of the city, marking Siena with invisible lines of unspeakable allegiance. Each citizen belongs to one: Tower, Caterpillar, Unicorn, Ram, Porcupine, Eagle, Snail, Little Owl, Dragon, Giraffe, Seashell, Goose, Wave, Panther, Forest, Tortoise or She Wolf. Colorful coats of arms are the insignias of each pocket sub-community, and one recognizes the street he treads by the flags that hang from sconces, windows and doors. These districts converge twice a year for the Palio, a furious horse race around the Campo without saddles, guard rails or guarantee that the rider won't fall to his death.

The single force capable of uniting the *contrade* is a collective, zealous hostility to the city of Firenze, situated to the north. Rivalry between the separated cities can be traced back to the thirteenth century when, during an era of almost constant warring, Siena lost a great deal of land in the hills lying between them. Firenze, to the Sienese, represents brutality, slavery and treachery. Although the battles were fought many years ago and are only now living in history books housed on untouched shelves in the stacks of college libraries, bad blood runs boiling through the veins of many of Siena's oldest natives.

There is a hazy distinction separating history from legend in the city. Piazzo Tolomei boasts a tall statue just off the main street, Banchi di Sopra, which runs from the main bus station and stadium all the way into the city center. Atop the pillar, a stone she wolf suckles two human babies, Romulus and Remus. The details of the figures have eroded over time, but the depiction is haunting. According to lore, the twin Romulus founded the city of Rome, but grew evil in his hunger for power and dominion. His brother, Remus, had a son named Senius who fled from his wicked uncle and established the city now known as Siena. Then there is Saint Catherine, the city's heroine and patron saint, who decorates the doors of many homes throughout the city, and the church of San Domenico boasts the tomb of her head and finger, relics believed to contain power.

Siena is a city set like a gem into a country that clings to tradition with a tight fist, refusing to be moved, refusing to be changed. In the shaded streets, behind thousands of closed doors and open windows, years upon years of life exist with an ardent, beating heart, carrying each day into the next. In Siena, history is king. And history, like the city herself, grows blurry with years, so it is difficult to distinguish what has come to pass with what collective memory has constructed from its own timeless longings.

1

Inside it was hot even though the window unit maintained an ongoing exhale to keep up with the demands in the hundred-year-old apartment with original ventilation. Jill moved around the room, her whole back soaked through with sweat, pieces of her hair stuck behind her ears like black leeches. She'd made the apartment in the DC suburb her own—the painting of dahlias over her desk, the memorial photograph of Teddy, his face smooshed down between his paws, gums sloppy against the wood floor, the rhododendron, the walls she had painted a sea foam green despite the lease she had signed forbidding her. It hadn't been easy turning the manila space into something livable.

The ten-day forecast called for temperatures in the hundreds straight through the week. She threw things haphazardly onto the bed beside the tremendous black duffel bag. Wiping her forehead, she stood back from the bed with her hands on her hips, admiring her pile. The phone rang.

"Hello," she said without looking at the number, lodging the phone between her chin and shoulder as she picked up a pair of jeans, rolling and wedging them into the side of the bag beside four other pairs of jeans, also rolled.

"It's me," Gary said.

"Hi, Dad." She glanced at the clock.

"Are you packing?"

"Yep." She paused, arching her dark caterpillar eyebrows, waiting.

"Listen," he said, "I won't make it over for dinner. I have a client meeting."

She nodded slowly, smirked. "Okay." She was watching herself talk in the mirror, observing the odd ways her face moved when she spoke, the way the tattoo below her collar bone moved slightly with certain words.

"Want me to order you something out?"

She rolled her eyes and leaned in closer to the mirror, traced the blurred lines of the lily she had designed. She still thought it was beautiful, even though it represented a darker time. She was a better artist now. "I can order my own dinner."

"What time is your flight tomorrow?"

"Hang on," she mumbled, reaching toward her dresser to pick up the plane ticket stuck between the pages of her passport. "Leaves at eleven."

"Why don't I pick you up at seven?" His voice had the bolstered quality he sometimes adopted when he stepped into fatherly roles, even now, when Jill was twenty-six years old, living on her own. She imagined him sitting at his desk, leaning back in his chair, away from pages of legal briefs he still insisted on printing, his narrow green eyes behind his glasses, squinting, the top button of his shirt undone now that office hours were over. He was nice looking for his age, fit, and his hair was still brown, but his face showed the permanent creases of deep exhaustion. "Should get you there by nine, but it will give us plenty of time to hit traffic and still make it."

"Sounds good," she said, picking up a pile of books and art journals from the desk. Behind them was the dated photograph of her mom, gathering dust. She ran her fingers over the glass, making parallel tracks, then wiped them across her chest. Her mother's expression always made her smile. She hadn't looked at the picture in a long time.

"Thanks—and good luck with the packing," he said.

Jill frowned.

"See you later." She hung up the phone, threw it back down on the stack of towels, and stared at it. It was the last time she would see him for months and he had found a way to be tied up. She turned on music—jazz with a bit of a techno beat. Removing her thick-rimmed black glasses, she rubbed her eyes. She pulled her hair back, twirled it into a low bun and fixed it against her head with a pen. Seated on the edge of the queen size bed she stared at the mess.

She had allowed herself to relax into him just a bit, when he'd asked to take her to dinner, to drive her to the airport, a rare instance of lowering her defenses. They typically saw each other once, maybe twice a month, even though they lived within ten miles and both her part time job and school were fairly close to his office in the city. But she was leaving! He didn't like her, she'd always known that, but in the past few months it had felt like he was trying to—she didn't know how to respond.

The last two times they'd met for dinner, conversation rested mainly on Jill's trip, and her job prospects after grad school. He'd also mentioned thoughts of taking a vacation together in January, but these discussions felt listless, neither one of them enthusiastic enough to commit. She'd noticed there were moments when it seemed he would start to say something, taking that small wisp of an inhale, but then he wouldn't. She wanted him to say it! Whatever it was he was trying not to say.

She recalled how in another time she would have pressed him, but she did not do that anymore—she had learned that lesson and accepted him to be a generally cold, stoic, one-dimensional person.

The confusing thing was that he had seemed to take an interest in her location choice for her final semester. Her options were Milan, Florence, Siena and Rome, and he had expressed an opinion—Siena!—from the beginning. There were only ten spots in that city, and she was unfamiliar with it, but he had nearly insisted. He helped her edit her essay, and even offered to write a letter to the dean of the university, whom he knew personally. Jill had refused the offer, but his participation in the process had been so unfamiliar—pleasant, but also suspicious, as if she were only waiting for the attached string to be pulled taut. It had been years since he'd displayed any kind of genuine interest—since she had stated her intent to earn a Master's in Art History instead of law or medicine, as if he could have been surprised. Looking into the cities, their histories, she had ultimately found herself drawn to Siena on its own merit. It was small, something off the traditional path of art study. In photos it looked cursed and exquisite all at once. She had never seen a piece of art from Siena. The other cities were home to icons depicted over and over on T-shirts, desktops in American offices, mugs, dorm room posters. Siena was under digested— there was plenty of room for Jill there.

Once she'd been placed there, it was back to normal. Her father's stiffness, which she had been accustomed to for years, felt fresh again, and even more confusing in the wake of that puff of interest he had taken in Jill's life. Was he pleased with her for going, or not? It was stupid of her to even crack that door of hope for him because now she was paying her dues.

She shook her head, as if thoughts were gnats that could be fended off, and ticked through items on her fingers, mumbling over her mental list—charcoals, several blank sketch books in different sizes, a few erasers. Most of her clothes. Her camera was already tucked in her book bag. Wishing she were a more organized person, that she would have thought to make a list with small boxes to check off, she stood up and surveyed. She spotted the program booklet tucked underneath her suit case and pulled it out. The aerial view of Siena's central piazza pictured on the front cover gave her a nervous, excited feeling. She was leaving for five months to live in Italy and study art, the very manifestation of her dream.

Her phone rang, drawing her back to the present. It was Zane.

"Hi," she said.

"Hi to you. Are you miserable? You sound miserable."

"No, sorry. I'm not miserable! I'm just hot and distracted and overwhelmed by this shit all over my apartment."

"Are you excited?"

"Obviously, yes," Jill said.

"So are you and Gary doing dinner earlier or later? I hope you say earlier so I can come over later."

"He isn't coming." She walked to the kitchen and opened a beer.

"What? Why?"

"He has work."

"You're kidding."

"Not kidding. So now I don't have dinner plans." She poured the beer into a glass, then ran the bottle under the water. When it was full, she turned off the faucet and poured the water into the dirt beds of each of the six succulents on the windowsill.

"I'll pick up something and come over in an hour or so. Any requests?"

"No, I don't care."

She had spent a year imagining Siena—its abundant art culture, the singularity and remoteness of the city, the bygone architecture, but most of all its ability to offer her an untethered self-sovereignty. Photographs had seduced her. It almost seemed haunted with its turrets and deep alleyways, and Jill was well acquainted with ghosts. Although the city was located right in the center of Tuscany, only miles from Florence, where she had vacationed with her father the summer before she turned fourteen, she had not heard of Siena before it was mentioned as an option for the semester away. She'd looked it up in travel books of Italy—the Palio, the picturesque hills of Tuscany, and the enchanting stone fortress had made her decision. A place offering sanctuary—from what? It wasn't as if she had a bad life, but she was tired, bored, oversaturated. Longing for something new. In Siena she could be whomever she deemed, would answer to nobody but herself. People there didn't know her, and that prospect felt like the empty space she needed to crack open her own head like a coconut and survey the insides. She'd felt claustrophobic, she had come to realize, for a long time, and the notion of five months alone was a freedom. She intended to capitalize on that freedom.

She remembered little from the previous trip to Italy—it was a vague storyboard of stifling heat and starvation as she was forced to eat dinner after ten o'clock each night. They had taken so many trips, visited nearly every big city in western Europe and certainly every cathedral, and vacationing with her dad was a little like being tied to the back of a horse and dragged around a paddock. If there was a museum, he wanted to see it. A guided tour was better. He traveled as an educational hobby. Jill had always preferred to wander—she loved to people watch and meander in and out of shops and streets without a guide, images from travel banked to be translated to pages with blurred edges, dusty lines, jet black pupils and ravens and jaw lines. She still preferred that, but in the past few years she had developed an appreciation of the museums and tours because the guides knew information she now found intriguing. Recalling her attitudes on their European vacations filled her with regret now. All of the work she had missed because she was too young to understand.

Jill pinned back loose wisps of hair, regretting her failure to schedule a haircut. She wiped the mascara from underneath her green eyes and practiced her picture smile. As a child she had been gangly, but now her five feet and eight inches seemed elegant, especially with sketching, where long, slender limbs were the ideal subject. Gary had the height. Everyone said she had parts of Lily's face, though she scrutinized photographs and tried to pull up images from memories but couldn't see it. It was too long ago.

Her thoughts returned to Lily, as they sometimes did at times when she innately felt the maternal absence. The emotions usually took her by surprise, like a dried out, washed up fish suddenly leaping up from the sand. It ought to be dead, you lean down to look at the marble eye, and jump back because the life is still there. She glanced down again at the framed picture her dad had taken with the long lens. Photography, pleasure in that type of creativity, was one of the only things she and her father had in common.

A thin sheet of ice coats the metal bar, my hands hold on tight. It's windy on the edge of the mountain, and the chair rocks front to back, making squeaking sounds against the cable. The tree limbs are covered with thick snow and ice, but they move a little, side to side. The icicles look like sparkly diamond earrings. I could paint them with glitter. I'm dressed for it to be very cold, my knees look like purple marshmallows, on my hands are the pink mittens with red hearts at the knuckles. My legs feel so heavy, and I'm scared if I move at all I'll slide right off the seat. But then maybe the tall snow piles below us will catch me, like the down comforter that sits in a big heap at the foot of Mama's bed when the sheets are being washed. Thinking of that makes me feel warm, and safer.

When we get to the top, don't forget you just stand up and lean forward.

What if I fall down?

They'll stop the lift. And it's your first try! She's smiling at me and she doesn't seem scared at all. She told me the first time she went skiing she was four years old! I am seven, and the only thing I remember from being four was my horse birthday party. Her hair is down around her face, held back with a blue ear warmer. She looks like one of the people in the brochure that has been stuck to the refrigerator for the past few months.

Just do what you practiced. Are you cold?

I shake my head, even though my face is. From in front of us, Dad turns around. He hangs his arms over the back of the chair and shouts, *Say cheese!*

Mom grabs me like she's afraid I'll disappear and blows into my ear. I am laughing and wriggling, and I forget to be nervous.

Don't fall, she whispers, *only birds can fly.*

The memory of that trip stood out as colorful and sharp where most others were only a foggy gray. Did the photograph serve as a signpost of the memory, or was it simply the only thread left between her present self and the self that had known her mom, held her hand, felt the soft skin on her cheek, heard the gravel in her voice? Jill's memories were anecdotes written in pencil, fading with time. Now she found herself straining to lock onto her mother's eyes, or the shape of her hands.

In the past she'd circled her father like a vulture, swooping down to grab any small mention of Lily, as if they were bits of rotting carcass on a charred desert. Early on after Lily's death, out of longing, Jill would resurrect her mother from the earth daily in conversation with him. Bringing up memories, asking questions, a younger Jill would probe desperately, building her understanding of her mother in snippets. However, as she grew and asked more, her father began to retreat, and she had listened to the slowly closing door creak shut and eventually found herself cast out, standing on the outside observing the fortress. She used to wonder what it was, the reason for his silence, for he often met her questions with anger and aggravation. If she was going to learn anything, it would have to be on her own. In college she'd tried with greater subtlety, but eventually grew weary of it, and then in one single day she had sealed herself closed. Now Lily had been dead for seventeen years, eight years longer than Jill had actually known her, and she had ostensibly let it go.

◼

The light pouring in from the small window reflects the floating dust. Stale air with the fading odor of mothballs feels poisonous. It's cold in the attic with the wind pushing through thin fissures in the outer wall. The floor beams are separated by pink insulation, so I balance, stretching my arm up, anchoring my hand on the sloped ceiling to root around in the mess. I've sorted through several cardboard boxes before finding the one containing the albums. Which album holds the photograph I'm remembering?—the profile of Mom, her blonde hair pulled back in a bun, her green eyes concentrated down on a painting, which is only barely visible in the corner of the frame. The professor suggested a close-up with at least half of the facial features visible and this one came to mind immediately. I didn't even bother asking Dad to find it.

The oldest album holds the photographs of Mom when she was younger, before I was born. I turn the pages back slowly to absorb the images I haven't seen for a few years, but which feel agonizingly familiar. There's a picture of us sitting outside Amigos Cantina, where Dad and I went just last night. It was pleasant between us, even warm. I think I've always attributed my loneliness to the quietness of his presence, but living away for the first time I think it may be the opposite. I miss his quiet reading of the newspaper in the morning, the Thai carry-out in front of Monday night football ritual, the way he mumbles when he's making eggs.

The photograph is in the second album, from when I was a toddler, and I slip it from the sleeve. When I go to tuck the box back in the corner I see a larger box, wide and tall, but thin, propped against the wall. It's like it's whispering to me. I open it and audibly gasp.

There are paintings. A few dozen soft canvases stacked like blankets, painted with thick, colorful boldness in ethereal images of faces, water, loaves of bread, snow, and Mom's name scrawled in the bottom corner of every one. I pull them out one by one, lay them over an old dresser, run my palm over the set paint, feeling its density in places where it has globbed like candy buttons, and where it thins out. For cold water she used golds, of all things, and it's brilliant. Her strokes are unexpected, and up close the paintings don't seem like they'll work, but standing back they do. Some canvases are better than others. Where did she get these images? I am stunned and full of pride. I knew she was a painter—she had taught adult classes a few evenings a week before she got cancer—but this trove is astounding. Here we've been living destitute on top of a gold mine. Her style is not like mine at all—much more colorful, blurred lines, more impressionistic, but the paintings are stunning. Refined. They possess the kind of dignity I've been working toward.

The door to the study is open and Dad's sitting at his desk, leaning back in his leather chair with his foot crossed over his knee, reading a book with a pen in one hand and a vodka tonic in the other. His office is dark, wood paneling for walls, and there is a large fire roaring in the fireplace. I've dragged the entire box down.

I found Mom's paintings. I didn't realize I was angry until this moment.

He looks up without moving, his linear gaze cast over the top of his glasses.

Why are they in the attic? We should hang them. But hanging them isn't really what I want, is it? I want to ingest them, to find a way to get them into me, make them a part of me.

He places the pen in the center of the book and closes it. *You need to put those back where you found them.* He speaks as if to a child ignorant of some propriety.

No. I'm offended now, on top of confused. *I want to keep them out. They're beautiful. Have you even looked at them?*

Of course I have. His voice is staccato and lower than normal, an indication of rising frustration.

Well it's crazy you're hiding them in the attic! I open the box and pull out the top canvas, aware I'm being dramatic. It's an image of a bridge over a creek, the whole scene blanketed with thick snow. The water in the creek splashes up over rocks as it rushes by. In this light I can see the way the paint captures the water's movement, the way it sprays up at certain places. There are a few trees, some with limbs fractured under the weight of the heavy snow. I look at Dad and he's not looking at the painting. He's looking at me. I finally have his attention. I place the image carefully on the floor and pull out another, a young woman's profile who I think looks like Mom, but I'm not sure.

Stop, Jill.

What? Another. There is an emotion flooding my head, clouding my barometer for sanity, and the emotion is anger. He has been keeping this from me, this chord that so obviously connects me to her. I've beat down the door looking for tiny clues and scraps to hold onto, to help me remember, to know anything at all about her, when all along this fantastic answer has been tucked away right above us! He's cruel.

He removes his glasses and runs his hands through his hair. *You don't understand.* I detect sadness, exhaustion in his voice, but it's eclipsed by my own, and this adrenaline.

You're right! I don't understand a fucking thing about anything because you don't ever tell me! You know it sucks not having a mom. I'm sure it sucks not having a wife, but that's your choice. You're cold and stuffy and miserable to be with! He physically recoils, as if the words were darts, and I'm momentarily disarmed. But then his face sets, and in his transient stillness I find fuel for this fire. *But it's not my choice to not have a mom and I have begged you to talk to me and tell me about her. To keep her alive—*

He rises from his seat, but his voice stays low. He seems huge, and the muscles in his forearms are sinewy and taut as he grips the edge of his desk. *Don't think for a second you can talk to me this way. I don't tell you things for your own good. It's better that you not know every detail. You're not the only one who lost Lily, Jillian.*

The fury in his face is frightening, something I've never seen in twenty-one years, but my starvation for any dialogue at all, any display of feeling, is somehow energizing. I stare directly into his shining eyes and shove the canvas across his desk, knocking his book to the floor. The next painting is of a house. Then a landscape. Another landscape. Snow again, heaping them onto the desk. And then, a portrait of a woman. Again, I think it could be Mom but it's all happening too quickly. His face, which has become unreadable so I can't fathom what he's thinking, winces. As if I've taken a knife to his cheek.

Stop, Jillian. Quietly. And then he shouts it again when I don't reply. The temperature in the study has changed. I freeze, sensing at once that he will do anything to stop me. My body is so tense I can feel his pulse through the air between us. I can hear his heartbeat, or maybe it's mine. We are teetering on the brink of a world into which we have never crossed, pulling at each other like a tug-of-war match. It is silent in the room but for the popping logs. I think he wants to hurt me. He won't.

I can't do this. I cannot. As these words come from him, from his choked throat in this split-second transition to sadness, I'm remorseful because he looks like a wounded animal. But then.

In a fluid movement he sweeps his arms down around the pile of art and gathers the paintings in a mass toward his chest in a gesture that seems loving, protective, and violent all at once, and heaves them into the large brick fireplace.

I'm stunned. I stand motionless, feeling my stomach turn over and over—I might actually vomit. The moment of hesitation condemns the canvases to the flames, fueled by the paint, leaping up around the images, causing the colors to run and blend, the face of the woman to morph into a grotesque puddle.

We don't look at each other, but as her paintings burn I begin to cry silently. Later I wonder if he, too, was crying. Silently I close the box, still containing a few paintings secure its locks, and leave the study hating him.

After she'd stayed angry for a commendable length of time, exhausting herself with an emotion requiring such active energy, she eventually ran out of resolve, and anger turned to dismissal. They began to coexist, with Gary occupying the outskirts of Jill's world, but he'd lost his last foothold—her trust. There was a period late in college, during the aftermath of her relationship with Aaron, when Jill had been forced to be more honest with him about details of her life, but once that was taken care of the lines went quiet again. As the distance between the day the paintings burned, a watershed, and present grew, her perspective had changed in some aspects. She'd grown up, and began to have empathy. She understood later, perhaps she'd even understood then, her raw insistence had been punishing, and she had apologized years after. But it was the moment of maximum capacity for the pressure cooker—the explosive burst before the slow release of air. After the burning, the energy she'd always felt in holding onto Lily had deflated slowly.

Now their interactions were cordial. She politely accepted his invitations to dinner once or twice a month, mostly because he was paying for her to be in school. They exchanged pleasantries, kept conversations focused on innocuous subjects and danced around the wafting ghost hovering overhead, ducking so as not to brush up against it, and pretended to be fine. There existed now between Jill and Gary a great ocean of unintelligible anguish and unfamiliarity. She'd always sensed something, some reason for his coldness, why he remained fortified behind the bolted door, but she had written it off and moved on.

Jill looked at the painting that hung over her bed, one she had not pulled out of the box that day, one of the only ones not to have been lost. A wide blue door with a rusted handle set in a wall of large, gray stones. The paint peeling from the door in a few places, sunlight reflecting from the small square window in the top. She loved this painting because the colors were soothing and the door seemed large, even though the canvas was only one foot by two. She also found it alive in a way. When she wasn't rushing, when she took even a moment to look at it, she found herself imagining the wider angle. Where was the door? What was behind it? There was nothing particularly interesting about it, and yet it breathed in her presence.

2

The doorbell buzzed as Jill fought to zip her suitcase, and she gave one final tug. Without any real confidence in its finalized contents, she dragged the mammoth to the kitchen.

"I'm coming!" she yelled when the doorbell chimed again.

"Hey there," Zane said, and kissed her as he stepped inside. He was still in his suit, his tie in position. He placed a brown paper bag and a bottle of wine on the counter. "I got sushi."

"Thanks." She'd been hoping for a cheeseburger or fried chicken, something quintessentially American. Zane loved to eat sushi. It always left Jill feeling vaguely hungry.

"Well, I don't know about you, but I'm glad Gary canceled. I get a little more time before you're gone for the rest of my life." He winked.

"It's five months." She began pulling small foam boxes from the bag and Zane opened the drawer beside the sink for the corkscrew. Jill marveled at the fact that he could still look completely put together at eight o'clock when he had been at the office since before seven in the morning. He still smelled like his aftershave. Had he re-applied it?

"You feeling good about your packing? Did you remember your toothbrush?"

She smiled. "Yes."

Zane poured two glasses of wine, and Jill carried the sushi to the coffee table and sat down on the red sofa. Her body relaxed and she sighed.

"How was work?"

"Fine. You know this client I've been talking about, the guy that wants to sell his property in Santa Barbara and buy into that startup—"

She nodded, taking a sip of wine.

"Anyway, he was in the office today. This meeting went on for way too long…"

She kept nodding, taking sips of wine, bites of sushi, keeping her gaze locked on his face as he spoke. She was practiced in the art of half-engagement, eyes on his, tuning back in once in a while for details. He could talk forever. When she realized she was doing it, she felt guilty. She wondered if the meeting went long because of the client or because of Zane. She considered him. Six years older. Or was it seven? He had a handsome face, she thought objectively. Sharp features, an angular jawline, perfect teeth. He was a bit skinny—she sometimes caught herself comparing his width to her own. The hair gel she'd grown used to. She'd never liked it when men used product in their hair to form that weak helmet, but it suited him. The first time they'd met, when he had asked her to dinner, he'd been wearing a baseball cap. He'd given the impression of being a very casual person, a little more frat-boy-grown-up than the guys she was usually drawn to, the kind of guy that goes to Tuesday night ball games and drinks cheap beer. Turns out he was there in a box, on the clock, schmoozing a potential client, and he'd purchased the hat at the merchandise stand just inside the entrance to the park. That was really the sort of guy he was, a composite of harmless egotism and a puppy-like desire for affirmation. But he made her laugh. He appreciated good art, and her art. They had a good time together. When he wasn't thinking about his work angles, he could be funny, content to be a little lazy. He was smart, steady as a barge.

"I'm sorry I can't drive you to the airport tomorrow," he said.

"It's really okay," Jill said. She refilled her glass. His was almost full. "I guess I probably need to talk to my dad before I leave. That'll give us a couple of hours."

"What am I going to do with you gone this long?"

"I don't know, see other women?" she smirked. He frowned. "I'm kidding. It'll probably make your life easier—you won't have to feel bad about working late, nobody to get back for. You can spend some time with your sisters, all your nieces and nephews." They had been recycling this conversation for months.

He groaned, leaned back against the sofa.

"Here," she said, and leaned forward to loosen his tie. "You're all wound up."

He leaned in and kissed her. "I'll miss you."

"You can come visit any time."

"I know, I just…" He sat back again, the moment drifting away. "I don't know when I can get away for that many days."

"I know, it's alright," she said. These conversations made Jill weary, as if they were fifteen years older, already in some interminable grind of life.

"You know if it works out, I'll book a flight that day."

They finished the sushi while Zane told her about two new temps they had hired, detailing his frustration and impatience. Jill found her mind wandering as he spoke, and chastised herself to pay attention.

"I hate to say this, babe, but I really need to finish packing." It was after ten and her eyes felt heavy. She had been yawning for an hour.

"I can stay over—I can help you."

She sat upright. "You're not going back in?"

"Well, I could. I have work to do," he said in a defensive tone.

"Always," she said, smiling complacently. "You should go then. I really need a good night's sleep, and I need to look back over everything."

"Okay, if you're sure." He was torn between disappointment and relief, and his effort to mask it was ineffective. "But I got you something." He reached into the breast pocket of his blazer, which was hung over the back of the kitchen chair, and removed a small box. Jill's stomach flipped over painfully, as if tackled to the ground and pinned there.

"You look concerned," he said. She smoothed her expression obediently.

"No, I'm just surprised—you didn't have to get me something."

Her heartbeat was in her throat; she was having a hard time breathing steadily, taking hold of every aspect of her being to maintain a posture of calm. He handed it to her.

"Should I open it?"

He laughed. "Yes."

The box was small and black. She removed the lid, turned it over and a velvet jewelry box fell into her hand. She looked at Zane again, and he smiled. She flipped back the lid.

Positioned in the box was a gold locket. The rush of adrenaline passed over her like a roll of thunder, and the muscles in her shoulders, neck, and chest grew limp. The locket was lovely—antiquated with some age spots on the edges. It was an elongated oval, about an inch and a half, and etched with flowers and vines on the front and back. The chain looked newer. It was stunning, something she would have chosen for herself.

She looked up at him and smiled. "Thank you, it's gorgeous."

"Open it."

Jill pressed the toggle on the right side of the locket and the door popped easily open to reveal two small photographs. Jill drew it up to her eyes. A very clear, miniscule black and white of her mom stared back at her on one side. On the other side was a photograph of Zane.

"Oh my gosh, where did you get this?"

"Your dad. I asked him for a picture of your mom."

"And he just handed it over?"

"He loves me, are you kidding?" His expression was playful and smug.

"I love it," she said, even though his presence in this fold of her life felt somewhat intrusive and their photographs side by side seemed anomalous.

"I can tell that wasn't what you were expecting to find in the box," Zane said.

She could feel a shade of color rising in her neck and face.

"I wasn't expecting anything."

"Jill." Engagement was something they had discussed around the edges, in the manner two people might discuss their projected tax return. They had been together for almost two years; she would graduate in a matter of months; he would make partner in the firm any day. It was the next step. However, the couple of times it had come up, she had been surprised by the anxiety that filled her. She knew she loved him. He leaned down and kissed her, reading her contained combustion as disappointment.

"I'm going to miss you," she said, because she couldn't think of anything else.

"I know. Call me when you get there."

"I won't have a cell yet—I get it in Siena. I'll e-mail though." She walked with him toward the door, yawning fully.

"I love you, Jill. Be careful."

Her face was buried in his chest as he hugged her, and she mumbled a reply. He left, and she closed the door behind him. She stood on tiptoe to watch him go and saw his back turn down the stairwell, his face illuminated by the glow of his phone.

Opening the locket, she held it up to her face. A photo she'd never seen, crumbs for a beggar. She turned on the hall lamp to see the photograph more clearly. Her mother, with her light hair, clear eyes, hanging from her neck like a saint was an odd comfort. She felt relaxed in the silence of the apartment, the wine having paved over her nerves.

She spent an additional hour repacking her things after Zane had left, going over a list she had decided to pen and debating over certain items of clothing and quantities of things like shampoo and razor blades. Her favorite T-shirt, worn so thin it was see-through at the edges, lay crumpled on her pillow, the two-tone sketch of Earth with small white print underneath faded on its front. *The Planet*, her ex-boyfriend's band that had become famous in the past few years since she'd last seen him, was a mix of grungy techno and jazz. Some of their sound was sort of painful, but she liked it because it was different and she had seen the genesis of many of the songs.

Usually she wore the shirt without giving Aaron a second thought, but sometimes her mind wandered back to that strange time. Memories of that period felt like a movie reel of another person's life. The disparity between Aaron and Zane was so stark it made her laugh. She rolled the shirt and tucked it into the bag. She considered a few novels, but ultimately decided their weight was too great a burden and left them on her nightstand. After eleven, when Jill was finally confident she had everything, her phone rang and she jumped.

"Hello?"

"Hey there, are you all packed?" Gary said.

"Just about. Late dinner, huh?" she said, doing the dance, flattening her voice.

"Yeah, I had a client meeting," he said. "Sorry about that."

"No problem. Zane brought dinner over."

"Oh good—well that was probably better." She didn't reply. After a moment, he continued. "Alright. Well, you should probably get some sleep. I'll be by around seven tomorrow."

"Sounds good."

"See you in the morning," he said, and hung up.

3

The galling beep of the alarm clock startled her immediately from sleep, and Jill rolled over in the dark to silence it. Laying her head back down on the pillow, she closed her eyes again, then quickly opened them, remembering herself. There was a strand of light around the frame of the door and the sound of water running thickly through the pipes.

Disgusted to find that her sheets were soaked in sweat, along with her black tank top and boxer shorts, Jill got up and stripped the bed, threw the sheets in the laundry, then took a shower. She considered the previous night as she got ready. Gary's dinner cancelation. The jewelry that wasn't a ring.

Fully dressed, Jill surveyed her outfit. Red flats and earrings that dangled close to her shoulders were accents that wouldn't bother her during a long day of flying. She lobbed her heavy leather book bag onto the edge of the mattress and unzipped it to check again that she wasn't forgetting any essentials. Another look around the apartment and at the last minute, as if prompted by some spirit, she grabbed the ski lift photo and tucked it in her bag, locked the door and headed downstairs.

In the car, after they had stopped for coffee, Jill spoke.

"Ask me if I have things."

"What?" he said.

"Specifics, like 'Did you remember your passport?'"

"Did you?"

"Yes, obviously."

"Okay, wallet?"

"Yes."

"Rain jacket?"

"Yes."

"Computer?"

"Mhmm."

"Computer power cord?"

She hesitated. "Yes."

"Sure?"

"Yes," she replied, recalling placing the cord in the outside pocket of her luggage.

"Art pencils?"

She laughed. "Charcoals?"

"Yeah, whatever."

"Yes, I have my art supplies."

"Pepper spray?"

"Dad," she said, rolling her eyes.

"You should take it with you," he smirked.

"I don't own pepper spray."

"Well you should. I've failed as a father."

Jill sipped on her Americano and pulled apart a warm blueberry scone. She was surprised to pinpoint she felt a bit angry at him. They hadn't had dinner together more than five times the entire summer, but she now realized she had allowed herself to nurture an expectation of something like togetherness before she left the country. That instinctive longing for family, as her counselor referred to it, had sprouted like a weed again, baby green sprigs underfoot before she'd even realized it.

When she was a child, they would eat dinner at the table every evening. Lily spent whole afternoons banging around the kitchen, and when Gary arrived home from work they would sit down and dim the lights, light a candle, turn on music. Those memories were stark to Jill, though those dinners had dissipated as Lily made more frequent trips to the hospital with the genesis of the chemotherapy treatments. They'd begun eating at the island in the kitchen or in front of the evening news.

National Public Radio reported on the attempts of American oil companies to stem the overflow of a well in the Gulf of Mexico. He had always listened to NPR. She did too. They hummed the musical interlude at breaks in the program. Often they discussed politics, world news, the economy. But not today. Her father drank his coffee quietly. Twenty minutes after merging onto the highway, Jill placed her cup in the console.

"Shit."

"What?" he said, glancing at her.

"I forgot my iPod." She closed her eyes, suddenly anticipating the plane ride with considerably more dread.

"I can mail it to you. They'll have headphones for you to buy. I'm going to give you cash."

"Dad—"

"Jill, don't be contrary. I'm paying for the whole trip anyway. Whatever I don't give you now, I'm sure I'll transfer to you later." She did not reply. She disdained it, desiring an autonomy she could not yet fund. As soon as she had her degree and a job, she would no longer accept his handouts.

Her father was, if not many other desirable things, wealthy. He was also self-made and had a proclaimed intention of shielding Jill from that gut-wrenching work of climbing the economic ladder. Coastal South Carolina fishing piers where he grew up helping his father mend nets and clean the underbellies of boats had fueled him to rise up, live a different life. He'd done it, working about a hundred hours a week, coming home only to work more. He had put himself through law school working nights stocking vending machines around Boston, and was a non-litigating name partner of a small, prestigious Washington firm with mugs, commercials on morning television, their frosted logo on their large glass doors. He handled cases for banks along the Eastern seaboard and, at the age of fifty, could retire and live a very cushy existence for another fifty years at least.

Gary's life was comfortable but not ostentatious. He still owned the three-story Victorian home on a street lined with enormous, lovely oaks, where he lived alone. The black Aston Martin with sand-colored leather interior was her father's one extravagance, his unspoken swagger. He nursed an affection for fancy cars, and she had inherited this love. Her four-year-old red Audi, a graduation gift, looked out of place in the lot behind her apartment building. She'd left it in his garage for the semester.

They spoke little during the drive, a sporadic course of conversation punctuated by long periods of silence when they listened to news reports. Jill kept her gaze out the window, mostly occupied by her own thoughts. She felt the urge to dissect her anxiety, but couldn't find the avenue and Gary didn't ask. She looked at her fingernails painted a dark maroon and second-guessed the color. At the airport the departures curb was crowded with cars a few rows deep. Gary squeezed his enviable car into a short opening, put the car in park, and got out to unload Jill's bag. She stepped out into the loud, hollow echoing of slamming doors, yelling, and honking. She stretched, unloaded her book bag, double-checked for the presence of her passport in the front pocket. She stood on the curb as he closed the trunk and stepped up beside her. There was something in his hand.

"Alright, Jilly. Be careful," he said, trying to speak over the din.

"I will." The use of her nickname softened her a little. "You too. Oh—you know what I forgot? To stop my mail. Can you do that for me? And maybe run by the apartment every once in a while to check on it?"

He nodded.

"Don't forget to do things like eat and get your house cleaner to come." She smirked.

"You know I've lived without you for eight years. Besides, missing a few meals is good for my waistline," he replied, patting his stomach. Jill rolled her eyes. He ran six miles every day before sunrise.

"Right. Well—" She looked down at her feet.

"I have something for you to take," he said, handing her the parcel she had noticed in his hand. On top, a small bank envelope was folded in half. "Cash."

"Thanks. What is this?" she asked, sticking the cash in her back pocket and surveying the small, flat object wrapped in brown paper.

Gary stammered, at a rare loss for words. "I—Jillian, I didn't tell you something. I couldn't decide and—well . . . This is your mom's journal."

"Oh—wow. Cool, where did you—I mean, thanks." She shook her head, pulling away the paper hastily. It was simple, a dark brown leather cover. There were overlapping circular watermarks on the back. A thin cord wrapped its way around the book twice, and the edges of the pages were slightly warped and folded. She looked up at him and the expression on his face, uncharacteristically human, softened her.

"It should belong to you. I didn't know when to give it to you, but . . . " His voice trailed off and he gestured with his hand toward the sidewalk, as if explanation could be found in the oil-stained cement.

She stared at him, baffled. His manner was strained and choked, so unlike his normal disposition that she felt uncomfortable. They didn't know how to do this sort of thing anymore, how to come together, how to deal with Lily—who she was, who she had been.

"Jill—" he said. It was as if the words he anticipated uttering gave him pain. "Your mom was in Siena when she wrote that journal."

It took a moment for the words to coalesce and make sense. They swirled into her brain and fused into meaning, taking on impossible significance. His neck grew red above his collar.

Her mouth opened stupidly. "What?"

"She studied art there. Like you. That's why I, sort of, encouraged you to go there."

Turning the journal over in her hands, Jill stared at the artifact with a singular voracity. She couldn't weigh what was more shocking—this extraordinary alignment of history and present, or the fact that he seemed to recognize this deep need she sheltered and respond to it, that he had orchestrated this. "Why didn't you tell me before now?"

He paused, looking toward the approaching security guard who was demanding people move along from the curb. "I don't know. I hope that this—" he said hoarsely, motioning to the journal, "makes up for everything I haven't said." His manner was unusually servile, but he suddenly stepped forward, almost in a lunge, and gripped her with an unexpected fervor, as if this was his last chance, as if his hesitation might negate any opportunity he might ever have again, as if he was losing her and he knew it. He pressed her head against his chest and held his hand to the back of her hair, placing a kiss on the top of her head. She let him, but her eyes were open and blank. It was the strangest feeling. She watched the cars move in and out of the spaces along the curb. "I do love you. Let me know when you land in Switzerland." He stepped back a few steps.

"Alright."

She watched him round the front of the car, sit down in the low seat, check his mirrors, drive away. For a few moments she stood planted to the concrete. The parking guard approached her.

"Ma'am, do you need some help? Do you know where you're going?" He looked at her with concern.

"No. Yes. I know where I'm going—sorry," she replied, turning toward the sliding glass door, unable to grasp the magnitude of the thing she now held in her hands. The walk from the curb to the airline counter felt like a solo underwater swim in a pool while a party commences on the deck above. She paused for a moment and swung the book bag forward onto her hip, opened it, and tucked the journal inside.

4

When I lift my toes and stick out my legs I still can't touch the seat in front of me. I try to reach, arching my back.

Jillian please, he says through an exhale. I stop, roll my eyes and look out the window. I am tired of being quiet and sitting still. It is dark under us, but if I look up it seems like there is an orangey light in the sky; maybe if I was drawing it I would use the Atomic Tangerine crayon. I start thinking about which crayons would work for all the colors in the plane. My seat is beside a door that says EXIT in big red letters. Scarlet or Radical Red. There is a handle and I wonder if I pull it, will the door just open? It seems too easy, like I could just yank it open, unbuckle my seatbelt—Wild Blue Yonder or Manatee—and jump out. Thinking of this makes me feel nervously sick in my stomach.

Mama, can I have my art bag please?

She nods and opens her eyes. She strains when she lifts her head off the seat. When she leans forward to get the bag from below the seat in front of her, the light from the ceiling reflects off her bald head, which shines like it's wet. It's hard to remember what her hair looked like. I think it was sort of brown and blonde, Goldenrod and Raw Sienna.

Suddenly mama is shaking, bouncing forward. I grab the big hand next to mine. *Daddy!*

He jumps like he's been electrocuted, grabbing a bucket from under the seat. She is throwing up, but it isn't loud and not very much comes out. He rubs her back and holds the bucket. When she is all finished, he takes it to the front of the plane and mama rests her head back again, her eyes shut. She hands me my art bag, which is Vivid Violet.

Thank you.

You're welcome, baby. She is smiling, but her lips cover her teeth. Her face is pale like yogurt. White.

The sky is lighter when I wake up. My neck hurts.

Are we almost there?

Yes, almost. He's looking at a magazine that's in front of every seat on the plane. Her head is resting on his shoulder. She looks better now.

Are you sick, Mama? I know she is, but I mean for now.

No, I'm okay now.

I pull my matching magazine onto my lap, and start at the end. There is a picture of a beautiful city. It looks like a castle, and there's a horse race in the center and billions of people watching. I would love to live in a castle.

Can we go here? I put the magazine across Dad's lap so she can see.

Her face twists up in a frown. She looks off balance or something.

No. Her stern voices makes Dad look up at the picture, but he looks away. It feels like he disappeared even though he's there, and everything is bad.

■

The personal screen eighteen inches in front of Jill's face jumped in and out of focus and only the left ear bud in her new set played sound, allowing her to hear the movie's conversation but none of the sound effects when the cars raced or exploded. She turned it off after twenty minutes and retrieved her book, *Michelangelo and the Pope's Ceiling.* She smoothed her fingers over the illustration on the soft, grainy cover. Instead of opening it she laid her head back and stared at the balding crown of a head in front of her and thought about the other book wedged in her bag.

After a day of layovers in two airports, an absurd path up and down the east coast, she had boarded the transatlantic flight out of New York in the evening. The woman to her left against the window, in the seat she had been assigned but which she had found occupied upon arrival, had been asleep since before Jill even boarded. To her right was a man who looked to be in his forties, dark hair, a chiseled face with a five o'clock shadow, dressed in a black business suit and loafers. He had glanced at her as he took his seat, and now tapped away at a glowing laptop. Her arms were pressed inside the armrests.

With the help of dozens of hours of therapy over the past five years, Jill had finally built a peaceful memorial to her mother within herself based on the information to which she was privy, her memories and some bits of intel her father had reluctantly shared. But now, suddenly, new information, a first-person narrative. Was it Fate orchestrating this divine collision? Her father? Some heavenly power? Her perception of Siena had shifted in the moment she had been handed the journal—her excitement at escaping for a few months to focus on art, mingled with nerves had been replaced by a different sort of fascination, a thirst for scraps to bolster, even reconstruct, Lily's history again. She was transforming back into the bloodhound, and she could feel the hair rising off her spine.

Lily had lived in Siena. In a way, that meant she was there now, pulsing through the city like the very lifeblood in Jill's veins. The fact that Gary had prompted her to choose Siena made practical sense, but he'd spent years holding a dark hood over her head and now, at once, pulled it away. She couldn't understand why. She couldn't understand him at all.

She had yet to open the journal, and its ignited presence had been the source of a palpable tension in her body for the whole day. There had been hours in the various airports when she could have begun to read, but she hadn't. Several times Jill had pulled it out and turned it over and over in her hands but the leather cord wound tight around it protected her—protected the words from her intrusive exploration. She had been stunned as Gary had pulled away from the curb that morning and thought she would open it as soon as she made it through security and read the entire thing in a day, but she'd felt bashful when she gazed at the book. She recalled her own journals—juvenile, self-aggrandizing, pointless—but also full of sentences and paragraphs she hoped no other living person would ever read, let alone her children. There were movies and histories made up of the embarrassing confessions of people who kept written records of their lives—seemingly lovely, harmless people turned out to be heinous, perverted, riddled with secrets. It felt like trespassing. The last time she'd kept one was during the time she and Aaron had been together. A person's journal was something meant to be hidden.

"Where are you headed?" the man beside her said, closing his laptop. He removed his reading glasses to look at her. His smile was charming. The watch on his tanned wrist looked expensive.

"To Italy," Jill said, facing him slightly. She sized him up quickly. It was a long flight to be seated next to a loner looking for small talk. "I'm completing my master's in Siena."

"What is your degree?"

"Art history."

He nodded, took a sip of his drink. Not jumping the gun on her.

"What about you?"

"Zurich, for business," he said. "I went to university in Florence and visited Siena. I've lived in New York since then. My best memory of Siena is the Palio. A horse race—are you familiar?"

She nodded. "Are you from Italy?" She had detected the hint of an accent, and then there was the way he said *I went to university.*

He laughed, shaking his head. The flight attendant came to their row with the drink cart. Jill ordered a Malbec, the business-man, a vodka tonic.

"Cheers," she said, smiling, raising her plastic cup. Was she flirting with him? She thought for a moment of Zane, the heavy locket hanging around her neck.

"I'm from Albania," he said when the cart had passed. He looked at Jill and she offered an apologetic expression. "Many people don't know where it is, even smart women earning master's degrees." There was a levity in his manner, and he focused on her intently. She was enjoying this. "The country is very small, borders Italy."

"Oh, okay. I'm sorry, I'm not great on geography," which was only partially true. He appeared clean and sophisticated, and she felt foolish. She loathed the way many Americans settled for ignorance when it came to the rest of the world and had always tried to do the opposite.

"The climate, terrain, people look very much like their Italian equal," he said, gesturing with his drink, "but an Italian would be none too pleased to think he was confused for an Albanian, or vice versa."

"I don't know if I get what you're saying."

"Oh, it's something in the way of Canada or Mexico's relationship to the US, the way the people view one another. Do you see what I mean?"

She nodded, and looked forward again, bereft of an appropriate reply, feeling her ignorance acutely. The comparison made her feel uncomfortable for some reason, defensive or embarrassed. Jill made a deliberate point of keeping herself abreast of what was happening in the world, reading the *Times* and a variety of political blogs, listening to talk radio, following the actions of Congress, but here she found herself in a conversation where she was unable to discuss an entire nation of people.

He pulled the airline magazine from the pocket in front of his knees and flipped back the front cover. "I'd venture to guess you'll meet some Albanians—it's very common for my people to go for education in Italy. You may see what I mean. I'm Pal by the way."

"Jill," she said, and they shook hands. He gave her a small smile, returned his glasses to their position on his nose, and reentered the invisible privacy from which he had only just emerged. She found it strange the way he had laughed when asked if he was Italian—it was a disdainful laugh, subtly bitter. He had released her from their conversation, possibly aware of her discomposure. She shifted forward again.

A cup of black coffee and a small package of cookies occupying her tray beside the journal, open. The handwriting was bold, sharp edges to the letters, as if it had been written with permanent marker, graffiti. There were eerie drawings of symbols and cartoonish characters. Jill flipped through the pages quickly, licking her index finger after every third. Words, words, words. Strange words she did not understand. Her name, then a page that only said *Soon I'll be dying* over and over, like the manuscript of Jack Torrance. There was a woman's voice then and she drew her eyes up to see Aaron walking down the jetway, carrying his guitar, gazing at her with unblinking eyes. She recoiled, and suddenly her father was seated beside her, telling her not to worry about Aaron.

She awoke disoriented and rattled.

The woman's voice came from the loudspeaker. Jill's tray was up, her arms crossed over her chest. She was breathing quickly, and looked to Pal and the woman on her other side, but they weren't paying her attention. The aircraft stirred with people waking, packing up, putting on shoes, closing laptops.

"Excuse me," she said softly to Pal. "I need to go to the restroom." She made it a few paces down the aisle nearly jogging, feeling the tightness of claustrophobia in her chest. Why Aaron all of a sudden? Was it simply because she wasn't with Zane?

"Ma'am," a flight attendant said from behind her. She spun around and recoiled in the fluid motion of a guilty person when he touched her shoulder. "We're about to land."

"Sorry," she said, and sped toward the stall, swiveled into the narrow door, shut and locked it. Her eyes betrayed her exhaustion, darkened with smudged mascara and the disquiet of her sleep. Jill tried to convince herself that she had not actually opened the journal, but she couldn't get her bearings. It had been years since she had seen Aaron, but the image of him in her mind was as clear as if he were really there, and her dad welcoming his arrival was so unnerving she physically shuddered. Her breath was thick, she felt greasy and smelled the thin layer of sweat.

There was a knock at the door.

"Ma'am?"

An ethereal voice spoke in German, and then repeated: *Ladies and gentlemen, welcome to Zurich. Please remain seated with your seatbelts buckled until we have landed and safely reached the gate. Thank you for flying Lufthansa. On the ground and above the clouds we have one focus: You. Nonstop you.*

5

Inside the terminal chrome chairs on gray carpet sparkled in hundreds of neat little rows in both directions. Wide panels of fluorescent light on the ceiling, directional signs in German, a sterile, metallic odor all seemed to assault in her exhaustion. She felt nauseated. It was not crowded, but men and women in business suits walked quickly by toting black streamline luggage. The passengers getting off her own flight migrated somewhat slowly into the airport, temporarily nocturnal creatures forced back into the light of day. Some plopped right back down in chairs, parents carried sleeping children whose drooling heads draped over their shoulders. A few Europeans and twenty-somethings meandered groggily, focused on glowing cell phones. The sun was rising, still close to the horizon, and Jill walked to a tall window and stared out on the tarmac, feeling very keenly her absolute foreignness. She found an Internet kiosk where she swiped her credit card and sent a quick e-mail to her dad that she had arrived, then one to Zane. She was suddenly ravenous.

Small stands and shops lined the walkway, few of which were open. She stopped in front of a kiosk positioned in the middle of the hall and approached the aproned worker who mumbled gutteral syllables. Jill smiled and pointed toward a sandwich behind the glass. Taking the metal tongs, the woman removed it and placed it in a paper sleeve. Wordlessly she returned her gaze to Jill, who pointed to a bottle of water.

"Sonst noch was?"

Jill nodded idiotically and gave a thumbs-up. Expressionless, the woman moved to the cash register and began punching at the keys. There were several people lined up behind her now. The total appeared on the small screen and Jill handed the clerk a five-dollar bill. Without opening her hand to receive the money, the clerk continued to stare with the same blank expression and an added raised eyebrow. Jill looked down at the money and felt her face grow hot.

"Oh, right," she said with a laugh for solidarity, and fumbled with her wallet to produce her card.

"Kein karten." She pointed severely to a piece of paper taped to the register with the symbol of a credit card, circled with a line through it. She glanced at Jill's tattoo.

"Oh, god. Sorry—I . . . " she shrugged her shoulders, and said. "I don't have any Swiss francs." She looked over her shoulder at a woman whose mouth was set in a line. Body language transversed all international lines. She grew hot with embarrassment, appalled by herself.

With an audible sigh, the cashier glanced at the people lining up. Jill shrugged, repeated her apology, and turned to leave, tripping over the rolling suitcase beside the woman to her rear.

"I've got some francs." A strong arm caught her as she went down and hoisted her easily. He looked to be about her own age with a cartoon face—thick lips, a wide forehead, coarse hair. He was very broad in the shoulders and wore a fitted orange T-shirt and jeans.

"Oh—thanks, it's fine. I'm not that hungry," she lied. She tried to move away from the stand.

"No, listen," he said, "I got this. I'll only be in Switzerland for three hours and I've got more francs than I need."

He had a way of butchering the elegance of the Swedish monetary denomination's pronunciation, spoken like the name of a midwestern uncle. Though his speech, disposition, and appearance would have seemed ordinary a day earlier, she found he seemed as alien to her as she herself felt in Zurich. She realized she was staring at him as such.

"I'll have one of those sandwiches too, please ma'am," he boomed, as if the language barrier were both physical and soundproof. The clerk glared at them, and Jill could almost feel the tension of the line behind her at her back.

After the stranger had paid for the sandwiches, they stepped away from the vendor. She thanked him again and wished him luck in his travels, but when she moved she felt him follow.

"Where are you going?" he asked, taking a sizable bite of his sandwich once they had taken seats.

"Italy," Jill said.

"Oh nice, me too. I'm Wyatt Kingston." He held out his hand. She shook it.

"I'm Jill."

"Where in Italy?"

"Near Florence." A lie. Feeling guilty because of the sandwich, she said, "What about you?"

"I'm heading to Siena to finish up a degree. It's a smaller city."

Her chin dropped. "Oh! Wow—well, actually . . . " It was too small a chance. "That's what I'm doing."

"What program?" he said with his mouth full of food.

"A master's in art history with Siena's Art and Architecture branch of the Italian-American Academic Exchange."

He smiled. "Me too." Her surprise must have shown. "Architecture."

"Neat," she stammered, and bit into her sandwich.

A shorter flight from Zurich to Florence, and the small plane touched down on wobbling wheels, its body creaking audibly against the pressure to come to a stop. It was a small, run-down airport, and a few dogs played out by the chain link fences enclosing the tarmac. Steps descended down to the runway when they stopped. They filed out, trooped across the pavement, retrieved their luggage from one of two belts, and made their way to the front of the building and out to the bus shelter.

Jill stood, watching Wyatt, seated on his bag with his eyes shut, head leaning back against the cement post, and surveyed him. He seemed harmless. Near her several men and women sat on benches with their backs against the Plexiglas walls of the shelter. The Italians were unmistakable, clad in dark fabrics, leather, metal. The ideal civilization for charcoal. She drew it in her mind's eye—sun low to just above the tree line, hazy enough she could look at it straight on; the blasé demeanor of the woman in black stiletto heels and big sunglasses standing with her black weekend bag; the dark cat slinking against the corner of the shelter, snaking its lithe body around the post. Jill prided herself on the ease with which she engaged people, but here she felt faulty. She could look the part, but she lacked that seamless self-possession. She was glad her book bag was made of slouchy leather rather than one of the popular outdoor hiking brands made of plastic and neoprene. Jill turned as an abrasive American accent drew the attention of everyone under the shelter.

Pristinely matched from green earrings, to skirt, to sandals, the source spoke, dragging a large Louis Vuitton suitcase embroidered with "Heather," with another matching one stacked on top. Her thick, orange hair against the sea of green gave her a sort of Irish caricature. The luggage bumped loudly along the rough pavement. A petite Asian girl who appeared disgruntled by her current company walked vaguely in her wake.

"It's disgusting," the redhead was saying, dropping her suitcase on the ground and planting her hands on her sides. An enormous diamond ring on her left hand reflected the early morning sunlight terrifically. Black stilettos eyed the American girl with disdain over the top of her sunglasses. "I mean, do you think they clean the restrooms? Ever?" The second girl looked around, vexed, and did not respond. Her eyes flitted around beneath her glasses. She appeared to be trapped in the conversation. "This bus to Siena had better be a little nicer."

They were standing in such close proximity it felt unnatural to pretend to ignore the pair, which is what Jill would have liked to do, when it was obvious they were all Americans. She smiled slightly at the shorter girl.

Their bus pulled into its spot along the curb and the four Americans loaded their heavy suitcases underneath. The redhead sat, and her unwilling counterpart slid in next to Jill. After everyone had filed on and found seats, the driver pulled the door to a close and lurched brazenly out of the parking lot without a sideways glance, nearly missing a gray Vespa who yelled something in Italian, brandishing a fist at the retreating backside of the bus.

If the bus was fitted with air conditioning the driver chose not to use it, and the odors of cigarettes, feet, and sweat mingled into a thick, repulsive combination. Cars, almost all very small, jetted around the streets, missing each other's scratched and dented fenders, bumpers, and side mirrors by centimeters. Scooters wove like squirrels through the narrow spaces between the cars, their drivers without helmets. The uneven curbs were blanketed with minicars parked so close to each other that they touched, bumper to fender.

"People drive like maniacs here," the Asian girl said finally. Jill had been distracted.

"Yeah, really. I'm Jill."

"Hey, I'm Ling. Any chance you're bound for IAAE?"

"I am."

"Cool."

"Where are you from?"

"New York. Where people also drive like maniacs. Brooklyn, actually. You?"

"DC," she said.

"My aunts live there. Well, technically Alexandria."

"Oh, Alexandria. Me too!"

"Nice," she said, then looked back out the window. Her glasses were large on her face so her eyes were magnified and seemed excessively disproportionate on her small visage. Her fingernails were painted teal, and she wore several bangles on both tiny wrists. The accessories had a ballooning effect on her presence. Ling reached into a small bag and removed a camera. It was old and boxy, with a short, flat lens protruding. She toyed with the dials, then pressed it to the window.

"Film?" Jill said.

Ling nodded without removing her eye from the viewfinder. A sticky film coated Jill's skin, and she was weary, but she felt something like freedom. A newness—she could be anyone and there wasn't a single person who would care. Ling did not know a single thing about her, and she could decide which truths to divulge, if any. Reinvention wasn't really lying, and neither was the shedding of pretenses. Unlike the girl across the aisle, her left hand was only accessorized by nail polish, and in this moment she could not have been more relieved. This was an opportunity to expand, as an artist and a professional, but also as an individual. She felt confident and motivated. Released.

They stopped for a few minutes, and the driver stood and straightened the tan pants on his narrow hips as the air hissed forth from the lowering vehicle. He lit a cigarette and stepped off the bus, followed by a few riders. Jill and Ling talked a bit about the demographics of their lives at home.

The second driver boarded and opened the windows, and when the bus lurched into motion again, the breeze began to flow and Jill felt her body slacken. Ling's head lay back she closed her eyes. Jill surveyed her. She wasn't typically quick to attract friends, but Ling had started talking about riding her bike all over New York, which Jill found impressively self-possessed. She was wearing checked Vans, her manner was direct and quirky, and she had known that Jill's tattoo was a charcoal drawing of a lily. When she was certain Ling was asleep, Jill turned toward the window and pulled the journal from her book bag, finally finding a privacy, pluck, and peace she'd not had for twenty-four hours. Wedging herself up in the corner of the seat and the window, she opened the leather parcel and surveyed the small, pressed together cursive writing without reading the words. No dates, sentences punctuated by dashes and ellipses, no introduction. Flipping through the pages, Jill was amazed at the length of the entries, and at once a plummeting feeling overtook her stomach, as if she were only moments from falling over some great precipice. She looked up to center her gaze, across the aisle and through the window, and watched as the scenery began to thin out into a countryside of voluptuous hills hued in greens and tans. Nobody watched her. Inhaling, she looked down again and read the first words.

6

I can't believe I have lived my whole life without Italy. People thrive here—it's a different world. Italians operate with this ease I can't even put my finger on, not worrying about anything, taking their time, enjoying food and so much wine, lingering around outside, confident, bold, happy. I have never felt this kind of peace, like I fit into the rhythm . . . It is seeping into me. The way I feel here makes me realize I've never been really content before.

Education is very different here. That's something I've learned so far. I have four classes—Italian language, Art History, and two Studio Art—one painting, one sketching.

Signing up for Ital. language was a whim, but I'm glad I did. Turns out the Italian I've taken at home is helpful, but not in the complete way I need. Signora Lucia is a little like a fairy with long, black, wavy hair to her butt. She sits on it when she sits, but for her, sitting is rare. Usually she paces and jabs the chalk at the chalkboard writing conjugations and vocabulary. The vocab is so random and unstructured because she just talks about herself, her life, her family, sex (I've never met an adult who talked about sex so openly! I absolutely love it because it feels so free) and her plans for the weekend—she goes out all the time even though I think she may be older. But it's strange, women here are ageless. Nobody seems old, but then I see a grandmother who looks to be about eighty carrying five huge bags full of food uphill. It's like "aging" is an overnight transformation.

I don't know the word for "food," but I know the word for drunk—"ubriaco." So far my favorite words are "assoluamente" (absolutely), "va bene" (means "sure, cool, it's good, it's goin good, i'm fine, i'm great"—a universal positive response pretty much), "bella" (obviously pretty but the way they say it is so charming, like "bEalla" . . . something about drawing it out. Hopefully I don't forget how they say it if I ever leave—which I might not). I'm pretty sure Sra. Lucia isn't married, but she talks about a variety of men on a regular basis. She speaks English the way I speak Italian, so I guess there are probably a lot of times that we miscommunicate. Several other Americans and Brits in the class, and she favors Americans. She'll shriek something in Italian for no reason at all, then she'll rub someone's head or something bizarre like that—would definitely not happen in America. She seems a little crazy, but maybe she's just Italian and happy. I'd be if I were her—teaching your native language, going home to your beloved dog and multiple handsome lovers. She's a mystery woman. Pazza!

Studio Arts are taught by a few artists that rotate. They speak ZERO English and most of the other people in the class are Italian or French. Some British, but there's only one other person in that class that doesn't speak Italian. The two male teachers like me—I think they make fun of me in Italian, but I'm going to assume it's not malicious. One is very very old. His skin appears to be disintegrating and his wrinkles are so deep he looks like a patchwork doll. Italian men DO age. The other one, Giovanni, is younger (and fiendishly handsome. God, he's handsome.) I get the gist of what they say most of the time. It's mostly charcoal and pencil in sketch, and then oils and watercolors in painting. The other teacher is a woman and she's a bitch.

My last class is Italian Art and my teacher is a woman from Milan named Fabrianna and she speaks perfect English because she lived in New York. I adore my classes, all of them. Doesn't feel like this can be real. At first I wondered if a year was too long, but now I don't know if it will be long enough.

I do miss Jodie. I think of having her here, sharing all of this with her, but maybe it wouldn't be perfection to her the way it is to me. It's weird, this is like the first thing we've ever really done apart—me going away alone while she gets married. It just couldn't be more different, and we've always been "two of a kind," but all of a sudden it feels like we are totally different. But maybe if she hadn't met Buck (what a name!), she'd be doing this too, or if I had met a guy, I'd be staying. I don't really think the latter would happen.

I keep wondering if she thinks she has to get married. Not sure if I ever came out and expressed that to her, even though I tried to. I don't feel like I know Buck very well—he seemed pretty buttoned-up and boring from the one time we met. Very smart. But also nice looking, in a way. I don't even think I really ever want to get married. I feel bad I'm not there to help—it's hard and expensive to call and letters take forever but they'll have to do. Plus it's fun to get mail from across the ocean. I got a letter from Mom today—they've picked out my maid-of-honor gown. Cranberry is not a terrible color on me.

I bought a 10-month Eurail pass—hard to part with that much money, but it'll be worth it. I'll travel during the winter break, plus I think I'll be able to go around Italy, maybe France and Spain during the weekends. There are two girls from London in my Art History class—Jillian and Claudette—who I think I'll do most of that with. They're great.

Wandering around the streets of this city has taken me to some pretty incredible vistas already. They sneak up on you. My favorite is Porta Pispini. It's all the way at the top of this one hill— I found it while running early one morning. Street sort of dumps you out to this flat little park area with an old swing set and jungle gym (which was kind of spooky in the foggy semi-dark). But I wandered over to the edge and looked out and the view took away my breath. The hills are unbelievable! Every other ridge has some beautiful villa and so many of the hills are covered in vineyards and those skinny cypress trees. That morning it wasn't totally light yet and there was so much fog—it sort of sunk down between the hills like lava or something—so thick. The danger is that it's quiet and makes me want to stay and think, and too much quiet thinking gets me going down the dark roads I'd like to avoid. I'm writing from there now. I'd like it to be a happy place. It's perfect, like Siena.

7

Jill stumbled and tripped over several uneven stones in the road as she dragged her duffel bag on its two small wheels, an insufficient support for the weight of belongings within it, trusting in the sufficiency of Ling's map reading. The sun shone white and beads of sweat ran singularly down the center of her chest and halted at her bra, which had chaffed a red, raw strip on her skin. Her glasses drooped toward the end of her nose, and she kept pushing them up with the inside of her arm.

Lily's voice bounced around in her head like crickets in a cage. It wasn't what she had imagined—the words and language were combative and flippant in a manner she couldn't ascribe to the mother she had known. The language could actually have been taken out of Jill's own internal monologue at different points in her life, and she thought of how intensely her father disdained that insolent quality she sometimes adopted. He would never have married a person like that, and yet . . .

Then there was her name, Jillian—surely the name of her mother's friend, the same as her own, was not a coincidence, but she had never even heard of the girl, the woman? She was alive somewhere, probably with children. Maybe grandchildren. Nobody ever spoke about her Aunt Jodie, dead long before Jill was born and rarely mentioned; she'd only ever heard a handful of vague allusions. There was no reference to a date either, which would determine Lily's age while authoring, so it seemed surreal, removed from life.

Streets swarming with people veered off from the pulsating *Via Banchi di Sopra* and she allowed her eyes to rove down each one. Venerable architectural intricacies decorated every meter of the landscape. She noticed hundreds of a single flag, violet and black with what appeared to be an owl perched in the center, hanging from every window and banister, and thick matching streamers draped loosely over the street. She snapped images into mental frames to sketch later, distrusting the views to keep, unsure she possessed the time for phlegmatic artistry. Bustling men and women on cell phones carrying brief cases, surprisingly like their counterparts in the District, unaware of the magnificence of their surroundings, walked with directness and intention, heaving sighs as they were forced to step around the bulky suitcases blockading their footpaths. Jill tried to pay attention to her steps to keep the suitcase as out of the way as possible. Her mouth felt cottony, she was desperate to stop for a bottle of water, but she was at the back of the group of her fellow students so she kept her eyes on the back of Wyatt's head and tried to maintain their pace.

Sloping downward, Via Banchi di Sopra eventually opened up into a large half circle even more densely packed with people. Jill craned her neck to discover the source of the holdup, and saw among the swarming crowd a group of twenty or thirty Chinese tourists in the center of the road, motionless, gazing at a woman standing at the foot of some low steps leading up to a wide sort of fountain with statues. The small tour guide, donning a wide-brimmed straw hat, held up a yardstick with a large red ball attached to the top and shrieked unintelligible phrases into a megaphone as Italians pressed around the sides of the group to get across the way. Not ten feet away, another group of tourists slowly followed a guide dressed in khaki cargo shorts, shirt and hat, soaked through with sweat, down a sloping alley. Jill nudged Ling, who was looking down at the map and tracing her finger along the roads. She looked up and laughed.

"That's so typical of Asians," Ling said. She pointed to the other group, disappearing. "I think they might be going to the Piazza del Campo."

"I'm turned around," Jill said. "Are we there?"

"According to the map—" she placed her turquoise index fingernail on the page and held it out for Jill to see. They entered a small, covered stone thru-way that provided temporary relief from the volume of the crowd and the blazing heat of late morning. The steep steps down were wet and flanked on both sides by crooked little shops carved into the alley walls, a jewelry store and a cafe. Jill's bag plummeted down the steps and she nearly fell, but at once the ground leveled again and she stepped forward into the sunlight and onto Siena's seashell heart.

Crossing the threshold to enter the Campo was an immediate implantation into the body, the movement, the cadence of the city. There was a heartbeat there, a rushing swirl of viability connecting the people. Jill gazed at the Torre del Mangia, the three-hundred-foot Tower of the Eater, shooting upward into the crystal blue sky, and marveled at the intricate carvings around the turrets of the Palazzo Pubblico, the squarish government building just beside, adorned with stone wolves fifty feet off the ground bounding forward with realistic fervor. From where they stood, the entire square was visible, rock pavers on the outer ring, brick at the center, graded downward to one center point that appeared to be a drain located just feet in front of the tower. Patterned in doubled zigzags, the red brick floor somehow curved in perfect parallel to the curvature of the Piazza itself, creating a mollusk within a mollusk. There were people everywhere, adults watching children play chase games, students lying on the ground with books held overhead as shade from the sun, a few dogs, men selling battery operated light-up rockets from sacks hanging from their necks. Stepping further, Jill turned in a circle, taking in the ornate patterns of the continuous bulkhead of building faces positioned around the fan of the Piazza like the rising seats in a baseball stadium, each one distinct from its neighbor in color, motif, and structural design. Her fingers itched for pencil and paper. Thousands of windows to private places adorned with flowering window boxes met as squares on an aberrant checkerboard, each one containing its own universe inside. Flags declaring contrada loyalties and national pride speckled the architectural backdrop of the Campo, and dozens of shops on the ground level beckoned visitors with wide panels of open doors and windows. Jill counted three gelaterias.

"Whoa," Ling said.

Jill nodded.

"Look—" Ling pointed down the Piazza toward the center, where several people stood in a large circle surrounding a group of boys no older than thirteen dressed in jester-like costumes. They wore tights, jackets with pouffed shoulders, hats, and cloth shoes in bold colors. Each one carried a large flag matching his outfit by a long wooden handle taller than himself. The Americans watched as the boys tossed the flags in the air and caught them again with graceful ease. The city was like a piece of medieval history, picked up out of centuries earlier and put back down in present day. She stood transfixed as the billowing flags launched like kites, then plummeted back to the earth.

The sand is cold under my feet and it feels wet, but the shoreline is far away, the sky has no clouds and the beach is wide. The wind is whipping at my head. Strands of hair from my braid are loose and they land in my eyes and mouth. Daddy did it, so it isn't as tight. My hair is very long. It's never been this long. I keep telling him I need a haircut, but he hasn't taken me because he's at work when the hair salon is open.

There is sand stuck in the cuffs of my jeans.

The air smells like salt and sea.

There are hundreds of seagulls standing like a troop of soldiers on the sand. I chase them and they fly away, but then land a little farther down the beach.

It's getting harder to hold onto the red kite. It floats nicely for a few minutes, tugging a little, but steady, and then all of a sudden it lurches, dives, twists, crashes to the sand and lifts up again. I love the beautiful tail with the four yellow ribbons thrashing around like caught fish. Usually I only feel the wind after the kite feels it. Maybe if the wind is strong enough it can lift me right up. I read a chapter book about a girl who was holding onto a white balloon and it started to rise up into the air and she forgot to let go so she floated across the whole world. That can't really happen, but just in case, I better remember to let go before I get too high.

I look back down the beach to where he is sitting. His jeans are rolled up and his hands are in the sand behind him. His hair is getting long too, like Uncle Steve's, and it is blowing around, but he never moves to brush it away. The wind has gotten me far away from him, but he isn't looking at me or the kite. Maybe he's looking at the ocean, but I'm too far away to see if his eyes are up, or down, or open. Sometimes I think he forgets I'm here unless I'm talking to him.

He doesn't like going to the beach much, but he compromised and came when it wouldn't be hot. This is the first time I've ever been to the beach in October. This is the first time I've ever been to the beach without Mom.

The kite lurches hard, I fall forward and accidentally let go of the string. My cheek stings immediately where it's cut by a shell in the sand. I push myself up to kneeling and start to cry because the kite is bouncing away down the empty beach so fast I'll never catch it. When I wipe my face, there is blood on my hand. It looks thin, like dense watercolors.

Jilly, he says. All of a sudden he's right by me. *How did you get all the way down here?*

I lost my kite. I'm covered in tears mixed with blood, dripping onto my white sweatshirt.

We can get another one. He is holding the sleeve of his sweater against my raw cheek, and he's holding me. It feels good—he's close to me, talking to me, remembering me.

We sit down in the sand, and I lean my head against his shoulder. I watch as the kite hops farther and farther away.

◼

"Here," Wyatt said, standing in front of a lopsided green door on Via Giovanni Dupre that looked more like an industrial loading dock than the other doors they had passed, each one a different height, color, texture—a mouth full of crooked teeth. "It's seventy-three, not thirty-seven."

"Well, knock," Heather said, and Ling stared at her with a blank expression. Heather's long hair had been ironed straight, but she had sweated in the heat and the strands framing her horse face had reverted to their natural texture. In the middle of each of her cheeks was a bright, rosy spot.

Wyatt rapped three times. They waited for a few moments, though nothing seemed to stir anywhere on the street, and he tried again. With that, the green door ached loudly and groaned inward revealing a wide, dimly lit room.

"Oh my goodness, you made it!" The woman flew from inside like a bat. "I've been flipping out for, like, an hour because I thought you missed the bus or you got lost! I didn't know if you'd even made it to Siena." She was petite with short dark hair, and she was panting. Her faded jeans stretched tight across her wide hips like elastic. "Come in!"

They followed her into a large, cavernous space without windows, and it took Jill's eyes a moment to adjust. She felt her forehead relax for the first time. The room looked more like a reservoir for grain than a classroom or an office. The floor was made of smooth cement, as were the walls, which curved upward to a circular dome-shaped ceiling.

Fifteen study tablet desks stood in three rows of five facing the front where Jill noticed a projector and whiteboard for the first time. What appeared to be a class schedule was scrawled in red ink: Italian History, Sienese Art and Architecture, Art of Italy, Structural History, Culture, and Italian Language. The woman hurried away to an adjacent room without a word, but she returned quickly, holding a stack of papers. Nobody spoke, and the students watched her move in a fervent drive to accomplish something unknown. Stopping suddenly, as if she had only just realized she was not alone, the woman halted and turned to the group, still positioned like a herd of sheep in the center of the room.

"You are in the right place? This is the Art and Architecture Master's Capstone with the Italian-American Academic Exchange?" The words came forth so quickly, ending suddenly with the intonation of a question, the adult students remained moronically silent. Only Ling nodded.

"Okay, fine. The others got here yesterday—they came in from Rome. They just left to get something to eat, and I guess they'll be back in a second. I'm Denise Smith, and I'm your program coordinator."

Just then, as if on cue, the other students entered, and the two groups merged naturally, making introductions, filling space with easy small talk, making threads of common connections to places and people back home.

Jill's attention drifted to the open door. There was a café across the street, and its doors were also open. She watched the barman wipe down the tables, the countertop. A woman sat at a window with a book. She thought of Lily, sitting in various spots across the city, penning her thoughts. It wasn't like home, where the landscape of the city was always changing, bulging with new architecture, restaurants, billboards, cars. Siena hadn't changed in hundreds of years. Perhaps Lily had walked by this very doorway and seen the very same café.

"Hey." The girl with a pixie cut approached Jill with a confident stride. "We're roommates."

"Right," Jill replied. "Isabelle, right?"

"That's me. And you're Jillian?"

"Jill's good."

"Cool. We also have two roommates from Albania. I think they're cousins. They go to the University of Siena."

"Oh, okay," Jill said, picturing Pal. Isabelle could read her hesitation.

"They're tiny, and they sort of hide." She laughed. "Do you need help with your stuff?"

"No, I can get it. Is it far?" Jill asked.

"Nah, less than a ten-minute walk. Probably less than five. It's on Via del Porrione, if you're familiar . . ."

Jill shook her head. "I have no idea—Ling navigated us here from the bus station by the stadium. I was just following blind. Sweating."

"Yeah, it's hot. Well, here," she said with a laugh, picking up Jill's book bag, "I'll at least carry this, and you can drag that monster."

Jill waved to a dejected Ling, who had expressed a hope they would be roommates, and followed Isabelle out the door.

8

Jill lost track of their route as she became submerged in fascination with the streets; their churches, statues, anomalous structures, textures, and stained glass windows. They sloped slightly downward, wound and stopped, forcing them to maintain one bearing, like being swept into a natural blood flow. Isabelle pointed right down a narrow cut-through where they turned, descended a few steps, and found themselves at the corner of a large, open square. To their right a wall about eight feet tall closed them in, and to the left a raised brick area like a stage, about the size of half a football field, stood empty with a sturdy roof above. Across the way, on the other side of the open space, were more stairs ascending to another street that looked much like the one off of which they had just turned.

"What's this place?" Jill said, craning her head to see over the wall.

"I don't know." Isabelle consulted a map she had removed from her shoulder bag for the first time. "Let's see... Piazza del Mercato."

"Is it an outer wall? I'm shit with directions."

"Looks like it." Isabelle found a small divot in the rampart where a bit of one of the bricks had crumbled, inserted her foot and grabbed onto a stone protrusion. Jill noticed a thin scar over the back of her ankle. Hoisting herself upward with athletic ease, her eyes just cleared the top. "Wow, nice view. Looks like California," she said as she surveyed the landscape Jill could not see. She liked Isabelle—she liked a girl who would climb a wall to confirm a navigational direction. Lucky, finding two suitable English-speaking friends in a new country in one day.

Isabelle jumped down, and Jill climbed up in her place. Unfurled land flayed open to the horizon, a series of rolling hills like the ones her mother had described in the journal lay still before her eyes. Textures and colors distinguished vineyards, fields, and patches of trees, and she could count the houses by the red terra-cotta roofs. She had seen the countryside from the windows of the bus, but the elevated view was stunning, graceful in its motionless splendor. Her hands twitched for her sketch book. As ever, she thought of the panorama as a drawing. She often failed to enjoy beautiful things for themselves, always seeing material for reconstruction on a page, memorializing while simultaneously draining its life, as a photographer often sacrifices what is real to take a picture that will only ever capture a shadow of the thing.

They continued on, and after a few more turns, just as the edge of the Campo came into view around a curve in the road, Isabelle stopped in front of a dark green door embellished with metal studs and a door knocker as big as her head. Jill's shoulder ached from the weight of her bag.

"Fifty-six Via del Porrione. Home sweet home," Isabelle said as she placed her hand in the half-heart handle and wrenched the door outward. Taking a final glance at the people passing behind her, Jill stepped into the cool, dark atrium.

Echoes of indistinguishable sounds bounced around the inside of the enormous foyer, empty but for a staircase at the far end and a grouping of mailboxes beside the door through which they had just entered. Doorbells for ten apartments were numbered, and the top two showed names—*Valentino* and *Muti*. The air was musty, and natural light came through a few small windows high up in the walls. Together Isabelle and Jill climbed the wide staircase to the first landing and turned toward the door on the left. Isabelle inserted the key and pushed her shoulder against the great wooden slab with the force of her whole body.

Number two at 56 Via del Porrione felt like a cozy den belonging to a very small person she could have read about in a fairy tale. The unit appeared to stretch the length of the building's outer wall beside a narrow back lane, on the other side of which, visible through a window, was a similar building of apartments or offices. To the far left, closest to the street, was Isabelle and Jill's bedroom—a miniscule space with two cramped beds, one of which was situated underneath a built-in shelving unit, giving the person in the bed less than three feet to sit up. There were several photographs taped on the cabinet doors. A suitcase sat in the corner of the room, and the bed under the shelves was made.

"Wow, it's really . . . small," Jill said, standing in the doorway.

"No kidding."

"Did you sleep in that one?"

"Yeah," Isabelle said, then laughed when Jill raised her eyebrows. "I'm not claustrophobic. I don't care. But I was genuinely relieved when you weren't fat."

There was a window to the alley, and a light bulb hung from the center of the ceiling. Jill wondered if it had at one time been a walk-in closet, turned by an enterprising landlord into a bedroom to double the rent. She dropped her bag. Outside their bedroom, a small dining area with a table and two chairs sat beside another window, this one allowing plenty of sunlight from the open air above the alley.

"No screens?" Jill mused.

"I noticed that too. People leave windows and doors wide open. Maybe there are no bugs?"

Cream-colored tile floors in the entire apartment looked new, though the white stucco walls and arched ceiling made in rounded patterns of brick reminded Jill of movies set in castles. Despite the hideous decorations and furniture, it was actually charming, inspiring that these quaint hideaways still existed.

The poky kitchen, which was more like a twelve-foot hall-way with countertops on one side, an oven on the other, and a window into the alley on the end, was lit with fluorescent bulbs. Hobbit-sized appliances were pressed into the corners. Inside the fridge, the top three of four shelves were stuffed so tightly with food that upon opening the door, Jill had to react quickly to catch the cascade of yogurt cups and chocolate bars. Down the hall, to the right of the front door, were four more doors. In the back corner was the door to Era and Lule's bedroom, which stood ajar. The room was spacious with two large windows into the alley where it widened, showing the clear blue of the sky, a closet, a television, and one big bed. To the right of their door, at the end of the hall, was a very tiny closet housing the washing machine. To the right of that was the bathroom with a Victorian-looking bathtub on pedestal feet and a white vanity and mirror with gold filigree leaves winding up and around as a vine.

Jill pulled open the final door to reveal a half bath that stayed dark even when she flicked on the light switch.

"A powder room," she said. "That's unexpected."

"Oh no," Isabelle said as she stepped into the small space with Jill, closed the door, and pulled a shower curtain that Jill had not noticed across the inside of the wooden door. Reaching down, she placed a plastic cover over the roll of toilet paper and pointed up at the corner of the powder room to reveal a spigot.

"Fancy," Jill said slowly.

"This place is so weird."

"Hello?" There was a knock on the door, and the girls immediately stopped laughing.

"Oh shit," Isabelle whispered. "I think it's Era and Lule. I only met them for about a second earlier."

Jill sat down on the closed toilet and bit down on her thumb to silence her laughter. Isabelle pulled back the shower curtain to open the door.

Two girls stood in the hallway against the opposite wall, frowning with concern, similar in extraordinary petiteness. One had long, dark hair, thick with gorgeous waves, and porcelain skin. The other looked much older in the face, and somewhat severe. The one with long hair began babbling quietly to the other in a language Jill did not recognize, gesturing emphatically with her hands. The rise and fall of her voice indicated her distress, and the other spoke back to her more calmly.

"Hello," Jill said, stepping forward beside Isabelle. "I'm your other roommate."

Silence. The girls continued to stare.

"Umm . . . " Isabelle began, speaking with precision and slowness. "Hey . . . I brought . . . Jill. Our fourth roommate?"

Boldly, the second girl stepped forward slightly and dug her hands into her pockets.

"Isabelle?" she said.

Isabelle nodded encouragingly.

Era waved her hand behind her in the other girl's general direction and looked at Jill. "I speak little of English. Parle Italiano?"

Shaking her head, Jill scrunched up her nose in apology. "I'm Jill," she said, pointing in the direction of their sleep-in closet. "I share the room with Isabelle."

Comprehension seemed to be dawning on the girl. "My name is Era," she said. "This Lule."

Muted, Jill looked from Era to Lule. In rapid speech, Era appeared to be informing her cousin that the two tall Americans who'd been locked, together, inside the shower, were going to be sharing their apartment. Lule's eyebrows formed an incredulous arch and, at the end of Era's speech, she nodded. The four girls looked around at each other.

"I am Lule," the second girl said after a moment, and nodded her head affirmatively, as if to assure herself that she had communicated her identity correctly.

"We are going now," Era said. She grasped Lule's hand and pulled her toward the front door. Each carried a backpack, and they waved as they flitted out the door, allowing it to slam shut behind them.

"Did you see their faces when we opened the door?" Jill said.

"They probably think we're lesbians." She shook her head, rubbing her eyes. "This is crazy."

"I like it."

Isabelle nodded in agreement. "It's good real estate."

Jill unpacked her clothes and stuffed them into the narrow dresser drawers Isabelle had left empty. In the stack of T-shirts was the one from Aaron's band tour. She stared at it for a moment, remembering her dream with vividness, then shoved it in, looking over her shoulder to see if Isabelle had seen it. The band had become popular in a certain niche of music enthusiasts; it was minutely possible Isabelle would have heard of The Planet, if she happened to be into that sort of thing. Last Jill had heard they were heading overseas on tour, London she thought. She didn't feel up to a conversation about Aaron. There was a square cabinet where she placed all of her art supplies. She set the picture of her mother on the ski lift on a ledge beside her bed.

"I'm going to nap," Isabelle said. "We have a program dinner at eight. Can you make sure I'm up?"

Jill agreed, picking up her book bag and turning off the light as she exited the room. It was an endless day, every hour doubled, but fueled with the intoxicating presence of adrenaline. Realizing she was walking quickly, she slowed. In the middle of the city she was alone. Finally, with her mind solitary in contented quiet, she could inhale the smell of it, she could capture and document the sights in her mind. There was nobody she needed to report to. There was nobody to suggest a plan. The architecture, the beauty of all that stone washed over her and she felt her throat constrict. Dust kicked up in front of her nose and eyes when a Vespa peeled off toward the Piazza to the left. Consulting the map she verified the point she had found earlier: Porta Pispini.

It was specific, an actual point on a map that she could find and see, a place where Lily had not only visited, but spent lengths of time. Black ink on unlined ivory pages was kindred to hearing her mom's voice again, the sound of which she knew she had forgotten long ago. Jill felt unrestricted. The lily tat-tooed on her chest was a mark on her skin, a stamp of closure, but the journal had opened the past up again. She felt a kind of allegiance to absorb every word her mom had written, memo-rize the lines and tattoo them on her mind. For years she had craved a knowledge that could only come from knowing a per-son, astute to the impossibility, and then this book had cropped up out of nowhere and offered her that intimacy, and perhaps an even deeper understanding than she would have had know-ing her mother face to face. The woman living in these pages seemed different from the Lily she remembered, a fact that was both uncomfortable and exhilarating. Lily in Siena reminded Jill of herself in certain words and suggestions. She spoke with a spirit of adventure and command, but the mother she remembered in her clipped and incomplete memories seemed deflated and sad much of the time. What had happened in the years between the journal and Jill's birth? Undated entries also begged the question of when Lily had been in Siena. Had she known Gary then? Had she been Jill's age? Younger? It was a time of her mom's life she had never even considered before. She felt certain her father would explain if she asked. He was waiting for her to ask. But the not asking, the mystery, was exciting. Her curiosity was awake again, hungry, a bear surfac-ing from a long hibernation.

Three men in dark suits sauntered gracefully by, flickering their eyes over to her. One smiled slightly as he returned his gaze forward, and she heard one of the others say something under his breath. Jill turned in the opposite direction toward Porta Pispini. Having taken a good look at the map, she entrusted the picture to memory and placed it in her back pocket.

She was sweating again, her jeans stuck to tacky skin. Making her way through the stone maze, Jill peeked in the open shop doors of a few cafés, produce markets, studios, and book stores. Very few people passed her as she moved outward to the city gate, a steep uphill climb.

Arriving at the top of the hill, breathing with heavy quickness, Jill walked through a large stone archway into the arms of the small clearing. Inhaling sharply, she slowed and gazed before her at the park described in the journal. Jill moved her hand to the locket that hung about her neck. She went back and forth on ghosts or spirits, but in the moment she allowed herself to imagine the unlikely and whispered a greeting. She made her way over to a segment of the wall shorter than the others, stepped up, and lowered herself to sitting, removed her sandals, and dangled her feet over the edge. Rotund, swollen clouds sat low in the cobalt sky, and the hills rolled upon themselves like folds of dough. She watched a small red car wind over the country road, coming in and out of view with the rise and fall of the landscape. Soundless moments passed by. The muscles in her body loosened as she relaxed, swallowing the vista over and over and over again until the sun began to dim.

9

Wednesday classes began later in the morning, but Jill woke up early and couldn't fall back asleep. She got ready soundlessly, then pulled damp laundry from the machine in the closet and balanced it awkwardly in her arms, moving toward the window beside the dining table. She pushed open the hunter green shutters and hung a few pairs of underwear, a pair of jeans, several shirts, and two bras, pulling the inner line toward her as the outer line dragged the clothes like an assembly belt, the rusted pulleys squeaking with every yank, enjoying the provincial task. She left the window open wide, grabbed her bag, and had one foot in the foyer when she saw Era standing at the top of the hallway. She stated Jill's name.

It was rare for them to cross paths. The cousins slept late, and when they came home in the evenings, they would eat dinner in front of the television, then retreat to their master suite to watch for the rest of the evening privately.

"Hey," Jill said. She stepped back inside and kept her hand on the door.

"How are you?" Her cotton pajama pants were striped pink and brown and dragged the floor. She squinted even though the apartment was dim, and her eyes appeared swollen.

"Good," Jill said. She tried to enunciate without sounding as if she was talking to a computer. "You are up earlier than usual."

Era nodded, then giggled. "Yes, I have work. Usual no mornings, but I work today at nine o'clock."

"Oh, where do you work?"

"Mac-Donald's," she said.

Jill nodded and smiled. "Cool."

"I want to tell you—is okay for my brother to stay here for some nights?"

"Oh," Jill said, drawing her chin back, trying to imagine where another person would sleep. "Sure, that's fine with me." She pointed to the couch.

"Yes, yes, if is good for you and Isabelle."

"Of course. Is he visiting from Albania?" She had done some research on the small country after she found herself living with two Albanians. She hadn't known Mother Teresa was Albanian.

"No, not a visit. He live in Roma—" She gestured at the floor, frustrated. "Um, he drive a car for people."

"A bus?"

Era shook her head.

"Taxi?"

"Yeah, taxi!" Her face lit.

"Okay, yeah. That's fine."

"Ok, thanks you."

"Sure," Jill said, and Era gave her a tiny wave, then retreated to the bathroom. She seemed nervous, almost jumpy, but maybe that was her way.

Outside Jill turned left toward the Piazza. She tried to picture Era working at McDonald's. That would be the reason she was absent much more often than Lule, who spent more time in front of the TV in their room or out with friends and boys. Era was also in school full time, Jill knew, and Lule only took English and Italian courses. She hadn't known about a brother, or any other siblings or family. She didn't actually know anything about Era at all. When she considered this, she made a mental note to ask.

After many mornings following the same routine, Jill could walk down her street and across the Piazza del Campo with her eyes closed to Fiorella, the understated café on Banchi di Sopra that she, Isabelle, and Ling had espoused in their first week in Siena. Delivery trucks full of milk, produce, and bread butted up against storefronts and rangy, muscled men unloaded their haul while restaurant owners unstacked chairs to set out around tables creating a secondary perimeter of the brick plaza. Jill now recognized the same people day after day—the squat woman dressed in all black crossing the space walking a matching black dog, the bald man with the thick gray mustache looking like a giant seated beside the same small, circular table with a newspaper and cup of espresso, offering a glance when she passed, the two panhandling gypsy women. She liked to think that she too was becoming a fixture during that time slot in that place each morning. Walking through one of several stone alleyways to the main road, Jill turned right at the Loggia del Mercanzia and ducked into Fiorella.

"Ciao," the barman said, lifting one eye as he spun around to pull two portafilters from the grouphead and dump the used grounds. The espresso's aroma felt thick in the air, and the shop was full of the locomotive sounds of the machine, the people, the revolving door. Jill smiled in his direction. Winking subtly, he refilled the polished filter basket with fresh grounds and set to work making her Americano. She glanced around for Ling, but she wasn't there. She would be taking advantage of the chance to sleep in. The shop was narrow and deep, full of brimming daylight from the glass storefront. Several men and a few women in business dress stood up at the bar, discussing the headlines from the morning paper, she imagined, strewn about the counter. Others sat at the few tables against the wall opposite the bar, tearing pieces from croissants and mindlessly sipping from ceramic mugs.

"Americano!" shouted the barman, sliding the cup and saucer toward Jill who stood, waiting on the corner of the bar closest to the back.

"Grazie," she said as he made eye contact, and handed him a euro thirty. He moved quickly, but it was also clear he saw her. As she watched his interactions with every customer, it appeared he had similar relationships with many of them, each one distinct yet understated.

"Prego, bella."

It was the satiating familiarity of this brief interaction for which she returned each morning. In some way, however small, he expected her, knew her, recalled her, indulged in her femininity standing out in the sea of business suits. She had almost asked his name once, but lost the nerve when his assistant barista vehemently chastised a man who had spilled his coffee on the newsprint. The opportunity had not since presented itself, though in some way Jill enjoyed the reticent distance between them, the sensuality of the scene. Finishing up her drink, she pushed the cup back toward the center of the bar, whispered, "Ciao," and pushed her way out of the crowded café.

Squatty cars reminiscent of college campus service vehicles rumbled down the street kicking up dust, and scooters wove in and out of people while the majority of Siena's morning traffic walked up and down the Via Banchi di Sopra heading for work or school or, on this day, the busy weekly *mercato*.

Her cell buzzed deep in her book bag, and she could feel it at the small of her back. She swung it around to her hip and dug the phone out.

"Well, good morning," she said, moving toward the edge of the road where there were fewer people. "What time is it for you? Four?"

"Just about. How are you babe? I miss you." Zane's voice came through clearly over some feedback in the line.

They'd played phone tag for four days. He would call her Italian number with a phone card, she would return with a text telling him the next time to call. Often the appointments she scheduled conflicted with his work meetings, especially now that he was working longer hours in her absence, taking dinner and breakfast meetings more frequently. Their communication was far more consistent over e-mail, which she found she preferred here. It felt easier to detail her days that way, where tone of voice was easy to doctor with punctuation. She had never enjoyed talking on the phone, and now she knew Zane had a greater need to feel she missed him reciprocally through her tenor. There were certainly moments she thought of him, thought he would enjoy an experience or meal. At times when cultural differences created humorous misunderstandings she thought of him especially, how they would smirk at one another, capture the irony in a glance. She did enjoy hearing his voice, the way it grounded her in something familiar, but she did not spend her time thinking of him or pining for him. Communicating with him took her out of the present, removed her from Siena, and she always felt an underlying urge to get back to it.

For a few minutes he told her enthusiastically about a conversation he had had with one of the senior partners at the firm, who had, without explicitly stating it, told him he would probably be offered partner by Christmas. She could tell he was in the office because he spoke quietly and tried to sound less excited than she knew he truly felt. This had been the goal all along—this firm, this time frame.

He asked her for a trip update, and she assured him things were the same. Art and history classes. Exploring Tuscany with Isabelle. He seemed fascinated by her friendship with Isabelle, almost surprised by the way Jill had connected with her. Isabelle was effortless. She was strong-willed and sometimes abrasive, but Jill found it refreshing. Part of their immediate amity was due to the fact that they slept three feet apart and spent almost every moment together, but Isabelle had assumed an attachment at the onset, leaping over typical formalities of habituation and treating Jill like an old friend. She was comfortable—with herself, the newness of her surroundings, all of the circumstances of her life. The fact that Jill still held her at arm's distance did nothing to impede her wide open disposition.

They talked a bit longer, and she thought of telling him about her hilarious Art of Italy professor, Weldon Grimes, but then he seemed to have to get off the line.

"I leave for New York tomorrow."

"Fun. How long?" she said.

"A week. We're trying to close a huge deal, so it'll be busy. I'll talk to you when I get back. I'll call you."

"Okay! Sounds good. Good luck!"

"Thanks, I'll need it." He didn't really feel that way. "Love you."

"Love you back. Ciao!"

He laughed. "Adios!"

Once she hung up, she rejoined the crowd moving up the street and thought about his fascination with Isabelle. Jill hadn't had very many close friendships. What was between herself and Zane was, she reasoned, a different thing entirely. They were romantically involved; it wasn't really a friendship. With Aaron it had been both, but the closeness between them had been toxic, and many of their most intimate conversations had been after his gigs when he was high and mildly drunk. Zane was robotic in a way—highly effective, operational, usually correct. But his emotionalism felt perfectly placed, like he was programmed to "feel this, now." It could feel dull, which was in some ways good. She'd felt so stable for the past two years. The few girlfriends she'd had in college she didn't keep up with. Occasionally the girls in her program would go out for happy hour and she'd join. She often wondered if her inability to make authentic friendships was derived from growing up with her dispassionate father, which had dulled her displayed emotional spectrum to a gradient of gray and blue. He had a few friends who came over once in a while for drinks, or to watch a basketball game or something, but that was rare. She wondered was it this experience opening her to a person like Isabelle, or something like the opposite?

Jill approached the top of the street at the Piazza Matteotti to find the entrance to the market. The crowd grew thick and ornery around her and finally, standing between the bus station and the soccer stadium, she spotted the tops of the canvas tents. There was nothing she intended to purchase, but she enjoyed isolation within a crowd, the dichotomy of aloneness in a throng of people, the images. She simply wanted to experience it.

During her first Italian culture class, the buxom Professor Memmo had come directly from the market, precariously balancing several plastic bags full of merchandise. Sweat dripped down her temples and, setting the bags down, she had collapsed into the chair at the front of the room, heaved a great sigh of exhaustion, and peeled her long, streaky, bleached hair off the back of her neck. Wiping the bleeding mascara from her cheeks, she had explained the market to them in her heavy Sicilian accent—an enormous flea and farmer's bazaar where any imaginable item could be bought for a price. She explained that it was over a mile long with hundreds, perhaps thousands, of vendors. Her emphasis was on the butcher, as well as a specific corral near the entrance that sold denim. It was their first introduction to Memmo. She'd been draped in a large black shawl, giving her the effect of an enormous bat.

Jill pressed forward in the throng, in between the hordes of women babbling in Italian. Elbows and long hair touched her from all sides. It was a clear day, crisp with fall, and the breeze that couldn't navigate the high walls in the center of Siena rushed over the market here. The first section of stands sold clothing. Studded jeans and bejeweled shirts hung from hangers upon display nets. Gaudy leather and velour materials fashioned clothes looking like costumes. There were hundreds of patterns and styles, a few hung as samples, the rest stacked in piles on tables. Jill moved on past dozens of tables covered in similar styles of clothing in lurid patterns, table and bed linens, hats, thousands of shoes, purses, backpacks, lingerie, and ant-like patrons crawling all over every mound as if it were the final day to shop. Ever. She hugged the outer edge.

Making her way through the teeming maze, Jill had the vaguest sense of approaching the Medicea Fortress, a garrison built in the sixteenth century as a port of protection from the Florentines, later demilitarized and turned into a public garden. Leather bound books drew her attention, and she stopped at the stall to run her fingers over the binding of one that reminded her of the journal that lay at the bottom of her book bag, under-neath her camera and wallet. She pictured her mother walk-ing through the very same market years before, and looked up imagining a view of the back of Lily's profile. They were bound together here, in Siena, united in their participation in its his-tory. How strange for Jill to think her own path was doubling back over Lily's, pressing it down, deepening its lines.

Rock steps downward afforded a break in the tents, and Jill moved into the section for food, immediately aware of the smell of cooking meat. She removed her camera from her bag, recall-ing the intention she'd had of taking at least ten worthwhile pic-tures a day to use later for drawing, and snapped a few frames of the sun filtering through the trees onto the tented stands. The source of the smell was a cart where a tall man stood flip-ping kebabs, sausages, and bratwursts. His face was livid red, and beads of sweat dotted his brow and ran down his temples. He did not speak, but another man, much smaller, barked out orders as he assisted. Five feet back, she stood rooted, watching their synchronized dance—flip, transfer, and bag—graceful, seamless motions to fill the orders of women shouting their demands like children. Flinging sweat in every direction, the master of the grill gave low grunts of acknowledgment as patrons called out *Grazie!* Catching Jill's eye, the butcher raised his eyebrows, and she quickly shook her head, stepping backward, stealing one shot when his head was turned.

The street was cooler in the lower stretch than other places in the market because of the shade provided by the hulking fortress, and she perused colorful stands full of tomatoes, glistening eggplant, bell peppers, flaking onions, carrots, celery, fresh leafy parsley and rosemary. There were truck beds displaying hundreds of types of cheeses, and some tables stood covered in unrecognizable cuts of meat. The colors were mesmerizing. One stand laden with four-foot-tall jars of pickled calves feet did not appear to draw many customers, and she snapped a photograph. The vendor looked at her suspiciously. Several carts full to overflowing with baguettes, rolls, and hearty loaves of bread smelled so fresh and succulent it made Jill's stomach twist. Stopping, she picked up a half-baguette and showed it to a very small, elderly woman wearing a pocketed apron, who whispered something she did not understand. Fishing out a one-euro coin and hoping it would be enough, she handed it over, and the woman gave her several small coins in return, then turned to her next customer.

Wicker baskets crammed with food hung on the arms of formidable women, and Jill marveled at the strength of some who looked old enough to be dead. Stepping backward to dodge an unswerving grandmother, Jill felt the jab of a bony shoulder of another person plow into her hip, and she spun to see a young boy hold up his palms in apology, then turn to disappear into the crowd.

In the next moment, several things happened. Jill heard a very deep voice shout something in Italian as the boy, almost invisible, stopped dead and turned back, eyes wide with fear. It was then that she noticed his dusty, bare feet, the largeness of his shirt, the sharp points of his clavicles. As he turned quickly to run, another figure, this one much larger, bolted from behind her, passed by on the left, and lunged at the boy, grabbing him by his stretched collar just before he had time to move his feet.

Jill watched as the man held onto the skinny arm and gruffly shouted at the boy, who wore a furious scowl and whose head now hung limply to his chest. Several bystanders ogled, clucking their disapproval, while Jill stood still, bewildered. Sudden comprehension dawned on her as the man held out his palm and the boy reached deep into the pocket of his pants and pulled out Jill's wallet. Flicking the child on the back of the head, the man shooed him along and walked back toward her. She flushed with embarrassment.

10

"Buon giorno," he said, standing before her with effulgent eyes, holding out the wallet. His face, which had been dark and stern while chastising the thief, was now calm, open, and warm. He seemed to gaze at her with a kind of wonder. There was an aspect of altruism about him, and he looked like the depiction of a person in a black and white photograph. He studied her face. "You must not be from here." The accent creamed his words, but his English was perfectly spoken.

"No, I'm not." She looked around to find the bystanders had lost interest and moved on.

"Come, sit down," the man said, motioning to a bench under a great tree in a grassy clearing just beside the market street. Jill moved toward the bench, clutching her wallet in one hand, the camera over her shoulder and the baguette in the other hand, trying to figure out how the boy had gotten his hands on her wallet from inside her fastened bag. Sitting, the man spoke again. "My name is Amedeo Perlo." She began to put her things back into her bag, and he continued. "Gypsy children are taught from a very young age how to steal. You must be very aware of yourself in the market. It is so busy, you may not even know it is gone until you arrive home."

Nodding, Jill surveyed the man, drawing him in her mind's eye. His clothes looked expensive, tailored and pressed. He was perhaps an inch or two under six feet tall, and well-built, as if at one time he had been in very near perfect physical condition but had allowed his body to relax with age. His eyes, the darkest shade of brown, stared deliberately, and his head was covered in stately, thick, peppered hair. He had dark eyebrows, and a deep five o'clock shadow already blanketed the lower half of his face. Articulated lines ambled out from his fathomless eyes and his countenance was delightful, almost amused. He was as old as her father, and handsome. His closed mouth suggested a smile, though his face remained straight.

"Thank you," she said, shifting forward.

"You are from America, no doubt." He paused, narrowing his eyes slightly. "East coast. What is your name?"

"Jill," she said, and shook his extended hand.

"Are you visiting Siena?"

"Sort of. I'm a student. I'm finishing up a master's degree."

Amedeo raised his eyes. "Very good. May I ask which program?"

"My degree's in art history." She hesitated. "I'm here with the Italian-American Academic Exchange."

He chuckled.

"So you're familiar with it."

"Oh, yes. I am on the board of directors. I serve as the . . . hm, how do you say? Liason to students. So you are Jillian Dunn. I read your application to complete your capstone here. Smart woman. Excellent choice."

"Well that's ironic," she said with a softening smile.

"Professor Bova is your teacher?"

"Yes."

"She is my cousin. Her mother is the sister of my mother."

"Oh, wow, small world," said Jill.

"Small world. I like this American expression." Amedeo looked thoughtfully toward the fortress, which stood unobstructed from where they were positioned. Here there was a break in the trees and the sun warmed and reflected on dew in the grass so each green blade glittered individually. "My family has been in Siena for hundreds of years," he said. "We never seem to leave! Except dear Anna, who went to school in Milan, then returned to be your teacher." Then added, "Anna Bova."

She nodded. He showed no sign of moving, so she continued. "Do you live inside the city walls?"

Shrugging, Amedeo gestured southward. "We live where it is not so busy. In the Valley of the Ram."

She looked at him.

"Contrada, my dear." Angling his face toward hers, he leveled their eyes and added, "You must know the contrade of Siena if you intend to be adopted here." Then he laughed, the most dulcet, splendid laugh, and Jill smiled. "And I know you are from the east coast of America, but where? I have been to California a few times, for wine business."

He perpetuated the conversation like they were old acquaintances, drawn into the deeper intimacy of rediscovery and a common background. He was uninhibited by Jill's inhibition, seemingly heedless of the time.

"I live near Washington DC," she offered. "A little south of the city—technically in Virginia."

A mournful shadow moved fleetingly over his eyes, snuffing the light that had thus existed there, and he nodded. "I know the place." He stood at once and looked at his watch, a motion that seemed to return him to his previous state of contentedness.

"Bellissima, I must be going, and I might assume you have a class to be getting to?"

She glanced at her watch, then nodded.

"Will you come for dinner with the Perlos this Sunday? In Italy family is a broader term—you must join one for the time you're here. You can meet my brother and sisters, my son, and the whole family. It will be bellissimo. You can bring your roommate—who is yours?"

She paused, all of her conventional skepticism flashing in warning, but nodded. "Isabelle."

"Prego!" He gave her vague directions to dinner, then, taking her hand, Amedeo raised it to his face, kissed it lightly, and said, "Darling, Jillian. Until Sunday!"

"See you then," she trailed off as he was already walking away. "Oh! What time?"

He turned and holding up seven fingers above his head, Signor Perlo shrugged, then pivoted with a nod and disappeared around the corner of the fortress.

11

On Sunday Jill woke to a sound like a rattling air conditioner and groggily walked out of her room to find Era's brother on the sofa, his feet dangling from the end like grape clusters on a vine, snoring. His height surprised her, and when she walked quietly to the kitchen she peered over to see his face, but his arm was flung over his head so she couldn't. He wore jeans, which seemed uncomfortable and indicative of his impermanence in Siena. She ate a cookie, got dressed and left, wondering what Zane would say if she told him about the brother. Of course she wouldn't tell him. When she returned from a walk, he and the cousins were gone, and there was no sign anyone had been there.

Isabelle returned from a shopping trip in the early evening with four new bras and five pairs of colorful, patterned stockings. She laid them out for display on Jill's bed.

"Do you think we should dress up?" she asked, standing in front of the small armoire.

"Maybe sort of nice? He seemed casual. Do you think he would've said something if it was going to be fancy? Maybe not." Jill grimaced in uncertainty. Isabelle pulled a sundress with capped sleeves from the rack, holding it up.

"What about this?"

"Yeah, that's probably good," Jill said, standing up to root through her own sparse collection. "This would be easier if I had all my clothes here."

Isabelle slipped out of her denim shorts and tank top and into the dress. Selecting a white peasant top and jeans, Jill quickly changed and ran her hands like a comb through her hair.

"Your tattoo is gorgeous," Isabelle said.

"Thanks."

"Did you draw it?"

"Yeah, I did." She touched the lily under her collar bone and thought back to the day she'd taken the charcoal to the artist, the way she'd felt his mutual respect. She had designed it with Aaron. That was the idea, anyway. Mostly she'd worked on it while he worked on his songs, each of them isolated gods in their own creative universes, company to one another. She'd designed his tattoo as well. Sometimes she wondered if he regretted it, the permanent stamp of her on his body, on his universe. She bore something similar of him; it just wasn't visible.

"Hey, did you see Era's brother today?" Jill asked.

"Hm? Oh, was that her brother?" Isabelle was pinning her hair back with bobby pins.

"Yeah, she told me Wednesday he was going to stay here a couple of nights."

"We talked for like a second. His name is Luan," Isabelle said. "He lives in Rome."

"Did he say what he's doing here?"

"I guess just visiting?"

"Yeah, that's what I would've thought, but when she mentioned it last week it didn't seem like that." Jill paused. "I don't know."

"They were talking pretty loud when I got home, but as soon as I opened the door, it was—" Isabelle drew an imaginary zipper across her lips.

"Do you have an address?" Isabelle asked as they walked down Porrione and turned right onto a nameless alley. They headed southward, in the direction of the Ram Valley.

"No," Jill said, and Isabelle looked at her.

"Then where are we going, exactly?"

"He said we'd see it," Jill said.

"Great."

Red and yellow flags with rearing, royal rams replaced the violet ones picturing the elephant with the tower on its back, affirming that they were, at least, in the correct section of the city. The girls wandered, passing side streets opposite wide open vistas of the countryside. Farther from the city center some houses were spaced out, offering narrow slices of a view to the outside of the city.

"Jill," Isabelle said, grabbing Jill's arm as she looked out over a wide panorama of the landscape to the south. "Do you think it's—"

Turning, Jill followed the direction of Isabelle's gaze opposite the overlook. Positioned down the center of the narrow street was a long dining table covered in a tablecloth with ignited taper candles in a row. Thirty or more chairs placed around the table were also covered in golden seat covers, and there were small bud vases of bright red flowers from end to end. Gold-rimmed china plates sat at each place, along with two goblets, silverware, and a rich ruby red napkin. Medieval torches hung high on outer walls, casting a flaxen glow over the whole scene, made more stunning because of the slowly descending sun. Amedeo had said *family dinner.* This appeared to be a movie set of a wedding reception.

Milling about the table and the street were a few dozen men and women, as well as young boys and girls running in circles, in and out of the alley, twirling ribbons and batons, chasing one another with play swords and soccer balls. Jill heard her name called out in a familiar voice, and turned to see, to her surprise, Amedeo coming into the crowd from a door just beside the set table.

"Jillian and Isabelle!" He exclaimed when he saw them, lifting his arms up in greeting. Motioning toward himself, he migrated to them through the crowd of people.

"That's him," Jill said.

"My god," Isabelle whispered before he was upon them.

Amedeo took Jill's shoulders and kissed her lightly on both cheeks. "Benvenuto! Welcome! And you," he directed himself toward Isabelle, "are the beautiful Isabelle. Yes?"

"Yes," she curtsied as he took her hand and kissed it.

"Welcome, welcome, welcome," he repeated, his saturated good spirits exuding from his glad tone. "I knew you would find us. This is my family. The Perlo family!" He waved his hand toward the crowd, and a few paused in conversation and turned to the visitors. Several gentlemen the same age, perhaps slightly older than Amedeo, lifted a hand in greeting, all smiling kindly, and returned to their conversations. The few women also gave nods, then moved toward a door. Having abruptly stopped running around, the dozen or so children looked shyly toward the girls, except for one young boy who ran up beside his uncle and stuck out his hand toward Jill and Isabelle. He laughed hysterically when Jill took it to shake, and running away, broke the trance of the other children, who then resumed their sport.

Four young men perhaps in their late teens and twenties nodded toward the girls, who smiled back.

"That is Dovio," Amedeo declared with pride, pointing to one boy, tall with longish hair, who looked to be about sixteen. "He is my son." Dovio smirked and lifted a hand.

Just then several women filed out of the door carrying plates of antipasti. One woman had an infant wrapped onto her chest, and its small eyes peered over her shoulder. The last to emerge, with arms full of wine bottles, spoke rapidly in thick Italian, and the other women roared with laughter. One of the younger men reached over to take a few of the bottles, then pointed toward the girls, and the women all looked up from the table where they laid their charges. A few appeared startled, and Professor Bova regarded them with mock astonishment, then winked. The woman who had arrived last approached them.

She draped her arm over Amedeo's shoulder, looked up at him and said, "Brother, these must be the guests you told us about?"

Giving a single nod, he smiled from her to them. "This is my sister Sophia."

"Beautiful! Too skinny," she said, stepping forward first to Jill and embracing her in a powerful hug. "You are Jillian, yes?"

"Yes," Jill said, surprised to hear her name.

"And you, beautiful golden hair, are Isabelle?"

Nodding, Isabelle returned the woman's hug, who then stood back from them and looked to her brother. "You only bring them here because they are so beautiful, little brother! Did he tell you he is forty-nine years old?" she said with grave sincerity, and then her face broke into a wide grin as the men standing nearby roared with laughter.

Amedeo shook his head. "I invited them here because they are students in my program!"

Sophia introduced them to everyone by name, though the names were delivered so quickly and behind the veil of such a thick accent that neither Jill nor Isabelle could later remember more than one or two.

After an hour and multiple glasses of wine, Jill was warm and mildly tipsy. They had been given seats near the head of the table where the three oldest men sat unmoving, sharing bits of family lore, tales of their fathers and grandfathers, which Amedeo translated. Though dinner had not been served, appetizers appeared every twenty minutes as the women moved in and out of the house, replacing empty trays and bowls with full ones.

"Here, let me," Jill offered, as one girl reached over her head for a tray.

"No, we can do it," she replied waspishly.

After she disappeared, Amedeo leaned over and said, "Do not take it personally from the girls. They are jealous because you look Italian though you are not." Jill observed the dynamics of a large family with the fascination of an anthropologist. There were so many people, and they spoke and interacted with more openness than she and her father ever had—arguing, interrupting, leaning in to listen, narrating stories with animation. To Jill, extended family was synonymous with acquaintance, or even stranger, and yet here it was not so. And this was only one family in a whole city. There had to be hundreds more dinners like this one happening elsewhere.

Sometime around nine, there was a call for everyone to be seated, and the children dropped their toys and ran to find places at the table. After a blessing in Italian the family shifted from speaking in Italian to speaking, in majority, English for the benefit of the guests. Dinner was just as lengthy an affair as pre-dinner had been, and each person, from the youngest child to Nonna Perlo, remained seated for the entirety. The constancy of chatter around the table was interrupted only by several boisterous outbursts of laughter throughout. Jill and Isabelle were bombarded with questions and jokes, and their companion wine goblets in equally convivial measure seemed never to go dry, even after they'd begun to modestly decline refills.

Jill pulled out her camera to capture a few frames of the evening and the food, and the family agreed enthusiastically to being photographed, under the vow that Jill would print copies for them as well. In all posed shots, she noted, everyone but the children smiled slightly without showing teeth, but the candids were marked by uninhibited grins and wide open faces. For a long time Jill and Isabelle listened to family stories, bursting for the telling at the introduction of new listeners to the dinner table, and they ate slowly for hours. When the barrage of food tapered and the empty wine bottles stood as sentry stationed about the table, Jill leaned back in her seat. Several children stared off into the distance, eyes glazed in exhaustion, and the two youngest boys slept silently, their cheeks pressed heavy on the table.

The grasses are tall, and bend over like bows, tickling my face. It's so sunny I squint and shield my eyes. The glen is warm because the trees block the wind. I am hungry, so Mama brought me outside for a while before dinner.

Jill, look at this, she calls. She sounds excited so I bound over to her, imagining I'm a deer. She is standing over a nest made in the ground with two blue eggs in it. Her long hair is braided and lies against Daddy's red jacket.

What kind of bird's nest is that?

I'm not sure.

We stare at it in awe for a few moments, and I'm hoping to see the eggs begin to quiver and crack the way they do in cartoons. I begin to worry the mother bird will miss the moment, so I look around for signs of her.

Has this nest been here for a long time? I ask.

I don't remember ever seeing it.

My stomach growls so loudly she looks at me with surprise, then laughs.

When is it time for dinner? I'm whining, and she hates that.

Soon, love.

We continue our exploration of the field, moving away from the house so only the chimney is visible above the trees.

Later I say, *Is anyone else coming to eat?*

Hm?

Miranda told me she has Thanksgiving at her aunt and uncle's house in Virginia and they have forty people. I think she said . . . forty or fifty. We were talking about Thanksgiving in school this week and how big families all eat turkey and pray and sit together. There is a boy in my class who is black and he told us that his family invites people they don't even know to eat with them! Nana's table in the dining room is really big. Why do we only have us here?

She is looking forward as we walk, but I can tell she's listening because her lips are moving like she's chewing something very small. That's what she does when she's thinking hard or sometimes when she is very sad.

I like that she always thinks before she answers me because I know that she is trying to be honest. Some grown-ups answer kid questions really fast, like Daddy. But she's always figuring a good answer to my questions, like I'm a grown-up too, so I don't mind waiting for her.

Well, every family is different. Some families are big, so they have lots of people to invite, and then there's a lot of extra love so they can have even more people. My family is very small. It was just the three of us, and then your dad came along. And now we have you.

I think about this, and deduce the only way to fix the problem is for Nana to have other kids, which she doesn't, or for me to have a sibling. I want a sister so bad because sometimes it is too quiet in my house. I want to have someone to play castle and horses and do art projects with. I am getting ready to make this suggestion when the cow bell rings.

I am running, leaving Mama behind me, thinking to talk to her about this idea later.

Blackness flecked with stars blanketed the sky above the rising fortress, and conversation had quieted to a lower murmur. Some of the children had been carried off to bed, tucked in homes piled above. Several people smoked cigarettes, and curls of gray rose up to form fluid cobwebs above the table. There was music coming from a record player that had not been audible before in the raucous din of dialogue, but now the grainy melodies warmed the evening as the embers of a dying fire. Jill yawned widely, covering her mouth, and looked toward Isabelle, whose eyes drooped. When she turned her gaze toward Amedeo, he drained the last crimson sip from his wine goblet.

"It is late for you? You are young!" he declared. He pointed to her. "Your tattoo, why do American women get tattoos?"

She hesitated, looking down to where the neckline of her shirt dipped so the edge of the permanent ink was just visible. "I don't know why anyone else does it. I've had it for years. I got it because it means something to me. It's a lily."

He nodded very slowly. She couldn't read him.

"You're studying art history—are you an artist as well?"

"Aspiring," she said.

"My cousin conducts an art competition for Christmas. You should enter something."

"What is it? Paint? Drawing?"

"Everything. Anything is admissible. It is for fun, and a little money. There is a reward for the winner. It is called *Arte per Natale*. There is a website."

She made a mental note.

"Jill," Isabelle said from behind her, laying a heavy hand on her shoulder. There was a desperate quality to her voice. "I'm so tired."

"Yeah," Jill said, standing, the unique density of drunkenness surging into her head. She didn't often drink herself to this state, and thought to herself she would have to figure out how to drink wine well while in Italy. Amedeo's head was tipped back, and his eyes were closed. Her attraction to him was strange—it wasn't romantic, but there was something acutely magnetic. She didn't want to leave. Shaking her head subtly she announced their departure.

"It has been a pleasure to have you," exclaimed Sophia. "We will see you again soon! Anna can keep you up to date on the family dinners, eh?"

Anna nodded. "See you in class Tuesday," she said.

"Molto grazie!" Isabelle exclaimed through a yawn.

"Ciao, ragazzi," Amedeo said.

12

Thought I lost this journal. The cops just returned my bag to me. Cash was gone, but that's it. This was still in there. The guy was Italian so he probably didn't read it. Bastard! They said someone found it in the corner of an alley and turned it in. I had to throw my bag away because it was torn. Makes me so mad! I loved that bag. The police were nasty about it, like it was my fault I happened to be mugged while walking home from the studio. I am so sick of feeling like it's my fault when stuff like this happens! I'm reliving the same nightmare, like I am ten years old again, but I absolutely refuse to accept the blame for this. I hope he was furious when there were only twenty euros. I hope he felt like a total ass. I'm so bitter, it's like chewing on iron, and I'm trying not to let it ruin my portrait of Siena. It could happen anywhere.

Catching up—Saturday morning I took the train north to the Cinque Terre (trans: 5 Lands). The coast snakes around over the Tyrrhenian Sea like the outline of a stubby hand, and at each of the five points there is a precious little town. J. and C. came too, and we hiked a trail from Monterosso to Riomaggiore. It rained until the fourth town. Spent a very uneventful night in the last town because it's not summer anymore, and that's when the trail is the busiest. Hikers must be their only source of income because there was hardly a person anywhere except for one sort of creepy Australian. C. almost spent the night with him, but J. stopped her. She's crazy. J. told me C's family is rich and she doesn't have siblings and she just does whatever she wants. J. is more down to earth. C. is sort of wild which can be fun, but sometimes it makes me nervous. Our hotel was on the water, so we went skinny dipping (FREEZING) in the dark and carved our names on a dock piling for posterity. I like leaving traces of myself.

We went to Viareggio for a day after that, which is a bum little beach town. Stayed in a cheap motel, but had great seafood. We found men and went dancing. These evenings when we go out we drink enough that I don't exercise much caution, and can't remember all the details. It's like I'm flying down a hill on a bike with no hands. Sort of exhilarating and terrifying at the same time. I haven't slept with anyone—the Italian men are a lot different from their American counterpart, and I'm just never going to be the girl that goes to bed with a guy who doesn't even know I'm an artist or where I'm from or some grounding detail about who I am as a human being. Sex isn't cheap!

Some of these little Tuscan hill towns are running together in my mind. San Gimignano, Volterra, Cortona . . . I can barely distinguish them now, and it's only been a couple months. I hate to think what I'll forget in thirty years! Should have bought a camera before I came. I've painted a piece that's the colorful architecture of Vernazza and I'm happy with it. My teacher said it's really good, but that the subject is overdone. I don't care, it's for me anyway. Painting here is so easy—the material is . . . from heaven.

Jodie's first letter came yesterday, but it was written almost a month and a half ago, so she probably hasn't gotten any of mine. Wedding plans are good, but Dad's drinking isn't. The feeling I got just reading her letter was so intense—my stomach felt awful like I was going to have diarrhea and it was hard to breathe. I had to put it down and walk outside on the street until my body regained its equilibrium. I didn't realize how heavy it felt until I wasn't there, but that physical repulsion is the norm when I'm home. He gets into the spiral and I can't sleep well or get through a day without that sick worrying. All this emotional fear or dread. I kind of hated reading her letter. I hadn't thought about all that shit for a while, but now I'm thinking about it. I'm trying to stop.

This journal is becoming my therapist. Necessary to change the subject.

I LOVE Studio Art—definitely producing my best work yet. The landscape is so inspiring here, the people, markets, architecture. Even the sky is better to sketch here than at home. I swear it's bigger. Language class is good because I'm actually learning Italian. Coffee is also a new thing for me—after a lifetime of being disgusted by coffee, I've made a commitment to like it (or tolerate it). I must, it's the way of the people. Have also taken up the national beverage, red wine, and I've been smoking a cigarette here and there. Smoking is one I could definitely hold onto, but I don't like the next-day taste in my mouth. Ha! Sounds like all I've gained from this place is a bag of vices. (It's all sort of fake, though, because I can barely choke down a tiny little espresso and still cough every time I smoke—the Italians roar at that one . . . but it's fun to try.)

Goals:

1. Become a "regular" at a café.

2. Carry on a conversation with an Italian.

3. Ride a motor scooter with an Italian.

p.s. I am happy here. Maybe it's the freedom—I have never felt this way.

13

No trace of summer lingered. The days grew shorter, turning into chilly evenings. Darker fashions, quieter nights on the Campo, and fewer floating pods of tourists. All of Siena seemed to gracefully relax her formidable shoulders.

"I'm going to meet Wyatt for gelato," Isabelle said, walking from their room to the bathroom. Jill sat at the dining table, the large pages of her sketchbook covering the top like a drape, her charcoals laid out. The image of the long table set between the high walls of apartments and homes, lined with wine goblets and candles, the three old men seated at one end was down on the page, but the texture of shadow was incomplete, so the scene appeared flat.

"Wyatt, huh?" she said.

"Yeah, Wyatt," Isabelle called out from the back of the apartment.

"You guys have been spending a lot of time together." She smirked for her own enjoyment, rubbing her thumb along the lines distinguishing the pavers on the street.

Isabelle came and stood over Jill's shoulder.

"Looks really awesome," she said, toweling off her hair. "Spot on."

"The shading's off," Jill replied.

"Well I wouldn't know about that, but I think it looks good. Is this the piece you're going to enter in the contest?"

"Maybe," Jill said, tilting her head for a new angle.

"Hey, what's the latest from your mom?"

Isabelle had a way of referring to the journal as if it were Jill's actual mom. She'd been candidly inquisitive from the first day she saw the article in Jill's hands. She had pried and asked too many questions, and initially Jill had resisted, tried to brush it off with casual replies, but she was insistent, genuinely interested. Plus, she possessed a certain nonchalant informality that negated the potential offense. Jill shared details selectively, and Isabelle didn't press for more. Isabelle's presence in the process of unbraiding the past life of Lily was somehow reassuring, like she would be there, able to extend a hand if Jill began to drown.

There was something she had read in an entry referring to "reliving a nightmare." It didn't stand out at first, but then her mom's tone had gotten sort of dark and she returned to it. The portrait Lily was painting of her family was colored with sadness, something Jill had certainly picked up on over the years—a general melancholia always plopped down on any real joy or humor. She'd always written it off, that it was simply her family's personality, trapped in the cycle of taking themselves too seriously. She fought against that in her own life. And yet, that small reference. *A nightmare.* And this unveiled alcoholism. Perhaps there were reasons for the sadness.

It was after eight when Jill knocked on the door to Ling's apartment.

"Hey," she said as the door opened, and then she retreated back inside. Jill followed her.

"No Ellie or Sarah?" she asked.

"No, they're at dinner," Ling replied. She grabbed her bag and slid her feet into a pair of flats. "Ready?"

IAAE provided the students with one cafeteria meal voucher at the dining halls for *Universita di Siena per Stranieri* for each weekday, and they typically used them for lunch before or after class. Although she hadn't eaten in a dining hall since college, and although her father was paying the bill for her semester and would gladly send her all the money she required, these meals were already paid.

It was a lengthy walk uphill, but at the top was a wide grassy lawn with an overhead view of the city. The building, like the rest in Siena, was an antique in itself. A piece of real estate like it in any American city would have been leveled and turned into expensive condominiums or renovated for preservation, but here the old school cafeteria remained, large and unusually modern with fluorescent panel lighting, colored plastic chairs and tables, and plastic utensil dispensers, servicing young adults with half-decent meals.

"Isabelle told me you met a guy," Jill said. They stood in the line for salads.

"Oh god," she said. "Rocco. We're friends. And no. I mean yeah, but it's not a big deal. We made out twice."

"Where did you meet him?"

"At the cafeteria," she laughed. "It was hilarious. He wasn't expecting me to speak English. Asians in Siena are pretty rare—unless they're tourists or straight from China or Korea or whatever, studying here. He speaks English, so it works. He's from Rome." They made their way over to some empty seats.

"Oh, there's my roommate," Jill said, nodding across several tables to one in the corner where a group of students including Lule sat. Extra chairs were pulled up to the table and a few girls sat on the knees of boys. They all looked young, heedless in the way young people are in packs, before they've been stripped of that electric arrogance. The table was a boisterous epicenter, everyone laughing and talking loudly, drawing the gaze of the students seated at tables beside them.

"Which one?" Ling asked.

"Her back's to us. Pink shirt, long hair."

"Oh yeah," Ling said. "Albanian?"

"Yep," Jill said.

They watched as two girls from a table next to Lule's, who had been glowering at the rowdy group, stood, walked to the table, and tapped Lule's friend on the shoulder. Words Jill could not hear were exchanged. The table grew quieter, only the girls speaking back and forth, and then one of the guys chimed in. A few students at Lule's table stood. They were speaking quickly and more loudly.

"What are they saying?" she asked Ling, who knew more Italian that she. Most people in the cafeteria were watching. Jill kept looking toward Lule, who stayed seated on the other side of the table from where the argument was taking place. She felt protective of the girl.

"Just nasty stuff," Ling said. It appeared to escalate, the instigators stepping forward aggressively, and some shouting, and suddenly there were two men in uniforms standing at the table. The volume decreased immediately, and the girls returned to their seats sneering. The commotion in the room quickly returned to normal.

"Whoa," Jill said. The girls at the two tables continued to cast threatening looks toward one another, but the security guards stayed nearby. Lule appeared quiet now while the rest of her table visibly rehashed the confrontation, maintaining their territory. She looked like a little girl, her mouth closed into a tight line and her eyes searching her lap. "What was that about?"

"I'm pretty sure it was girls being bitches. That table with your roommate," Ling nodded in the direction, "is all Albanians. Those other girls are Italian. They're just being racist, ragging on your roommate's friends because it's easy." She took a large bite of her salad.

"The whole Italians versus Albanians thing is . . . I don't know." Jill shook her head.

"Typical? Or racist? I think that's the word you're looking for." She chewed for a while. "Rocco was literally just explaining this to me. It's like, Albanians come to Italy, and other countries too, like Greece or whatever, for school because what they have in Albania is shit. And you know, Albania is known for a lot of messed-up stuff like drug cartels and human trafficking, et cetera, even though obviously there are plenty of good people there. He was saying that a lot of Italians think Albanians cause all the trouble here—they don't work hard, they're leeches, take jobs from Italians, stir up problems, stuff like that. They're also typically Muslim, and Italians are Catholic." She rolled her eyes behind her square glasses, took another bite, and with a mouth full of food said, "It's just good, old-fashioned racism."

"What does Rocco think of Albanians?"

"He's racist too; he grew up here. Like, white people are generally racist toward Asians, or blacks, or whatever because you're raised in it—you almost can't help it. I'm racist in my own ways, although living in New York dulls your expectations of any one type of person, honestly. I don't think you choose to be racist. I think it's more like you have to make a really conscious choice not to be. Rocco's like that, I guess, trying not to be."

Jill nodded. Her previous ignorance about the country felt reprehensible now that she knew people from Albania. Racism, which had always been unconsciously defined in her mind as white against black, took on new shade now. The roommates just a few yards down the hall from her were under fire here, living in a completely different Italy, fighting.

On weekend evenings students banded together to populate bars or to loaf around the Piazza, bringing new life to the ancient bricks and stones, drinking Peroni and smoking cigarettes as the sky faded to its darkest blue, and then began to lighten with pink and peach. It was a new generation painting on another layer of history on the same old architecture. Ling's apartment had a narrow balcony overlooking the Campo where they squeezed in and leaned against the iron guardrails playing cards and speaking in all the languages shared between them late into the night. It was a constant flux of people. Jill felt like a younger version of herself, as if she were reliving undergrad, that period of time when there was no real responsibility to anyone. When she thought of Zane, and her life at home, she'd begun to feel a sense of claustrophobia. Here she was less unusual as an artist, surrounded by people like her.

Friendships established there in the heart of the city, within the walls draped with bold banners, where unlit torches jutting out overhead made everything look like the scenery of a movie about knights and royalty, took on a certain dreamlike quality, breathed with a fleeting sort of breath. In the late and dark, when the wine bottles had been emptied, they parted company and traipsed through the alleys to their apartments, and as they slept the night's events faded. In the morning everyone returned to his own place, his routine manner of speaking and living. Between classes Jill frequently passed Reynaud, Ling's neighbor who worked at a bar and often showed up on her patio at three or four in the morning, but in the daylight they never exchanged words, only nodded curtly.

"We do the same thing every weekend," Ling said, staring blankly across the Campo to the lit tower against the velvet sky. "We hang around, drink, stay in Siena. We need to go somewhere. Let's go somewhere next weekend, okay?" Her words were soft and round from the alcohol, her lips like putty.

"Where do you want to go?" Wyatt asked. He was smoking a very thin cigar that looked unnatural in his massive hand, his brown leather work boots propped up on the iron rail that prevented them from casting off the edge to the bricks thirty feet below. When she focused on it, it made Jill's stomach drop down out of her body, so she tried not to.

"I don't care, there's about two hundred places. We could go to Venice."

"We're going to Venice with Weldon," Isabelle said, yawning. She had already fallen asleep once.

"I want to go to Spain," Ling said.

"For a weekend? It's too far," Wyatt shook his head. "Stick to Italy."

"What about the Cinque Terre," Jill said. She had been loosely planning it in her head but hadn't mentioned it to the others. The idea of traveling there alone, hiking the trail by herself like a sort of pilgrimage was appealing, but she was not so blind she couldn't recognize the idealism of that plan, the vanity. She had brought it up in an e-mail to Zane, and he'd emphasized the importance of traveling with companions, afraid she'd make acquaintance with an undesirable character and be abducted. It was absurd, really, but with the others it would be fun, and besides, Lily had been there with friends too. Once she'd started in on the journal, Jill hadn't wanted to venture from Siena, totaling the number of days she had there and counting backward. The fresh knowledge of her mom set against the unchanged backdrop of the city made her feel a bit frantic, as if she only had these months to be with Lily again. But Cinque Terre had also meant something to Lily, and she had not been afraid to leave the city. Besides, Jill kept reminding herself that the journal would go home with her, and that relying on the apparition of ghosts was pathologically weird. They agreed to go the following weekend.

The news is on; Brian Prost is discussing the recent scandal with one of the presidential candidates. I'm not watching, but I like the way his voice sounds. He laughs a lot, which dad thinks makes him sound ignorant when it's a serious topic. But I think it makes him sound cheerful. I know he has four children.

I hear the dead bolt slide with a *clack*, and the sound of the door creaking to open. The twelve footsteps, the pause where he flips through the mail, the five more.

Hello.

Hey, Dad.

Hanging out with Brian?

This is what he says to me every day when he gets home from work, like he's making a funny joke but has amnesia. I smile dutifully.

I need you to sign a permission slip for school. I slide my homework over and pull the paper from the folder. The entire seventh grade is going to a nature camp for a weekend in March. The nature part will be lame, but sleeping over will be awesome. Miranda and I are going to try and sneak out of the cabins and go down to the creek where anyone else who can escape will go.

He comes around the side of the table and reads the document. I watch as his eyes fall on the section that requests parents to volunteer to chaperone the trip. They continue down to the signature line. He picks up my pen and signs before he realizes the ink is purple. He looks at the felt tip like it's a strange new discovery.

He gets a beer out of the fridge, twists off the cap, and takes a long swallow. He loosens his tie with the other hand and slides it out from around his neck. The same routine every day. *How was school?*

It was good. School's always good. Work is always fine. There's no room in this dialogue to tell him about Cal Dougherty, how he asked me to go get ice cream, or that I started my period last week. Plus, I'm not sure if that's something I should tell him. I got Miranda to buy me pads.

How was work?

Fine.

His eyes are on the television, still discussing the scandal. I don't know what it actually means.

I have a project for English. I'm supposed to write a three-page essay, double spaced, about a person in my family that's interesting or famous or cool or something.

Mhmm. Maybe he isn't really listening. Perfect timing.

We are supposed to interview other family members about the person we choose. I think I want to write about Mom. I can interview Nana and Grandad and you. I think I would need one more person—it's supposed to be four.

He's looking at me now, and his mouth is closed. So he was listening. His jaw is locked in position so I can see the bone curvature under his ears. He's thinking.

Alright, he says. I feel myself relax a bit. I wasn't sure if he would say yes. Sometimes he's less uptight. And then, lately, there are times he tenses up and avoids me. *Also, so you know, I booked us a trip over Thanksgiving.*

You said we weren't going anywhere this year. It's like three weeks away! This was when I was going to do my interviews.

I decided we needed a vacation. It's been a while.

It has been exactly three months. We went to the Grand Canyon right before school started. I do not need a vacation.

Where are we going? Because there's no point in arguing.

London.

Really?

Yeah, what do you mean really?

We've been to London twice. We should go somewhere different.

Where would you like to go, Jill?

This is a normal sort of discussion—overseas travel on a whim. None of my friends' parents do this kind of thing. All of my friends have mothers.

I don't know. We've never been to Italy.

He contemplates this, nodding up and down very slowly. *I don't think so.*

Why not?

We don't speak the language.

I roll my eyes. That has never hindered us before. *I want to go to Rome.*

Why?

What do you mean, why? It's Rome, dad!

I already booked London. We'll keep it in mind for another trip.

14

Panting thick exhaust, the old train pulled into the station, slowing to a crawl until it lurched forward, exasperated, and finally stopped. The doors facing the platform of the Monteresso station slid apart, and Jill stepped out just as her mother had all those years ago when it had probably looked precisely the same: a simple concrete slab, the old building with a small café and a bathroom, opening up to the widest view of the ocean she'd seen since visiting Montecito three years ago. Perhaps Claudette and Jill had been like Isabelle, perhaps they had traveled on the same train with the same stops. How was it that these places could be so dependably static, and yet, not? Full of different stories, different people, different climates.

The five coastal towns comprising the Cinque Terre perched precariously cliffside on juts of rock and earth over the Tyrrhenian Sea. They were connected by a lengthy dirt hiking trail and were frequented by thousands of nomads on foot every year. The places themselves were inspiring enough, but to Jill they felt sacred. She had begun to nurture a sense of ownership of a land where she was a foreigner, as if Lily's brief bout of tourism had purchased for Jill a deed to the place, as if her mother's stint living in Italy lent her own visit more credibility. Realistically, she did not belong in Italy at all. She had no Italian ancestry. It was the uniqueness of this experience shared with her mom that fueled a hunger she had spent a lifetime trying to quell. How could she explain it? She wanted more, a greater understanding of the past, the whole picture—of Lily, who she was, where she'd been. So much so that the pain of it was actual, as if she had missed the sense of sight or hearing for years, and suddenly found it coming back, pushing her senses to overstimulation.

Later she wandered the small town as the sun began to set. She walked along the crags overlooking the ocean and noted the layers of gray comprising the thick clouds. The outward curvature of the land gave the horizon the illusion of extended width. Two sailboats, tiny white triangles, moved slowly toward one another. Jill sat down with her book bag and watched the frothy navy and white waves smack against the rocks. Setting perfectly in the west, the sun glowed like a backlit orange and Jill thought of Zane. She replayed their last evening together— the jewelry box. Touching the locket hanging from her neck, she tried to imagine he was here with her, sitting beside her. He would probably be commenting on the architectural brilliance of the towns—built into the sides of the cliff face like ears on the side of a head. He would also probably dislike being unable to communicate with locals, and the relatively narrow range of food options. Sitting there she acknowledged the certainty that he would propose—likely when she returned for Christmas. Of course he would, she had expected it, but now the thought filled her with an anxiety she couldn't rationalize.

What would her father say if she told him she was marrying Zane? Her father. She had never asked him for opinions on things like relationships or the future. His advice was reserved for the practical matters, like car maintenance and saving for retirement. Personal things she dealt with alone. It was early afternoon for him—he was somewhere in the direction she faced. That sun would soon pass over him, then set. He certainly wouldn't notice it, or think about Jill having absorbed it first. He would be working. She could understand that a bit better now.

At first she hadn't thought about him much, only when she wrote brief e-mails with the factual details of her classes. The more she read the journal, though, the more often he came to her mind and she wondered when he'd first known this part of Lily's story. It was difficult for her to separate her dad from a Gary a few decades younger. Had he read it before Lily died? Did he understand how different she had once been, the change that had taken place at some point after she was in Italy? Had he, too, been different in those days, whenever *those days* were? What had inspired him to hand over the precious treasure after all the years she had begged for information, followed by the years they both sat silent on the issue? Jill had called Gary a total of three times since landing in Europe, and each conversation lasted no more than ten minutes. She told him facts: classwork, who she hung around with, what they did, where they went, the food, the apartment, the weather. He in turn told her the things she already knew about his schedule, leaving out details either because he thought she wouldn't care or, more likely, because she was not a person by which he desired to be known.

He did ask her details about the city of Siena, responding with some evidence of interest, and in those moments there was a comfort in hearing his voice, like an anchor tethered down through the depths of the ocean into firm sand. They had not discussed the journal, however, and until he did, she wouldn't mention it. She would read it all the way through at her pace and perhaps someday they would speak about it, but for now she preferred to exist alone in the private world she shared with Lily.

Running her fingers over the leather cover, Jill watched the sun sink to meet the horizon like a deflating neon balloon, dip lower below the line, and quickly disappear into the distant ocean. She turned and gasped at the sky to the east. Garishly colored in a spectrum of pinks and oranges, it now looked more like canvas than atmosphere. Dashes of clouds, as if open paint cans had been flung haphazardly through the heavens, created molten streaks and gashes, and she felt the reflection of color in the hue of her face and eyes. A chill traveled over her flesh and she crossed her arms tightly. It was a greeting of camaraderie, a deep affection from a mother for whom she had always longed, closer in this moment under the blushing sky than she had been since the day she'd left Jill for good. She felt a physical presence. Mesmerized, Jill reached for the leather bag without removing her eyes from the marbled artwork and took a sketchpad and some colored pencils. She balanced on a large stone and used her knees as a table. Her eyes flicked up and down quickly like the shutter of a camera, and her hands scrambled to take possession of the canopy above.

Lacking the same power with the pencils as it did with charcoal, her thumb couldn't blend the color the way she wanted. She tried to erase, but it only marred the picture more. She moved to perch on the bench in an effort to capture the fringes of light reaching toward the coast as limbs of a great tree shading the lapping waves, turning the entire ocean into a coral colored pond. It was dissipating. Evaporating. The colors changed too quickly for her hands to follow, and she felt the familiar anxiety that preceded a missed image.

Within minutes the sky was a darkening purple, and the drawing looked childish. She cursed aloud, tearing the page from the book, flexing her hand to crush it, and shoved it into her bag. The waves lapped quietly, but otherwise it was silent and Jill thought fleetingly of the time. In a town like this with few restaurants open for service, it would not be difficult to find her friends. Her hunger was only a dull awareness.

When all color had drained out of the night, and she was left as a shadow standing beside the black ocean under the great chasm of sky above, she began to cry. A reserve somewhere deep within her opened and flooded her from the pit of herself upward until it hit her in the face and her eyes filled with all the tears she had not shed for many years. It surprised her, the ferocity of missing. Time had not dulled her feelings; she had merely closed them in a chest and locked them down. Clutching the journal, she hung her head and cried with her eyes open, allowing her shoulders to shake, allowing herself to weep freely, not holding back the way she usually did, constricting the deluge with the back of her throat. Alone on the beach, she whispered to her mother, lifting her eyes to the stars hoping against her belief, hoping in a god in whom she did not really believe, that Lily could hear her. Then she wiped her face, opened and closed her mouth, composing. Too much time by herself.

Jill wandered up one of the wide streets of Monteresso, peering into restaurant windows. Most were either closed or nearly empty. The wind whipped down the hill and through the street like water through a pipe. She found her friends in a small café and ducked in.

15

"Where have you been?" Isabelle whispered. "Were you crying? Are you okay?" Besides Isabelle, Ling, Wyatt, and Rocco, there were five other strangers.

"I'm fine," she whispered. "Who are they?"

"Met them at the hotel—they're South African." Her eyes lifted. "Their accents are unbelievably sexual."

Jill laughed, and found an empty seat. Over dinner they exchanged basic information with the group of young men traveling on a month-long break between military tours. Wyatt joked exhaustively about the disparity between his studying architecture and the duty of protecting the freedom of a nation, wearing camouflage and wielding guns, but the dynamics within the group were wonderfully balanced to make conversation interesting.

Jill was seated across from Thomas, a striking man with blonde hair and blue eyes, who kept catching her gaze with his, smiling slightly. He was talkative, but not overly so, and it became clear through several understated deferential nuances from the others that he held some sort of military command. Throughout dinner she was distracted by their presence, the way she felt her femininity being drawn to the surface. It had been a long time since she had felt that way. The only place she could truly recall that feeling was in the months she'd spent with Aaron in college. It made her nervous, as if the ground were rumbling beneath and within her.

"Let's go find a bar," one of the soldiers, John, suggested when they had finished dinner a few hours later, when enough wine and limoncello, which the owner had brought out to them on the house, had rendered them warm and relaxed. The air in the streets was cold but refreshing after such a long time in the restaurant.

"It's kind of late—we're hiking tomorrow," Jill said, not because she meant it, but because the presence of the strangers combined with the slackness in her brain was making her nervous.

"God, Jill. That is not you talking." Isabelle's arm was linked in Jill's, a buffer, also fuel.

"I saw one earlier that's open," John suggested, and they followed.

The small bar was full of people—all the people in Monteresso, apparently. Italians that looked like locals, wearing short sleeves and loose pants. Beach sort of people. Also travelers, a mix of skin and hair and height and language. Stephen, one of the soldiers, ordered a round of drinks, distributed them as they came off the bar, and toasted to new friends. Wyatt got louder, showing off for Isabelle in the presence of new competition. There was music, some vague notion of people dancing, holding drinks, moving bodies slightly to the discreet bass.

"Why does it seem like every time I look at you, you look away?" Thomas was behind her, leaning into the bar, speaking into her ear. He left a small distance between them—he wasn't encroaching, but the gap was narrow enough his intent was clear. He was flirting—he had been all evening—and her capacity for resistance was waning. Men usually backed off from her for this reason—her aloofness, the metallic edge in her voice.

Without turning her body, only her head, "I don't know what you mean." She caught his eye. Then felt his hand, his fingertips light on the small of her back, and the gentlest pressure to turn her toward himself. Facing him now, with only a foot between them, she studied his face. There was a scar over his lip. His eyes were dark brown, and his hair fell thick over his forehead. No military haircuts in South Africa. He was smiling as if he was enjoying a game.

"That's better," he said.

"So you're the boss, huh?" Conversation to distract herself.

"Everyone has a boss in the military. I'm on a rung. But you're studying art, and to me that's more interesting."

"Why's that?"

"Well, in the military everyone is following orders. Only Command from the very top of the ladder can exercise creativity. But art is the opposite. Every artist is a creator, calling the shots, writing the story."

"That's sort of true." This was sobering talk. It was obvious he was intelligent, which stimulated her own mental acuity. "Not exactly though. Art is creative in a way, but you're always building on something. It's like, maybe you saw something in nature and then tried to capture it. Or maybe some other art has inspired your piece or your style. Nobody is original." She tried to gauge his interest, and he seemed present in the conversation so she continued. "I don't think you can really say artists are creators. It's more . . . narrators I guess. Or record-keepers. With unique spins."

He laughed and threw back the end of his beer.

"I would be honored to take you for a walk down to the beach. I'll be chivalrous; I won't try to take advantage of you."

"I . . . um . . ." Jill hemmed, glancing back at Isabelle, whose arm was lounging across Wyatt's back. She pictured Zane. In her mind's eye he was in a slightly crumpled suit, his regular after-work attire. He smiled at her; he loved her. If he were here, she wouldn't even be having this conversation.

"You can say no."

His eyes.

"Okay."

"Okay?"

Was he expecting a different response?

"Let's go," she said. As she followed him out the door, Isabelle caught her eye, registering surprise on her face.

When they reached the rocky sand, just feet away from the spot where she'd stood only hours before in tears, Thomas stopped and stepped out of his shoes, leaving them beside a boulder. They began to walk slowly.

"From your discussion of artists, I gather you don't just study them."

"I sketch some. A little painting. Nothing brilliant. How long have you been in the military?" Back and forth, a protective measure.

"Thirteen years. I enlisted when I was eighteen."

Fast calculation.

"That seems like a long time."

"It's gone by quickly."

"Do you like it? I mean, that's probably not the right question. Are you happy to be in the military? Would you do it again, is what I'm asking."

"Yes, to all questions. It's a family business—my father, his father, my brothers."

"I feel sorry for your mom."

He laughed. "She's used to it."

They made their way down a natural pier made of rocks. Jill crossed her arms and wedged her hands in to keep them warm. The ink black sky unyielding, impervious, shone only one large half-moon glowing with a thick halo. She was conscious of his proximity. It occurred to her this wasn't a discerning move, wandering around a foreign town, virtually deserted, with a man she didn't know who had the body of a buffalo, but she was enjoying it. Him. He was standing a few feet from her, looking over the edge. Frothy waves collided with the boulders, smacking loudly, then diminishing to bubbly, retreating pools. She found she wanted to talk to him. He was kind. Present. Responsible. Lovely.

They sat at the water's edge for what felt like a little while. Jill wanted to know what it was like to have a tour, or to be stationed in a strange place. He wanted to know about the United States, somewhere he hadn't been. About the political system, the military there. She could answer some political questions, but few military. He was very intelligent, but in such a way that she didn't feel diminished. There was something grounded about him, as if he was solidly rooted. Confident, unafraid of the tide of his life. They'd flirted over dinner and drinks, but now the conversation felt different.

"I realize you don't know me. You don't know my last name. It's Hammond. Thomas James Hammond."

"Jillian Dunn. Nice to meet you."

"Well there, now we're very well acquainted. I told you I wouldn't take advantage of you, and I won't. But I am about to lean in and kiss you—I'm giving you fair warning. It's just…" he shrugged. "I can't help myself, you are too beautiful."

Before she had time to register, to think or speak, his hands were light on the back of her neck, his fingers in her hair, and he was kissing her. It was soft, the kiss of a gentleman. A first kiss. She'd forgotten that feeling. He didn't pull away when their lips separated. Their faces so close she could smell the beer on his breath.

Thoughts, red lights, memories swirling. She looked into his eyes. He was a stranger.

"Kiss me back, Jillian," he said.

And she did.

16

It was windy and slightly overcast in the morning when they entered the hiking trail heading south from Monteresso. A small wooden sign etched with Vernazza and an arrow pointed down a dirt pathway. The path was carved into the sloping coast, halfway between the foaming sea below and the high edges above, and at the first curve of the trail the town disappeared behind them.

"I think my dad is coming next week," Isabelle said. She held her hand out to the side, letting the leaves run through her fingers.

"Oh, I didn't know he was coming at all."

"Me neither," she said. "That's the way he is."

"How long's he staying?" Jill asked.

"I don't know, probably a few days. He has business in France and Italy, so he's combining business with pleasure." She accented her voice for a dramatic flourish.

"Will your mom come?"

"Nah, she's been to Italy, and she is busy with my step-dad's kids' stuff. Step-mom duties."

Jill nodded, and tried to imagine a life where Lily was married to another man with other children.

"Is Zane going to come? Or your dad?" They moved to the side of the trail, now ascending, as a group of three women passed them heading northward.

"My dad hasn't mentioned it," Jill said. "And it's up in the air with Zane. He's really busy at work all the time. Not the vacationing type."

Isabelle looked at Jill with raised eyebrows. She and Wyatt had found Jill with Thomas down by the beach the evening before. In the darkness, they'd called her name from the road, and she had separated herself from him, disentangling her hands, standing up from the bench on the point. Jill had been so flustered, as if their voices had awakened her from a dream. She'd shouted, *I'm coming,* collected her bag and begun to walk toward Isabelle. Thomas had placed his hand in hers for a moment, but she'd quickly taken it away.

She had lay in bed by the open window long after everyone else was asleep, listening to the ocean crash into the rocks, finally nodding off around two-thirty. She sorted through feelings, resurrecting an image of Zane and willing herself toward a paddock of guilt and anxiety, but realizing ultimately the thought of him made her feel rather flat. When she allowed her mind to go down the alternate road, there was instead a vague sense of appealing openness.

The view was ocean to the west and a lofty, hovering coast on the right, and without warning a thrust of the trail would arch out and back, and the next town appeared. Built into the vertical faces of the seaboard, the buildings grew on top of each other, a rainbow patchwork of architecture, a child's Lego creation in pastels, compressed into a small cove. The trail descended first into Vernazza, then Corniglia, and then Manarola, sister hamlets blending together like the frames of a vivid reverie, and they stopped to explore the seaside squares where fishing boats moored in the tiny harbors. From the street, the town was all overhead, built up, and dozens of stacked clotheslines hung between windows, socks and T-shirts like carnival flags. They found a restaurant with tables overlooking the water in Vernazza and the manager, accustomed to patrons arriving on foot with luggage, showed them a corner where they could drop their backpacks. They ordered Peroni in bottles and Caprese sandwiches.

After they'd finished and sat for some time enjoying the majesty of the colors and the sea, Ling and Rocco wandered off to take pictures and Wyatt went to find a gift for his mom. Isabelle and Jill walked down to the waterside and sat in the sand.

"Do you still have a headache?" Jill asked.

"Not really. I took Advil. Do you?"

Jill shook her head. It did feel good to sit, though. Her body was tired.

"The Cinque Terre is giving Siena a run for her money," Isabelle said. She had removed her shoes and was skimming her toes along the top of the water. She had not asked Jill anything about the night before. "It reminds me of Santa Barbara."

"I've never been."

"Well it's not really like this, but it sort of reminds me of it. But this place is like, not real life. People actually live here! Do you think if you lived here you would still wake up, walk outside every day, and think it was the most beautiful thing you'd ever seen?"

Jill turned back to look. "I bet you get used to it."

"I think you're right, and that is sad. Are you gonna draw it?"

"Maybe," Jill said. "But it's the colors I would want to get right, and colors aren't my thing." She recalled the previous evening, the crumpled sketch. She had almost forgotten the sunset, her tears, compartmentalizing and stowing everything before dinner.

"Whatever," Isabelle said. "If you can draw you can draw."

"No, it's not like that."

"I'm not an artist, so I wouldn't understand?" She said, mocking.

"I didn't say it," Jill said, and smirked. The colors of Lily's paintings had been brilliant, perfectly mastered. She thought of them, subconsciously pulling at the locket around her neck. "So," she wanted to redirect the conversation, away from all of the things bouncing around in her head like pinballs. "What about Wyatt?"

"Wyatt?" Isabelle mimicked Jill's suggestive intonation.

"Well?"

"Wyatt is Texas, which I don't do."

Jill laughed. "That's stupid."

"No, it's actually smart. Texas people are one hundred percent physical, no intelligence."

"That's the dumbest thing I've ever heard. Not to mention the fact that you and Wyatt are together on a very regular basis."

Isabelle shrugged.

"Are you into him?" Jill said.

"Oh, I don't know. He's funny."

"That's it?"

"That's the best part about him." They observed the water for a few minutes. "I have to ask you."

Jill looked at Isabelle.

"Did you get his number?"

"What?"

"You know exactly what."

Jill looked back toward the ocean.

"No."

Isabelle nodded. "Okay then."

The next day Jill woke up and sat in the bed against the wall, staring out at the low, gray mist over the ocean, wishing there were someone to deliver coffee. The water looked different, as if the night had dulled it, removed the diamonds from its surface. Her body was sore in a pleasing way, her muscles taut from the hours they had spent hiking down the coastline. Isabelle and Ling were still asleep, so she pulled her charcoals and sketch book from her book bag and started on a new image.

She drew out the frame of her window, straight, perpendicular lines. The day before, during the hike, she had batted all the factors around in her head. Zane and Thomas, the moment in time when she'd sat on the point over the water as a silhouette with a strange man beside her, feeling deliriously free, another time, when she'd thought she was about to be engaged. Oddly, her mind had also wandered to Aaron. She had felt crazed, guilty, discombobulated. Yet, in the stillness of the morning, she felt somewhat detached. Untroubled. She moved on to the water, still and textured.

The water's expanse toward the horizon was motionless. The way of the clouds, thin and long. Her relationship with

Zane was a decision she'd made. He was stable and smart, and loved her. Before him, she'd gone on countless dates with a wide variety of men and nothing satiated her. Then she'd met Zane. He worked for her, they fit nicely together. She did love him, in his way. But then, like crocodile eyes, beads on the surface of the pond, other notions emerged from time to time. Perhaps there was something better. When she allowed her imagination freedom to roam, she imagined a different sort of love, something with more at stake. Was she afraid of letting him down? She certainly wouldn't tell him about this one night in the Cinque Terre when she slackened in the embrace of a stranger from South Africa, a stranger who had somehow, in one evening, unearthed her. Or perhaps it had been happening gradually. Her hands moved gently, easily over the page, and in minutes there was the likeness of the open sea from her window. In its simplicity the drawing satisfied her.

She sat alone on the ride back to Siena, citing her headache, and opened the journal on her lap, finding the page where she had left off a little less than halfway through. It was a welcome distraction redirecting her focus again. She read a few sentences at a time, stretching them out like putty, and was immediately transported. Her gaze settled outside the window as land raced in the opposite direction. She relished the words in a way, but reading them also gave her an agitated feeling, and thinking of her father reading it was worse. The author of the entries was a stranger. This Lily had despised her home, hated her malignant relationship with her parents and the fact that Jill's grandfather had been an alcoholic. There was a biting edge in Lily's voice, and even though Jill wanted to know it all, it made her nervous. She had her own skeletons—she thought of her relationship with Aaron, the things she had said to him, and even more toxic, the things she had felt toward him. Her feelings toward her father. There were things she would never tell anyone, very least of all her daughter some day in the future. It was unnatural to know a parent from before one's own birth, but she couldn't stop because for twelve years she had longed to understand her mother, to fill the vast emptiness of her history with story, and now was her chance. She came to an entry that caught her attention. It was different from the others at the first sentence.

17

I met someone. I'll get there.

I've accomplished one of my three goals and become a "regular" at a café. About two weeks ago I turned down this side street near the Duomo that, oddly, I'd never even seen before. That keeps happening—finding streets I've passed but somehow never seen. This city is like a haunted castle in that way, I swear some of these things disappear and then appear in new places. Anyway, I turned down the street and found an itty bitty café with a bright blue door. I was starving for lunch—had just been painting at the Duomo with my class. I walked in and I knew it was meant to be. It was this cavernous little room, the ceilings were so high, but the space was narrow. Wide windows at the apex of the roof let in such great light. There were four tables and a bar counter where a tiny woman was standing, maybe in her forties, and it was all so quaint. She was small, the place was small. Adorable. I wanted to set up my easel right there and start painting. I really did! I ordered a square of pizza with eggplant on it and it was incredible. Hot and fresh, the best red sauce I've had, thick crust, cheesy. She must have just made it.

I sat down with my pizza and the woman actually came over to sit with me. She spoke pretty good English, and that surprised me since most of the Sienese don't seem to speak it, or else they just won't speak it to me. She's the friendliest local I have met by far—some are stand-offish, but I can understand that. My Italian is abysmal. I wouldn't want to talk to me either. Her name is Rosa *and she owns the place with her husband, Leone, whose family has lived there "always." That's the word she used. Thousands of years maybe! I've gone back several times, when I have time because it isn't exactly on the way to anywhere I ever need to go. Rosa is always there and she gives me an eggplant pizza whenever I come in the afternoon, even if I don't ask. It's cheap—half a euro for a slice. If I come in the morning I get a cappuccino (unless it's late morning, because it's very gauche to drink coffee with milk at that point?). I've been once in the evening and had a beer. It's just called Café Duomo. Original. Maybe I'll help Rosa with the marketing. She has three sons, all off at school in Milan. Maybe she is older than 40. She looks young.*

There was a guy reading there when I first found it, and I met him. Ha! What luck. He was there again the second time I went, reading an English book about Thomas Jefferson, and that obviously caught my eye. He is very handsome—dark hair and eyebrows. He's less trendy than some of the Italian men I've met. Very casual, but also very put together. I haven't figured out how they pull it off—looking debonair, but also relaxed. Men in the States are not that way, it's one or the other. You're a banker or a lumberjack, but not both. Anyway, I was looking (very conspicuously) at the cover of his book—I think I was actually gaping, which is humiliating, and he looked up to take a sip of his coffee and saw me. He actually started laughing! I'm a classic fool! When I sat down with my coffee, totally avoiding his look, he came over to my table and struck up a conversation. It was nice. His English is incredible, though my Italian is improving a lot and we switched between languages. He clearly did that for my benefit—absolutely charming. He is from Siena—his family is in trains. That is what he told me, whatever being "in trains" means. I didn't ask because at that point we were in Italian. Anyway, we talked for a long time and when I left, he asked me to have dinner. We did. We went out the following evening (this was a week ago or something) and had a ball! Stayed out until four—dancing at this little bar up near the Piazza Matteoti! He is a great dancer, and I got several dirty looks from some Italians. There were no other Americans at the bar, but a lot of French and Spaniards. Lucky I can dance, or else I think they would have chucked me out. Dancing to Europeans is so passionate, it's spiritual. And it was so warm and fun and he just stuck with me the whole time, like he was really there <u>with me.</u> Maybe the best night of this trip so far. Actually, maybe the best night of my life. Wow—I'm gushing. Didn't mean to. We've had dinner again since. And we're meeting up this weekend.

Back to reality . . . received a letter from Jodie yesterday and got all the details about the wedding. Only a few months away now and she's really happy. Three pages of wedding plans, details, times, colors and flowers. Guillotine, please. I think I'll elope. She and Buck are going to be in Paris for two weeks on honeymoon— I should be back here by the second week of their trip and they want to come see me in Siena at the end. That will be fun. I want Jodie to see this place. I miss her.

Late for class now—supposed to do charcoal today, which I generally despise. No color. Ciao!

18

Professor Weldon Grimes taught Italian History, the class that felt least pertinent to her degree but which perhaps she enjoyed the most. He was a peculiar man. His Cockney was thick, a paste in the mouth, a choking hazard, and he spoke of his tiny hometown of Romford, England, as if it were the Queen's birthplace. The first time they had met him, the Wednesday of their second week of classes, his week-and-a-half lateness due to his having been held up on "business," he'd offered a brief autobiography.

"My mother was from Belgium, my father from England. They are dead now. It was an explosive, volatile union with only one child produced in the throes of passion, myself." He had bowed slightly. The students sat more attentive than ever. "They are never married because she hates the name of Grimes, and my father could not convince her otherwise. She was a very stubborn woman." At six feet, four inches tall, the professor, who preferred to be called Weldon, was visibly imposing with his full head of graying hair, his perfectly perched spectacles, a cycle of bright orange, red, and yellow pants, and an odd wool jacket that he switched for plain T-shirts in the heat. His accent, so confounded between its sources, required the listener to pay very strict attention, yet he spoke at such a volume that people passing the open-doored classroom would often poke a head in to find its source. Weldon was passionate about the whole world and its past, had attained PhDs in Italian History, Belgian

History, and British History, and made a living teaching students in programs such as IAAE in countries around the world. He gave the impression of someone who had enjoyed life to its limits, drank a great deal of wine and Scotch, and entertained numerous women of a wide variety in the course of his intrepid life. In the small city of Siena, Grimes was a single mistuned key on a grand piano.

Weldon's eccentric and unwieldy thought processes often took discussions of Italian history on strange and nonsensical paths, frustrating the note-takers who tried in vain to keep an outline of the lessons. After the first class, Jill had closed her notebook and given up on lecture notes in favor of listening to his stories, histories, and rabbit trails. When, a month into the semester he presented their first test, she was glad to see one lengthy essay question that read: "In your opinion, who was the greatest Italian leader between 1200 and 1500. Explain." She received a B.

The class met on Tuesdays, Wednesdays, and Thursdays from three forty-five until seven in the evening, though they had yet to begin on time and Weldon often dismissed them for a fifteen-minute coffee break an hour into class. After one such interlude, they returned and sat.

"Okay, children," he began, and they grew quiet immediately. "I have a project for you. My degrees are from the Sorbonne, Cambridge, and Universitat Heidelberg, and from each one I learned about the history of our species differently. History is dependent on perspective. There is no such thing as objectivity.

"You must will interview one or two or three, or fifty locals for an un-American perspective on an historical event. It will be best you find educated people, you know, because it is so hard to get good conversation from the ignorant." He turned and walked back to his desk, sat down, and began to read from a heavy book on the desk.

Heather raised her hand and began to speak. "What are the parameters of this project?"

His inscrutable gaze lingered on her face for several moments before he responded. "What do you want with parameters?"

She flushed. "I just mean, what are we supposed to do with our information? How do we present it? And how many questions do you want us to ask?" It was obvious she had more questions, but his expression corked her.

"It is your decision; it is your project."

With October came shorter, colder days. By the time they were dismissed from class, the darkened street was alive with students and working class people on their way home to make supper, warm up, and settle in. Isabelle and Jill walked up Via Banchi di Sopra toward the small grocery store located on the Piazza Matteoti beside Era's McDonald's. Amedeo had mentioned this abomination to Jill, informing her that it was only in recent years the city had allowed the American chain inside the walls. He called it a "black mark." She wondered what he would think of the fact that she lived with two Albanians with an extra on the couch. From the few conversations they'd had, he didn't seem like the sort of person who would concern himself with the business of hating an entire people group, but then again she didn't really know him. She had considered interviewing him for Weldon's assignment.

"I'll get milk, cereal, and pasta toppings," Jill said as they entered the store. It was after seven but still jam-packed with shoppers, pressed so closely to one another that if you missed something going down the aisle, you were unlikely to make your way back upstream.

"Yep, I have laundry detergent, toilet paper, pasta, and wine." The roommates broke to assemble their baskets and check out as quickly as possible. Heading for the back of the store, Jill moved slowly, poking her arms between people to grab her items. They met ten minutes later at the checkout belt, and Isabelle pulled a handful of change in euros from the outside pocket of her shoulder bag and handed it to Jill. People stood so close that one person's groceries could easily end up in the bag of the next person. Jill could see the empty earring hole in the back of the woman's lobe beside her.

It was dark and windy on the walk home, but the street was still busy. Jill kept the toilet paper tucked close under her arm, and shifted the heavy bag between hands every so often. Each open storefront glowed orange and cast its shadow of light to the ground. Doors were kept closed now that the freedom of summer warmth was gone, so every time someone walked in or out of a restaurant, the noise from within would rush out with a burst, then be sucked back in when the door swung closed again.

As they entered the Piazza, a jubilant song rang from the inside of one of the restaurants, followed by a loud cheer, and the girls peered over their shoulders for the source. It was a bar showing the Siena versus Milan match. The restaurant overflowed with fans in their sweaters and scarves, arms draped over each other, swaying to their fight song.

"Anything interesting from your mom's journal?"

A woman talking on a cell phone walked straight between them, her voice scraping them as it passed like keys on a car.

"She mentioned this café near the Duomo where she used to hang out. I might go see if it's still there." Exhausted from internal processing, Jill continued. "It's really strange to read—she may have been younger than we are. I sort of have her confined to what I remember, so that's like four or five years maybe. She probably wasn't even really like that; I mean, I have these weird details and memories, and it's only in the last few years I can sort them out and they can start to make sense. But then I read this, and it feels like I didn't even know her at all."

"Doesn't your dad fill you in?"

"It's weird with him," Jill said. This would be an exercise of restraint and honesty. "He's a nice guy. He is a *good dad*. But he's also—I don't know. We don't have a good time. We're not close."

"When did your mom die? What was her name again?"

"Lily," Jill said. "She died when I was nine."

"Of what?"

"Cancer."

"God, I hate cancer."

"Yeah," Jill said, finding Isabelle's frankness to be something of a relief.

Via del Porrione was crowded, and a few small cars beeped their pithy horns for pedestrians to move out of the way, to no avail. Stopping in front of their great, green door, Jill dug the large bronze key from the front pocket of her book bag and inserted it into the lock. Together, the girls slipped through the doorway and pushed it closed behind them, suddenly muffling the cacophony outside.

"I just think it's really cool," Isabelle said. "That you get to have this intimate information. I think about my parents, and how if they divulged the deep, dark secrets of their youth to me, it would be a total sham. Like, they would never tell me the truth. Not because they're bad people, but just because I know I would never tell my hypothetical kids about a lot of the stuff I've done. Or actually, *thought*. You can paint decisions and actions in an excusable light, but you can't glamorize your thoughts." Isabelle inserted the key into their door and pushed it open. "Is there anything juicy in—"

They both stopped in the doorway.

Era was standing beside the door to their room, which stood open. They habitually closed the door upon leaving, a small act to assure some measure of privacy in the apartment shared with strangers. She had been speaking quickly in Albanian when they opened the door, but she now stared at them, her face drawn into a portrait of horror. "Luan," she whispered.

There was rustling from within their room, and then Era's brother appeared. He didn't acknowledge the girls but walked past his sister and toward the kitchen.

"Hey," he said.

"No, no, no, no," Jill said. "Not 'hey.' What are you doing?" Her eyes followed him, the casual, juvenile slump of his shoulders, his emotionless expression. He did not look up, and it was Jill's first interaction with Era's brother, so she was unsure about his command of English. She looked to Era who had not moved an inch.

"Era, what were you doing in our room?" Isabelle said. Her voice was calmer than Jill's.

"I'm sorry," she began. She rubbed her hands down the sides of her thighs the way one does in a public restroom when there are no paper towels. It was as if her feet were planted to the spot in cement. "My brother is looking for something."

"In our room?" Jill said. Her voice was taut, a tenor understood across all languages.

They stared between each other for several seconds, none knowing what came next. It occurred to Jill that she had trusted Era initially because she was mousy and quiet, not thinking she could pose any sort of threat. In reality, they didn't know the girl at all.

Luan, who had retreated to Era's bedroom, returned wearing a jacket. He muttered something to Era, and she flicked her small eyes to him, giving her head the slightest shake. He repeated himself, and moved toward the door without looking at them. Jill and Isabelle had not moved, and to leave he brushed Isabelle's shoulder with his broader one. As if his motion had suddenly snapped her back to attention, Era scurried to the door and grabbed her bag from the coat rack.

"I am sorry," she said again, then slipped by sideways.

They turned and watched her move down the steps, then turn.

"What the hell was that?" Jill said.

Isabelle shook her head slowly. "I have no idea."

"If she comes back tonight . . . "

"Yep."

19

"Okay, here's the story," Jill said, pulling groceries from the bags and setting them on the counter, handing Isabelle a knife, a cutting board, and the vegetables. They had discussed the strange encounter with Era and Luan to death for twenty minutes after combing through their room where they found nothing amiss, and finally quit without headway. As she unpacked the sausage, she spoke.

"It's not that complicated. My mom had cancer for a year or so before she died. Around middle school I guess I started asking my dad questions about her, but he avoids the subject. He's not really . . . open about stuff." She paused, looking at Isabelle, who nodded and threw the onions into a pan now simmering with garlic and oil. "This went on for years. All during middle and high school. I'd ask him about her, he'd ignore the questions. I got really mad about it for a while, and I used to scream at him to tell me, but he still wouldn't. We had one major fight early on in college." The dark study, the wall of books, the fireplace, the running oils as the canvases burned—it was all so vivid in her memory. She thought about the expression he'd worn just before she turned and left the room, a stunned Jekyll surveying the damage done by his alter-ego, Hyde. She too had felt like an animal that night. "He's stubborn; he can be an ass. We both are actually. It's been a Cold War ever since. We're nice to each other, but it's like we're colleagues or something."

"It's weird he won't tell you anything." Isabelle added the rest of the chopped vegetables and filled a pot with water to boil. "Like, I get that it's sad for him, but at the risk of sounding like an insensitive bitch, it's been a while. Do you think he's like trying to hide something?"

Jill's eyes found Isabelle's briefly, then returned to the sausage. "I have no idea. I don't think so. Gary's not nearly interesting enough to have secrets. He's a workaholic in a love affair with nice cars. And I mean, I haven't asked in a long time. "

"So back to the journal—"

"Right, so he hands it to me at the airport's curbside drop-off. It was really strange, and he drops this vague bomb about my mom studying in Siena, or doing art here, or something."

"I find it almost unbelievable that you didn't know your mom had been here."

Jill shrugged. The sausage and onions sizzled loudly in the cast iron skillet. She pulled the cork from a bottle of Chianti they'd opened the night before and split the remaining wine between two large glasses.

There is a cadence of life that draws a person in, always rhythmically moving forward, and the simple thing is to be swept along and lulled to a kind of peace, never looking back; the difficult thing is to put a foot on the ground and fully wake, breaking the rhythm to confront what has passed. In her case, her foot had been forced. She had moved on in life, until now.

"Are you finished?"

"What?" Jill handed her the glass.

"The journal."

"No, I'm trying not to rush. I kind of want it to last while I'm here, you know? It's like she's narrating it." It was the truth—Lily's recollections of the Piazza del Campo, the views at Porta Pispini, Riomaggiore; the sights she'd recorded were vivid because Jill had seen them for herself. The details Lily had assumed from memory were completed for Jill in person.

"When was she here?"

"I'm not sure. My dad didn't say, and the journal's not dated."

"Was she in college?"

"I don't know," Jill repeated. "She was taking art classes, but she never says a year or references him or anything." What Jill did not say was that it felt like her mom was so caught up being away that her time in Siena was a separate timeline from the rest of her life. If she hadn't known the outcome would be her own existence, she would have assumed Lily never left Italy.

"This is a very bizarre story," Isabelle said.

"I know."

Sticking her fork into the boiling water of spinning noodles, Jill lifted one and pulled it out, dropping it quickly on the counter top. Blowing off her scalded fingertips, she picked it up again and put it in her mouth. "It's done."

Isabelle and Jill sat down at the table and turned on the television for the eight o'clock hour of American night shows with Jay Leno and Conan O'Brien. A haze of steam rising from the oiled noodles and sauté warmed their faces as they ate without talking. When the television switched back to Italian, Isabelle turned it off. Swirling the last few sips of wine in the bottom of her glass, she gazed at Jill thoughtfully.

"What?" Jill said.

"Are you scared of what you'll find out?" she said.

"I'm not scared," Jill began. She sifted words, defining feelings through a sieve in search of the correct one. The journal sat in her bag, a glowing live wire. She wanted to read it, yes, but she realized now as she sat staring at the black TV, she also didn't. What was it Gary hadn't told her? Why had Lily changed? After a lifetime of unanswered questions buried in silence, the voice of her mother was like a narcotic. She could easily become addicted, but the repercussions could be subversive—discovering something new would mean the secure confines of her self-erected kingdom could be shaken, even leveled. The pretense that the journal was an insignificant addition to her world wasn't going to hold up.

"I don't know, maybe," she said finally, then stood up from the table and carried her plate to the kitchen.

The studio is loud with Mozart and painting students talking to each other and the jackhammer across the street putting in new light posts. Everyone's back is to me, and Mama is walking around between easels, stopping to say things to the artists I can't hear, stooping down to them, wrapping them with encouragement in the way she does to me. The window is open because there's a cool fall breeze.

My hair comes down from my braid and tickles the sides of my face, around my eyes. I push it away with the back of my wrist and accidentally brush my shoulder with the paintbrush, missing the smock, leaving a brown gash on my pink sweater.

They're painting animals. At the front there's a sample of a donkey she painted. She was doing it last night in the kitchen, humming to the commercial jingles while Dad and I watched a television show where different people are in a contest to see who can do the best in the wilderness with only a few useful items. She had her head propped up against her left hand, and painted with her right. I watch her, but she never notices. She doesn't notice things when she's painting. She did not make a single mistake, and it is the most beautiful picture of an animal I've ever seen. Its fur is rainbow, sort of. But it looks right.

I'm trying to copy hers, but the legs look like posts and the bit of hair between the donkey's ears looks like a crown.

She comes back to me and peers at my attempt. She is smiling.

Do you like it?

No. I know I'm whining, and she looks at me with an expression that warns against it.

Why not?

It doesn't look right.

Who's to say what's right? She is looking at me, not my donkey. *Art is personal expression. Nothing is right or wrong. Why don't you try a different animal?*

Like what?

What's your favorite animal?

I think about this. The first thing that comes to mind is an ostrich with the obtuse body and skinny neck and legs. *Ostriches.*

She laughs but doesn't challenge me on it. Until today my favorite animal was a dolphin. *Well, try that. Get a new paper.*

I don't know how to draw it.

Call it up in your memory and give it a shot.

She walks away from me to the front of the studio and brings the class to attention. She is talking about brush strokes and paint density and water ratio. Her words hit me separately,

unconnected, and I don't listen to a single one. I disagree—
there is right and wrong. Some things I draw and paint look
awful. Everything she paints is beautiful. When I get mad and
crumple up my papers, she always says it takes practice, but I
don't want to practice. I'm not patient like her!

I start with the body, a floating ball. Then the neck.

It was a Wednesday, the air was clear and crisp, and Jill made
her way toward the Duomo. A few brief visits had given her a
chance to wander small side streets around the cathedral, and
she had located one turn that seemed closest to what Lily had
described in her journal, though she had not actually had time
to venture down it. Jill sometimes imagined it was hundreds of
years earlier in the city, without the modern touches of colorful signs, cars, electric lights. She imagined the stones rattling
during battles, the streets teeming with carts and horses. It was
easy to envision.

She had received another e-mail from Gary asking about
what she had been up to and, for the second time, about her
progress on the journal, which he'd added as a postscript. She
had typed a few replies, deleting each one. What was there to
say? *What's the whole story, Dad? Why the holdout?* He was giving her a green light, but she didn't proceed. Words didn't seem
to form the right sentences, and she'd discarded her reply.

The steps to the massive edifice were wide, made of a
marbled stone, and a few people sat reading, conversing, eating sandwiches, accustomed to the grandeur—it was no more
than another park bench. Part of its towering face was covered

in scaffolding and an enormous canvas with an image of the
building printed on it, as if it could trick a tourist into thinking he were looking at the architecture dead on, except that the
printed sky was an unearthly blue, slightly greened from the
heat of the sun. Half of the actual face was visible, and the tri-
angular apex at the top with its circular window like a ship's
portal reflected the cottony clouds. Jill stood at the base of the
steps leading up to the three great doors of the cathedral and
looked around. A small band of boys ran in circles in the street,
chasing pigeons with slingshots. She moved to the left, crossing
the stone square toward the narrow street, and walked slowly,
considering each door and storefront.

Reaching a dead end where she would be forced to take a
left or right, Jill turned around and realization struck her blind.
It was as plain as if she'd been coming there her whole life—the
blue door from the painting hanging above her bed, propped
open, the entrance tall enough for a full-sized elephant to walk
through, so recognizable she laughed. Faded and barely legible,
a wooden sign hung beside the door that read *Café Duomo*. She
stood still in the middle of the street until someone bumped
into her shoulder, and she backed all the way up to the wall
opposite the door. Leaning against it, she continued to stare.

It was all real, sound now emanated from the black and
white score. The journal, the stories, the art classes, the trip to
the Cinque Terre, Claudette and Jillian, Jodie and Buck, the
wedding, the alcoholic father, the wild teacher. Her mother. It
was all real now that the Café Duomo with the blue door stood
solid and palpable in front of her, while at the same time that
door hung over her bed in her apartment back home. Sucking
in a thick gulp of air, Jill realized she had been holding her

breath for several seconds, and her reverie broke as a young man stepped out of the café and into the street, glanced at her ghostly face, and turned away from her. She walked slowly toward the door, took another deep breath, and entered.

The café appeared precisely the way Lily had described it years before—down to the tables. It was different than what she'd pictured, as the reality of a thing is always different than what is imagined; but the familiarity was satisfying like a movie made accurately from a book, where one is finally able to enter that beloved world that he has only imagined in his mind's eye. Light from the high window fell on a few patrons seated at tables, eating slices of pizza and drinking Coca-Cola, sipping on small cups of espresso. A young woman behind the counter stood wiping the inside of the glass display case with a grayish cloth. She didn't acknowledge Jill until she approached the bar and waited quietly.

"Ciao," she said, pulling her head out of the case full of pizza, croissants, and paninis.

"Ciao," Jill replied. "Vorrai un pizza."

"Questo?"

Pointing at the last piece with whole slices of tomato over fresh, melty globs of white cheese, Jill said "Si" when the girl touched it with her silver tongs.

"Grazie," Jill said. She paid for the pizza and a Coke and sat down at the table nearest the door. She took a bite and was surprised to find it bland and dry.

She watched the room discreetly, keeping an eye on the girl behind the counter. Jill compared the scene to one that might look vaguely like it in America, though in American cafés coffees were served in much larger cups made of paper with plastic lids and cardboard cuffs to protect the drinker from a burned hand that might result in a lawsuit for the franchise owner. Lunch, like the coffee cups, was also much simpler here—a plate of pasta or a slice of pizza. Fewer options and fresh ingredients took the focus away from the food. Two gentlemen sat comfortably playing a slow game of chess and drinking espresso. Seated with his back toward her, the older of the two leaned casually against the chair, while the other sat forward, his chin propped between his thumb and forefinger. They reminded her of Amedeo. Speaking softly, they seemed much younger than the whiteness of their hair, and she watched them as she waited.

As Jill took the last bite of her pizza, an old man came in through the blue door, shouting goodbye to someone on the street. Approaching the counter, he slipped around the side and began talking to the employee in less than hushed tones, speaking so fast and with such a thick accent that Jill couldn't make out a single word. She watched them obviously. After a fast exchange, the girl removed her apron, took the pin out of her hair so it fell down past her shoulders, kissed the man on his leathery cheek, chirped "Ciao, Nonno," and went into the back.

The old man took the gray rag and wiped the counter. He restacked espresso cups and plates, examined the newspaper. When he had taken a seat on the stool beside the register, Jill approached the counter.

"Ciao, bella," he said with a smile.

"Ciao—" She dipped her face minutely. "Do you, by any chance, speak English?" The question came out hard and fast, and she couldn't decipher the expression on the man's face.

He smirked and tilted his head, surveying her. "Some."

"Okay, I'll try then." She felt suddenly overheated. "My name is Jillian." She stuck out her hand. Taking it, he brought it to his face, kissed the skin on her knuckles, and let go, raising his eyes, which sparkled with youthful playfulness. Blushing, she nodded, uncomfortable in a way she rarely felt.

"Sono Signor Gavarola," he said.

"Signor Gavarola," she repeated. "I have a strange question."

He nodded again, maintaining the unflickering half-smile.

"A long time ago a woman—or, a girl—came to Siena. From America. She was maybe my age, maybe a few years older or a few younger. I don't know. She was a little shorter than I am." Jill stood up, leveled her hand with her eyes. It was stupid, she realized then, so unlikely. "She had wavy blonde hair. She was beautiful and . . . an artist." The more she said, the more doubtful she became. The Signor did not indicate a response, so she continued. "Painting and drawing—that's why she came I think. To study the Italian technique."

"Italy is the country for artists," Gavarola interjected.

"Yes, I agree," Jill said, expelling air with a strange gust of laughter. "Okay, well this girl used to visit a café. It may have been this café. In fact, it had to be this . . . one." She stopped, raising her eyebrows.

"I see."

"She used to talk to the woman who owned or worked here. An older woman. Rosa." She had saved the name for last, knowing that the mention of a name would resolutely determine the existence of the woman, of both women. If he knew the name, if a Rosa had once worked here or been affiliated with the café, she was mere steps behind her mom. If he did not, she feared it would all evaporate.

The old man maintained his posture, though Jill detected a small tremor across his face. When he didn't speak for a few moments, she looked stiffly at her feet. Raising her gaze again, she said, "I was just trying to—"

"Rosa died six years ago, ragazza. My wife."

Jill's eyes burst wide. "Oh my gosh. She was your wife." The possibility had not entered her singularly focused mind. She hadn't really believed it could happen—crossing paths from the past, yet Jill felt the crushing weight of disappointment that they were both gone. Two ends, both dead.

"We are married forty-one years."

They were strangers, Jill and the old Italian restaurateur, each processing the singular agony of loss.

"I'm sorry," she whispered. And she was sorry—for him, but also for herself. She had come so close. This was the right café, a specific place where her mother had been known by an actual human being. Thinking that Lily had stood where Jill stood now, had talked to this man's wife, and now both were buried in the ground, made her want to scream.

"This is life." Looking deeply into her eyes, he smiled. "Why do you ask about the girl?"

"She was my mom," Jill said flatly. "She's dead too."

"Sit down. I will get you espresso."

Obediently she moved toward the table nearest the counter and sat, her hands folded over the red and white checked cloth. He sat down and slid a small cup and saucer toward her.

"I am Leone." Jill perked up.

"She wrote about you."

"I remember your mother. Lily. You resemble her."

"You knew her?"

"Not well. She came to sit with Rosa many afternoons. How they talked and laughed! Rosa painted some, they exchange ideas, and Rosa helps Lily with her Italian. She was so terrible with the accent, and she ask the signora to repeat words thousands of times. Rosa fell in love with your mama, so beautiful and kind. She wants to stay in Italy forever, I remember."

Jill nodded. "Do you know why she didn't?"

He looked at her with strange curiosity. "No. She is suddenly gone. It is vague in my mind, but I remember how Rosa mourned her leaving, how she missed the girl. We had three sons. Lily was a daughter."

"When did she leave?"

"Sometime in the winter . . . or early in spring? I don't remember. I am an old man, Jillian, and I have lost my wife and my oldest son. Time and sadness has wiped away many memories. The gift of age is the numbing of some things that are painful." He touched his heart.

A customer walked in, and Leone excused himself. Jill glanced up at the clock and realized with a start that her class had begun ten minutes ago. "I have to leave," she stammered to him, muddled by the wild run of her thoughts. "I have a class now."

"Who is your teacher?" Leone asked over the bar, suddenly cheered.

"Weldon Grimes. He's British."

"He is an unruly man, drinks like a shipmate, and tells stories better than an Italian."

Jill placed her saucer on the counter. "Yeah, he's crazy. Oh!" she reached for her backpack. "May I take a photograph of you, here?"

"Si, va bene."

Removing the camera from the bag, she stood back to capture Leone in front of the counter with the walls reaching up behind him to the glowing ceiling. He stood still, maintaining the characteristic slight smile, and she took a few shots.

"I'll be back," she said, returning the camera to the bag. "Maybe we could talk a little more."

"It is my great pleasure, bella. Please, you will come back and bring your boyfriend."

"Okay," she said, smirking. "Thank you, Signor Gavarola."

"Prego, ragazza."

20

It was over a week before Jill or Isabelle saw Era, and it seemed as though Luan hadn't returned either. Between her job and school, she spent most hours out of the apartment, but it seemed like she hadn't even come back to sleep. When Isabelle asked Lule, she only shrugged. Isabelle had gotten the impression that the girl hadn't really comprehended anything she'd said.

In the middle of the day, Jill returned home to retrieve a paper she had written on the art in the Torre del Mangia for Professor Bova. Era stood in the kitchen over a pot of boiling water and jumped when Jill said, "Hi Era."

"Hi Jill." Her face flushed.

"How are you?" Jill approached the kitchen. Her body filled the better part of the doorway, unwittingly cornering Era. The small girl sunk a bit, cowering like a dog that has been caught pulling scraps from a trash bin.

"Good."

They looked at one another with faltering reserve. Jill lodged her thumbs between her shoulders and the straps of her book bag. "Is Luan gone?"

Era nodded, giving the pot a stir. They couldn't know each other, Jill thought. Their best chance was an exchange of simple phrases and answers to questions. She considered that it was her own ignorance of only knowing English that prevented it. It was uncomfortable talking even now, but one question was unavoidable.

"Era, why was he in our room last week?"

"I'm sorry," she said quickly. "I'm very sorry. I try to tell him no for going in your room, but he will not hear me. He just go in."

"Why?"

"He did not take—" she gestured with the spoon, "—he is stealing nothing."

"Alright," Jill said. They had looked through their things and come to the same conclusion. She continued to stare at the girl, but it seemed like she was finished.

"Why did he go in there?"

Era closed her eyes and lowered her head slightly. She seemed to grapple not with her inadequacy of language, but with the substance of her reply. Jill waited for such a long moment she almost spoke, but Era took a deep breath.

"Is very hard for me to explain to you," she said, suddenly aged. The bright eyes she usually wore grew instantly dull, as if she had removed a tight plastic sheet from her face. There was agony in her expression. "Albania, my country, it is beautiful. The beach there is so pretty, and the people look like Italians. But in the last years," she gestured with her hand, rolling it backward, "it is very bad there. Sometime—um—years ago? The government change from communism."

Jill wanted to stay firm in her insistence Era explain her brother, but she was intrigued.

"After that, everything is crazy. Albanians come to Italy and come to Greece because it's close and they look like—" she pointed to herself. "Is better life in Italy because there is jobs and land and schools are good."

Jill leaned against the doorjamb. She had never heard Era speak so much, and she realized now how she had reduced her. She was foreign, she was still in school, she worked at McDonald's, she shared a bed with her cousin. Jill had painted her inferior, and felt suddenly ashamed.

"When did you come here?"

"I come here some years ago. My brother Luan, he come to Roma first, and then I come and stayed with him for four years and make my Italian very good, then I come to Siena for school."

"How did you learn English?" Jill said.

Era laughed. "My English is bad!"

"Not really, actually." Jill smiled, thinking of her abysmal Italian and the half-hearted efforts she had put into learning Spanish in high school, a skill considered valuable for some vague idea of a changing landscape in America someday, not because it was a tool she would ever require for survival.

"I learn from some friends, they teach me. I look at books. And soap operas in English." She laughed again, embarrassed. Jill wanted to negate her shame.

"You just have one brother? Luan?" Jill asked.

"I have one sister, and she died when she is eleven. She steps on a land mine. My other brother, he is in Albania still. My mother is also in Albania."

Stunned, Jill nodded, trying to reconfigure Era's words, in case there was any chance she had heard incorrectly.

Era turned the black dial on the stove face, then removed her pot from the heat. She looked like a child with small hands, thin, muscled arms, short hair; but her lined, darkened face contained the evidence of her life. She poured the pot out into a large colander in the sink, and the steam rose around her head like a cloud, the water rushed down the drain, and a pile of small, colorful potatoes was left glistening like gems.

"How old are you?" Jill asked.

"Thirty-one," she said. "I am getting old!" Some of the light returned to her eyes.

Jill laughed. "Hardly."

Era moved the potatoes to a large bowl, doused them with olive oil and salt, and began to smash them with a whisk. When she had finished, she scooped some out and put them in a cereal bowl.

"Do you want some?" she asked.

"No, thanks."

Era picked up the bowl and turned to Jill.

"I don't know why Luan goes in your room that day. I don't know what he is doing there. I told him never to go in again." She said this looking Jill straight in the eyes.

Jill nodded. "Okay."

"I have to go eat, and I going to work then."

"Oh, sorry," Jill said, and stepped aside of the doorway so Era could walk past. The girl walked down the hall to her bedroom, her feet falling without sound, her body with the lightness of a ballerina. Jill could hear the mattress squeak, and then there was the sound of Italian coming from the television. Era hadn't answered for Luan, she thought, but she had explained something. Jill simply wasn't sure what it was.

It was a week before she could return to Café Duomo due to a few added excursions around Tuscany with Weldon, as well as each of their four professors demanding an essay apiece for the mid-term. When class dismissed Thursday evening, Jill checked her e-mail to find a short message from Zane, suggesting he might be able to come for a long weekend, but it was the same weekend as the program trip to Venice, so she wrote back with a brief apology and explanation. She imagined him opening the reply in his office, and found she couldn't anticipate what his response would be. Jill stood, folded up her laptop and stowed it. In the lobby of the offices, the other students milled around and questioned Denise about the upcoming trip. Rachel was speaking loudly about a guy she'd met and gone home with Tuesday night, glancing about for a wider audience. Veronica and Heather stood around a desk in the corner discussing their plans to meet up with a couple of students they had met from Germany. Jill went out with them sometimes, but the game was to meet and hook up with men, and while she had allowed her better judgment to fall overboard with Thomas in Monteresso, she had no intention of making it a habit. "Be careful," Anna was saying, standing just a few feet away, hovering over the border distinguishing professor from friend. They all liked her.

Jill slung the backpack over her shoulder, wrapped a scarf around her neck, and stepped into the cold air. The sky was dark, but as she walked toward the Campo, the streets grew yellow with the light emanating from restaurants and shops. She walked under the flags bearing the crowned dolphin to delineate the Contrada of the Wave, and they drew her gaze upward. The walls stretched up to the night, the thousands of windows closed to the cold. They would all be open in the morning, allowing the raw, bitter air to sweep in and carry away the odors and sickness and staleness of indoors. Jill passed people walking briskly, wrapped up in thick coats, hats, and scarves. She pulled her own collar tighter around her neck and face.

On the Piazza a three-man band played a slow, mournful song, and Jill slowed for a moment. The first sat on a stool and beat lightly on a djembe wedged between his knees. Another stood with a guitar, the artery for the trio, playing the central tune of their song. Tonight they were the only people idling on the Piazza. The tallest man stood with a cello. His thin arms, rippled and sinewy, came out from the rolled up sleeves of a flannel shirt. His face, darkened with stubble, almost gaunt, looked young except in his eyes, which were wrinkled.

A ladybug is crawling over the toe of my shiny black shoe. It seems like she's floating because her feet are invisible under her body. She turns toward me and moves closer to the top of my foot but stops when she gets to the edge, where she will have to take a giant step down onto my skin. She won't. Suddenly her wings spread open like the tiniest hang glider and she lifts off. I lose her.

When I look up I remember what is happening—I'm at a funeral. Frieda told me at our last appointment that I easily lose track of what is happening sometimes because I am protecting myself from reality. I don't understand what that means because it doesn't feel like I'm protected. It feels like I am totally alone. Also, I think I understand that reality means the things that are actually happening, and I am positive that my mom is dead now, and I'm thinking about that all the time. Frieda says I am very observant for a nine-year-old too, which makes me feel like Harriet the Spy. She thinks this will make me a better artist.

Underneath an enormous weeping willow tree a man is playing the cello. This is the instrument I wanted to play when we were first deciding, but mom thought it was too big for me to take to school on the bus, so I picked violin, which I detest because the sound it makes hurts my ears.

There is also a woman playing the violin, but it doesn't sound horrible. It might be the viola, actually, I can't tell from where we are standing.

Someone, or something, has dug a hole in the ground. If I took off my shoe I think I could throw it straight into the hole because I wouldn't have to have good aim. It's pretty big, and a perfect rectangle. The opposite sides are the same length, but the two sets of sides are different lengths. I would use a tape measure and addition to find the perimeter, which is something I learned in math class this year. There are gravestones all over the place. It makes me think of Halloween, because our neighbor puts fake gravestones in her yard and has dry ice to make smoke, to make it seem scary. But it's July, and this is a real graveyard.

The music is changing, and all the people are shifting and turning. I look to Dad to see what to do. He is wearing black sunglasses so I can't see his eyes, but I look in the direction he is facing.

Six men are carrying the big box, shiny and black like my shoes, through a walkway in the middle of the people. I know mom is inside the box because this morning when we were eating Dunkin' Donuts, Dad told me what was going to happen at the graveyard, and then we saw her at the viewing. The box must be very heavy if it takes six men to carry it, because when she died she was very small and Dad carried her around all the time by himself. One of them is my Grampa. One of them is Mom's cancer doctor. I'm not sure if I know the others.

The violin music is the only sound—everyone is silent.

I want to run away.

The graveyard is on a hill, and I can't see the edges. I'm a fast runner, even faster downhill, and it would feel good to run as hard as I can. But I promised Daddy I would be the most obedient today, and I don't want to leave him. He can't run away. I always tell him we are a team. Frieda told me that when Mama died. She said, *Now you and your dad are a team.*

They fix the black casket to some kind of ropes attached to metal poles over the hole. The pastor is speaking, holding his Bible, but I am not listening. I'm staring at the box. I feel afraid for her, because it would be scary to be stuck in there, but then I remember she is dead. She won't know. I feel my throat tightening, and it hurts because I am trying not to cry. Suddenly I feel Dad's hand around mine, and he gives it a squeeze.

I look up at him, and he is smiling down at me with his mouth, but I can't see his eyes. His forehead is sweating. The box with Mama inside begins to descend on its own, like someone has hit a button somewhere. It goes lower and lower, and then I can't see it. I am frantic; I scream and start to lunge toward the edge, but his hand becomes a grip and I can't.

People moved quickly, heads down, crossing to get out of the Campo that had become a natural wind tunnel. Jill wove through the crowd, into the street, and came out in front of the Duomo at the edge of the Eagle Contrada. There was soft sound, almost like chanting, coming from inside. Strange, all the music in one evening. Perhaps she simply hadn't noticed it before. She turned away and found the blue door. It was heavy to drag open, and inside the cafe was busy with customers.

The same girl was behind the bar, only now she smiled and carried on flirtatious conversation with the men seated before her like students. Sensuality permeated the people, as if they, as a nation, had been excluded from the lessons learned in Eden. Amedeo's grandfather had even behaved this way. It was somewhat discomposing at first, and then enviable. She slipped into a seat at a twelve-inch table by the door, the only opening in the small café.

"Prego?" the girl called from the bar, fixing a catlike stare on Jill.

"Café," Jill replied, afraid to try ordering anything more complicated from across the restaurant. An infinitesimal nod was the only indication her request had been heard. The girl delivered the drink, and Jill waited.

"Buona sera bella!" She heard his voice before seeing him come from the back. "I have waited for you for all the week!" Signor Gavarola stood across from her.

"Buona sera," she said, rising. His rough face kissed both her cheeks. Most people she found only made contact with the air. His commitment to the gesture spoke of a dated gallantry. "I've been so busy, I'm sorry."

"I have found something for you. I wait to give it to you all week. You wait." He went around the back of the bar and exchanged a few words with the girl, then disappeared. In moments he returned and handed Jill an envelope.

"What's this?" she said, sliding her finger under the sealed lip.

"When you leave last week I started to think about all this things I have not think about for many years. You have—" he hit his head lightly a few times, "—make all my memories come back in my brain. I have not think about this things for many years! I went in my old boxes and find many things from when we are younger, and I find this picture."

He reached out for the envelope, too eager to allow Jill to be the one to open it. His fingers, thick like jib sheets on a sailboat, struggled to wriggle into the opening so he licked them and tried again. Finally he tore through and a picture slid out onto the table face down. He drew it toward himself so it fell from the edge onto his lap. He flipped and slapped it down in front of Jill, subduing it with finality, and on his face was a thin smile. "Va bene."

The photograph of two women had been taken just outside the blue door on a warm, bright day. On the left, a middle-aged countenance with dark hair pulled back. She had an angular face, thick bangs, high cheekbones, and dark eyes behind rimmed glasses. She wore a polka-dotted blouse tucked into a green high-waisted skirt that revealed her slender frame. Rosa was stunning, even in the normalcy of her conservative dress.

On the right, the sun reflected from the shining blonde hair of the shorter woman, smiling broadly, wearing a brown dress and a blue scarf. That scarf! Stunning, more stunning than Jill had ever seen her. There was a halo of light surrounding her head. She held a pair of large sunglasses in her hand in midair, as if she were only just taking them off her face, still bringing them to her side. A picture in motion. Lily.

"She is your mother. She looks the same as you! Only with blonde hair," Signor said, tremendously pleased with himself.

Jill felt cold. She picked up the artifact and studied the two women. She had seen pictures of Lily from before her birth, and from her early childhood. She looked to be in her early twenties here, not very much different than Jill at this very moment. Perhaps younger, in the face—what was it? A freedom, an openness, some angelic quality of purity? She had forgotten about that scarf, and it was strange to remember it now. She gazed past Signor and to the place just outside the window where the picture had been taken. How anomalous, seeing this image here, now. Present. Past.

"I can't believe you have this," she said, feeling a terrific imbalance of sadness and wonder. "Did you take it?"

"Hm?" he said.

"Did you take the picture?" She pressed the button on an invisible camera.

"Oh, I do not remember if it was me, or another person."

Jill nodded, and placed the photo back on the table slowly.

"Oh no, no," he said. "This is for you. I have hundreds of pictures—you have this."

"Grazie," Jill said, picking it up again, overcome with a possessiveness.

"I try to find the letters, but there is so much," he said, leaning back in the chair.

"Letters?"

"I think your mother writes letters to Signora."

"She did?" Jill's heartbeat quickened, immediately addicted to this new medium of discovery. "When?"

The old man shook his head, squinting, as if her questions had suddenly taken on a physical nature, as if her asking was an affliction. "I tell you, I don't remember. I am very old now, these things happen a long time before."

Jill nodded, then leaned in. "You really don't remember? Can you try?"

"I tell you what I know," he said in a raised voice, his expression turned stern. "I have to work; I am sorry. You have the picture."

"Yes, thank you," she said, and stood as he stood. "Thank you," she repeated, "so much. I cannot tell you how much this means to me."

His face softened a bit. "You come back and eat, bring your friends!"

"Okay," she said, remembering as he returned to the back side of the bar that she'd intended to ask to interview him for her project. She would have to wait on that.

The carpet is squishy under my feet, the color of the red wine they sometimes drink at dinner. Without her, he usually drinks something else like beer, or a clear drink with carbonation. The light isn't very bright; it's freezing cold and everybody is whispering. I am standing as close to him as I can and sometimes put my hand in his pocket. I do this when I am afraid of getting lost. I want to go outside—it is sunny and there's a breeze. Inside I feel like I will explode. People I know are acting so strange, only speaking to us with weird voices. I guess this is because today is the funeral, and that's a strange thing too.

You're not going to have her look, are you? Grandma is whispering to him, but she always whispers loudly so I always know what she said.

He nods. His face looks tired. He isn't looking at her; he has that look like he's staring at something nobody else can see.

She'll be traumatized. This is a word I've heard a lot in the last few weeks. I need to look it up in the dictionary. I think it means sad.

Mom.

After a little while we walk over toward a huge, black box that's propped up high, and I can't see in. The top is open.

He squats down so his face is right in front of mine. His eyes have been red all week. I am staring at his face, and I think suddenly he looks like an old man, and that is something I never thought before. *Remember what I told you, Jillian?*

I nod. He has told me a lot of things I need to remember and think about and do today, mostly about being quiet and good, but I think I remember everything, so I nod.

He lifts me up.

She looks like Mom, sleeping. Her fake hair is pretty. She is wearing more makeup than usual. She looks very small. She is dressed in church clothes and a blue scarf she only wears for special occasions. I think again about the sky outside. This scarf is the same color as the sky!

I want to climb inside and sleep next to her, even though I'm not tired and there are all these people here. I miss her. I start to cry because I miss her and because I can't touch her even though she's right there. And I am crying because I'm afraid of her dead. This is the first time I've seen her in two weeks, since the day she died. I saw her that day just for a minute because she died really early in the morning. Dad said I didn't have to go to swim practice that morning, which I was mad about because I love swim team, but then he said I needed to go say goodbye to Mama. I didn't understand, and then I went and sat with her and she was hardly talking, but she had her hand on my wrist. There was a nurse there, and Dad was standing behind me. She closed her eyes just like a slow blink, and then it felt strange, the way it feels inside your ears when you are flying in a plane and you hold your nose and push air out and it's like a stopper was in them, but then it's not. But it was the opposite.

I look at Daddy and don't know what he is thinking. He doesn't look sad or mad or anything. He doesn't look like anything. He isn't crying. I look at her one more time before he puts me down.

We finally go outside, but there is still the quiet, and it makes me nervous.

21

Jill woke up and gathered the blankets to her chin. The temperatures were descending with sinister dependability, night by night, giving way to chilly mornings. She lay still with her eyes open, listening to Isabelle's puppy snores. The photograph of her mom was taped up next to her bed, and she stared at it—waiting for it to offer just a little bit more. Was that too much to ask? It had been warm that day, maybe summer. She wondered where the dress had ended up, separated from the scarf. It was strange to think that Lily could have woken up similarly, even in the very same apartment, just a few decades ago. That was the axis of Jill's wonder—her mom's life, which had always been sort of vague to her, was now quite clear, and remarkably like her own. At least at this point.

A volume of brand new information—she had never known that her grandfather was an alcoholic, though now he never took a drink when everyone else did. When did it change for him? She'd certainly never known any details about Jodie, who had apparently been Lily's best friend, her only real friend it seemed. Jill was like her in that way. It seemed to bother Lily, not knowing Buck very well. This was most clear because her tone toward him seemed jealous in a way, as if his presence was pilfering bits of Jodie, as if her sister were an abandoned house where Lily had taken up squatting. There was an immaturity in that, she thought. When Jodie died, Buck had faded away. Nobody talked about them. Jill wondered where her father would come into the picture. Perhaps it was a budding romance with Gary that had ultimately anchored Lily in the US. Sometimes, if she could forget the storyteller was her own mother and the fact that she knew the end of the story, Jill pulled for Lily to remain in Italy where she was happy. The gap between the known and the unknown was shrinking, but nothing was simple—the not knowing or the knowing.

A few days before, when Jill had narrated the experience at Café Duomo, Isabelle had asked her *do you think you'd feel a lot different about this whole study abroad experience if it hadn't become a quest for finding Lily?* She'd paused on the question ever since, trying to pinpoint her original intent. She circled around thoughts of Zane and her father, her life at home—the relief she'd felt even leaving for the airport. She recognized now her desire for escape, if only for a short time, and to leave all of the dead weight behind her. But her relationships were not dead weight—it was a terrible thought, a selfish, naïve thought.

When her father had handed her the book, she'd been surprised, certainly intrigued, but she hadn't imagined it would unearth that longing she had buried in the recesses of her heart years before. At first she had seen the act of his giving it, more than the thing itself, as the miracle, a rare event of tenderness for which she had spent years waiting, then eventually given up. Then she had felt known by him, that he had encouraged her to come to Siena, that he had waited for the right time, or what he saw as the right time, to shed new light on Lily. Now that she was immersed in the pages, however, she found it was also the journal itself—a direct answer to that deepest desire, as good as talking to her mom after the draught of information she'd endured. It was drawing her into an old story, by nature one she should never have known. Lately Jill felt a vague sense of trepidation about the whole thing, like becoming immersed in a novel in which it's clear the plot is heading for a breaking point. She thought about what Isabelle had said. Had she turned the antique into a talisman? Her quest for the elusive grail? Lily's journal was enlightening, but still just an image of a person she never really knew, and it was dangerous to put her chips on an expectation for anything more. At this point, it really hadn't explained anything other than the debilitation of Lily's family, her intense loyalty and allegiance to her sister Jodie, and the biggest surprise, the general hostility of her mom's younger self, her bitterness. Meeting Leone Gavarola, finding he had known *that* Lily, Siena's Lily, had fanned the flame of her pursuit, but still, it was only a pursuit of shadows.

She rolled over and forced her eyes shut, but it would be impossible to fall asleep again. Getting up, she grabbed her towels and walked to the bathroom. All of the windows were open and the white squares felt like ice underfoot. She dropped her towels outside of the powder room and closed herself in, pulling the plastic cover over the toilet paper and drawing the thin curtain across the wooden door. It took the water a few moments to warm up, so she pressed herself to the wall like an insect. When it was finally hot, she stepped underneath the spigot and exhaled, relieved as heat permeated her body from the outside in. She finished, dressed, and sat down at the table while the apartment was still quiet.

The charcoal she had started the night before of Leone was coming along, but the challenges of his facial structure made her want to switch to the inanimate. In the photograph he was smiling, content in his memories now that age had allowed the painful ones to fade. But in Jill's mind there was also the frustration of his loss, the way he chided her for pressing him for information, his disappointment that he has grown old. She was surprised to see when she stepped back from the drawing that it looked very good, the roughness of his chin, the way his shirt draped over his narrow shoulders. But the face was still blank—an empty white oval.

The Via Banchi di Sopra was unusually slow in the mid-afternoon hours. Some shops and cafes were closed for a late lunch and would reopen in the early evening. Jill watched a young mother with two perfect, dark-haired boys who continued a few steps ahead of her. The younger of the two repeatedly punched the older one, taller and lanky, in the arm whenever the mother was looking the other way. The older, becoming irritated at his attention-grubbing sibling, tried to ignore him, but eventually retaliated with one swift, hard hit to the side of the head at a moment when the mother had turned to scold them for bickering. Grabbing the older boy fiercely by the arm, she berated him hotly. He mumbled a few words, but she silenced him, and he didn't try again for defense. When they started walking again, he scowled at his brother for the treachery. She tried to attach the age to her own memories. Occasionally she imagined what it would have been like to experience life with a sibling, but the concept was foreign.

On Via del Montanini, just north of Piazza Matteoti, Jill opened the door to the art and camera supply shop, and a small bell jingled. Tiered shelves of different colors and sizes of paper lined the wall to the left, and beyond that were hundreds of mediums, brands, colors of paints. There were samples of custom frames along the back wall, and on the right several hung paintings and drawings. Tables held buckets of paint brushes, pens, pencils, rulers, and other artists' tools. Jill ran her hands over the soft brush heads.

"Ciao, va bene?" the cashier said as he wiped a very expensive camera lens with a cloth.

"Si, grazie," she replied, looking around the store. She stopped in front of a photo kiosk, inserted her memory card and scrolled through the photographs, selecting a few to print. She picked up two boxes of charcoal, opening each to check for broken pieces and evaluate the thickness of the pencils, and selected one, as well as a few large sheets of thick paper, some regular pencils, a new eraser and, on a whim, a cheap sleeve of basic watercolors. She paid and walked a few doors down to the stadium's ticket booth. Earlier the soccer match between Siena and Florence had come up in conversation, and she had offered to pick up tickets. Two men in front of her took several minutes to select seats, and she watched a pick-up game between several teenage boys on a solitary patch of grass. A few girls stood on the sidelines as spectators. A couple of young men walked by her and hissed in approval, and she smirked, turning back to face the window. Just as the teller waved her forward, she heard her name in a familiar voice. "Bella Jillian!"

Amedeo approached with a broad smile.

"Why do you stay away so long?" he said, hugging her to his side.

She laughed, cheered by seeing him. "I don't know! I didn't know how to get in touch or anything. I wanted to send you a thank-you note for dinner, but I didn't know which apartment was yours."

"Consider me thanked. No letter is needed. I knew we would run into each other again. It is the nature of the city, very intimate. You never lose a person in Siena. Have you been well?"

"Yes, I'm great." She thought. "We've been to Pisa; we hiked the Cinque Terre."

"Beautiful, yes?"

She nodded.

"I have not done that since I was twenty. Maybe twenty-three. Too many tourists in the summer, too cold in the winter. Too rainy in spring. Perfect in fall, but life is busy. Are you planning to attend the soccer match Sunday against Firenze?" he asked, drawing out the name with the phonetic elegance of a born Italian steeped over a life in buttery linguistics.

Jill glanced toward the counter where another man now stood purchasing his tickets. "Yes, a group of us. I need five tickets. Isabelle and I are going, and then three other friends."

"Good! The football match is at two o'clock. You and your friends should join us for dinner afterward."

"Oh, thanks! That's so nice of you to offer," she said. "With your whole family?" She extended her arms.

"Perhaps not. Fewer family members. We will go to my house. Pray to Saint Catherine that Siena wins, or else the mood could be very sour."

"I'll start my vigil now. Should we just go there straight after?"

"Come here, right where we stand, and we will all walk together," he said. "You were saying something about buying tickets?"

"Yes," she said, stepping up to the window. The teller's expression brightened, and he raised an eyebrow.

"Amedeo!" he said. "Va bene?"

"Si! Va bene, amico. Tu mama? Va bene?"

"Si, si. This is your friend?" the man asked, politely switching from Italian to accented English.

"Yes, a good friend. She wants five tickets to the match. What can you give her?"

Directing his gaze to the computer screen, he went about clicking and muttering "Si...non...non...non..." to himself. Amedeo glanced at Jill and winked.

"Five tickets. The best in the stadium, Siena side, for my friend Amedeo, his friend!" he exclaimed. "I sell them to you for one hundred fifty euros. This is a good deal."

"He is telling the truth. This is a good price."

Nodding, she handed the man her credit card. "Grazie mille."

"Prego, bella," he replied.

Once Jill had tucked the tickets into her book bag Amedeo accompanied her back toward the center of town.

"Are you considering entering a drawing with *Arte per Natale*?"

"I have a few projects underway. A couple of landscapes and a portrait."

"Are these images from Italy or from your home?"

"They're from here."

He nodded, his eyes focused on something else. It seemed he was perpetually distracted by a secondary train of thought, always wearing a slight smirk in response to his private world. As they approached Palazzo Tolomei he slowed, pointing to the entrance of a bank located inside an ancient city mansion. "Here is where I stop. I will see you and your friends after the game Sunday, okay?"

"Sounds great."

"Va bene. Tell your friends to come hungry. Only coffee Sunday before the game. Ciao, Jillian. Be good!"

She watched him push through the rotating door and tried for a moment to put a name to the feeling she had toward him, but after a moment she gave a physical shudder of refocus and turned down the street.

A river of people coursed through the wide street in the direction of the stadium, almost every one wearing something to denote his regional team allegiance. The most popular accents were scarves around the neck, red and purple for Firenze; yellow, black, and white for Siena. Boisterous men shouted and jumped up and down with explosive energy, and the crowd collectively ignored a fistfight between a red scarf and a black scarf on the corner of Via Banchi di Sopra and Piazza Salimbeni. Wyatt stuck out like an island in his orange polo shirt and blue shorts, his dress and fashion and stature so unlike that of Italian men. It was as if he was dressed in costume. An American woman with some awareness of herself, especially a brunette, could float into Italy and discreetly alter her style and hair, makeup and jewelry to pass for European if she didn't speak, at the very least. Wearing shirts a little looser, a little lower, fewer colors, heavy metal earrings, vintage shoes and rings, Jill and Isabelle had adapted well. Wyatt, however, had no desire to alter his style.

Buses of Florentines arrived on the piazza, honking for football fans to get the hell out of the way, and were received with jeering and cursing. Everyone shouted, some out of enthusiasm and unbridled excitement, others to be heard over the din of the mob. Jill's eyes moved quickly in all directions. She had never seen Siena this way—electrified, hostile, pent up, ready to erupt.

"We need to buy scarves," Isabelle said loudly, pointing toward a cluster of carts selling various souvenirs and Siena football apparel. They could have been walking into a university football game in Louisiana or Madison Square Garden to see the Knicks, the cadence of this kind of sports event, this level of intensity, falling into a common sort of ritual. Once they'd purchased and arranged their team markings, Jill and Isabelle linked elbows and pressed back through the crowd toward the stadium entrance. They followed Rocco, who led them to the main entrance and showed the tickets to a woman in uniform. She raised her brow, looking Wyatt up and down, burning him with eyes that judged his colorful garb, then turned to point to a center section of seats underneath the scoreboard behind the Siena team bench.

"No way!" Wyatt said. He and Rocco led the way to the section, then to the fourteenth row, seats eighty-nine through ninety-three. The stadium, large and deep, overflowed with people, all vaguely uniform in scarves, sunglasses, and dark hair. Siena, a city of little consequence on a world scale, filled her gargantuan complex with ease. Bright sunshine beat down over the massive crowd and warmed them in the deep, wide bowl. It was a perfectly clear day. The stands pulsed, alive with moving color and sound, and Jill gazed all around, aware of a conversation between Rocco and Ling about the regulations of European soccer. Suddenly a voice came over the loudspeaker, in rapid Italian she did not understand, and was cut off by an exhilarated explosion of cheers and applause erupting from the stands as the Sienese players ran onto the field, pumping fists and waving in circles to their ecstatic fans. Again, the voice came over the loudspeaker and Firenze came onto the field, welcomed by a surprising volume of cheers, quickly over-powered by boos and shrieks from the Siena side. After more from the announcer, from which Jill pulled only a few words, the game started at the sound of a horn and everyone stood. The effect of a collective enthusiasm was contagious, and Jill joined in the cheers and jeering. They never sat down.

After the final whistle, masses of people surged toward the exits creating an impassable bottleneck and, as their seats were close to the field, the five friends stood still for a long time, discuss-ing the dramatic points of the match. Siena had pulled out a narrow victory, two to one in the final minutes, though thirty seconds before the final buzzer Firenze's World Cup champion, Luca Toni, had nearly scored again.

Jill led the way to the ticket booth, and they found Amedeo. He propped his hands lightly on Isabelle's shoulders and smiled at Jill, his whole face, into the center of the eyes, drawn into an exuberance. His affection was warm, what she imagined to be fatherly.

"Isabelle, lovely to see you. And Jillian, buona sera. Va bene?"

"Molto bene, grazie," she replied in her best Italian.

"A victory for Siena!" Amedeo cried, throwing his hands up in the air. "It was a good match." He wore jeans and a black sweater, more casual than his customary tailored suit.

"Amedeo, these are our friends," Jill said, and introduced them one by one. When she told him Rocco was from Rome, the two men were suddenly submerged in a conversation in rapid Italian.

"He knows my uncles," Rocco explained when they finished.

Amedeo was delighted to discover Ling was from New York. "New York University, I was there in, let me think—no . . . Listen to me! I can talk all day standing on a street corner forgetting that you are in Italy and you want to eat! You have never had food like you have here. It is fresh and perfect, not like what you have in the States. My family has gone back to start on dinner—we'll eat with my mama and sister's family, okay? Not such a big crowd as last time. Anna cannot be there today—she is in Milan to visit—but Sophia is glad you're coming back," he said to the girls. His speech seemed accelerated by the energy of the mass of people surging around them.

They followed him down streets off the main drag toward the center of town, eventually turning to head south until Jill recognized the ram contrada flags strung between the buildings. It was the street to which they had come a few weeks previous, and she mentioned it under her breath to Isabelle, who nodded in recognition. Moments later they turned into the empty alcove where the dinner table had been set up, stopped in front of an imposing cherry wood door with rod iron darts, and Amedeo announced, "Casa nostra!"

22

It was a courtyard atrium with a view of the sky, decorated with several potted plants and flowers, and two small chairs sat in a little grassy patch in the corner beside a watering can. Amedeo led them to a staircase and up to the first landing, placed his hand on the door, and said, "This is the house of my mother and father. Mama is upstairs helping Sophia cook. You did not meet her last time. My father died just a few months ago. He was very old, very happy. Happier now, I think," he said, then continued up the steps, stopping at the next level. "This floor is my sister's, Sophia, and her husband and children. Dovio and I live on the third." He gestured upward, then followed his hand. At the next level the stairs ended. He rapped three times on the door, an announcement rather than request for entry, then pushed it open. Jill went first, and stopped in the foyer. Amedeo followed, waving for them to come after him.

His home was much larger than it seemed from the outside, plunging backward. The crown molding creeped a few inches toward the center of the ceiling, a thick, complicated carving of vines. The ceiling itself was painted crimson with a pattern of thin gold latticing. As they walked further into the apartment, Jill noticed each painting. There were drawings, oils, some photographs. She stopped in front of a landscape of Tuscany, and her eyes followed the raised bumps of oil paint. The furniture was antiquated and simple. The aroma of garlic and pesto poured out of the kitchen rolling on steam, right into their noses and mouths, and Ling's stomach gave a loud lurch. Their eyes met and Jill pressed her lips together to stifle laughter. Following Amedeo, they walked down a surprisingly long hallway. Jill tried to conceptualize the view from the street, which direction the building stretched and how much of the city block belonged to the Perlos. In the dining room Amedeo led them to the table and left them. When he was gone, Ling spoke.

"Well this place is stunning."

"Enormous," Isabelle whispered. "And can you imagine how old?"

Amedeo returned, followed by Sophia and her husband Charlie, an American. Dovio came in next, held up a hand, and sat, and finally Amedeo's mother entered. She walked slowly, and everyone was standing to be introduced and shake hands. Nonna Perlo was short and round, with graying hair. She took the cheeks of both boys in her hands, kissing them on the forehead. She greeted Isabelle, then saw Ling and Jill, who had been positioned slightly behind the others on the back side of the table. Her face changed. Her eyes drew together as if being pulled up with a threaded needle. She turned her head to Amedeo and spoke something in fast, indecipherable Italian. Sophia replied, but Nonna didn't look at her, she kept her eyes focused on her son. He spoke in a sharp, cold tone. Jill watched all the eyes of the Perlo family grow simultaneously stale. The old woman's hand flicked up toward the girls, and Jill and Ling glanced back and forth between one another, each with a look of defense. Jill looked down at her chest—the tattoo was clearly visible, and she tugged the neck of her shirt over to cover it.

"Mama loves guests!" Amedeo said suddenly. Nonna drew back within herself like a hermit crab, sat in her seat, and the moment was gone. Jill looked at Ling, matching a baffled expression with her own. It was almost as if she'd imagined it. "Especially the boys."

There was a strangled quiet.

"Isabelle and Jill," Sophia said, propelling them. "Introduce us?"

"This is Ling, Rocco, and Wyatt," Isabelle said, pointing to them in succession.

Surveying them, Sophia reached forward and removed Wyatt's hat, revealing his matted hair. "Why do you hide this beautiful head of hair?" she exclaimed, holding his chin in her hand. "Handsome." But even Sophia's most charming conversationalism didn't assuage that momentary strangeness.

After introductions, they all sat and Nonna Perlo and Sophia went to the kitchen to retrieve several pizzas. Ling and Jill exchanged another quizzical glance. Had it been Ling? Or Jill? Or both? The guests narrated their approval as they ate, and answered hundreds of questions. Sophia and Nonna, who at least pretended to have let go of whatever dislike with which she had begun, basked in the praise of their guests.

"Dovio, you're in school?" Wyatt asked, redirecting the conversation. Dovio nodded. He had been quietly listening throughout the meal.

"Dovio is an accomplished violinist. He has played in cities all over Italy and France," Sophia added.

The young man shook his head once, a smirk on his lips. He had the same dark eyes and engaging gaze of his father. He was skinny, the sort of gangly cypress of teenagers who have not yet grown into their adult bodies.

"Go get your violin for us," Sophia said as she stood to pour more wine into each glass.

He looked at his aunt skeptically, but Amedeo echoed her suggestion, and then all of the guests were cheering him on, begging him to play. Shaking his head, he left to retrieve the instrument. He returned moments later, pushed his chair back from the table and sat on the edge, leaning forward slightly, his feet rooted to the ground, one slightly in front of the other. He drew the violin to his chin, lifting his head a few inches, and allowing the lower bout to rest on the inside of his shoulder. He ran his hand over the neck gently. The boy handled the instrument with incredible precision and tenderness. With the violin in his able hands he seemed older than sixteen. He raised the bow and began to play. The expression on his face did not change—acute focus without a trace of strain. The music resonated beautifully, starting off soft and slow, and swelling, then retreating again. It was a rueful song, and his shoulders moved with its story, as if the action of his entire body was required to produce the sound.

Jill watched Amedeo. He expelled intensity, an electricity of pride. The man's body moved slightly with the cadence of the music, and when he opened his eyes she saw they were wet with tears. She felt a pang of jealousy. Dovio's music, his art, his passion; the gentleness with which he held his instrument, the meticulousness with which he moved his long fingers, the way he closed his eyes to feel the spirit of his piece migrate up out of his chest and flow into his shoulders, arms, hands—she found she could relate to him. She knew what it was to channel beauty into a medium, to wield her instruments with grace to produce excellence, to feel her whole self moved by the act. His family was proud of him, his entire encompassing family, wearing his music like a badge of identification. A gallery. She had not even recognized how acutely she longed for it until this moment, sitting in the nucleus of Dovio's audience.

When he'd finished, he set the violin in his lap and smiled slightly as they all clapped and praised him for his talent. He blushed, just a normal teenage boy again. He was embarrassed, perhaps a little annoyed at his father and aunt for making him perform, but underneath those fleeting feelings, Jill imagined, was a spring of confidence and love from which he had always grown.

After dinner Dovio excused himself to go play soccer with friends, a tradition following a win. The girls helped take the dishes back to the kitchen, and Wyatt and Rocco accompanied Amedeo and his brother-in-law, Charlie, out to the porch to smoke cigars.

"How'd you meet Charlie?" Ling asked once they'd put some things away and settled into the kitchen.

"Oh, my Charlie. He is a banker. He was working with banks in Chicago, but he came to Roma for a work trip. One day he comes to Siena because he loves history," she said. "He meets me at the bus station. He falls in love with me in one day! He quits his job in America and moves to Italy—the man is wild. We are married two months later, and Amedeo finds him a job in the Siena Bank."

"Do you have kids?" Jill asked.

"Si, two daughters at boarding school in Bologna. They come home in summer and for December." By the time the dishes were dry and put away, they had polished off another bottle of wine, liberating their tongues to make conversation easy. Nonna sat in a backed chair in the corner silently, as if she were in and out of sleep. The light grew flaxen from the fixture on the ceiling as the daylight in the windows disappeared completely. They sat on the kitchen stools around a tall island.

"This place is beautiful," Isabelle said in a moment of quiet.

"Grazie," Sophia nodded. "It is not always so nice, Amedeo fixed the building for us. Is been in the family for a long time, but it was very old—like all buildings in Siena. Needing new kitchens, roof. You know."

"Was he married?" Jill said bluntly. She had wondered from the first dinner.

Ling smirked.

"What? I'm just wondering."

"Oh, yes," Sophia said, shaking her head. "Dovio's mother died when he was only ten years old. Gabriella. She was a beautiful woman, in her face and in her heart. Amedeo knew her from the time he was a very young boy. The mothers and fathers planned for the marriage—what do you say in America?"

"An arranged marriage?" Ling said.

"Yes, like that. Only not so strict. Amedeo had to choose yes or no. It took him some time, but they finally are married. They are very happy. Very, very happy." She had a way of switching to present tense as she began to live the past. Sophia stood up to retrieve a framed photograph from the hallway. "Here."

The photograph was crisp and looked professional, but the colors were warming to reveal its age. It had been taken on a rainy day, and Amedeo stood beside the woman, his hand around her waist, pulling her toward him, bending to kiss her cheek, holding a colorful umbrella that glistened wet in his other hand. Jill was surprised by their youth in the picture. Amedeo's hair was completely dark without the flecks of gray. He was handsome then, as now, and Gabriella was lovely in a nondescript way—petite, smiling with her mouth closed in a slight, contented expression. Her face was simple, somewhat closed, contrasted with the strong features of her partner. She looked happy, and he looked proud.

The fire is lit in the hearth, dwindled down to a gentle, quivering line of flame. The rest of the house is cold, but in the study, with the doors closed, it can warm up like the inside of an oven. A log gives a sharp pop, then crumbles from the top of the pile. My eyes watch and grow watery and unfocused.

I straighten in the chair and sit back. My posture needs attention. I walked past a mirror in Macy's last week and realized I was standing like a hunchback. Sarah Franklin's hunchback is really sad. She has some crazy scoliosis, but sometimes I think *What if I end up like that?* Dad's always telling me to stand up straight.

This essay. The blinking cursor, mocking in consistent readiness. *Start typing now. Now. Now. Now,* with irritating rhythm. His computer feels large and foreign. Even his keyboard is different than mine. I thought a change in scenery might jumpstart my brain, but it hasn't so far. Once I get the first paragraph I'll be good. Even the first couple of sentences. Then I'll know where I'm going with it.

It is the worst kind of prompt. *Write your personal statement. This is the opportunity to tell us who you are, what makes you unique, why you are different. Maybe you have had to overcome diversity. Maybe you have lived in uncommon circumstances. Maybe you grew up on Mars.* Liberal arts colleges, trying to be witty. *We want to get to know you. (600 word limit)*

The obvious answer is to use the "My mom died with cancer" line, but I don't want to get into college because an admissions counselor pities me.

I sit back in the chair and run my fingers over the carved edges of the desk. The drawers have small swinging pulls I flick up and down. I pull on the one in the center and it moves. The drawer has my attention. I sit upright again. It isn't locked.

I glance around the room as if there could be hidden cameras, as if he is sitting in his office at work looking at the feed of me in front of his desk. I know he won't be home for hours.

The drawer on which I have mindlessly tugged hundreds of times in my life only to find it locked opens with some resistance, as if the edges don't quite fit together. So he does open it. I am staring at piles of paper, a few small boxes. I glance at the door again.

There are personal letters tucked into the original envelopes. Some were mailed—there are return addresses I don't recognize, names I have never heard of. A few I have. I flip through a few in the stack and though it's tempting to open them and read, I don't. There are lines I won't cross. I open a box, and inside are mom's rings. I place them in my hand and run a finger over them. I try to slip them over my ring finger, but my knuckles are too big, and I am afraid of getting them stuck, so I return them quickly to the box. Someday they'll be mine. I picture them on her petite hand, and suddenly I can picture her hands with a visual clarity I have been unable to find in years.

There are a few other small boxes, our social security cards, some official papers registering our cars, the house, insurance documents, financial papers, all in a thin file folder. At the back of the drawer is a stack of photographs.

I pull them out and begin to flip through slowly, moving the top picture to the bottom of the stack, trying to distinguish an order, a reason for the preservation of these particular relics in the locked desk drawer. Some stick together, as if they, like skin, have fused over untouched time. I am surprised to find several are photographs of me. I am ten, dressed up as Nancy Kerrigan for Halloween. I am in my soccer uniform, maybe seven? I am very young on the beach, squatting at the edge of the ocean, peering down at a gathering of shells where the froth recedes back to the incoming wave. The first time we went to the beach without her.

There are a few pictures of Mom. Mostly before cancer, when she still had the blonde hair. There is one of her with no hair at all. She is sitting on a park bench—maybe when we went to London to see that specialist—and her bald head is wrapped in a lovely floral scarf. She is wearing big sunglasses, and her face looks very small. She is somehow glamorous, in spite of her proximity to death. It was only a few months she was bald.

I stop on this photograph: it is Dad. He looks like another version of himself though, and all I can think is he is *happy*. I have rarely seen this look on him. In memories before the cancer, when our life was good and normal, even then I don't think his expression looked like this. I bring the picture closer to my face because it's not completely focused. His arm is wrapped around Mom, but there's something strange about it, about her. This might be the oldest picture I've ever seen of them together. She looks pleased. Radiant.

I stare at the picture for so long my eyes begin to burn. I haven't blinked. Something about this picture won't let me go. Her expression, her stance—like they are brand new to me. Finally I flip quickly through the rest of the photos, looking for this Lily, but I don't find her again.

━

"What happened to her?" Jill asked, staring at the lost faces.

"It was horrible. She was driving her car from Firenze to Siena—she used to teach some in Firenze, mathematics. A car hit her, and she died then."

"Oh my god," Isabelle said. "That's terrible."

Terrible. A terror. To Jill it felt entirely personal, a repetition of a cruel fate, a calculated disaster, a shock she understood intimately. Two happily married people, one child. Mother dies, kid and father are left alone. Father stays alone forever and kid—she didn't know what happened to the kid—she felt detached from that now. She thought of Dovio.

"Many women wanted to marry my brother," Sophia said frankly. "They tried for years, but he will never marry again, I think."

They sat quietly for a couple of minutes, not uncomfortably. Nonna Perlo stood up and walked out of the kitchen. Jill wondered how much she had understood. "It is silly to be sad over something that happened so long ago, now. We will go outside on the porch to see the top of the tower."

"Oh, you can see it from here?" Ling said.

"Ragazza, si! We are high here in brother's house—you can see the Torre anywhere. Bring your glass!" She led them down a new hallway, and they passed several doors open to bedrooms, a study, a bathroom, and another small kitchenette, and out to the porch where the men sat in chairs positioned in a wide arc facing out.

"This view," Isabelle said, walking toward the railing. Thousands of little rooftops lay below them as a covering of pavers over the city, as if they could have stepped off the patio and walked across to the Campo, opened up beyond, glowing in a halo of light, featuring the tower rising up like a lighthouse. From where they stood the tower seemed smaller. Clouds like stretched cotton covered the sky reflecting light from the city, and the moon was a fuzzy half-circle. "I didn't realize we were this high."

"It is beautiful," Amedeo agreed. "My favorite spot in the city."

Music played from speakers somewhere deep in the apartment, washing the evening in a kind of cinematic backdrop, and Jill sat down beside Amedeo in a chair facing the skyline.

He gave her a sideways look. "Was Sophia interrogating you?"

"No," she laughed. "She's really funny." Then changing the subject. "Dovio is amazing." So many reasons for this.

"He has a gift. You should hear him perform some day. It surprised me when he was younger that he chooses mournful music. He has always been a happy person, so I tried to steer him to play that way, but I think it is the way he expresses his sadness from the inside." Amedeo touched his chest.

Jill nodded, staring at the city lit in an unearthly blue. She found his capacity for emotion fascinating, as if he sat in an observable petri dish.

He continued as if she wasn't there. "It is six years since my Gabriella died, and still it feels like only just a moment ago she was here, waking up beside me with the sun on her face." He glanced at her, breaking his trance. "Listen to an old man talking of love."

"Sophia said your marriage was arranged," Jill said. "What was that like?"

"It was probably not like what you think. It is different here in Italia, more like a puzzle, and parents trying to fit their children together. I had a choice."

"Were you in love?"

"I loved her. Perhaps I was not 'in love,' as they say."

The man's eyes glistened the same as they had the first time she had spoken to him, evidence the layers of his history ran deep.

"Do you believe in being 'in love'?" she asked. He looked at her intently, exposing her. How had she ended up in this conversation with a stranger the age of her dad? She wanted to laugh, to diffuse the awkwardness she felt, but then he nodded.

"I do."

She turned her gaze back to the bell tower and considered this. Her parents had never been in love, she suddenly felt sure. She thought of their relationship objectively, her memories like clues. They weren't in love. Not that Jill had a great gauge for that sort of thing. She thought of the photograph in Amedeo's foyer and considered that perhaps to love someone was enough.

How strange, she thought, that the Dunns and the Perlos had in common such unique experiences. Did this same phenomenon describe her own relationship with Zane? Was what they had enough for her? Sitting there, she wanted Amedeo to hug her in a rush of childlikeness that felt foreign, a thing that floated back to her like the wisps of a blown dandelion—it was a feeling she used to feel around Lily.

"Why do you have us over?" she asked. "Like, these random American grad students?"

"I'm on the board!" He laughed. "You think it is strange for me to invite foreigners for dinners?"

"Sort of," she admitted.

"This is not unexpected here. In Italy, to share a meal is—" he drew the fingers of his hand together—"life. How do I say it? Community, it is important. People knowing people. Family, of course, but also friends. It is different than in the US. When I have been in America it seems business is first, knowing people is secondary, or even third. Here I think it's different. People are first, everything else follows. Do you understand?"

Jill nodded.

"When I met you in the market," he continued, "you seemed a bit lost, and I am a father. But then it was fate—I always adopt program students. I also love art, artists. You are one. Then I met your friends, and the rest, well. Here we are."

"Lucky for me I got pick-pocketed," she said.

"Lucky for me as well."

Late that night, back in her apartment, Jill sat at the dining room table working on a new piece, finally sure of what she wanted to enter in the art competition.

23

"The new olive oil is released now, every year," Professor Memmo said. She had arrived at the program offices carrying an enormous glass jug of the greenish liquid. It was thick, and a floating haze hovered near the bottom. She hoisted it onto the table at the side of the classroom with a vigorous grunt. On her forehead was a glaze of sweat despite the frigid morning.

"The olive vineyards have spent the year producing and curing the oil. This week Italian families will buy a whole year's supply, even five or six jugs. Oil is used in everything, never butter, and this is why we have the healthy hair, skin, nails."

"It's kind of weird that Italians only use olive oil, but right next door in France it's all butter for everything," Ling observed.

"To you it's hard to understand. The closeness of countries here is like your closeness of states, and tradition and cultures bleed together there. But in Europe the cultures of countries are unique. France united in independence, Italy united, Switzerland united—all singularly. Europeans value culture as a treasure to be preserved. You see?"

Between classes Jill and Isabelle walked to the grocery store to buy some of the fresh oil for Isabelle to send home to her step dad, who aspired to one day become a chef. They stopped at a few other stores, then returned to the offices and walked into an animated conversation among a few of the girls. Rachel's arms waved wildly above her head as if she were swatting away a swarm of flies.

"Well I don't care if he is the goddam King of Rome," she said. "If he thinks he can screw me and then spend the next night with someone else, he can go to hell!"

Ling seemed to be only half listening as she clicked through e-mails on her laptop, nodding and murmuring "Mhmm" every so often. The others egged her on, flanking her, agreeing, children cheering a schoolyard fight.

"I have been trying to tell you for weeks, Rachel," Heather said. "These men from Europe don't respect females. They think they can just use and abuse. Especially American women. We have a reputation for being 'easy.'" The adjective was delivered with an emphasis indicating absurdity, as if the notion was completely unfounded.

"Drama," Isabelle stated, inserting herself. Jill could tell she would make sport of it.

"The guy I've been seeing is cheating on me," Rachel said. She had a way of looking around the room when she spoke to someone, only making fleeting eye contact.

"Lying bastard," Isabelle said, her cheeks twitching.

"He's an ass," Veronica said, then walked through to the next room and sat down for class. The troop of girls stared after her blankly.

"On a brighter note," Heather inserted, looking directly at Jill and Isabelle, "I was just telling these girls I ordered a custom leather skirt this weekend from a boutique in Florence, and I'll pick it up in two weeks." They nodded. "It's gorgeous. Three hundred euros, and I say that is nothing for a genuine custom

Italian leather skirt. I'm considering boots to match. So if you want the name and number of my man, let me know." Lifting her bag over her shoulder, she followed Veronica.

Isabelle mouthed, "Genuine Custom Italian Leather," flicking her head back and forth with every syllable, and Jill smirked, rolled her eyes, and took a seat beside Ling. Within a few minutes Professor Bova strode through the door. Her hair was feathered around her face, and there was a touch of natural rouge in her cheeks, nearly imperceptible indicators she had been rushing. She was, as ever, a portrait of composure and elegance in patent leather stilettos—a different breed of Italian—though she did resemble the Perlos in the nose and eyes.

"Good afternoon," she said, setting her slim, leather bag on the table beside the lectern. Her eyes flicked across the room. "We seem to be missing our only ragazzo?"

Jill hadn't noticed Wyatt's absence. She looked at Isabelle, who stared straight at Anna. She apparently had.

"Well, we'll begin. I imagine he has a good reason." Wyatt's exclusive claim on maleness had its perks.

With the lights extinguished, the cavernous room was completely dark, and Professor Bova started a slide show—image after image of thirteenth century art found in the historic buildings throughout Siena. Jill observed with fascination. There was a common crudeness to the images, the cartoonish depictions of faces, murky dark colors, a sense of medieval cruelty and doom. Man's penchant for created beauty had grown into something else entirely, yet these ancient works of art lay wedged in at the foundation, solidified in their functionality, sturdy under the weight of centuries piled on after. The professor expounded upon each image, offering background and clarity. The students listened in silence.

An hour into class the room flooded with light, washing out the image of the slides on the white wall, breaking Jill from her trance. Wyatt slinked in and took a seat.

"It's nice of you to join us, signor," Anna said.

"Sorry, Professor," he said, and did not offer an explanation. She gazed at him with an inscrutable expression for a moment, then continued.

He was wearing athletic clothes, a jacket that made a kinetic sound when he moved, and his hair was slick with sweat. He glanced at her and she wrinkled her forehead in question. He wrote something on his notebook, then held up the corner slightly so Jill could see a scribbled soccer ball. He smiled.

With Dovio? she mouthed.

Wyatt nodded.

She returned to the slideshow, finding her place in the visual litany of slides again, and began to daydream.

Her art would fit somewhere, a minute glimmer in the tapestry of all time. Lily's too. And the art that would come in the future. And Wyatt's architecture, Ling's photographs. All collating into humanity's anthology of creating. If civilization came unglued or divine powers sent some cosmic flood again, her work would be found amidst the rubble, possibly thought crude and archaic. There was a sense of being part of a whole as an artist—even though the moments spent at work were isolated, internal, and full of self-glorification and hatred. So much of that perceived seclusion was an illusion.

24

I swore I would not get involved with an Italian because they're supposed to be so terrible. Seedy and obsessed with sex. Claudette is always saying to get involved with a German, if a European at all. But this boy! He is smart and well read. And he knows painters. We spend a lot of time together, and his friends are so fun! I wrote to Jodie about him. I won't get too involved. He can only be temporary—for the duration of my stay.

I feel myself grafting into the city now. When I got here I felt like an awkward foreigner. But it helped to make friends with Europeans—they've sort of shouldered me in and I pretty much only hang out with European student types. They're charming and drink slowly all the time, smoke a lot. I can't get into that—the taste of it on my breath in the morning makes me gag. Rosa says I'm becoming an Italian, except for my blonde hair. I've gotten a lot better at Italian, and I go sit with her for a couple of hours three or four times a week, just talking. She remembers things about World War II. Definitely older than forty. Her father was a soldier and she talks about what it was like in Northern Italy during the war. She's not from Siena. Leone met her when she was in school somewhere (I forget) and brought her back. I think . . . some things get lost in translation, but I usually nod even if I'm missing something.

It's really cold now, and Leone says it will be a very cold winter. He expects the coldest one in a long time, and some of the vineyards are worried about the crops. This year's olive oil was not as good as some years', according to Rosa, even though she had me dip some bread in and I couldn't tell a difference. They seem to qualify years and time with things like that—how the oil was a certain year, or the heat of a summer, the chill of a winter . . . never seem to say an actual year, "1943," for example. In descriptions nothing is specific or precise. Descriptions are sort of like song lyrics. They speak in rhythms and lovely cadences, but sometimes they don't really communicate anything concrete. Italians are so interesting.

I started thinking about the possibility of extending this year. Rosa said that her brother-in-law would hire me to work at his vineyard as a hostess for travelers and wine tasters because my English would help. The vineyard is ten miles outside the city, and she said he has quarters for people to live. It's tempting. She said he'd teach me about working on a vineyard. I guess it's probably like this everywhere, but it's much easier to find a job through a connection than just by looking around. I would have to get a work visa or something . . . she wasn't sure about all that and seemed sort of taken off guard when I mentioned having to do that. I think she thought I could just start working here. Oh, Rosa. Maybe if the Italian government didn't know . . . but I keep on asking myself if I could really leave Jodie for that long, and if working in Italy is just a feeble escape attempt. Escaping from Connecticut is a glorious thought, but I do also love it here. Finally spoke to Mom and Dad this week. First time since I've been here, although I did send them two letters. We talked about the weather, honestly. The weather. Also about Nana, who apparently doesn't remember anyone, including Mom. I regret not being there for that, and I am afraid she'll die before I get home. When I'm there for the wedding in a few months I vow to go see her in the nursing home. I, LILY, VOW TO VISIT MY NANA. There, it's in stone.

25

A last-minute decision to travel for fall break, largely based on available cheap flights and the fact that Isabelle's father canceled his trip just days before his scheduled date of arrival, deposited the roommates in elegant Paris, where the rest of their friends had planned to be for the past month. By noon just a few days after booking the tickets, they had checked their bags into the small hostel on the Left Bank and were milling around the *Arc de Triomphe* and the miles of fashion that surround it. The street was strangled with shoppers, but it was sunny and the sky was a deep, clear blue. There was an understated energy there, a fluid rushing coursing around and through the people, one which did not disturb the calm. Like an undetectable undertow. On each side of the street was a wide sidewalk with tables and chairs dropped around implanted trees where people sat eating crepes and sandwiches from the box stands along the road.

"Bonjour," Jill said when she and Isabelle returned to the room with three double-stacked bunk beds.

"Oh, it is indeed a bon jour," Wyatt said. "Where've you ladies been all day?"

"Shopping," Isabelle lifted her bags.

"Oh, jealous. Where'd you go?" Ling said.

"The Arc." As if she possessed the rights. "All around there."

They walked to a restaurant near the hostel and ordered *boeuf bourguignon* served with warm baguettes, then went for a long, pleasurable walk to the *la tour Eiffel*. When they arrived the monument sparkled with flickering lights to announce the top of the ten o'clock hour, and they stood beneath it, staring up into the tower's skeleton. Colossal beams crossed over each other in an iron plaid, and a never-ending staircase wrapped around the inside. Long lines of people waiting for tickets to the elevator stretched out beside the tower. Rocco began to climb, so the rest followed up the hundreds of steps to the first tier. On the landing Jill snapped several photographs as she worked to catch her breath, mesmerized by the night lights coating the landscape. She'd seen it before, but the Eiffel Tower was still stunning in size and intricacy, a center point for both tourists and Parisians, lending its dignity to the city as the star at the top of the tree.

By the time they reached the upper tier, Jill had a painful side stitch. She stood against the railing looking down the long stretch of park where thousands of people moved around like tiny bugs. She imagined them lying back in the grass, drinking wine from paper cups, taking pictures, buying food and souvenirs, sleeping, kissing. And then she thought of the same people, looking up at her, just a black speck. She had thought the same thoughts as a child, but it felt as large now as it had then.

The waiter is wearing a tuxedo. I have eaten in restaurants where waiters wore tuxedos before, but I was dressed up too. I am just wearing jeans and sneakers. There's a smudge of chocolate on the cuff of my sweater from an éclair I ate after lunch. I roll it over so the waiter won't notice.

Well, what do you want to eat? He's smiling, like we have a secret, but I'm not sure what it is. He can be embarrassing, but he's less embarrassing than a lot of my friends' parents.

I can't read the menu.

Oh, okay. It's standard stuff. There's roast pheasant, duck, a sausage dish, steak tartare, escargot.

I am cold, and tired from walking, so I ask if there is French onion soup, which there is. *I'll have that.*

He orders wine and an appetizer, and the waiter walks away. He seemed snobby when we got here, but when Dad ordered the wine, he started smiling and acting friendly, so the wine was probably expensive, but I'm still sure I won't like it.

This is fun, isn't it?

I smile, nod. We have been on historical walking tours for two days, and he is the only person I have to talk to. It's the second time we've gone overseas just the two of us. When we went before, with Mom, it felt like a great adventure. Now it's not like that. I am also missing the freshman formal, two soccer games, and the speed-painting competition to raise money for diabetes.

But it has been sort of more fun than I thought. He seems happier here. Actually happy isn't really it—that's not the right word—just a little bit more like he used to be. Not so silent. We're both quieter now. Without Mom there just isn't a ton to say. He asked me about boys, which was embarrassing, but he has never asked me about boys before.

After dinner we walk looking for dessert crepes. We find a cart near the Eiffel Tower and I get Nutella and bananas and he gets powdered sugar and berries. We sit down on the grass and after a little while, when it's nine o'clock, the tower starts to light up. It twinkles.

How do they make it do that? Are the lights turning off and on?

I guess so.

Mom would love this. As soon as I say it I wish I could take it back. He's probably better here because he isn't thinking about Mom. I think he's usually sad or angry or quiet because she's dead, and he's remembering that all the time. We haven't talked about her on this trip, and he's been good. But I want to talk about her! I feel like she's an animal inside me, clawing me up.

Yeah, she would.

I glance at his face, and he is smiling. Phew.

Her first trip to Paris felt far away. It had been their best trip together. For all of his faults, for all of their lack of communication, and for all of the strange silences between them, she had presently and consciously loved him. It's easier to love the people closest to you from far away, where the individual scales are invisible, blending into the beast as a whole. She thought of him now, sitting in the leather reclining chair beside the glass door to the back porch, his specs perched on the end of his nose, reading some book on revolution in the workplace or American history. It had taken her years to be able to step over the fence between them and begin to understand. Her counselor, Frieda, had been her saving grace. Jill's pediatrician had referred her just before Lily died, and they had continued to meet throughout her childhood and into college. Jill still e-mailed her when big things happened, though she no longer functioned in a counseling role. Her practice was for children. Frieda had helped Jill to be able to see her father's pain through the fog of her own.

"Pretty unreal," Ling said, suddenly beside her.

She nodded. "I know. I was here when I was younger, but it actually seems bigger. It's the other way, you get older and everything shrinks. But not this. It's like, as you grow, it grows."

Ling began to explain the process of Paris's acquisition of the tower, which she'd read on a plaque on the other side of the landing, until Wyatt and Isabelle found them. They gathered up Rocco and Veronica, who were reading other bits about the construction of the tower posted around the landing. When they reached the bottom, Ling went to a shop on the street nearby and bought a few bottles of wine. They sat for a long time on the lawn passing them around, mostly discussing Weldon Grimes and their staggered headway on his project to interview locals. They discussed what they all referred to as "our city"—Siena—even though the discussion was almost exclusively based on the commonality of being foreign in Europe. They found a small restaurant near the tower where they bought *pain au chocolate* and *beignets*. Jill found herself returning to Lily's discussions of possibly staying abroad longer—there was this freedom, this collective disconnection from life at home—and it was refreshing. Also impossible for her. There was a shade of guilt, knowing Zane was there waiting for her to return while she returned over and over to Thomas and the odd grief she felt in knowing she wouldn't see him again. At two in the morning they returned to the hostel, thoroughly exhausted, where a teenager with headphones over his ears buzzed them in.

As they walked up the darkened steps to their room, Jill scanned the wall of the stairwell, where hundreds of flyers had been hung, taped over one another, layered like shingles. There were advertisements for services and language tutoring, printed pages looking for roommates with the bottom frayed, each pullable tab with a phone number to call, lost animal notices, posters for new exhibits at museums and current and expired dance performances.

She came to an abrupt stop, and Rocco slammed into her back. He cursed in Italian, looked at her blankly, and stepped around. She tore the colorful poster from the wall and walked back down the steps into the light of the foyer, incredulous she hadn't noticed it before.

The Planet
30 Octobre
8h00
a Femme de la Lune

The poster was dark, all black and purple like a bruise, and showed the cover of the album titled "These Silent Places." It was the most recent one, the one she didn't own. Below it was another photo of the five band members, Aaron standing with his guitar on the right, his hair longer than she'd seen it, his expression aloof, his aquamarine eyes somewhat vacant. She drew the tour poster closer to her face, but it was small and there was nothing more to be seen. It was a photo of only limited pixels, not real life, though it felt as if he were suddenly standing before her.

"Um, do you know where this place is?" she asked the boy at the desk. He didn't hear her, so she walked up to the desk, set the poster down in front of him and rapped her knuckles beside his computer. He pulled the headphones from his ears and stared at her.

"Do you know where this is?" She placed a finger beside "a Femme de la Lune."

"Oui," he said, nodding with a smile, obviously delighted.

"Where?"

"Pigalle."

She shook her head.

He grabbed a map from the desk, opened it, and pointed to the ninth *arrondissement*.

"Do you want to go?" he asked. He was maybe seventeen years old, still skinny, his body not quite substantial enough to fill his height. The quality of his flirtation made him seem even younger. Jill tried to imagine herself in high school meeting him. She would have been charmed.

"I—um," she said, looking not at the boy but at the poster, shaking her head slowly. "It's tomorrow?"

"Yes," he said. "I can get tickets for you." As if he were a concierge at the Four Seasons.

She considered this. Why would she go? She'd never loved their music in and of itself—it was loud and abrasive—and there certainly wasn't anything to be gained by seeing him. Chalk it up to irony and replace the poster. And yet, the part of her that nurtured a belief in fate, in the alignment of individual paths for a larger purpose, whispered *go*. It had been five years. No, six. She couldn't not go, it was all too strange.

"Yeah, that'd be great. I need two. How much?" She pulled out her wallet. She could change her mind.

"I can get them free. It's okay," he said. He looked her up and down unabashedly, then smiled again.

"Thanks, that would be awesome." She winked, but when she turned around her expression narrowed with her thoughts.

26

The next morning there was a different clerk at the front desk. Jill hadn't mentioned anything about The Planet to her friends under the rationalization she wasn't sure the boy would come through with tickets. In the event he did, she wasn't even sure she would go.

They took a bus to Versailles. The palace was famously Brobdingnagian, yet at the same time Jill found its elegance possessed a kind of delicacy. The six students stood at the ticket window outside the iron gates reading prices.

"Damn," said Wyatt. "That's expensive. Thirty euros to see inside."

"It's historically crucial," said Ling. "It's not that expensive. You've obviously never been to New York. It's very standard for a museum."

Wyatt yawned. "I'd just go get some breakfast. A little chocolate croissant?" He nudged Isabelle, who was looking at a brochure.

"I'm good with the gardens, and that's cheap," Jill said. The sky was light in the morning under the climbing sun, overexposing all the ivory stone and greenery. It was warm there, in the arms of the castle shielding them from the wind. It would be chilly at dusk.

"I'm going inside, I don't care if I have to go alone," Ling said.

"I'll go inside," Veronica echoed.

Rocco agreed.

Isabelle, who had been inside Versailles before, and Wyatt elected to stay with Jill in the gardens, and they made a plan to meet at one o'clock on the outdoor terrace for lunch.

Ling, Veronica, and Rocco filed into a long line behind a group of tourists who had just descended from a neon bus while the others purchased the cheaper tickets from a booth with no line and made their way through to the back.

The gardens, like Alice's wonderland, drew them into an illusory endlessness. Hedges created a maze for losing oneself, and marvelous white stone statues of nude figures, military heroes, and detailed animals decorated the grounds. Several empty pedestals, home to damaged or crumbled sculptures now under restoration, invited them to become statues. Jill took a few pictures when her friends posed themselves dramatically, making faces where the stones would never dare, admonishing them to get down whenever voices neared for fear they would be expelled from the place. Isabelle nearly ran straight into a statue of a man lounging on his side, his smooth, perfect rear displayed, his gaze directed off into the distance. She stood beside the cold glutes, her back to Jill, her head turned to the side for a dramatic over-the-shoulder gaze, and Jill took the photograph. They decided to play team hide-and-seek with no limits, and Isabelle spent an entire hour looking for Wyatt and Jill, hidden in the low limbs of an ancient tree on the south corner of the gardens. They were children, trapped in a mystical, endless playground, its power erasing their age awareness and returning them to an old, wonted reverie. By one they were famished, met the others at the place they'd predetermined, and bought dry, overpriced sandwiches from the trolley. They found a spot by the rectangular mirror pool to sit and eat. It ran perpendicular to the back side of the castle, and a raised stone bench ran the way around so hundreds of tourists sat without crowding. The mallards customarily residing there had left for the cold months, so the pool was as still as a mirror.

It was late in the afternoon when they returned to the hostel, weighing the importance of a nap or shopping, making plans for the evening. Jill was quiet, and felt her fingers tingle when it was the boy who knew Pigalle seated at the desk again. She intentionally loitered in the lobby perusing the corkboards covered with posters until her friends ascended the steps.

When she approached, he held up two tickets with such obvious self-satisfaction that Jill laughed.

"Ah, merci!"

"Do you have another person to take?" he asked eagerly, as if he'd been waiting the entire day to ask this singular question.

She had considered this. She knew Ling would go with her, but the entire day had passed, and she hadn't mentioned the possibility. If lives could overlap, if the universe was flexible in its adherence to time, she would have liked to take Lily. The old Lily. She felt sure the old Lily wouldn't have judged her. She would have found the whole thing a hilarious adventure. It would also probably be nice to take the Lily of Jill's youth. She would be level-headed and allowed Jill to lead, simply exist as a support beam. Some kind of combination would've been welcome.

"I could find someone for here—" he gestured to the desk.

"Oh, no. I'm sorry. I'll be meeting someone there," she said. It was not untrue. The boy's face fell slightly as he handed her the tickets. She took his hand, pulled him toward her, and gave him a light kiss on the cheek. "Thank you."

He smiled with satisfaction and nodded. On a map he had behind the counter, he highlighted the way she should walk, explaining it was about two kilometers.

When Jill entered the room, she found her friends lounging on their bunks.

"We have a plan," Isabelle said. "We're going to nap for an hour, then head toward the Left Bank for the evening and find a place to eat there. Ling has the Fodor's book, so if we can't find something the adventuring way, we'll resort to that."

"Cool," Jill said, making her decision in a split second. "I actually have plans tonight."

"What?" Ling snapped her head around. "Without us?"

"Yeah, don't take it personally. I found out a friend from college is here in Paris, and we're going to meet up."

"Why doesn't she come out with us?" Wyatt said.

"Yeah, I um . . . " Jill didn't correct him. She couldn't remember if Isabelle knew anything about Aaron. "I think I'm going to join in on some plans with their friends. I'll mention it though—maybe we could meet later or something?"

"Whatever," Ling said, and lay her head back on her pillow, bringing her guide book up over her face.

Jill walked over to her bunk, grabbed her toiletries, and walked out of the room to the bathroom.

"You're being weird," Isabelle said, suddenly behind Jill in the dark hallway.

"What?"

"Who's this 'friend'?"

"Just someone I know from school," she said.

"I doubt that. You're all defensive."

Jill laughed.

"It's a guy, isn't it?"

She turned and Isabelle was staring her right in the eyes, her feet planted in a dueling stance.

"Yes, this person happens to be male. What the hell is this, an interrogation?" Defensive.

"Because you're acting totally weird, it's written all over your face."

"I apologize," her tone completely unapologetic. "This is dumb." She inserted a few coins and the shower turned on. "I need to get in—only have a few minutes," and she closed the door, isolating herself within the miniscule bathroom. She stripped and stepped under the warm water.

There was a certain peacefulness in walking the Parisian streets alone, a privacy. There were plenty of times in Siena when she walked alone, but there she felt familiar. Plus, in Siena there was the added distraction of Lily's journal. She hadn't brought the journal to Paris primarily for fear of losing it, but also with the intention of escaping for the week. Evidently she'd escaped from one ghost only to fall into the arms of another. All afternoon she had considered The Planet's gig.

■

He is sitting on the third step from the bottom and right beside his boot there is a discarded cough drop covered with tiny ants devouring the sticky, medicinal sugar. Red cough drops—and candy, anything with red food coloring—give me migraines. He looks up at me again. There are dark, ugly circles under his eyes, and his skin is pale, especially under the fluorescent light in the stairwell. Moths flutter above us, making strange shadows like fairies. The moment is awful, but the air is fresh and cool, a perfect evening.

I don't get it, Jill. Just all of a sudden.

This was all a mistake. I'm not this kind of person.

He flinches. *What does that mean? What kind of person?*

Like . . . I don't know how to say it. I don't know exactly what I mean. Unfiltered honesty is the only way. *You are doing this band, which who knows if it will ever go anywhere? And it's drugs and booze and women and music, and I have an education. I want to travel, and be an artist, and work in a museum. I mean, someday I might like a family, I don't know!*

He's nodding, looking down. His elbows are propped on his knees, his hands together in a fist like he's praying. His hair is messy, and looks like a little boy's hair from the back.

I'm sorry, Aaron. I shouldn't have let it get this far. In hindsight it was so stupid, getting involved with a person like him, but it had been fun and passionate, something completely different from the norm. A thrill. A rebellion.

Jill, I love you. He looks at me again, and I feel sick to my stomach. Second-guessing. I look around the stairwell, out to the parking lot of his complex.

I shake my head. *I'm sorry, I don't love you.*

I turn and walk down the landing, straight down the steps and to my car. I turn it on and drive away without hesitating. Once the parking lot is behind me, I pull over and weep.

He had quit stalking her after she had made herself perfectly clear. "Stalking" was a cruel term—he'd loved her and had not wanted to let her go. He had texted and called and hung around outside her classes because he wanted to make up to her whatever she felt he had ruined. "Stalk" was a word everyone else had used. She hadn't really felt that way. After that conversation, she hadn't heard from him again. She tried to remember if she'd even told Zane about Aaron, that was how irrelevant it seemed in her present life.

It wasn't long after that Aaron's band went from a local grunge outfit to an international sensation—she had gotten away from The Planet only weeks before they were discovered by an LA agent perusing open mic nights in Nashville to find new talent. Jill's roommate Mal, who detested the genre, had been the one to tell Jill after she'd heard it at the university newspaper office. The band was a from-the-ground-up, grassroots success story, a vision of hope for similar green musical crews. To Jill, however, The Planet was simply Aaron.

Oddly, seeing the photograph on the tour poster tacked up in the hostel stairwell had awakened Jill, as if dunked in a tank of cold water and brought back up into the moving air by the nape of the neck, alert, sober, oriented to a different sort of reality. Parting ways with Aaron had not broken her heart, really. She had felt disgusted with him by then. But now, so far removed from those strange nights of patchy recall, Jill felt a pull of affection toward him.

It was clear where the band was playing when she turned a corner and saw a mob of people pressing toward one very small door. There were several men scalping tickets, and she got rid of her extra with the first one she saw for twenty euros. She tucked the money into her back pocket and slid into the crowd between a group of rowdy teenagers. Acquiring tickets to the show might have actually been a challenge. When she approached the door, she handed over her ticket and ducked inside.

A long bar against one wall was packed with customers opposite a rather small stage at the front of the space. There were a few tables, but everyone stood, shouting to be heard, ordering drinks from five barmen running to keep pace with the demand. Clearly they hadn't anticipated the turnout this early in the tour. It was packed already, even without the line of people standing outside still attempting to enter. Jill ordered a beer and found a spot against a wall close to the stage. She spotted Aaron's guitar—the same one, to her surprise—on its stand fewer than twenty feet from her, and she could feel it in her hands. The smooth neck, the weight, the grit of the strings on her fingers. He had tried to teach her so many evenings, shirtless, lounging on his sofa, correcting her finger placements, watching her face as she concentrated with a playful smile always on his mouth. She was awful with music, and instead of retaining any of his instructions she had only retained the memories of that subtly heated intimacy.

"Bonsoir," a man said, approaching her from behind so it surprised her when he was suddenly standing so close she could smell the cigarette smoke on his jacket mingled with cologne.

She nodded and smiled.

"I see you're here alone?" He was tall with dark, coiffed hair. He spoke accented English.

"Yeah," she said.

"It's too bad you've got a drink. I would have bought you one."

"It's fine. I'm here with the band," she said, and inched by him to find a new place to stand.

After a few more minutes, the lighting changed and the crowd began to cheer. The band members bled onto the stage from the darkness behind. She squinted to make them out—Derek, Sam, Squid on the keyboard, and Paul. There was a guy she didn't recognize who sat down behind the drum set. They'd never been able to keep a drummer. Aaron came out last, draining the last of the water from a bottle, and he threw it behind him. He wore a Tennessee Titans t-shirt she recognized, and she smiled, feeling a shred of misappropriated ownership. The sound in the bar was deafening, too intense for such a small space, and it had a numbing effect on her ears. Jill watched Aaron—he was smirking, as if it was all a big joke. Paul, lead on the microphone, introduced the band and a fresh wave of cheers exploded. Jill laughed out loud. They all picked up their instruments and started, filling the space with electrified sound, and played the intro to a song she'd never heard.

They played for two hours, with one extra song at the end when the crowd refused to release them. Some of the songs Jill knew, a few she'd never heard. A bit of the sharpest edge to their sound was gone, replaced by friendlier beats—more people friendly. They appeared largely the same as the last time she'd seen them together. Aaron's hair was long, as she had seen on the poster, and it made him look younger. The drummer was obviously more talented than the guys who used to play with them. It was strange, seeing such a loyal following in France, when they had never been able to sell out a bar in Nashville. They'd always been collectively goofy, not the type for fame.

Jill ordered a third beer when the show ended and sat down while every other person surged forward to secure autographs and pictures with the band, watching the circus from a high-dollar sky box. She couldn't see them as celebrities, but she thought there was probably a contingent of people behind every famous person feeling the same. She wasn't sure why she stayed. She had told herself going into the evening that she'd see the show and leave. She had no reason to speak to him, and no idea what sort of feelings he held toward or against her. The beer was only half gone, but she stood. Putting on her jacket, she turned around.

"What the hell?" he said. He was smiling like a boy, the pieces of hair around his forehead sweaty and stuck together, swinging as he shook his head in disbelief.

She laughed, then shrugged. "It was just . . . providential."

They stared at one another for a moment. She looked into his eyes and found they were clear.

"You're clean."

"Yeah, I am. Manager's rules."

"Smart guy," Jill said.

"Girl."

"Oh." She nodded.

"Why are you here?" he asked, as if snapped out of a dream, terminating the banter and flipping their roles.

"I'm in Europe finishing up a master's," she said. "Just visiting Paris this week. I saw a flyer—I thought it'd be cool to see you guys on tour."

"Yeah, it's awesome," he said. "It's amazing. We've been to London, and then we're going to Spain and Australia. A master's. In what?"

"Art history."

He nodded. "Yeah, you wanted that."

It all felt like too much mystifying success and intersection to be real.

"You look beautiful," he said. "Older or something."

"Thanks, it has been what? Six years?" She shook her head, and because she didn't know anything else to say, made a move to go. "Well, congratulations Aaron. And all of you. I mean, you did it."

"Yeah, well, hang on. If I can just let 'em know, you want to grab something to eat?"

Jill hesitated, cast a glance behind him. "I don't want to make you—I wasn't even going to say hi—"

His expression faltered, and she couldn't tell if her words had wounded him. It was an uncomfortable feeling, knowing him so well, flipping through volumes of memories in her head, all the while acting as if they were just meeting. Somehow it was the same sort of clumsiness.

"It's up to you. I'd love if you wanted to come."

She looked him in the face, all of their relationship strung up like drying laundry on lines running between their eyes. "Okay, yeah. I could probably do that."

"Alright, sweet. I'll be right back."

After walking for a while, they sat on a park bench overlooking a small playground with two child swings and rusted monkey bars. The glossy red windmill of Moulin Rouge stood tall just beyond, its halo of light stretching up like open arms to the night sky. Jill held her crepe close to her face so the steam warmed her nose and cheeks. Aaron's arm lay draped behind her on the back of the bench, his hand almost touching her shoulder.

"This whole thing—the tour, your album, the fame. It's insane. I can't believe it." He was different—and so was she, but she'd known her own life would lift off. She had never imagined he would move on, go forward. He was thirty-seven now.

"Thanks, that's really nice to hear," he said.

"I didn't mean it like that—"

He smiled. Fishing a cigarette from his pocket, he nodded. "Yeah, it's fuckin' unbelievable. It's uh, you know, not something I ever really thought about."

"Is it good? I mean, are you good?"

He turned his face toward her with a look of confusion, then turned back to the park and shook his head. "You being here . . . I mean, you just showing up at my gig in France and asking me if I'm good. It's like, what are the odds of that?" His face was strained. She almost spoke. "But yeah, I guess I'm good. I had to get clean, sober up. I hadn't been clean for a long time— sorta forgot what it's like thinking with your whole brain." He laughed. "It's shit for writing music though, you know?"

She smiled, nodded. She really didn't know. He was so terrifically different from her it seemed impossible they could even be having this interaction, but she felt the pull to him, the same as before. Who was she? Who was this person wandering around Paris in the middle of the night? The distance she had put between herself then and now, which had seemed substantial enough, felt suddenly narrow. She didn't do these sorts of things. She was predictable. She went to bed at ten o'clock.

"I know I was messed up when you were around, but I did love you."

She was picturing a charcoal she had drawn of Aaron, an image of his profile against a pillow where he had fallen asleep with his clothes still on, down to his shoes. She remembered the moment because he had looked like a different man then, all of the truth of his youth in his face replacing the lines she usually saw there. She wondered if she still had it somewhere, if it had wisely hidden during her Aaron purge. She'd forgotten these emotions, how concentrated they were at the time.

"I know." Her mind was slipping back into the two-sided battle. The thing that had ultimately pulled her from him was the drug abuse, and she could tell from his eyes he was telling the truth about being clean. She was drawn to the artist, the music, the color and vivacity of his dreams for his future. And he loved her, or he had. They were practically kids then, at least she was. Seeing him now, as an adult, she could keep her feet planted. She was wiser, and he seemed to be too. His edge was gone, softened like a soaked sponge. But she was situated in herself now, she'd grown into it. Hadn't she?

Suddenly he kissed her. A full, gentle kiss with all the tumult of emotion she felt frothing inside her. When he pulled back, they stared at each other.

He laughed, wiping his lower lip with the back of his hand. She noticed a bracelet then, a thin woven thing made of many uncomplimentary colors. She touched it.

"What is this?"

"Oh," he spun the bracelet around mindlessly. "My daughter mailed it to me."

Jill sucked in her breath and physically recoiled.

"You have a daughter?"

Aaron looked up with a whip, stunned, and stared back into Jill's retreating eyes.

"Yes . . . I . . . yeah."

"How old is she?" But something inside her knew right then.

"Eight."

27

"It's not that far," Ling said. "We could just walk."

Isabelle groaned. "It's like two miles, Ling."

"Oh my god, that's like the longest distance known to man." Ling rolled her eyes.

"We can take the Metro," Wyatt suggested.

"It's our last day in Paris—we should walk and soak it in," Ling pleaded.

"Jill, what do you want to do?"

"I don't care. We can walk," she said. "Or the Metro's fine."

They walked. Jill stayed toward the back of the group, listening to music on her iPod, which her father had mailed a few weeks back. She looked around eagerly, trying to appear as though she was intentionally observing every statue, vista, fountain, and café. Behind her sunglasses, however, her eyes were unset and everything before her was taken in as a sort of blur.

He'd had a daughter the whole time, and she hadn't known, hadn't even nurtured an inkling of knowing. She was a fool! Even worse that in one night she'd cracked that door open again, allowed herself to consider him in a fresh light. She couldn't recognize herself. She'd kissed Thomas, and then Aaron, and in a month she'd only spoken to Zane four times. The man she was planning to marry.

"You can't avoid me all day," Isabelle said, suddenly dropping back from Wyatt to be in step with Jill. "Where did you go last night?"

"I told you; I met up with an old friend."

"Yeah, I don't buy that. You're wound up."

Jill removed her earbuds and shook her head. "I went to see a band."

"Okay."

"The bassist is a guy I dated at the end of college."

"Okay," Isabelle said, but this time her tone was completely different, as if she already understood the whole story. "Serious?"

Jill shrugged. "In its way."

"He dumped you."

"No, ironically," Jill said. "I dumped him because he was a deadbeat stoner. And then I saw him last night. He's clean, he looks good . . . he kissed me."

"Alright."

"And then he told me he has a daughter."

"What?" Isabelle's face was openly appalled. "Like, a recent daughter? That you didn't know about?"

"Old enough she could make friendship bracelets better than me, which means she was around when I was."

"Shit."

Jill arched her eyebrows. Her attraction to him had been dormant for long enough she'd thought it extinguished. The sense of relief she felt around him, that forgotten notion of feeling like that version of herself—free, artistic, unhindered; opposite of the current—predictable, secure, and comfortable. And then the added reality that Aaron was a father—it didn't add up. How had he never told her this crucial detail of his life in the thousands of hours they'd spent intertwined? He had kept it from her intentionally. It changed the memories, as if she could wash them in a swampy, dark green filter, like the raw olive oil. She'd left him on the bench looking over Moulin Rouge. He had not begged her to stay.

The art of the Louvre, the variety of time periods and types, all meticulously placed according to era and style throughout the wide corridors and the many stories, offered everything from ancient Egyptian mummies to Van Gogh. Despite the ongoing internal somersault, once inside the museum she was swept up in the art, an ideal distraction—a candy shop full of enticing chocolates, lollipops, cookies, truffles to sample and savor. She cherished seeing the *Mona Lisa* firsthand, walking around the display room to experience her following stare, and the beauty of *The Raft of the Medusa*. She was alone, and had been for hours. She had wandered until she was lost underneath the skylights and the walls, spaced for the ideal aesthetic, solitary among masses of others speaking French, Spanish, Italian, Russian, Chinese. Not English. It was the isolating nature of her entire experience of the continent—to be surrounded by people, yet feel totally companionless. The symphony of languages was, in different volumes and rhythms, a white noise backdrop. It was an aloneness in the world without the melancholy of being alone.

It was early in the evening and the inside of the museum glowed with soft, warm light. Backtracking, she looked down the hallways she had walked through. They hadn't made a plan to meet. The museum closed in three hours, so at the very least she knew she could find them then. Peering down the halls and into corners she could not find a single companion, and even looked in the café with no luck. She turned on the archaic cell phone provided by the program. There was a voice-mail from an Italian phone number. Finally, walking from one era to the next, Jill heard giggling from a side corridor removed from any artwork. Approaching the window, she discovered a small nook with benches, hidden from plain sight, with a view of the Louvre's courtyard. She peered in.

Wyatt and Isabelle sat on one bench, Rocco, Ling, and Veronica on the opposite, laughing in a delirious stupor. Wyatt had his head pressed up against the window, his hat in his lap, his hair matted up like tail feathers. He was laughing so hard he shook, and Rocco had his chin in hand, also laughing. Isabelle shook her head slowly, smiling.

"What are you doing?" Jill said, amused.

They looked up at her with simultaneous faces of guilt.

"Jill," Isabelle sputtered. "We've been here for like seven hours . . ."

"We all love art . . ." Veronica said.

"But god, Jill, this place is so boring," Isabelle interrupted. It was like she was drunk. "It's literally sucking my soul out of my body. How many paintings of the Virgin Mary could there really be?"

"Listen, I can't even pretend," Wyatt said.

"I have been dragging them," Ling said, Jill's only companion in the art concentration—the others studied architecture.

Jill slid onto the bench beside Wyatt and shook her head. "You all are pathetic." But she was smiling.

"Excusé moi." A deep voice, like the movement of velvet over skin. The effect of two policemen in uniform was immediately sobering. They all sat up straight and wide-eyed, unwittingly conveying their innocence to whatever crime they would be accused of having committed.

"Qui est Jillian Dunn?"

"You're looking for me?" Jill said. She raised her hand half-way in nervousness, as would a child.

"Are you Jillian Dunn?" the officer repeated, this time in perfect English. His face was straight, his expression erased. The second officer stood still.

"Yes," she said. She was afraid to look at her friends.

"We need you to come with us."

"What?"

"There is a security office on the first level."

"Did I do something wrong?"

"Please come with us, mademoiselle," he said.

"Can we come?" Wyatt said, the first one to stand up.

"No, only Jillian. You can wait in the lobby."

She stood timidly, felt the heat rising in her neck. The first officer moved forward, but the second waited for her to pass, as if ready for her to try and run. Jill looked over her shoulder. She only caught Ling's eyes before the officer quickly ushered her away.

They took an elevator underground. The officers didn't say a word, and Jill followed suit. Hundreds of seconds to imagine what she could have done, why she now found herself in the basement of the Louvre. It was fluorescent lighting, speckled floor tile, beige walls, and low, drywall ceilings stained with amoebic water marks along the way, the heinous underbelly of the world's finest museum. She turned over possibilities like stones in her hands. It had to be something to do with Aaron. When she reviewed their interaction in her mind she tried to find the place where he could have lied, and tried to imagine what could have transpired when she'd left him. There were doors to offices, most of them closed now that it was evening. Or what if it was something about her dad—he'd died in a car accident. A shooter had walked into his office. There were people that hated him, who had sat opposite him in court and landed in jail. It wasn't beyond the realm of possibility. She looked at her watch. Closing was in an hour. **SÉCURITÉ** was printed in bold, black letters on the door, and they entered. The first officer gestured for her to sit down on a wooden chair beside the desk, then disappeared. The second busied himself at the desk talking to another man, not in uniform. A few other uniforms and suits wandered about, but nobody paid attention to her. The office was surprisingly large, with a few desks and several doors open to smaller offices. The absence of windows gave the space a dismal, claustrophobic feeling.

A few moments later the officer returned and motioned for her to follow him down a hall and into another office. Inside a woman in a drab suit was sitting at a long table. She wore a severe expression, and appeared to be sorting through a file of documents. Behind her, a man wearing baggy corduroy pants paced. He had a beard and his hair splayed out from a severe cowlick at the back of his head like a child who has just woken from a hard sleep. It was clear this was not an office but a room for things like discussions and, like on television shows, questioning.

"Hello, Ms. Dunn," the woman said. "Please sit down there. Thank you." She dismissed the officer with a wave. "I am Detective Smith. This is Detective Feurre."

She was American, he was French. She tapped her acrylic manicured fingernails down hard on the faux-wood table. She seemed perturbed, as if the whole encounter was a wretched inconvenience. The man stood behind her looking over her shoulder at the documents.

"Do you have any idea why we have you here?"

"No," Jill said. She thought about what it would be like if she threw up then, on the table and the manila file folder full of documents. She easily could.

"Your passport number was picked up yesterday morning in coordination with an illegal border crossing."

Jill stared at her. She felt the pulse in her whole body, quick and firm, as her mind jarringly shifted gears at full speed.

"Do you understand what I'm saying?"

"Yes," she said. "Where was it?"

"The Italian-Albanian border." Detective Smith stared at her pointedly. Jill knew the stance. It was an accusation, a threat of knowledge, of consequences.

"I obviously didn't know that was happening."

Silence. The heat kicked on and rattled through the old, aluminum innards of the building. The sacred Louvre, a world-class destination, just a building like any other, with heating ducts and a damp basement.

"The person in question is related to a girl who, we believe, is your roommate in Italy. Era Dosti. Her brother, mother. It seems it is a family operation."

Era's name sunk to the pit of her stomach with the heaviness of a boulder, and Jill's eyes unfocused. She blinked, then nodded slowly. The detective called it an *operation*. It was an absurd thought, so unlikely. And yet, copying her passport number would have been as simple as walking out with one of her socks. She never took it out in Siena. Jill had the passport in her book bag now, as they spoke, so it hadn't been stolen. She considered this.

"I've got my passport here." She pointed to her bag, slumped beside her chair like a pile of laundry.

Feurre seemed to awaken. He nodded at her. "Show us."

Jill fumbled with the buckle, her cold hands shaky and slick. She produced the passport and pushed it across the table. Feurre picked it up.

"Have you met her brother?"

"Yes," Jill said. "Well, one of them. Luan."

"Do you know how he would have gotten access to this information? If he made a copy?" Detective Smith said.

"I guess he did. It was in my room. I don't carry it around with me all the time in Italy. I know he was in my room once—" They looked at her with renewed suspicion. "No, I walked in on him coming out of my room when I got home from class once. With my roommate, who is here." She pointed up. "You can ask her."

Feurre and Smith looked at one another, carrying on an entire analysis without speaking a word. Jill wondered where Luan was. If Era knew about any of this. She suddenly thought of her father.

"We're dealing with you here because of your American citizenship. Because you're here now in Paris someone needed to speak to you. Italian police got in touch with Parisian police and your name was flagged. The Louvre security contacted us when you arrived today. Clearly this case is impertinent to French government, but because I'm here, they called me to find you. Do you understand?"

"Yes." She was beginning to calm down, to see she wasn't in trouble. The detectives did not treat her as the problem, rather as a somewhat tiresome addition to it. They also knew about Era, the fact that they were roommates, and the fact that she'd entered the Louvre. With a clearer head, she began to think it seemed like a lot of attention for the issue at hand. Illegal crossings from Albania could not possibly be so extraordinary they would dabble in multiple international legal systems to investigate. Identity theft, too, seemed like an issue whose responsibility would fall more on the shoulders of the person under siege.

"The perpetrator is being prosecuted in Italy now. He is claiming he was trying to get his mother into Italy, where he and your roommate have been living for some time, without using her name." Smith was talking with a certain insouciance now, as if Jill weren't there. "His brother is tied to drug cartels. We can't be sure he wasn't passing the information to those avenues."

Jill nodded dumbly. There it was, the importance, but it seemed so improbable.

"Is there a phone I could use for an international call?"

Smith stood and picked up the folder, not looking at Jill, as if she hadn't heard the question. She exited the room, leaving Jill with the silent Feurre. He lit a cigarette.

"You don't know anything about this. All of this trouble coming out of Albania?"

"No, not really."

"Your roommate's brother—Edi Dosti—look him up. He is a bad guy."

Smith returned with the phone and glared at the cigarette in Feurre's hand. Jill dialed, and the detectives stepped out.

"Hey, where are you calling from?"

The sound of his voice was a relief. She explained the situation, trusting him, speaking quickly for fear he would panic, but was stunned by the composure he exhibited when she told about being led to the security office and put in holding. He let her tell the whole story, and as she unloaded the events she found she felt emotional, close to tears. The result of coming down from the adrenaline. When she finished, he asked questions about phrases and vocabulary used by the two detectives. He also took down their names, and the names of Era and her siblings. He asked her about pointed details she had to think to recall—when had she seen Luan in her room? When had he first come to stay at the apartment? How many times had he been there when she had seen him? What had Era said about him? She could tell from his line of questioning that he was mentally compiling a legal brief. She responded with complete honesty.

"I'll come," he said, as if speaking to a child. "I could be there by Sunday."

"Oh, my gosh, no. You don't need to come. I'm fine."

"Jillian, you can't use your passport."

"They're going to give me a document to return to Italy, and Detective Smith said the US Consulate will send me a new passport with a new number in like five days."

"Where'd you tell them to send it?"

"The program offices," she said.

"Smart."

"Thanks."

There was a long silence, then a deep exhale across the Atlantic.

"Maybe you should come back."

"What? No, I'm not coming home. I have seven weeks left."

"I'll think about it."

"You'll think about it? I'm not sixteen."

"Stop, Jill. I paid for it so I can make you come home."

Initially he had sounded kinder, like a shadow of his old self, but the shadow had evaporated as the conversation progressed. She certainly wouldn't be telling him anything about seeing Aaron. Leaving early hadn't crossed her mind. There was still almost half a journal left, and the rest of the undiscovered things of the city, not to mention the rest of her degree. She had art to create and more streets to see. Italy was just sinking into her, becoming familiar.

"You can't really make me." A default to a younger version of herself.

"When do you leave Paris?" he said.

"Tomorrow."

"Have you thought about what you're going to say to your roommate when you get back?"

She thought, then sighed. "No."

"Well, you'd better."

28

*R*osa *took me to the church of San Domenico for the first time.*
So strange I haven't been there before. It would be a place to
sketch. It's oddly sort of empty I guess. Like there's a whole big
open space that should be full of pews or a fountain or something,
but it's just hollow with tourists milling around. It's fascinating.
The church is famous because supposedly there are body parts
("relics") of Saint Catherine of Siena, who was a very pious, spiri-
tual young woman in the city. They say that the church has her
actual head and finger (WEIRD). I don't know. Again, a fault
line in my translation skills could have messed that up because
that is really hard to believe.

This is a spiritual city, but I'm not exactly sure what that
means. I thought the massive, ancient churches would be more
like artifacts, dry and cold and desolate. I've heard that a lot,
that there isn't real "feeling" in European churches, but every
time I step into a church here it's like someone struck a gong
deep in the heart of me and it reverberates. I can't explain it—my
vocabulary! Spiritual things—God, I guess—was never really my
thing, obviously, even though Jodie's always telling me I should
go to church—their church makes me feel so uncomfortable.
But I want to go to church here. I love to sit in a pew when it is
completely silent and stare up at the front with the stained glass
windows and all those thousands of little candles people light to
send up wishes or good feelings or thoughts to their dead fam-
ily members or saints or something. They really believe in God.

And sometimes when I sit in a church here I think I really believe in God too. It's like I can actually hear his voice. People say God speaks to them. I don't think I believe that, but maybe he's sort of around you and inside you like breathing in deeply when you're standing in thick fog. I kind of wanted to be an atheist, but I don't think I can in good conscience. I think God exists. Maybe I need to work on figuring that out. Add that one to the list—

29

It's snowing on Christmas Eve. People keep saying we are having a white Christmas, and Daddy said that's a reference to an old movie that we will watch tomorrow because it's a classic. When we get home, we're having steak for dinner and dulce de leche cake for dessert.

The church is very warm and my legs feel itchy with the thick stockings, but I don't squirm or complain because I want her to keep bringing me. I like the slow music; it's like the music before a play, a little bit spooky. I never understand any of the words because the priest speaks in Latin, which she said is a dead language, and I don't understand that at all because I can't figure out what an alive language would be either.

Church is strange. Everyone is very serious and looks unhappy. I don't know why the priest wears the robes, or why people go eat a piece of bread and drink wine. She told me that it is the body and blood of Jesus, who is God's son, which kind of scared me. I didn't tell Daddy because I thought maybe he wouldn't let me come. I guess he doesn't come because he thinks it's weird too. I don't know why we come. One time I asked, and she said, *To be close to God*. That didn't make any sense because I don't think God is on this planet. Then I thought if she asked me why I went, I would say, *To be close to you*. But she didn't ask me. I also love to look at the stained glass.

A woman dressed in dirty, gray clothes walks down the aisle and passes us with a cane in her hand. She is limping, and I watch her go all the way to the front and sit down with a loud thud in a chair on the corner. I look up to Mama with wide eyes, but she isn't looking at the woman. She's looking straight ahead, and she is crying. Nobody around sees her, and I feel nervous. I stare at her face, but she doesn't see me looking. One time she told me that sometimes people cry even when they are okay, but they just need to let some sadness out.

I reach up and put my hand in her hand. Her fingers close around mine.

My boots make craters in the snow. I don't feel cold, and the sky looks like pink cotton candy. It is very quiet because no cars are driving, and most people are home eating dinner already. Daddy told me that it feels quiet when it snows because snow muffles noise.

Do you think Santa will come tonight?

Yes, he always comes on Christmas Eve. She is smiling now, holding my hand.

I hope he brings me Molly. Do you think he knows how to make an American Girl doll?

I'm sure he can figure out how to have his elves make any toy. But you know, Santa might bring you something different.

I know.

We turn onto our street. We will pass eleven houses before we get to our house. Usually I count down from eleven.

Why were you sad at church?

Hm?

You cried. Suddenly I feel nervous for asking.

She doesn't say anything for four houses, and we're almost home. She is looking up at the sky.

Christmas is a happy and sad time for me, Jilly. I have had happy Christmases and sad ones, and I remember them all, so on Christmas I take a little bit of time to be sad. Then I spend the rest happy, like you! I'm happy now.

I nod, still unsure, until she puts her arm around my shoulder. And then suddenly she stops and picks me up. Her face is close to mine, our noses touch, and she smiles.

Want to race?

Yes! She puts me down, we turn, and line up our toes.

Go!

November unearthed a different kind of cold—damp and gray replaced crisp and clear, and in the city of stone there was nothing but humanity to absorb the impact. Indoors it was warmer, but not enough—the air floated inside and outside without impediment through fissures and cracks in the old architecture. After sunrise fog lingered dense in the streets like ghosts. That often colorless morning sky ran into the stone architecture to create a fathomless height of insipid tones. People walked through the city in high, dark boots, pants, long jackets with the collars flipped up to protect their necks, and the dark hair. Fall turning toward winter in Siena was unforgiving, the cold digging in deeper with every passing day, only occasionally relenting on a misplaced sunny afternoon.

Jill stepped out of her apartment door and pulled thin, red gloves over her fingers. Her hair, bedraggled and in desperate need of a cut, acted as a scarf on the back of her pale neck, and she wore jeans tucked into brown boots she had purchased for herself for her birthday just before the trip to Paris. She was twenty-seven now. She stopped into Fiorella for an espresso, then headed up toward San Domenico. Her mom's thoughts on spirituality were fascinating. The Lily she'd known had gone to church every Sunday, even when she was sick. When they went on vacation, her mother would pull out the telephone book, turn in the yellow pages to church listings, find one close by, and go to the earliest service. She didn't discriminate—at home she went to Catholic mass, but she'd attend a Presbyterian service, a Baptist service, she'd even gone to a black gospel church once in Atlanta. Jill had often accompanied her for the time alone together. After church they would get donuts and coffee— Jill would drink only a few sips, so Lily would think she was mature enough to handle true, intelligent conversation. Gary didn't ever go, but it never seemed like an argument. Church was Lily's. Work was Gary's. After Lily died, Jill had avoided church. Even as an adult, on occasions requiring her to attend— weddings of friends, Christmas Eve services with Zane's very Presbyterian parents, she felt wrong, like walking through the house of an acquaintance without him. Moving quickly to try to shake the cold, Jill consulted her pocket map once to be sure of the street, then turned down Via della Sapienza.

San Domenico was enormous and straight like a box, look- ing something like a municipal building from the outside. She mounted the stone steps, pushed the door open, and was greeted by an unearthly, hushed chanting and also somehow a great deal of silence. Standing just inside the doorway, she allowed her eyes to adjust from the light morning outside to the darkness within. It was just like her mother had said—empty. Only now, so early in the morning, there weren't even tourists to fill the spacious interior. Its largeness was surprising. Far to her left, at the front of the church, a section of pews held a sparse gathering of a few Catholics attending the service, the source of the chanting. That was only about a fifth of the space, and the rest was wide open. Jill moved toward the back wall and began to walk slowly along the outer edge, absorbing the paintings and glass cases containing lamps and books, a variety of artifacts with small plaques displaying names and descriptions written in Italian so she understood little. On the wall opposite where she had entered, Jill found the display of the relics of Saint Catherine. She gazed down into the glass case at the wrapped fragments and wondered if they were the real thing, or if the real relics were buried somewhere deep beneath the church for preservation. Her skin rippled from the chill in the air. She was unmoved. If anything, Jill thought the ritualistic display of body parts bizarre and moved on.

People were leaving the pews and the low murmur from the priest had ceased, so Jill moved closer to the front, slowly, walking against the wall with her thumbs hung on the leather straps of her book bag. Step after step she moved around the entire perimeter. Some of the paintings were beautiful, and she recognized names of artists from her Art History class with Professor Bova. Stained-glass depictions of biblical history were a puzzle for Jill, who remembered some stories from Sunday school as a child or biblical references from English classes, but not enough to place with certainty. When she had circled the entire outer wall of the church, she turned and walked to the center of the floor and looked up. She closed her eyes, willing herself to feel something.

But, nothing. Nothing quickened the pace of her heart. The only feeling she had was a gaping longing for her mother that was growing wider, reopening. Despite the beauty of the church, its grandiosity and repute, she didn't care about it. The tension of the past few weeks was as constricting as humid heat, and she longed for someone to unburden her, to answer the questions, to delineate the truth from illusion, the right and wrong, the yes and no. She walked to the last pew and sat down. Three rows ahead of her a very small woman with hair like cotton sat with her head down and her hands placed on the back of the pew in front of her. Jill watched her sit silently and still.

What was it Jill wanted? To be moved spiritually? To have her own awakening? Maybe she simply wanted to feel something that her mother had felt. It was the whole thing. Walking the streets, knowing the cafés and corners, painting the country, learning the Sienese dialect were all things that she now shared with her mom, who was still so far away. When Jill closed her eyes she tried to see Lily here, but she could not. She could only cut her mother out of her own childhood memories and paste her to this place, sitting on the Campo, flirting with that boy, holding his hand on the Via Banchi di Sotto, but that wasn't right. There were two different people. Lily who had written that journal was completely different from Mrs. Dunn, mother and wife. She couldn't connect them.

When her father had handed her the journal, Jill had imagined it all playing out differently, as if reading it would have the power to bring Lily into sharper focus, solidifying the things she'd known and refueling her near empty tank of untapped memories. She had counted on the journal entries to explain it all—why things were never quite right in their small family—but it did not. Instead it was estranging them further, adding to the mystery. She wondered if Gary had known—if he'd anticipated the book to be an artifact to bring closure.

Something didn't make sense, and it all felt wrong, but now she couldn't decide which side was right—Lily in Siena or Lily the mother. Touching the corners of her eyes, Jill stood and walked very slowly to the back of the church, took another look around, and left. Outside she removed her camera from the bag and snapped a few shots of the church against the western valley, still blanketed with dense fog, as the morning turned brighter and brighter.

When Jill and Isabelle had entered the apartment the day after everything had come unglued in the Louvre, they were silent. They'd stood at the door listening. Isabelle shook her head silently at Jill.

The detectives hadn't given her any solid information when Jill had asked about Era specifically—what had happened to her? Was she in trouble for her involvement? She had no way of knowing if Era had or hadn't known the truth about Luan, though it seemed unlikely she hadn't. She wasn't angry.

Jill set her things down in front of the television and walked down the hallway toward the bedroom with the big windows and the big bed. The door was shut, but when she pressed her ear up against it there was no sound.

"Nobody home," she said when she returned to the living room.

"Weird, but not surprising." They had discussed all of the possibilities on the plane.

Jill took her bags to their room and threw her suitcase on the bed as she noticed an envelope on her pillow. It was sealed, and there was nothing written on the front. She sat down and opened it. The text was printed in a small font, a dull grade of ink growing lighter with every line.

Dear Jill,

> *My friend is helping me write the letter, for making sure it is correct with English. It is very important to be correct. I leave it on your bed because I will not see you.*

> *I am terrible sorry for all the things that happen to you because of my brother Luan. I did not know he takes your documents and writes down your numbers and name and information private. I did not know until after you leave on Friday and I do not know how to talk to you.*

> *I want to explain this thing to you.*

> *I have one other brother. His name is Edi. He is living in Albania for his whole life. I told you some things about Albania, but is really worse than what I say for some people. My family have many sad things because I have an uncle who is very bad and is the boss for things with drugs and sex and violent. He is the cousin of my father. He has much money, and he wants my family to do this too, but my father always say no. My father was a good man, but he is dead for fifteen years. When he died, my uncle spend time with Luan and Edi. Luan is older, and smart. He was already*

doing good with school and wanting to go to Italy. Edi was always angry all the time, this is his way. Angry for everything. He is mean to me, and my mother, and his teachers, everybody. But he loves uncle because he is powerful and strong and has money. Edi hated my father because he think father was lazy and not making much money, but almost all rich Albanians is because they are doing something bad.

    Edi spent these years working for my uncle and he does many many many bad things. He has a gun and this is his power. My mother is little and silent. This is hard to explain in the letter. She is like a small bird, is the only way I can say it. But small birds can survive, there is place for them in the world. She is mighty. She loves Albania because this is the country of her parents, and parents, and parents. You understand, is how you feel about the USA. You have strong fist on the place you live. My mother is this way. But now it is dangerous because only Edi is there. She starting to think maybe is not good for her living alone, we are in Italy, my father is dead. She think lately she wants to leave, but my uncle is not letting her. He need her because he use her to hold on Edi. Is this making sense? It is hard to say what I mean with this bad English. Family is very important to Albanians—this is your whole name, your family. Edi is angry and stuck in bad things, but he loves the family. Love in a different way. It is not love like romantic. It is love like a kingdom.

    Luan is trying to get my mother to Italy without uncle and Edi knowing. This is why he take your information—trying to use it for my mother. I know he is

wrong, but also, a little bit, he is right. I hope you see it
better now.

I am sorry for it all, Jill. I am in Roma now with
Luan, and he is in jail for some time. Lule is staying in
Siena. She have had no involved with this.

> Your friend,
> Era

Three times Jill read the letter, and the part that struck her with the most force was *I'm terrible sorry for all the things that happen to you*, as if the inconvenience of being detained for an hour on a leisure trip to Paris, having to have a new passport printed and delivered to her, were somehow comparable to the circumstances of life for Era. She sat still, chilled, for a long time.

When she opened her laptop, there was an e-mail from Zane. It appeared her dad had spoken to him about the events in Paris before she'd had the chance to tell him herself. He was concerned, but she also detected a sense of frustration in his language, indignation that she had failed to call him. She had thought about it of course, after she called her dad, but it felt like too big a task to explain the whole thing. More advice wasn't what she'd needed, rather space to think—about all that had transpired in the French city. She wrote a quick explanation without an apology, and sent it.

30

"The vineyards," Amedeo said, "are the lifeblood of Tuscany." They were walking along the outer rim of the Wednesday market, and he rattled off information, always teaching. They'd met up, as usual, by chance, though the frequency of such chances called the alleged spontaneity into question. She had begun the assignment for Weldon, electing to research the effect of the 1991 fall of the USSR on Italy. Amedeo had a strong command of government and history, and had insightful answers to most of her questions. Jill listened, watching her feet pass over the stones to avoid catching a toe on a protruding edge. She ate an apple, and the juice absorbed into her gloves as they wove around and through stalls. "Have you been?" he asked.

She shook her head.

"I will take you Saturday. My cousin has a vineyard near San Gimignano. Do you know of this place?"

"Yes," she said.

"Okay, why don't you bring Isabelle?"

Isabelle agreed without hesitation—every time they'd gone along with Amedeo accompanied by Sophia, it had resulted in at least a five-course dinner—and Saturday afternoon they met Amedeo at his apartment door and walked south toward the wall. They stopped at an arbitrary, oddly wide door several blocks from his apartment. He inserted a large key into the keyhole, pushed the door upward, and revealed a small Mercedes-Benz.

The girls climbed into the back and Sophia sat up front, griping about the meager leg room with a twinkle in her eye.

"Do you see this cousin often?" Isabelle said as they wove slowly through the narrow street.

"Only when we have the whole family for a big dinner—he is always coming for food," Sophia said, "never just to see his aunt and cousins. If there is a feast and wine, he will be there, this much is sure."

Amedeo laughed, shaking his head. "Sophia is bitter toward our cousin because he did not use her art for the design of his wine label."

She hit Amedeo on the arm. "Va! You are unfair, brother. It was beautiful! The label now looks terrible. He would have sold much more."

Once they moved outside of the initial suburbs of the city and into the countryside, the land began to roll like waves and they sped over hill after hill. Jill watched Amedeo's face from her position behind Sophia. His salt and pepper hair faded around his neck and ears to white. There were aging lines on his face, down under his ears, and extending from the corners of his smiling eyes. Riding in the car felt unearthly and new, fresh to the senses, and in the presence of the siblings there was a levity, a familiar warmth. They flew past the terra-cotta roofs and long stretches of vineyards that could be seen from the city walls where they looked like checkerboards, now close enough to reach out and grab the wire cages around the vines. Colors so precise and vivid they looked like paint. The sun beat down from a cloudless sky burning off the fog, temporarily alleviating the season's bitterness.

They pulled up to an enormous stucco house, white with a circular drive. The shuttered windows were propped open and each one framed a window box overflowing with green vines. There was a massive wooden double door with iron fixtures in the shape of lion heads holding hoops for knocking. The lawn appeared professionally manicured, and Amedeo knocked four times, then called out, "Lucca!"

Moments later a man opened the door, beaming. He was taller than Amedeo, and heavy. His face, though bearded, did resemble that of his cousins, but he looked older.

"La mia famiglia! Prego!" He hugged Amedeo first, slapping him hard on the back, then embraced Sophia with a kiss on each cheek. She returned his affections, her anger forgotten. Who are the friends?"

"Hi, I'm Isabelle."

"She is from California and knows about wine," Sophia added.

"Va bene!" he replied, taking her hand for a kiss.

"I'm Jill."

"Prego, bella. You are both from America?"

They nodded.

"Va bene!" He turned to Amedeo. "Come in! You want us to show the friends around the vineyard?"

"If you have the time," Amedeo said.

"I have so much time, nothing but time. I used to harvest the grapes with my own hands, worked like a mule all day and all night, every season. Every day, even Palio! No longer. I am an old man and have hired my sons and their friends and now," he slapped his protruding stomach, "I drink the wine, eat cheese all day, and I grow larger! Not you, though, cousin. You look the same as when you are twenty-eight years old."

Touching his hair, Amedeo raised his eyes sarcastically.

They followed Lucca through the house and met his wife, a quiet woman, small, but she disappeared quickly. Jill and Isabelle walked out onto a porch off the back of the house with a spectacular view of the three harvest fields comprising the vineyard. Lucca explained the harvest season, the process of using the fields alternately, the condition of the current year, and his projections for the upcoming wine. He spoke fluidly and seemed often to be speaking directly to Amedeo and Sophia, forgetting about the girls, alternating between disseminating information for their education and disclosing details of financing and stock measures to his cousins. The vineyard was a Perlo family business, and the way the men spoke of it gave Jill the impression that Amedeo's and Lucca's financial lives were tied very closely together.

Staring out over the wide landscape, the girls did not speak while the conversation lingered on the trade, shifting in and out of Italian. Eventually they moved down to the storage cellars, located in a building about one hundred yards behind the house. Lucca showed them the colossal barrels for the wine, the presses, dozens of empty bottles to be filled. In the cellar Lucca showed them hundreds of bottles of wine, stacked and organized by year, and gave each girl a Reserve from 2004, which he claimed was the year of "heaven's grapes," translated by Amedeo. He spoke using eloquent words, as if conducting a sort of performance. He even carried himself with an inflated chest.

Eventually Lucca led them to the fields where he ambled down the rows of vines, fingering the grape leaves gently, discussing his theories of watering and planting, as learned from his father, Amedeo and Sophia's uncle, on this very earth which had been in the family for hundreds of years. Migrating to the third field, he explained to his cousin his concern over a disease that had killed a portion of that particular space, and they dropped to their knees in the dirt of the field. Gently they turned over the vines, the leaves, and rested comfortably on their haunches as they spoke quickly and vehemently in Italian.

"This is very important," Sophia explained quietly, gesturing to the men. "A disease on a vine can spread and kill a crop. It is very dangerous for the grapes."

Tilling the earth with his fingers, Lucca kept his eyes locked on his cousin as they spoke. As Amedeo leaned down to examine the lowermost leaves, the muscles in his back tensed beneath his pressed shirt and sweat marks grew between the shoulder blades. The sun was uncharacteristically hot now at two o'clock where the breeze didn't blow. Isabelle and Jill left the others and walked slowly up and down the rows, Jill a few steps behind her friend, taking pictures of Isabelle's blonde hair against the dark vines, the green leaves, and the clear sky, pictures of her hands brushing the leaves, of her boots walking through the uneven grass, the infant buds. Eventually they all moved back toward the house for a very late lunch. They sat around a table on the patio, and Lucca's wife brought out hot gnocchi with rabbit sauce, a platter of sliced meats, tomato salad, bread and wine, but did not stay to eat. The sun drooped in the sky, and the air grew chilly again. Lucca, Amedeo, and Sophia relived childhood memories of long games of hide-and-go-seek on the vineyard that only ended with the setting of the summer sun, and late dinners on the porch with their siblings, parents, and grandparents. They spoke lovingly of the yearly grape harvest, how everyone participated in the picking, the sacred days, and the years of bountiful yield. They cursed the devil's year—the year of no grapes, when Nonno's father had slept under the vines twenty nights in a row, praying to Saint Catherine and the Mother Mary for a miracle.

"Have you always lived here?" Jill asked. "On the vineyard?"

Lucca nodded.

"And your family," she looked toward Sophia and Amedeo, seated beside one another, "was in the city?"

"Yes, my cousin had the better life," Amedeo said, smirking.

"No, no! We worked hard, while you played and threw flags."

"Ah, ah, ah, you wouldn't speak blasphemously, cousin," Sophia chided.

"Hang on," Isabelle said. "The flag thing. These kids do a flag routine or something?"

"It is an important tradition in Siena, from centuries back," Amedeo inserted quickly, a rise in his voice. "It is like, for you, how young boys play on soccer teams or football teams. In Italy they do this too, but Sienese flag throwing is like a team. It brings honor to the family. For me, the ram is a very precious symbol. Each contrada has its own seal, flags, and costuming to match."

"Who gets to do it?" Jill said.

"It is passed through the family. Dovio is a flag bearer in the Ram Contrada, as I was, but he has aged out."

"Oh, he never mentioned it," Isabelle said.

"He is humble, like his mother." And then a quiet beat, when nobody knew the thing to say.

"So what did they do during the Devil's year?" Isabelle said, sweeping in like a wind, smoothing the sand. "For money?"

"Ah, interesting question," Lucca answered. "My mother loved art; she liked to draw. When the grapes were very bad, my mother and father entered art selling. When the grapes improved, they kept the art for a hobby. Now we have a fine collection in the house, a nice addition for visitors to the vineyard."

"I would love to see it," Isabelle said. "I'm sure Jill would."

"Come," Lucca replied, standing.

"I will come," Sophia said. "I have not seen the paintings for some time."

The gallery was a small, dark room in the second story of the house. The paintings were hung with museum precision, with small lights over each and a plaque underneath. The display was remarkable, with paintings by Giovanni Lanfranco and Giacomo Guardi beside canvases erected by local artisans. Lucca explained them individually, and Sophia added the details he overlooked.

"We must show Isabelle the wine museum," Sophia said when they'd taken a turn around the room. "It is another room like this one, with artifacts from the vineyard."

They moved to the next room, but Jill ducked out and returned to the patio where Amedeo stood leaning into the balcony, holding a glass precariously over the edge. The light had begun to change, growing warm as the sun set unhurriedly outside the great glass doors that opened onto the porch, and the air had turned cold again.

"Your family is so interesting."

"A long life, a great deal of history, many memories," Amedeo said.

She nodded and they stood quiet for some time. *A long life.* The way he referred to the longevity of his family as a single entity.

"What about your family, Jillian? You don't talk about them."

"There's not much to say," she said after a moment. Her family seemed venial in comparison to the Perlo dynasty all packed within a forty-mile radius.

"Everyone has roots." He took a seat as he said this.

She thought for a few moments, looking out. The rich sky and earth shone orange and pink as if made of metal. Where were the clouds? There were rarely clouds, she thought. No bugs or clouds. Amedeo sat with his fingers pressed together in front of his chin.

"My dad Gary's an attorney. He's . . . very smart and practical. He loves cars, makes a lot of money, watches football." She laughed. "I don't know! I have a boyfriend."

"And your mother?"

"She's dead."

He closed his eyes for longer than a blink and nodded. He seemed to feel emotion very deeply. It made her feel exposed, embarrassed for him. "What was her name?"

"Lily," she said, staring out over the hills. *Lily.* Speaking about her at home had always felt wrong in a way, as if the verbalization were an insolence. But Lily had lived here, found some sort of actualization in this city. She had been a painter in this nest of artists. She had found joy only here. She should have perhaps remained here, but didn't. Here it seemed the offense was in not speaking of her mother. This was the place for celebrating her memory.

For several minutes they watched as the colors grew dark and long shadows from the house fell over the vineyard. To Jill, Lily's death was a part of history, the essential scaffolding of her life, but as Amedeo seemed to absorb the sadness for her, she considered it freshly for herself as well.

"May I?" Jill said.

"Certo." He reached for the wine and poured her a little more, then topped his own glass.

"Why did she die?"

The way he asked, the *why* rather than *how,* could have been a translational error.

"She had ovarian cancer. She was diagnosed when I was eight, and then died a year later."

"Your father and I have something in common then."

"Pretty shitty thing to have in common," she said, laughing humorlessly.

He nodded. "What do you remember?"

"She was an artist," Jill said. "I used to go with her to a studio down where she taught pottery and painting classes to hippies and stuff. My parents referred to her work as 'part-time,' I remember that. She used to read out loud to me before bed and made up different voices for the characters. She was pretty quiet most of the time, except she got sort of sarcastic and smart when she was teaching the art classes. She used to take me on walks through this big garden and park near our house with picnic lunches. It's all very vague to me, but then every once in a while I'll have a vivid memory sparked by something I see or hear. It'll be clear as day. Do you know what I mean?"

"I do."

"But in general, honestly it's kind of hard to remember. I mean, I was a kid when she died, and I think I blocked the last year of her life out of my memory because it was just . . . miserable. I'm sure I glorify her in my mind because I can't get a hold on the reality of what it was like, what she was like." She shook her head.

"Does your father speak of Lily?"

"Not really. But it was very strange, just before I left to fly here, literally an hour before, he told me that my mom had actually been to Siena, she lived here for some time, a long time ago, I mean clearly. Before I was born."

"You did not know this?"

"No. He just handed me this journal of hers from when she was here. Isn't that weird? Like he was angling for me to come here just so he could give it to me at the right time—going for the dramatic I guess."

Amedeo was nodding, shaking his head at the same time. "And you have read this journal?"

"Well, I'm reading it slowly. I want it to last while I'm here, you know? It's like I get to kind of walk through her life here. She wrote about this café, and I found it over in an alley behind the Duomo. I've gotten to know the man who owns it, and his wife was a good friend of my mom's. Stuff like that." She looked out over the landscape again. "Isn't that strange?"

"Perhaps she wanted you to find her."

"Yeah," Jill said. "Maybe."

She sipped the wine. There was the beginning of light-headed relaxation warming her shoulders, hands, and face. She knew her cheeks and chest would be slightly rosy. She touched the tattooed lily unconsciously. The idea of fate, or of some author of the wider scope of humanity's story, a god, had always seemed like nourishment for desperate people—a comforting answer to an uncomfortable question of belonging, or purpose, or the reality of life whose true answer was a bleak, dark void. She didn't believe in it, not because she was above it, but because she'd never felt particularly convinced anyone or anything, any cosmic force, would have any interest at all in the happenings of billions of tiny people on a tiny planet in the universe. This thought, the thought of her mother's spirit somehow living, existing in the between space, leading her in some direction, was farfetched and went against her saner judgment. And yet. Here she was, looking out over the splendor of the vineyard at dusk, wondering if it was more farfetched to think there wasn't some epic in which she now found herself. She thought of Lily in church, the way she'd carried church around with her like the string to a splendid kite.

"And what do you think of the woman you have discovered? Is she as you remember?"

"Actually, no. I've honestly thought it could be a mistake, that maybe the journal isn't even hers!—she seems much younger and more free-spirited than she was when I was young. Does that make sense? Is this translating properly?" She laughed.

He nodded.

"I've been surprised. She's fearless and adventurous, and I don't remember her being that way. And there are things she wrote about her family that I never knew."

"Are you happy to learn these things?"

"I don't know yet." She looked at him. "You have this big, wonderful family with so much happiness and everyone loves each other. I just had my mom and dad, and now it's just my dad. It's very isolating, or, like . . . it's hard to explain."

That was what Era had said about her family too—it was hard to explain. Family was hard to explain, any kind of family. At least half of Tolstoy's first line of *Anna Karenina* was true: *All happy families are alike; each unhappy family is unhappy in its own way.* Era's small face returned to Jill's mind, and she wondered what would happen to her mother. To Luan. Edi.

"Everything is magnified," she said, returning to her train of thought. "My dad was always telling me to let sleeping dogs lie. I think it's just hard to deal with stuff when we only have the two of us."

"This makes sense to me," Amedeo said. "I am thinking your dad is very wise."

The next morning before class, Jill pulled on a few layers and some gloves and took her cell phone to the park she had found on Lily's recommendation her first day in Siena. It was early still, cold and quiet as she made her way up the hill and crested at the playground. Her hair was down and wild, and high on the crown of the city the wind whipped suddenly, then stilled, over and over. She sat down on a swing and pushed herself easily with her toes creating tracks in the dirt.

Gary had e-mailed more frequently in the weeks following the events flushed out at the Louvre. She knew he was now in Los Angeles on business so it would be late, but not irrationally so. She selected his number, one of three programmed into her phone.

It rang three times, then a half.

"Gary Dunn," he said.

"Hey, Dad." Certainly he recognized her number.

"Hi, you're up early."

"Yeah, I wanted to call before class. You're in LA, right? It's what, like ten o'clock there."

"I'm in a cab heading back to my hotel. Just finished dinner with a client. To what do I owe this phone call? It's unusual to be graced with your actual voice."

Jill laughed. It felt good, hearing him. The familiar way of joking, his transition from business tone to casual. She wondered if he felt the same. She tried to imagine an evening like the one she'd had at the vineyard, where they sat for hours, talking and drinking together.

"I don't want to spoil you," she said. "I'm calling because I was thinking about the Era situation. With Luan and everything."

"Okay," he drew the word out like a line between them, reading her trajectory by the framing.

"What Luan did was wrong . . . I'm not trying to say it wasn't, but that letter's on my mind—"

"Jill, we aren't pressing charges. We haven't taken any aggressive measures. We have truly done every possible thing to lift our hands." Back to business, referring to them as "we," suggesting he was her representation. "It's between Luan and the Italian and Albanian governments now. It's his lawyer's job to help him. You need to let it go."

"Dad," she said with more emphasis than she knew she felt. "They have nothing. They were trying to do something good. Who even knows what will happen to their mom if she can't get out of Albania. Did you look up their uncle? Because I did. He's in the news for being involved in really terrible things."

She could hear the sigh over the thousands of miles as if he were standing before her. "It isn't your responsibility. It doesn't matter what the circumstances are; Luan broke a serious law that went international in two directions. The legality of something like this is incredibly complicated, Jill. You don't understand. And to be honest, I don't fully understand. I don't often deal with the nuances of European laws, but I do know it's not an easy fix."

"You're a lawyer! You're supposed to be able to help." She recognized the naïveté, how unrealistic it really was, but he was at bat. If he would only try, merely look into the possibilities, take a swing, she felt he would shed all of the disinterested, superior garb into which she had always projected him and become a bigger man to her. She wanted desperately to believe that he would have the courage to take action.

"Not with this kind of stuff, Jillian. I can't do anything about this. I'm sorry."

She watched as wisps of clouds rushed overhead, and shivered.

"Fine."

They were quiet on the line for a moment, and then Gary spoke.

"I am sorry."

"It's fine," she said. "I'll talk to you later."

"Okay." There was a quiet beat. "Talk later."

31

Professor Voce made an example of my painting today! I have the hardest time understanding him, but he came around my canvas and muttered something under his breath. Usually he's ranting about the changes a painting needs, but he just took it from the easel, walked up front, and started telling the class about how amazing it was. That's what I think, I definitely heard "magnifico" or something. He was ranting, but Phil told me he was ranting at everyone else, saying mine was good. My style is definitely changing, sort of becoming my own, like my own personal voice is emerging. It's really exciting!

I didn't even realize today is Thanksgiving. No pilgrims or turkey greeting cards at the grocery store. Sad to miss: Buck, because it's really strange not knowing him and he's about to marry her. He really does seem to be the perfect man. When I get Jodie's letters I read them and they don't sound like her or something. She uses more proper language and she tries to sound adult in her decisions and reactions. I just want to talk to her! Jodie.

Glad to miss: everything else. Jillian asked me about Thanksgiving and I told her that it's typically a really nice American holiday for families, but ours aren't, i.e. "Well, last year my dad was drunk on Jim Beam and my mom hid for two hours in the upstairs bathroom of my aunt's house." Clearly too much information, but we were drinking (irony) and all laughing, but she knew it wasn't funny. It doesn't matter, I don't care what she thinks of them. I wonder if Buck will take the ring back when he meets everyone and figures out how fucked up our family is. Jodie told me she's worried in her letter. I would be too! Also sad to miss: stuffing and cranberry sauce with rum. I'm going to attempt a Gran's spice cake tonight for my roommates, who obviously don't celebrate Thanksgiving. Apparently Italian flour is different, and I don't trust the butter, so it might be horrible. The nuts are fine. If it works, I'm going to make another one for my date this weekend.

I've been thinking about how I fit in here more than at home. It's something like . . . nobody's faking—anyone will say, "hey, my life is shit" or "my family is completely unraveled" or "I can't afford to buy lunch." Same conversation, I was telling Jillian that in CT it's like television. Everyone's family acts very normal and functional and perfect. Moms actually play tennis with their daughters and people get along. At least they say they do, but who knows. That's the thing! It's like a collaborative, full-scale cover-up and everyone's lying for their own self-protection. Like in the ten years I've been friends with Becky, I've never seen her parents speak to each other. They're around the same house, out to dinner, but they talk through the kids. It's like they are living two isolated lives on two sides of a thick piece of glass but they have enormous oil paintings of their family sitting on the front porch. Wish that was the problem with mine. They just shout and bitch at each other about the pointless things, then avoid avoid avoid the things that actually matter! Jodie loves to think they're better than most parents, but they aren't. She's got this naivety safety net, which is why I'd never even think of telling her—or anyone— about Uncle Ronald. Since Dad flipped out when I even hinted that Ronald isn't just the best uncle on earth, I know it's a dead end. I always thought if he knew the kind of things his brother had said to me and tried over the years, he'd lose it but now I think

*he'd stand up for him over me. Ronald will be at Thanksgiving.
Another great reason not to go. Every time he sees me he still just
gives me that same, thin smile and calls me "Lills" and pretends
like I didn't break his nose to get away from him. Someday I'll
write a book and use his line "I fell on a watering can." I think
he thinks you don't remember things from age 10. Moronic ass-
hole. I remember things from long before that. I hate him. I have
thought about how I would kill him, and sometimes think I could
actually try. He's just always . . . haunting me. Only consolation
is he never seemed interested in Jodie at all. She should be glad
she was chubby. That's sick. The whole thing is sick.*

*The good thing is I know what kind of mom I'll be. I'll be
honest and I'll trust my kids. I just hope I don't have girls. I think
I'd ruin them, like I am. Sometimes I wonder if I'll even be able
to have kids because some cosmic power (God?) may be looking
down thinking OH NO, definitely not her. Probably will, but it
makes me scared to think. And then I think maybe I would be
better off if I couldn't. I'll let Jodie do the normal family thing and
I'll stay here. God, I'm so edgy. My family is probably glad I'm
away. And then suddenly there's a really GOOD guy in my life
and I'm not even sarcastic or mean around him. He is so sweet
and wonderful and his eyes . . . gushing. I told him about Dad,
and it didn't scare him off, though he didn't understand "alcoholism" so I had to explain, which was funny. Can't imagine not
even knowing what it is. They just don't live like drunks here.*

*I can't believe I'm writing this garbage out—I've never done this
because doesn't writing it sort of immortalize it? Maybe I need to
burn this journal once I'm done. Or I guess it just is . . . the way
it is. Truth is truth, and I've never been a liar.*

32

Weldon took the class for an extended weekend trip to Venezia. From the onset of choosing IAAE's Siena program, the excursion had been one of the most exciting aspects for Jill, but it was only heightened when she had a framework to conceptualize Weldon, and then experience his theatrical presence for five uninterrupted days. He treated his authority with indifference, making it perfectly clear he felt it unnecessary to keep tabs on them, that they were adults, and that if they did find themselves in an emergency situation the best bet would be to phone the police.

He lectured in motion, moving them through the narrow streets of the sinking city, across Saint Mark's square and into the cathedral, and the instruction turned at every corner into discussions directed by their tangential questions on the city itself, its history and traditions including an array of mysterious love affairs and murders. He explained Carnivale, the notorious annual spring Halloween festival in Venice, in great detail when they passed the most famous mask shop, and took them to restaurants they never could have discovered, hidden in basements and upper levels of discreet, faceless buildings.

Throughout the trip Jill kept her camera in one hand, beguiled by the juxtaposition of the architecture whose very disintegration was the framework of its magnificence, having left centuries of visitors bewitched. Venezia, like an elegant grandmother wearing diamonds as she is pushed about in a wheelchair, was the very quintessence of the tragedy of mortality. What appeared to be puddles of rainwater in the streets were in reality evidences of the rising tide against the literally sinking city, a grim, slowly moving reaper creeping up, inch by inch. It was as if the whole city had been divinely designed for the inspiration of artists.

Jill had expected to be moved by Venice, its canals and tragic structures, and while the visual uniqueness of the place seemed too picturesque to be real life, when they returned from the brief trip, she found Siena felt familiar, better, more beautiful. Not "home," per se, but a bit like a very long novel that has taken months to read, whose cast of characters and plot genesis seem to have grafted you in. She knew Via Banchi di Sopra, the main thoroughfare sloping gradually down toward the Campo with faithful curvature, first to the left slightly, then to the right where it leveled and flayed out with the dozens of shops opening onto the road. She found she could anticipate the uneven places in the stone underfoot and noticed the changing window displays at the clothing and panty boutiques tapping into the seasonal motifs of snowflakes and baubles. A voice she recognized called out orders from a boulangerie they passed daily, and the smell of roasting chestnuts hit her at the same place as always.

Familiarity was not, however, synonymous with ownership. Siena was merely a host. She hadn't earned any rights there. It was the history, the bloodlines, she reasoned with herself, forming a barricade difficult to surmount. The language, most of all—the walking through a crowded street, thousands of sentences swirling in her ears, and hearing only white noise. Fragments of conversation in English would amount to an interesting collection of bizarre, overheard discussions over the course of the day, but in Italy the sounds of language were more like instruments playing an overture of a production in which she was the central character. The affection she'd felt immediately upon arriving in Siena was turning into an attachment of some kind, and she felt a shifting in her core, like plates below the surface of the earth, but she was still a stranger.

After reading the most recent journal entry, one that had made her feel sick to her stomach, but which she could not quit, Jill had closed the book deliberately and wound the leather cord back around. She'd been on the train back from Venice, and the Tuscan landscape, which flew by like art class slides, was ordinary now. Jill had been thankful for the fact that her classmates were asleep and there was no one to interrupt her thoughts. There were only a few pages left, but she hadn't wanted to read another word.

Information she'd rather unlearn. Ronald, the decrepit great uncle who sat at the head of the table at Thanksgiving and smoked cigars indoors, was a pervert and a predator. She'd never really spoken to him, other than a customary hello after a year or more of fully forgetting him. He was frail now, with a face covered in sun spots like splattered paint—she tried to picture him as menacing but couldn't. Lily had torn herself away from her home and planted in Siena—the people, the pasta, the wine, the Palio, the music, the dancing, the language, the men, Rosa, Leone, the café, and in not a single entry did she speak of a desire to go home. Now it made sense—who would want to return to a family in which they weren't safe?

Jodie and Lily had been closer than sisters, but they were both dead, and in their deaths, the most intimate history had vanished. Fleetingly she had considered writing to her grandmother, but she was nearing ninety, pleasant and diminishing, growing marginal in her withdrawn disinterest in discussing more than the systematic ebb and flow of weather patterns, and would not be a good source of insight, especially in light of the truth that they'd never protected Lily from their own deficiencies, much less anything else. Jill pitied them—to have lost two daughters so young. The weight of a lifelong tragedy felt heavy, and strangely Jill's thoughts returned to her dad. Perhaps her drawn perception of him—emotionally narrow, dull, absent, workaholic—could have been concluded too hastily. By marrying Lily he had, either knowingly or not, entered a substantial mess. It seemed fitting, in light of the journal, that Lily had married a stable, even boring man. Perhaps boring had been appealing. He'd been brave, maybe, to go there and embrace the ugliness. She was suddenly eager to talk to him about the timeline—when he came into the picture, when the journal had been written.

Jill slid the thick page into the cardboard sleeve, careful to keep the top arched so the lines and shading wouldn't smudge. By the nature of the piece, misdirected lines and dark dust would be negligible, but there were the places where the cleanest bit of page was necessary for the effect, the ivory white gleamed through with an almost imperceptible glow. If she had to erase, the purity would be lost.

She turned when the door squeaked open. Lule stepped in and hung her jacket on the coat rack, then leaned her small body against the inside of the door as she slid down the zipper of her boots and pulled them with some effort from her feet. Her face was red from the wind.

"Hey," Jill said, taking a roll of tape from the table.

264 | WITHIN THE WALLED CITY

"Oh, hi Jill," Lule replied, straightening, as if suddenly keen on perfecting her posture. "You drawing?"

"Yes, I just finished a picture I'm entering in a contest." She selected words with calculated deliberation, trying to find the simplest avenue to communicate without dumbing it. The language barrier, harder with Lule than it had been with Era, caused her to infantilize the girl, though she was probably about Jill's age.

Lule nodded, smiling slightly. The girl picked up her boots from the floor and walked back to her room. It was baffling. Era was gone, but Lule was still there. They'd assumed Era supported her—she did not work, only went to school and ate food Era used to bring home from McDonald's or the grocery store, and yet here she was, living in a nice apartment in the center of the city.

Jill followed Lule and leaned her ear against the bedroom door, then knocked.

"Si," Lule said.

Jill pushed the door slightly. Lule was seated on the bed eating chips.

"I wanted to ask you. Where is Era?"

"Era?" Lule repeated.

"Yeah, where is she . . . living?" She motioned a pitched triangle roof in the air over her head.

"Oh, um. Era living in house of her brother."

"She is? She's living in Rome?"

"Yes, in Roma," Lule nodded her head assuredly.

"Oh, ok. Thanks," she said, and her mind rotated the possibilities. She turned to leave, then quickly said, "With Luan? Is she living with Luan?"

"No, Luan in Albania, Era in Roma. He has to go—um, police they take . . ." she motioned her hands, fists full of chips.

"Is he in jail? Do you know what I'm saying? Jail."

"Jail," she repeated, obviously bewildered.

"It's okay," Jill said, then gave a little wave and stepped back into the hall. She stood at the doorway to the kitchen and watched a bird perched on the window sill. It was outside, but also inside, its wiry little leg within the reaches of their heat. If it didn't move, she could walk over and touch its gray feathers, the sharp yellow of its beak, neon against the bleak stone outside. She imagined the shutter, if blown by the wind, would crush the small bird with ease. She quickly moved to shoo it away.

Carrying her drawing against her side, Jill walked through the Piazza and then north toward the office where entrants were instructed to bring their pieces. Consulting her map, she passed Fiorella, then turned down a short narrow street that opened to a small square with several storefronts. Siena was always doing that—presumptuously hiding its treasures. She found the place, then buzzed for entrance. A lock clicked, and she pushed the heavy door.

The firm was modern inside with furniture and art featuring hard, straight lines and angles. The lighting was bright but unoffensive, glowing from hidden fixtures. A long desk positioned just inside the doors formed a barrier between the door and the rest of the office, and behind it sat a young woman. Jill approached her and peered over the desk. The girl wore all black, and charcoal outlined her eyes with the same severity. Her hair was pulled into a tight ponytail, drawing back the skin of her face. There was a small granite nameplate that said *Alessandra*. She looked up at Jill, seemingly nettled.

"Ciao," she said.

"Ciao, I have a drawing for the Arte per Natale contest." She held up the envelope, whose presence in the office seemed crude.

"Follow me," Alessandra said, and stood. She led Jill down a hallway past several offices and conference rooms. There were no walls, only enormous pieces of glass to separate space. In jeans and boots, Jill was an oddity, but not a single person gave her a second glance when she passed. At the end of the hall, Alessandra lightly knocked on a door before pushing it open, and ushered Jill inside. Lucca stood behind the desk.

"Ah, Jillian. I am always wondering, will she come with art for the contest? Amedeo is telling me, 'Si, va bene, she is working on it!' but I do not believe him until I see you."

Jill smiled, softening into the comfort of being known. The office was small, but there were several windows along the back wall looking out over the Duomo. She craned to see if the café was visible.

"Grazie, Alessandra," he said, and as the girl exited the room, Jill noticed her expression had lost the shade of superiority.

"Here it is," she said, holding the bulky envelope.

"Prego, show me." He was eager, as if hers was the only submission he'd received, though she saw a large stack on a table behind the desk.

Laying the envelope on the counter, Jill grabbed a pair of scissors sitting on the desk and ran the sharp edge of one blade along the opening, separating the pieces of tape she'd just applied. She pressed the sides together gently, the slit opening like the mouth of a snake, and pulled the piece out so it lay on the desk in front of Lucca.

The image was dark, a shadowy room. Two women sat at a small table in the corner of the room. The profile of one was almost visible, but ended at her jawline, and only the whiteness of that sliver of her face could be seen. The other, whose face was positioned directly toward the artist's vantage point, too had a blank face. Eerily, Jill had used shading and fine pencils to bring the bodies to life, even to the edges of the face with the brow, the cheeks, ears, hair, but the oval faces had been left untouched by the deep gray of charcoal. Other figures on the page were black, shadowed.

"This door," Lucca said, hovering a finger over the piece, "I know it. This is Café Duomo."

"Yes!" She looked up at him.

"This is where I go for lunch when I'm here in the city—where I have gone since I am a young man. It is peaceful there, si? Not so many tourists. Leone Gavarola is a good man."

Jill nodded, unsurprised by the tentacles of that river of familiarity flowing between the natives of Siena.

"This charcoal is beautiful," he said. "What is it called?"

"Lost Lily," she said staring at the finished product. Behind her Lucca's face drew back in contemplation. He nodded slowly, struck.

"It's beautiful, like I say again."

"Thank you." She took the piece and slid it back into its envelope. "So is this your office?"

"No, no. I don't have offices in the city anymore. This is Amedeo's office! He lends me this one when I come to the city for business, maybe once or twice a month."

"Is he here?" she said hopefully.

Lucca looked at his watch. "No, he is out."

"Oh, okay."

"Sometimes he goes for ice cream. He is a traitor, loving the McDonald's with the candy and cookies inside."

"McFlurries?" she laughed.

"I don't know. I can't believe it! We all stomp our feet when the American excuse for *restaurant* comes to mar Siena, and my cousin is putting money in the bank! Italia, the nation of gelato, and he eats soft ice cream from a paper cup." Lucca shook his head. "Somehow he is always eating this, and still with the physique of a man at thirty."

"Okay, well maybe I'll stop by there. Thanks again," she said, placing her fingers on her art, feeling that sense of parental safeguarding she sometimes experienced when one of her works left her grasp. They exchanged the traditional kisses to the side of the face, and she turned to leave. "Oh, when do we know? Who won the contest?"

"It will be in the Siena paper, two weeks before Christmas. You'll still be here?"

She nodded. "Thanks."

Outside Jill wrapped the wool scarf tightly around her neck, chin, and ears and zipped the tails into her coat. Dropping her submission off had given her that wonted exhilaration that came with executing her art with explicit purpose. She did not require a contest, a reward or payment, for motivation to create, but it elevated the work for her, added an element of dignity to the time and precision she had poured into it.

The omission of facial features had happened almost without her intent. It wasn't that she had trouble with creating the authentic likenesses of eyes, that perfect shading of the bridge of a nose, lines coming in to form a mouth. In fact, it was the opposite. Those fine details were a skill she had always come by with relative ease, whereas many of her artist friends found them to be the most troublesome. Only lately it was the expression of emotion that confounded her. She felt herself stuck in a rotation of second-guessing, as if she no longer possessed the right to assign feelings to the people she drew. Her own heart felt turbulent here—full of joy and anticipation, freedom, clarity; also confusion, sadness, longing for family in its intended sense. That tumult found its way into all of the people she tried to capture on paper. She had stared at empty faces, dissatisfied, until the decision to leave them blank was the only viable option. The final product, as she'd looked at it with fresh vision in the novel background of Amedeo's office, was adequate. It would brand her work from this period.

McDonald's in Siena was not so different than any one would find in America, though the furniture was wooden rather than hard plastic, and there was penne with marinara and pizza on the menu. Even though she'd come for the purpose of finding him, Jill was amused to see Amedeo seated in the back of the restaurant, leaning against the corner formed by the window and the wall, reading a book and holding a McFlurry. She approached the table.

"Hello," she said playfully. "I seem to remember you saying that the existence of a McDonald's inside the walls of Siena was a blight on the city. Or, what was the word you used?"

"Bella, Jillian," he said, "I am ashamed! I love the Baci McFlurry, I can't stay away. Sit down." He gestured to the seat across from his own."

"What is a 'baci' McFlurry?" she smirked.

"You can only get this in Italy! Can you believe that?" He held the cup out, looking at it as if it were a jewel. "Baci is an Italian truffle—chocolate and hazelnut. It is this, in a McFlurry. It is only sold close to Christmas. This is *cielo*. This means 'heaven.'"

"I'll have to try it."

"Go, go get one!"

"Oh, not now. Maybe I'll bring Isabelle."

"Va bene, but don't forget," he said, settling back in his seat.

"Well I was at your office, dropping off my sketch, and Lucca said you'd be here. It's a beautiful office," she said.

"Thank you, yes. It is a nice place to spend the days. You finished your submission! I want to see it. I will be returning to the office next. I'll look then."

"Oh no," she flushed a little. "I'm embarrassed."

"Don't be," he said. "I will love it."

She had tried to examine the piece from her mother's perspective and thought maybe Lily would have been pleased with the skills her daughter had developed—artist to artist.

"So you just sit here?" She was changing the subject.

"Yes, I enjoy it. The coffee is okay! It's different from the rest of my life. It's a different sort of people, eating here. Working here."

"Do you know the employees?"

"Some," he said. "If they want to be known."

"My roommate works here—well she did. I don't know what she's doing now."

"What is her name?"

"Era Dosti."

His forehead wrinkled with interest.

"She's little, tiny." Jill held up her hand, thumb and fore-finger separated by an inch.

"Albanian," he said.

Jill nodded.

"I know her, she is here all the time, until the last few weeks. I hadn't been in, and when I came this week, she was not here. I was thinking maybe she went to see family. They don't live here, her family?"

"That's right. So you'd spoken to her?"

"A few times. She is very nice, hardworking."

"Yeah." She shifted. "I didn't know anything about Albania before. This is shameful, but I honestly don't even think I knew where it was. But it seems like there's, um, like a lot of tension or . . ." She was being diplomatic, trying to avoid accusation.

He laughed humorlessly. "When you are raised here, especially with my generation, you learn that *gli Italiani* are supreme. Italians hold themselves up on a pedestal in the world—we have Catholicism, Roma, the Vatican, the Pope. The food is exquisite and pure. Land, fashion, even soccer. The English word that is coming to my mind is *elite*."

Jill nodded, considering this, and mentally reframed his words to reflect the American sentiment of supremacy. In Italy there was a pride standing from the past, a Stonehenge of power with its foundation in the existence of thousands of years of dominion on a world scale. Americans, though, lacked the depth of history, the longevity, so nationality was more or less born of the nation's present identity, its current dominance.

"Of course, you know and I know this is foolish. There is no universal aristocracy, and when I left Italy as a young man to travel to Australia, the United States, Germany, Japan, my head was inflated with these notions of superiority. It did not take many years to realize the foolishness of it. I think Americans have this experience sometimes, going into the world for the first time. No country is 'best.' Some are better, but not one is the best.

"Albania is a pathetic country. When the Communist government fell, Albania was like a ship overturned in the middle of the ocean—people swimming and drowning and nothing to hold onto, only bits of the mess. What do they do? Look for land. And here is Italy, here is Greece—places to land. They come here, crawling on shore without much." There was an obvious tint of distaste in his language. "Many Italians despise this, not wanting the mess, afraid of losing jobs, afraid the perfect Italian culture will be dirtied. I understand, and also I don't. It is largely because of fear. Do you know what I mean? Italians who hate Albanians are afraid. It was worse twenty years ago— I see people coming around. Lucca's wife is Albanian so he employs many, many Albanians on the vineyard, at the estate."

"Wow."

"Yes," Amedeo said. "I used to have my own prejudice, and then he fell in love with Inez. She is a severe woman because she had a hard life. She changed the way we see Albania, even the way we see Italy. They are a strong, hardworking people. Like your roommate."

Jill decided to tell him the whole story, from meeting Era, and soon after, Luan, to the latest conversation she'd had with Lule. When she finished, he was quiet, nodding slightly, over and over, as if the motion of his head would shake up an answer to the problem.

"When you told me her name—Dosti—I did not believe it could be relation to Edi and the infamous Dosti family." He shook his head.

"I just feel like someone should do something. They have nothing."

"There is very little you can do here," he said, sounding just like her father. Jill sat back in her chair. "The bureaucracy. Some things you cannot change, Jillian."

She had imagined he'd have a different response.

When he finished the ice cream, they stood and left the restaurant, which had grown busier as the afternoon wore toward evening.

"What do you charge for an original charcoal?" he said, offering his elbow.

"Oh gosh," she laughed. "A thousand euros."

"They must be in high demand!"

"I'm kidding. I don't know, for you? Nothing. You've fed me enough."

He looked her in the eye sternly. "You do not owe me anything."

"What sort of thing are you in the market for?"

"Oh, who knows? Artist's choice. And I insist on paying."

"I'll see what I can come up with,"

They walked back toward the Campo, her hand resting lightly in the bend of his elbow.

"I'm leaving for a few weeks, and returning a few days before Christmas," Amedeo said.

"Oh my gosh! Will I see you?"

"I come back the twenty-second. I will see you then."

"That's the day before I leave."

"So you and Isabelle and your friends will come for dinner, va bene?"

"Va bene."

She would be leaving Siena, returning to life as she'd left it, and the thought gave her a vague sense of panic. In naïveté, she had allowed herself to forget it was temporary, to let those first threads of roots begin to weave their way into the Italian soil.

33

On Thanksgiving it rained all day, a heavy, sideways downpour unusual for fall in Chianti. Once she had arrived back from class, wrung out her coat and pants, and changed into sweats, Jill returned to the charcoal of the Perlo's street dinner, the first time she'd ever visited their family. In hindsight it was an evening where she had experienced some envy, but also hope, inclusion, curiosity at the dynamic. If she could perfect it, she would give it to Amedeo before leaving Siena. The sky produced a white noise, and a draft hovered over the floorboards like a moving ghost, so she wrapped up in a blanket. It was quiet but for the rain. Isabelle was with Wyatt, Lule was out.

The e-mail she'd received from Aaron that afternoon had been the only remarkable event of her Thanksgiving.

Hi Jill,

It's been all these years, and I imagined what it would be like if I got the chance to talk to you again. I stayed away because you asked me to, so I was really surprised when you showed up at our show in Paris. It was cool of you to come, but I wasn't sure why you did. You were adamant about us never talking again back when we broke up. But don't get me wrong, I was glad to see you. Am I allowed to be sending this email?

I'm sorry I never told you about Francie. She's really cool. I've made a lot of bad decisions in my life, but then one of them produced this awesome, smart, pretty, funny daughter. She's got a really good singing voice too, so I like to take credit for that. I won't see her much while I'm on tour, but hopefully when I get back and get my life together, I'll have her on some weekends. I didn't see her for a while because her mom wouldn't let me near her. But I'm getting better now, so she's thinking about it.

I know I was a sorry piece of shit when we were dating. It was a bad time for me. I'm sorry about the drugs, and dragging you into that world—that's about as low as I can go, I guess. I regret that that was the time of my life you happened to enter.

E-mail me back if you want. I'm on tour in Europe for the rest of the year. Then I go home. Hope to talk to you, Jill.

Aaron

She'd read it twice, then moved it out of her inbox so it wasn't staring her in the face every time she looked. It unbalanced her, crept into her mind. What was it she felt for him? His e-mail was a crowbar, effectively prying open those places she had deliberately soldered shut. She had always known that the appeal of her relationship with Zane was in part due to its predictable steadfastness. He was normal, his job was straightforward and stable, he was never going to surprise her. But when she felt that opening toward Aaron, she could remember the way she had felt moved by him. She had felt something similar in just a few hours overlooking the water with a man she hardly new. She had never felt that with Zane, and she wondered now if that was the very reason why she had allowed him to infiltrate her protected world.

She phoned Gary when she was sure he would be on his way home.

"Gary Dunn," he said. His voice seemed hollow, as if he were standing across a large, empty room, and she could hear only the echo of the real sound bouncing from the ceiling.

"Happy Thanksgiving, Dad."

"Happy Thanksgiving back."

"What are you doing?"

"Driving home from Grandma's. I left there about an hour ago."

"How was it?"

He laughed, which made Jill laugh. Their entire family dynamic contained within this one phone line.

"That good?" she said.

"About as good as you could imagine. Sheila is pregnant."

"What?" Jill said, transported back to the normalcy of home, family news. Sheila was Gary's younger stepsister. "Who's the baby daddy?"

"A man named Glen. They're talking about getting married. So there's that little family reunion to look forward to."

"Great," she said. "I can't wait for it."

Pause.

"Everyone was asking about you. I told them you were doing great, loving Europe. Maybe never coming back."

"Nah, I'm coming back."

Jill imagined the thickness of what lay unspoken. By her statement she alluded to the fact that the intention she had of returning home was pitted against the opposite intention Lily had had all those years before. By the silence on the other end of the phone, she wondered if her father was thinking the same thing. She weighed her words quickly, unscrambling them like Scrabble tiles on the wooden ledge, in an effort to say what she meant to say, what she was thinking. She opened her mouth to speak, but he beat her to it.

"Did you read any of your mom's diary?"

"Diary," she repeated, half laughing. It was a childish word, grossly misrepresentative. "Yeah, I've been working my way through it." So it was on the table then. When he didn't immediately say anything, she added, "A lot of messy shit in those pages."

He sighed. "Yeah, a lot of shit. Are you—um, do you have any questions?" He cleared his throat. She pictured him wearing his blue tooth, driving in the dark, his face lit up by the neon glow on his dash.

"I don't know. I mean, yeah, I probably do. I don't know."

Silent beats.

"Did you finish?" he said.

"Not yet. I took a break. Kind of felt overwhelmed by all of it."

"Okay." In the quiet space, she couldn't think of anything to say. "I know it probably feels strange to you. But try to remember, it's your mom. Even though some of it doesn't seem like her, it is Lily." That sensitive, paternal manner of speaking he brought out from time to time, like gilded china at Easter. "I was conflicted about letting you have it—maybe you can see why. I don't want your perception of your mom to change, but I also think you deserve to know her, and her whole story. I didn't always think that, but I do now."

"Alright," Jill said. "It's just weird to read because she seems a lot different than she was when I was little. Like, she is *crazy* or something, and so angry."

Gary chuckled. The sound surprised Jill.

"People change. I wasn't always as uptight. And you were a lot different before—" he stopped. "Well just finish the journal, then we'll talk more."

"Alright," Jill said.

"Are you celebrating Thanksgiving?" he said.

"Just dinner with people in my program."

"Turkey?" he said skeptically.

"Whole chickens. And I'm making a pumpkin pie because Isabelle's stepmom sent her canned pumpkin and nutmeg."

"Do you know how to make pumpkin pie?"

"I looked it up on the Internet."

"Well I guess I'll leave you to it."

His way of moving toward goodbye. "Alright, thanks Dad. Happy Thanksgiving again."

"You too, Jill. Talk to you soon."

"Bye," she said, and waited to hear the deadening on the other end of the line. She placed the phone on the table beside her. Watching it, as if she were waiting for it to stand up on feet and walk away, she thought of the day she'd missed. Jill had only attended the Dunn Thanksgiving ritual twice, and the last time she had been a senior in high school. Each fall her father w   mention it as a possibility, then plan something else the next few weeks. He'd once told her that he hated together with them because it made him feel like an outcast. They were all coastal South Carolina people, born and raised, working class, calm. He was the one who had "strayed," moved, gotten married to an artist, and stayed away. He was the only one with money, and consequently received requests for financial assistance from cousins and aunts and uncles, sometimes people so far removed from his immediate family he had never even met them. It alienated him. The widower label made him a spectacle to the "normal" ones, and the fact that he kept his only child from their gatherings gave them even more to talk about. When they went together they were a force, but he had gone alone. For the past few years they'd gone out, and then Jill had started attending Zane's family dinner, to which her dad was always invited, and to which he always politely declined. Jill wasn't exactly sure what he did on the day. It surprised her he'd gone to South Carolina.

Raindrops pelted the alleyway like firecrackers. Umbrellas passed underneath, and she thought how strange it would be if there were only umbrellas floating, no people. She pulled her blanket tighter around her shoulders and fingered the locket around her neck, again opened it and stared at the photograph of her mother. Somehow he had found Lily, and for reasons she didn't understand, had let her into his life. There was something in him, too, that she had found reason to marry. Jill imagined she could see into that part of history, could have this written narrative of that time too.

She knew it was cowardice, but it had been a relief to take a break from reading the journal. It was tucked away in her closet underneath the summer clothes she hadn't worn in months, out of sight. Every time she thought of retrieving it, finishing the last pages, something stopped her. She would finish eventually, but in the last few months, when she had let the glorification of a past that wasn't even her own take over her focus, she had begun to lose the narrative of her own adventure. This was her time in the stone city, not Lily's, and she only had a month left to savor it. In letting the words lay idle, Jill had felt her mind compose itself.

What would her story be? She tilted the charm toward the light so the shadow fell across Lily's face and Zane's was illuminated, and stared at it, searching it for something, some yield from the past two years. All she felt was a logical calculation. She'd missed his mental acuity, their conversations, the ease of having him around. But she didn't miss him. Was it Aaron she missed? Or was it her individualism?

Her pinky nail slid right into the oval and she wedged it beneath the photo of Zane. With a gentle flex of her finger, it peeled out like nail polish and fluttered to the floor.

The first Monday of December Jill and Isabelle stepped out the door onto Via del Porrione to a man perched on a high ladder across the street. The ladder was propped against the side of the building with orange cones placed around the base. He wore a worn, leather tool belt low on his hips and a thick bundle of some kind of cord wrapped over his shoulder. Reaching upward he fastened one end of the strand to an iron peg and worked quickly to secure it. Around the curve they saw, spaced evenly apart every twenty-five yards or so, strands of white lights draped about twenty feet above the ground. Isabelle gave a childlike squeal of delight. "It's going to be so Christmas-y!"

"Let's buy a tree," Jill said.

"Is that a thing here?"

"Probably not. We could go cut one down."

"If you go find a pine tree and cut it down with a knife from our kitchen, then I will put that tree in the center of the living room."

"Wyatt will help me."

"Go for it," Isabelle said. "I'd really like to see this." The girls kept their hands stuffed into mittens, shoved deep down in their winter coat pockets. Swirling smoke of breath rose up in front of them as they walked, and they ducked into Fiorella for afternoon cappuccino between their apartment and class.

They took their time with the coffees and a shared croissant, watching people come in and out from the back corner. Some people talked to one another, but mostly suited men stood silently drinking espresso and reading about soccer from the newspapers strewn about the bar. The girls enjoyed the afternoon fashion walk at the café. The women were elegant, and stood balanced on impressively thin heels and wore tailored skirts and blazers. Gentlemen with heads of thick gray to black hair carried hard leather briefcases and spoke in commanding Italian. Jill's barman flirted discreetly. When they couldn't extend their refreshments any longer than another sip, they drained the cups, finished the bread, and exited with a "Ciao."

"Three weeks left," Isabelle said as their uphill pace slowed. She was looking up at the large window of a stationery store, which had been sprayed with white paint to look like snow drifts in the corners.

"I know, I'm trying not to think about it." Jill turned to Isabelle. "What about Wyatt?"

She laughed. "That's out of left field. I didn't even tell you this—he asked me the other day—if we were dating."

"What'd you say?"

"I rolled my eyes, which annoyed him."

"I can see why that would be annoying."

"I mean, it's a long haul, Texas to California. It's not like we can see each other on weekends. It isn't like we're serious; it's just been like, a fun fling."

"It's definitely of higher quality than 'fling,'" Jill said.

"No, it's not a big deal."

Jill came very close in that moment to bringing the conversation around to Aaron and his e-mail. Jill had spent the night and morning going over his words in her mind, sifting them like sand falling through the spaces between her fingers. She had released Aaron, largely closing their relationship out of her present mind because she knew he had been a poison in her life. And she vividly recalled the disgust she had felt toward his sordid lifestyle, how it had struck her suddenly, as if she was broken out of a trance. The fact that she could have even fallen for such a person—And yet, the moment she'd seen his tour picture on the littered wall of a hostel in Paris, there was again that pull from a secluded space in her heart. That was why she'd gone to the gig, and agreed to linger with him afterward. When he had revealed one enormous detail, she had felt betrayal, of all things. How could he have kept something so integral to his life from her? Yet that line of questioning was no longer hers to demand, nor was his loyalty.

34

I met his mother last night—terrifying. She's small, but she's fiery. I tried speaking with my best Italian but she wasn't really trying to make it work, so it was more like half-Italian translated through to a woman with her ears glued shut. He kept on catching my eye and whispering not to worry in English, "She's just like that." I guess . . . He says it's hard for her because I'm not Italian, which I think is the most ignorant thing I've ever heard. His siblings were there too, and his father. He was quiet and sweet, kept smiling at me from behind his wife. The food was great.

I'm a little nervous about getting involved with him. Claudette says that's stupid because I'm already involved. Seriously involved. She thinks I'm in love. I'm not in love! But I do feel happy. The greatest secret nobody knows, to quote e.e., is that there is something about him. Around him I'm something I haven't been in a long time—it feels like careless or delighted or just . . . what is it? I feel myself becoming softer because of him, like I'm being deconstructed. He doesn't expect anything from me, he is tender and kind, and that look. I don't—I can't put my finger on it. I've become a hateful person in some ways, but he makes me see that, and pulls me out of those dark places. I am afraid of this feeling! I've got a system that works, but it depends on NOT folding. So there's this weak, soft part of me that wants to give in and get "involved," but I'm trying not to because that feels like folding. It doesn't make sense! I'm not here to fall for a guy, I'm here to . . . have an adventure I guess? Find a new start? Develop as an artist?

Enough. New subject: Christmas. It's a week away. The decorations here are so beautiful. We even bought a little tree and I strung popcorn on dental floss to decorate it. Babo Natale, Italian Santa, came to the Campo last week and all these precious kids were running around shrieking. I have a plane ticket to go home for the week that I DO NOT want to use. That means I'd be going home in December, then again in February for the wedding, then again at the end of the year. I'm not pining away for the holidays with family. Got a letter from Mom this week. I like seeing her handwriting—the slanty print with the loops at the bottom of the letter "p" and "y." She was talking about Jodie's wedding and how crazy it's been. She spent a whole side of a page raving about Buck. I really do need to get some time with this guy—going home would give me a good opportunity for that, and it's so important to Jodie, and to mom. She mentioned he would be spending Christmas with us because he doesn't have a great time with his own family. It's laughable he thinks it would be better with ours. Jodie said one of her favorite things about him is the way he supports her, the honesty between them. Guess that means he's in on all the secrets. That's impressive—gives me hope for the future.

I'll need to decide about Christmas in the next few days. I sort of have, but I feel guilty. I can get a half refund on the tickets and I'll send dad a check for the loss. He will be mad. Jodie will understand, Mom will be sad. I know they want me home, but this is my time. I may never be here again . . . unless I decide to move here. I will miss the snow on Christmas morning. I'm sure

I'll also be sad to be without Mom's cinnamon rolls—that's what Buck should really be looking forward to.

Maybe I'm in love. I'm writing his name. Amedeo.

35

Jill stared at the words, the isolated sentence printed at the bottom of the page, and felt her chest fill with her swelling heartbeat. A dampness formed at her hairline and her body felt hot. She unzipped her coat. She flipped the page, then another. Blank. She turned back to the last page she'd read and stared at the ink, then looked out the bus window. That was it, and she was stunned.

Amedeo. It was a common enough name, but she knew. Maybe she'd known before? There was something peculiar about the way they'd connected, almost magnetically. She tried to think back on their conversations—when had she first said Lily's name? He knew! He knew, of that she was certain, but he hadn't said a word. Why? What had happened to separate them? They'd been young, perhaps. Naïve. She'd mentioned Lily was dead now, how had he responded? She couldn't remember. It had never occurred to her to observe his reactions.

She turned the journal's page again, in case she'd missed something. Just like that, the narrating voice was extinguished, cut short, incomplete. The ending was left wide open. She flipped through the empty pages several times. There might have been an error—the writings erased? Impossible. *Like I'm being deconstructed*, Lily had said. As Florence's lights shrunk away behind the bus, Jill closed the journal and placed her hands on the cover and breathed in deeply. She needed to talk to Amedeo to piece together all the unanswered details, but he was gone until Christmas. There were so many answers, but also a gaping hole in the totality of the narrated story. But what had she expected? It was not as if a person's life was cut up into finite chapters with wrapped endings. She watched the lights bleed over the river as they drove out toward the no-man's land between the cities.

It was an oddly satisfying feeling of loneliness, the suspension between what had happened years before, independent of her, and her own future, somehow also unfolding regardless of what she had hoped to be. She had become the ghost, peering in on two narratives, weightless, transparent, hovering amid time in places she did not belong, greedily observant. *Like I'm being deconstructed.*

Compared to Siena's simple Christmas trimming, they had found Florence audaciously bedecked. The larger city lay vested in great swaths of red, gold and green and the strands of lights draping the streets were thicker and brighter than those of Siena, formed into the outlines of festive stars and shapes. A great tree stood in the Piazza, beautifully lit and decorated with fine ornaments. Christmas was everywhere in Florence, and the mood had been contagious. They had come to the larger neighbor city to purchase Christmas gifts for family members and friends from home, not because those things were unavailable in Siena, but because the spirit of shopping in Florence was much greater and more extensive here. Instead of one jewelry store, there were twenty stands, and rather than a few stationery shops, there were hundreds. The girls had meandered slowly, bartering prices, trying things on one another for size and color. The day was gray and dry, wind cutting through their coats, and they had sat over dinner for a long time before trekking back to the station to board the bus. After a long week of classes, papers, and cold weather to wear on them, the other girls were asleep, so Jill had retrieved the journal from her book bag and opened it for the first time in weeks.

She listened to Nat King Cole's and Bing Crosby's Christmas songs through the small earbuds, and the juxtaposition of the Italian hills with the old songs she'd known for years matched her disorientation. They didn't belong here. She pressed her forehead against the glass and the cold seeped into her brain. Closing her eyes, the nostalgia of the music swept through her, and Jill thought of her father, who listened to this kind of holiday music throughout the month of December. She tried to imagine talking to him about all of this. In her mind's eye his words were clipped, his demeanor closed to her. And yet, he too had read the journal. As possessive as she felt of this history, it was just as much, if not more, his. What would he do if he found out she knew Amedeo? Or did he somehow know that as well? He'd fed her the journal like cheese in a mousetrap. Had it been manipulation? What was his angle?

The cessation of entries was too sudden. It didn't make sense to approach the top of a roller coaster with the foreboding *click click click*, and at the top, at the brink of the descent, be asked to unbuckle your seatbelt and exit the car. Had Lily gone home that Christmas? What had happened then? Somewhere in the space of time between the wet ink on that last page and Jill's birth some critical shift had happened because the mom she'd grown up with was a different woman than the voice in those pages. She had expected it would be explained, that had to have been the reason Gary had given it to her, and yet she found no answers here. She'd been waiting for a moment, but maybe the changes in Lily had happened gradually. Still, she wanted the end of the story.

Classes wrapped up on Thursday afternoon. The students took written exams for Grimes, Bova, and Memmo, though Professor Grimes carried on a sporadic conversation with the class throughout the testing period and told them at the end that he would grade their tests "with an easy red pen." Anna's Art History exam was tough, a slideshow of images they had seen throughout the semester that she clicked through slowly to let them write down the name, location, year, artist, and description. Afterward the students left the IAAE offices and walked to a tiny bar up the street, packed inside, and toasted Peroni to the end of a great semester. They tried to speak only in Italian and laughed at their mispronunciations and improper word usage. With a week left in Siena free of courses, homework, and daytrips, they all had plans for the ways to spend their last days.

After beers, they split up and Isabelle, Ling, Wyatt and Jill made their way down the Via Banchi di Sopra to meet Rocco for dinner. On the busier streets the city was lit with a halo like the crown of a birthday cake from the glow of the Christmas lights. The small metal cart selling roasted chestnuts at the intersection of the main road and Piazza Salimbeni puffed steam as if the machine itself were smoking a large pipe.

They ate pizzas at Due Porte, then walked back toward the Campo.

"I'm gonna run by a store real quick," Jill announced just as they reached the Piazza.

"It's like ten o'clock," Isabelle said.

Ling looked at her skeptically.

"I need tampons."

"Thank you," Wyatt said.

They curved away, and Jill continued straight. She found the familiar cross street, passed through the alley, and turned out on the other side in front of the Duomo. The Christmas tree was preposterously huge, scaled to the cathedral, dressed with small blue lights that took on an eerie quality when they bled together, rather than the festivity of the white ones decorating the rest of the city. Jill turned down the side street, walked a few paces, and stepped into the warm, bright Café Duomo.

The tables were full, and people lingered around the bar, leaning against it, crowding one another. There was a soccer match on the television in the corner above the door to the kitchen. Jill looked around the restaurant to find an opening, somewhere to sit or stand.

The same girl was working behind the bar, moving quickly between the espresso machine, the refrigerator, and the register. A young man brought slices of pizza, plates of pasta, and sand-wiches out to people seated at the tables. A small table near the bar opened up, and Jill quickly swooped in.

It was a few minutes before the waiter approached.

"Prego," he said.

"I'll have a water. And a slice of pizza," she said when the he stared at her with a nettled expression. Before he had a chance to walk away, Jill added, "Also, is Leone here?"

"Yeah," he said dismissively as he rushed away to another table before returning to the kitchen.

It was Milan against Rome, in Milan, and the stands were packed. The volume was up on the television so she could hear that violent stadium din rising up around the pitch. She'd grown warm in the café, so she shed her coat and waited.

Leone emerged from the back and greeted the patrons around the bar with jovial affinity. He stood talking for a few minutes, looking up at the television, and commenting on the game. In his singular sobriety he entertained conversation while discreetly looking around the restaurant. The waiter handed him a plate with a slice of pizza, and whispered something in his ear. He turned in the direction of where Jill was seated, spotted her immediately, and smiled.

"Bella notte," he said, and she stood as he approached. "Sit, sit, sit. Here is your pizza. Are you wanting wine or beer or anything?"

"No, no, I'm fine." She hadn't even wanted the pizza.

"Prego. You have stayed away for a while; I keep waiting to see you here."

"I know, I'm sorry. I've been meaning to come back, but we've traveled for school and everything, squeezing it all in at the end of the semester."

He was nodding, smiling slightly. She had trouble reading his expression.

"I'm going home in a week." As soon as the words escaped her mouth, Jill felt an unexpected surge of emotion. Looking at Leone, she thought of the first time she'd entered Café Duomo, seeing the blue door exactly as it had been described in Lily's journal, exactly as it hung over her bed. She had walked through the streets of Siena first in summer, sweating and dusty, and then in the gorgeous, refreshing air of autumn, and now hunkered against the frigid cold. A lot had changed in four months—she had changed. She'd left home with the hardness of years of calluses, grown within her as defense from her disappointment, loneliness, and confusion. She hadn't recognized it. Only now did she see the difference—the openness, as if her heart had softened from stone. An infant vulnerability. "I wanted to ask you a few more questions for the interview project."

"Yes," he agreed. He sat down. "It is busy; we have to talk fast, okay?"

"Yes, okay," and she ploughed into her final few questions. They were brief, extra really, but she had wanted to come back once more, to put a bit of closure on the place. She'd felt overturned since reading the end of the journal, floating over water, waiting for Amedeo to return and anchor her again. When she finished, she said, "That's it. Thanks!"

"I'm glad you came here. I have waited for you. After I find the picture I gave you, I began to open old boxes and drawers, and find other things from Rosa. There was a box of letters, from years and years. Her whole life she was keeping every letter. I read some, some I did not. She has a letter I wrote her convincing her to marry me!" He laughed. "It is still hers, you know? It is private. But I find one letter from your mother, Lily. I have been keeping it for when you return."

He stood and walked back through the crowd, leaving her stunned in her chair. Returning, he handed her a flimsy envelope addressed in that script that was now so familiar. There were several stamps in the upper right corner, and ink in various places detailing the journey the letter had taken. The return address was in Connecticut.

"As you see, I have no use for this now. You can take it."

"Okay," Jill said. She had not touched the slice of pizza and her glass was full. "Did you read it?"

Leone nodded and stood, momentarily distracted by the game, and Jill followed.

"I'm very glad you came here to find Rosa. Because of you I went back to the old letters and photos for the first time in many years. There were things I forget. God bless you, going home." He leaned forward to embrace her and kissed her quickly on the forehead. "When you come back to Siena, come to Café Duomo."

"I will."

"Okay," he said.

"Okay. Thank you for everything."

"Va bene." The man winked, then walked back to the bar.

36

She sat down on the cold brick of the Campo and looked up at the tower. It was a clear night, lit by the moon and the glow of restaurants. She sat Indian style with her hands planted behind her for several minutes, grasping the ground, tempering a surge of energy. Dozens of people passed walking briskly.

She removed the envelope from her book bag, then the letter. There were two sheets of plain, lined paper covered in pencil. Some of the graphite had been rubbed away Jill noticed, around the edges. She could just barely make out the *Cher Rosa*. As she began to read, she sensed a difference in tone immediately.

> *As you can see from the return address, I went home to Connecticut. I left on Christmas, the day after we went to Verona. I am sorry, but I didn't have time to come say goodbye. I know that by the end of this letter you'll understand.*
>
> *It's hard for me to write to you at all. I miss you. I miss Siena, I miss so many things, and I thought for a while I would stay. I had decided not to go home for Christmas. But the morning after our trip there was a telegram for me that said my sister Jodie had died. Imagine, as you showed me Shakespeare's setting of the tragedy of Juliet, my own sister was inhaling for the last time. I have spent so much time trying to figure out where we were exactly, the precise moment when her life was extinguished, what were we doing? Our*

*day together in Verona was magical, one of the best
days of my life, until I got home and it was lost to me.*

*I can't stand it, I wanted to scream and run so
fast and far away at first, and then I got home and
there was this silent darkness. Sometimes I can't
even breathe. Jodie was the bright one in our family.
I described her to you so many times in small ways,
and I realize I never fully told you how perfectly lovely,
kind—how GOOD she was —because I was always a
bit jealous of that aspect of her. We look the same, but
we are so different! I feel wretched now, for any bit of
love that jealousy robbed from me, and I want to tell
you those things so you know. I'm sorry I didn't share it
before.*

*My heart is broken. I feel void of anything that
used to give me joy—as if Jodie's death killed every
good thing. Can you understand this? I am not planning to—*

She'd reached the bottom of the front page, and when she
turned it over, the writing was all rubbed away between the two.
Holding it up higher, Jill tried to catch the bright light from
the restaurant to her back, but it was no use. She could make
out a few words, but no sentences. Running her fingers over
the pages, she felt the smoothness of the rubbed out pencil. She
turned over the second page.

*—and that is all too much to take in. My life is
upside down.*

*I hope you'll come to visit. Maybe seeing you
would help me find a bit of myself that's lost, even
though I know there are some things I'll never be*

*again. If you came, I would take you to New York City.
Please write to me at this address if you want to. And
understand that meeting you, knowing you in Siena,
was one of the highlights of my life. Please pray for me.
Strangely I find myself hoping in God, if he is real, now
more than I ever have. I feel like I'll have this painfully broken heart forever and I don't think I can stand
it. I've wept writing this. How can the entire universe
change all at once?*

*I keep thinking, what will Siena be to me? It is the
city where I became an artist, where I saw the potential
of life. In that city, just stones under the sky, I believe I
began to love for the first time.*

Pray for me,
Lily

Jill read the letter through again. Her body grew numb. An
old man walked very slowly across the Piazza arm in arm with
his wife. His back, rounded at the top like a hill, and his news-
boy cap winking at his age. She was taller than him, and stood
up with perfect posture, seeming to contain the strength they
both required to exist.

There it was, the moment that had changed everything
for Lily. The voice in the letter was a different voice than the
journal's narrator, like reading the writings of two unrelated
people. Her mom had never said much about Jodie that she
could remember, and she had always reasoned that the sisters
must not have been close, that Lily's failure to introduce her
memory to Jill's life was because she hadn't found it important.
Jill opened the locket and looked at the photograph there. It

wasn't that her mom had ever seemed depressed—perhaps time had dulled the pain. She mentioned God in the letter to Rosa, and Lily's faith in God was something Jill thought of as a pillar of her mother's identity. Her spirit had simply been a shade of blue—melancholy, calm, thoughtful and, Jill thought now as she tried to place all the information together on a storyboard in her mind, always secretly dreaming. Amedeo would return in a few days, and she felt frantic to speak to him.

The floor is damp, like it's rained inside but a few days ago. I can barely reach the string to the lightbulb but I jump for it and finally catch it. The light comes on with my landing. There are boxes everywhere. Two old bikes in the corner, a workbench with tools covered with dust and spiderwebs. It smells cold, like outside, and I try not to feel worried when the tall metal box lurches and starts to make a loud sound like a lawn mower.

She said to look underneath the stairs. I pick my way through the mess and duck my head under. There is a big box with the word **PHOTOGRAPH ALBUMS** written in black. I am proud to be able to read the word photograph. I open it.

Nana said my baby pictures are near the top in a pink book with a bunny on the cover. I see it immediately, and remove it. I try looking through it, but it's dark there, so I set it down and start to close up the box.

There is an album that says **Girls—high school/college**. I am curious about this. College seems like a very long time away for me. I take this album too, and then close the box.

I sit down on the bottom stair because the light is bright there. The first page of this album has a picture of Mom, and she looks so young, and she is pretty, and she's standing with a girl that looks almost exactly like her, but with wavier hair. I almost can't tell them apart. They're wearing shorts and short sleeves and there's a lake behind them. Underneath the picture it says "Lily and Jodie, first day of summer at Camp Yuriko, 1977." I stare at this picture for a long time. Their similarity is shocking. I have to hold the photograph up high to see the differences. Mama's nose is narrower. Her sister is a little shorter and her hair is darker.

Next page. More pictures. I can't believe how pretty they are. I always think Mom was pretty before she had no hair, but she seems like a person in a movie in these pictures.

She will be so excited. I run up the stairs with both books, and come into the kitchen where Mom is sitting at the table. She's wearing socks and slippers and fleece pants and a big sweatshirt even though it is so hot in Nana's house, especially in the winter, which is weird.

Look! I put the album right in front of her on the table. I'm panting from running up the stairs in twos. *I found this in the box with my baby album!*

She stares at the book and doesn't open it, and I don't understand, so I open the book for her so we are both looking at Lake Yuriko. I admire her, and then look at her face. Her eyes are squinting the way they do when she is just back from chemotherapy at the hospital. I think that face means she feels bad. I look at Nana, and she seems nervous. Mom makes a little smile with her lips closed and looks away, out the window. She doesn't touch it. I turn the pages, but she isn't looking. Tears prickle the back of my eyes. I stand there in front of her so confused I want to ask *Why?* But the look on their faces makes me know it would be better to leave. I pick up the book, return to the basement, and put the album away.

At two in the morning a noise outside jerked Jill out of fragmented dreams of Leone, the bar at Café Duomo, and a letter hundreds of pages long, written in a language of symbols she couldn't read. For some time she listened to Isabelle's breathing, steady and deep, her eyes fixed on the ceiling lit only by the moonlight from outside the door. Eventually she got up and walked into the dark living room. Switching on the floor lamp beside the table, she opened her laptop and secured the connection to the Internet. Her inbox was empty. She clicked the icon to compose a new message and the screen opened before her. Holding her breath, she typed "Dad" in the recipient box and her father's e-mail address appeared: *WGD@dhcorp.org*. She hit the tab key and the cursor moved to the subject line.

The letter had opened the door a bit wider, and the paradigm shift made sense. She had known, of course, Jodie had died, but without any details. She had never understood the connection of siblings, but it was clear that losing Jodie had shaken Lily at a foundational level. Jill stared at the blinking line and closed her eyes tight, then opened them and typed, *If you have a minute* . . . She was disoriented. Hitting the tab key once more, the cursor moved to the content space and she began typing.

Hey Dad,

*It's hard to believe Christmas is just a week away.
I know you're all wrapped up in the holiday cheer,
making cookies and singing carols . . . Bah humbug?
I'll be sad when my time here is over, but I am looking forward to seeing you for the holidays. Please don't
worry about getting me anything, there isn't anything I
need or want. I bought myself a gift (a really expensive
leather bag—you can just "give" me that). Let's just
make a big dinner and drink wine.*

I can't sleep. It's the middle of the night here.

*So Mom's journal. I've been reading it all semester,
which you probably guessed. I haven't asked you about
anything or mentioned it, but I've read it slowly and
thoroughly. I got to the end where it just all of a sudden
stops. This whole time I've sort of gotten this weird
feeling about the journal, the stuff she writes about.
I never knew about Grandad and everything else . . .
kept thinking it would all explain itself in the end, but
then it just stopped.*

*I didn't want to ask you about anything because I
wanted to figure out Mom here, by myself. I've found
a lot of the places she talked about in the journal.
Anyway, when it just cut off I was so confused.*

*But here's the crazy part—you know that woman
that tutored mom in Italian? Rosa Gavarola. Well I
found that café, and the lady is dead (shocker), but her
husband isn't. I got to know him a little bit. He's not
nearly as charming as his wife sounded, but he remembered Mom. He gave me a picture of the two of them.
He also gave me a letter she wrote after she left Italy.*

302 | WITHIN THE WALLED CITY

> *It was written to Rosa, it's undated, like everything*
> *else (damn artist brains), but it seems like she wrote it*
> *just after she left, explaining about Jodie. That's pretty*
> *much it. Also looks like it was the beginning of her*
> *believing in God, which is weird.*

She stopped. It was the fact that over the course of the semester, Lily had become a friend. She felt as if she'd been listening to a peer, getting to know her, empathizing with her pain, her personality, her frustrations, the artistic filter through which she observed and documented all of life. But it was a new person, not her mom. People were always changing. Life would never be so boring as to stay static—it was a tapestry of the unforeseen. This is what she had gained from this secret period of Lily's life, miraculously documented as if for Jill alone. Lily had given Jill something, a dose of passion, a shot of adrenaline. It wasn't the Lily she'd known as a child; it was a different Lily, one who had opened her. And in the opening Jill was raking her hands over and over through the mess, trying to figure out who she was anymore.

> *I guess I should thank you? I was mad when the*
> *journal stopped because it felt like manipulation, to get*
> *so emotionally involved and then have this cliffhanger,*
> *but it's hard to be mad after reading what Mom wrote*
> *in that letter. I've got it, so you can read it when I get*
> *home. I suppose you opened up this . . . issue? History?*
> *Conversation? After more than ten years of being a*
> *lock box about Mom because you felt like I was ready.*
> *I spent a long time really pissed off at you, but I get*
> *it that it's hard for you too. I know you gave me the*

journal so I'd figure stuff out while I was here, which is cool and charming I guess. I'm also guessing you're aware that I'm coming home with about a thousand questions and I want answers to them. You're the only one who knows, so you have to tell me now. Okay?

See you in a week,
Jill

She debated the ending, and typed out a post script.

I also met that guy, Amedeo. The boyfriend. How weird is that? I have actually gotten to know him—he is on the board for my program. He's neat, you'd probably like him.

37

Four days passed and Jill floated between the consciousness to do and experience every aspect of Siena for the last time, waiting on Amedeo to return, and the unanswered e-mail to her father. It troubled her. For ten to fourteen hours every day he sat at a desk with his computer on. During the others he carried his smart phone that buzzed or chirped every time a new message was delivered. He never neglected to respond to any form of communication. He had most assuredly read it and hadn't replied, and it was driving Jill crazy. The e-mail was by far her most open attempt at honesty in half a decade.

Anna Bova had the entire class over for dinner on Monday evening. A long antique table filled her dining room, and there were chairs enough for everyone, though the teacher lived only with her husband and two cats.

Clinking her fork against her wine glass, Anna stood up and the din of conversation fell off. "I am so glad you are all here in my home, and that you all chose to come here for the semester. Most students go to the bigger capstone cities and miss the history and uniqueness of Siena. It has been a pleasure to be your professor, and to close our time together—" she brought her hand to her mouth in mock devastation, "I would like each of you to say what, other than your degree, you will take away from Italy."

Jill looked around the room. Most people looked down at their plates, or into the deep red of their glasses. They had stepped off the bus in August strangers, and were now leaving as something different than friends. A shared experience, an elixir of the highest potency, binds mightily with unseen cords.

"I know mine," Wyatt began. "I never appreciated truly exquisite cuisine." Everyone laughed as he pronounced his statement with delicate inflection. "I mean, that sounds dumb, but Italians kind of worship food; they don't settle for mediocre crap like we do. I think that's pretty awesome."

"The longevity of Italy's art history is truly incredible," Ling said. "Seeing this artwork that has been around for hundreds and hundreds of years, and the progression, how artists have grown and changed, and the value of life has been depicted in all of its growth and change. I feel like I've gained a broader perspective of art, and I am glad for that. I'll take that back."

As they considered answers and shared, Jill's mind returned over and over to the people. It was something about the Italian people she wouldn't forget. The warmth, the richness of emotion, what felt like a general contentment. In a break in the conversation, she was surprised when Isabelle spoke.

"The continuity of families. Just the way generations of people continue to bring life to this city that could be ruins by now. I mean, in America it feels like it's every man for himself and family isn't nearly as important as career or creativity or growth or money, whatever. It just seems like in Italy, people care more about keeping families strong than any of that. I like that. I'd like to take that home with me."

Responses to Anna's question led to retelling dozens of stories highlighting the humor of coming to a new city, speaking a different language, having unknown roommates. They broke for dessert, and split up to sit in the living room, a few people to smoke on the veranda.

Anna approached Jill and Isabelle. "I guess you'll hear about the art contest in the next few days."

"Yes, I think so." She'd nearly forgotten. "They post it in a few days I guess."

"How many people entered something?" Isabelle said.

"Lucca told me they had two-hundred forty-eight pieces. It's a record. I also wanted to tell you girls—I talked to my brother yesterday. He asked me if I saw you again to tell you he hired your friend's family to work at the vineyard, starting in February."

Isabelle and Jill exchanged puzzled glances.

"I'm not sure," Anna continued. "He said you have a friend, Albanian, and somehow Amedeo and Lucca know this friend needs work, her mother and brother too. Does this ring the bell?"

"Oh my gosh," Isabelle said. "You're kidding."

Jill stared at a smiling Anna, too stunned to reply. She replayed events and conversations back through her mind. She had been helpless to help Era, even to contact her. She had certainly never imagined this.

The evening was an isolated moment in time that allowed them each, and together, to revel in the experience now coming to a close. On the walk home Jill kept her arms wrapped tightly around her waist, her hands tucked underneath her armpits to try and thaw her fingers. The city's stone encasing made the cold seem heavier and deeper. It permeated even through the soles of her shoes, and the bottoms of her feet were white and grayish-blue by the time they arrived at the apartment. Somewhere, Jill imagined, Era and Luan and their mother were breathing easier, hopeful in this divine second chance. She wondered if human miracles had arms powerful enough to reach a person like Edi, to draw him down from a throne of power and evil and bring him back to the simple love of his mother and siblings.

Upstairs Jill checked her e-mail again, a habitual motion now, thinking perhaps her dad had been away for the weekend in a place without any service or Internet connection—unlikely, but after Monday there was still no answer. She frowned, scrolling down to the bottom, then checked the spam folder.

"What are you so stressed out about? You're hovering," Isabelle said, pulling a sweatshirt over her head and rubbing her hands together.

"Waiting for an e-mail from my dad," Jill said.

"You have literally checked twenty-five times today."

"I just sent him an e-mail about the journal. It's the first time I've really mentioned it, and I thought he would have replied like, in a second."

Isabelle nodded. "Okay, well I'm going to bed."

"Me too."

She stood, and moved to close the computer, but stalled. Staring at her e-mail, she sat back down, pulled up the message from Aaron, and hit *reply*.

Hello again,

I'm going to be honest with you, this has been one of the strangest times of my life. There are so many things I could tell you about. I think you'd be interested, which is sweet and appealing. I'm glad I had the opportunity to see you on tour, makes everything come around full circle in a way.

I'm not sure exactly why you e-mailed, but I have spent an inordinate amount of time thinking about you since I saw you in France. Mostly, I think about your daughter, and trying to place her in your life during the time we were together. I actually can't believe I never knew about her—I think I thought I knew everything about you.

I wasn't going to write back, but I want to tell you this: I'm not interested in you. I don't trust you. I'm not saying it to be a bitch, I'm sure you're different now, I mean, you seemed different. But I'm just tired of this sort of thing—always settling for something, which usually turns out to be mediocre instead of great. I've spent so many years of my life with an underlying desire for something great, you know? A solid family, honesty, fun, energy, but it's like there's always been a lid on the pot. I'm tired of that. I guess you can probably understand that in a way.

Please don't write me again. I'm happy for the way things have gotten better in your life, truly. I wish you the best with the band and your daughter.

Best of luck,
Jill

Tuesday was December 22, the day Amedeo was due to return, and the results of the *Arte Per Natale* contest were posted outside his office. Isabelle went with Jill in the morning. With no obligations or responsibilities and a sunny sky, they had the whole day to wander the city, to walk the streets that had become so familiar, to absorb them fully, remember the details. There was a small group of people gathered where the results hung, and Jill waited for a break in the crowd, then pressed forward to read the small print.

There were pieces designated for first second and third place, each rewarded a cash prize. Out of the fifteen runners-up, her name was listed second-to-last. She stared at the page, then looked around her. She was disappointed, but not shocked.

"Well?" Isabelle said eagerly when Jill emerged.

"I was a runner-up."

"That's amazing!"

"No, it's not." Jill laughed. "There were fifteen. Oh well, it was fun."

"You totally should have won."

They walked back out toward the center of town, taking hundreds of pictures, many of which they would delete in months to come, when the frantic grip on the singularity of their semester had loosened. They captured children on the Campo, charming old doors, contrada flags, storefronts, and vistas over the countryside where they perched on the wall. They stopped in a tiny café for a square of pizza and sat on the fountain steps just beside.

"I'm going to break up with Zane when I get home."

"Shit. Wow, I mean. Okay. Why?"

Jill stared down the street, the hard, cold stone she'd grown so accustomed to.

"I just don't want . . ." she shook her head. "I don't know. I want something else I think. I want to feel different than all that."

Isabelle's eyes were hidden behind mirrored aviators, but her face looked toward the street. They ate quietly for a few minutes, then got up and began walking back toward the apartment.

"Maybe it's a good time to tell you this, then."

Jill looked at her.

"If soldier Thomas counts for 'different than all that,' I got his number."

On the ascent up Via del Porrione, they walked by Lule, arm in arm with a boy.

"Oh!" Lule exclaimed, crossing over to the other side of the street and grabbing Jill's arm. "Happy to be seeing you! There is a man who waits for you."

"What?" Jill said.

Lule stared at her with a blank expression, as if she could not possibly understand what she could have miscommunicated.

"There's a man in the apartment?" Isabelle said.

"Si."

"Who is he?" she said.

Lule shrugged.

Jill looked incredulously at Isabelle. "Okay. Thanks," she said. Lule joined back with the boy, and they walked away. Jill and Isabelle wordlessly jogged the remaining twenty yards to the front door.

"She just let a man into the apartment?"

"Amedeo? Who else knows our apartment?" She inserted her key into their door and pushed it open.

38

A frigid breeze came through the windows, which stood propped open, and Jill's father sat at the dining table in the corner, facing away from where the two confused girls stood, agape. As he turned toward them Jill examined his face. He smiled slightly, and she sensed in him a discomfort, a hesitation—it was insecurity. She was too surprised to gather the words to put a sentence together. She moved toward him.

"Surprise." Gary rose to his full six feet. His black wool coat on top of the pressed shirt gave him the appearance of an Italian in street clothing. He hugged her. He smelled fresh, like his deodorant, and his hair looked clean—how long had he been here? The display of affection surprised Jill, but the familiar size of him, the feel of him, was welcome, like something from a different lifetime.

"It's pretty cold in here."

"Dad, what in the world? What are you doing here? Why didn't you tell me you were coming—I just sent you an e-mail like four days ago and you never replied."

"Why don't you introduce me to your friend?"

He always rode shotgun.

"This is Isabelle, my roommate. Isabelle, this is my dad. Okay, now . . ."

"I wanted to see it for myself," he said. His demeanor was controlled, the insecurity she'd sensed was gone.

"When did you get tickets?" she asked.

"It wasn't hard." Evading the question.

She shook her head at the strangeness it was to have her father standing in the dining room of her apartment at Via del Porrione, the way it felt like an intrusion, an unnatural blending of oil and water. The softening she'd felt, the way her heart had begun to open, had been a relief until now. He'd blindsided her, and she hadn't prepared. Why couldn't they talk to each other like normal people? He stood somewhat awkwardly, with his hands deep inside his coat pockets. She noticed then a small piece of rolling carry-on luggage propped up behind him. He looked younger in a way.

"So you just decided to come."

He nodded.

"Well, I think it's great!" Isabelle chimed in, bringing Jill back, reestablishing civil equilibrium. "It's so nice to meet you."

"It is very nice to meet you as well. Jill's told me a little about you, glad you could keep an eye on her." He was putting on the *parenting* hat.

"Not sure I can say that," she said. She was trying to be charming, giving Jill a few moments to collect herself. "Well, I can let you guys have some time if you—"

"No, we can all go for a coffee or something," Jill said, because it all felt so unnatural she was hesitant to be alone with him.

"Jill," Isabelle said frankly, "your father just flew across the ocean to see you. I'll grab a coffee with you later."

When Gary did not object, Jill shrugged. "Alright, Dad. Would you like to go for a coffee?"

"Love to."

Isabelle pardoned herself, and walked back out the door, throwing Jill a mystified expression as she pulled it closed.

"So," she said as they walked, "how . . . is work?"

"It's going fine."

"Nothing too exciting?"

He smirked. "Nah. Defending businessmen is dull."

Jill smiled, and they drew back into their solitary places again. She felt they both would rather have been jogging to the café. He hadn't explained his sudden appearance. She selected a place on Via Giovanni Dupre with a fireplace and tables they rarely frequented, away from the Campo, easily accessed by the cut through at Piazza del Mercato. The silence between them was like a force field.

In the wordless spaces of the past twenty minutes her wheels had turned quickly, trying to process. It was no coincidence that he'd showed up four days after that e-mail. Her father was not a spontaneous person, nor had he ever surprised her in her life, but she couldn't imagine what he could possibly have to say that could not have waited for three more days, or else been written or spoken over the phone. Four days ago she'd wanted to talk to him, but his sudden presence in Siena made her nervous.

A waiter waved them casually in the direction of the hearth, and they chose a table so close to the fire the empty wooden chairs felt as though they'd been roasting over the flames. For the first time in hours Jill was warm. They both ordered a café Americano, and Gary also ordered a croissant, and the waiter was back in moments with the steaming cups and pastry. He asked her questions about Siena—factual queries—to pass the time. They had spent their entire lives just the two of them, and silences were not uncommon, but now there was a sense of something impending, like the warm smell of rain before the sky turns gray and thunder begins to rumble. Jill shifted.

"I guess I owe you an explanation," he said.

"Yeah, well."

"Why I didn't, um, respond to your e-mail." He looked into his cup. His eyes were averted, betraying his position.

"And why you showed up here three days before I was going to see you at home."

He nodded, taking a bite of the croissant. Once he had swallowed, he nodded his head slowly, up and down, like a child's toy. It was his way of preparing, active thinking. She knew this, and waited without a word. Finally he spoke.

"This whole thing, it's all just very complicated, Jillian. That journal of your mom's—it actually sets up a story you've never heard, but it's vague, so you probably haven't put all the pieces together." Jill sat back in her seat, holding the ceramic mug in her hands just below her chin. He continued. "It ended abruptly, like you said. I didn't even find it until after she'd died, in a box of her old papers and paintings. I knew a lot of the story, but that journal was new to me too." He sipped his coffee, then returned it to the table. Jill watched his leathery hand, the dark hair creeping up the back of his wrist toward his knuckles, toward the gold band he had never taken off. She imagined him reading the journal in his study. Had she been young? In college? She knew better than to interrupt him—he tended to spook. His speech was clear and paced.

"Lily decided not to go home for Christmas that year, even though Jodie begged her to come. She made the decision a few days before the twenty-fifth. I don't know what she was doing on Christmas, but somehow a phone call got through to her, maybe through Rosa, who had at that point kind of adopted her."

"The letter said she received a telegram."

"Wow," he said, halting as if she'd clothes-lined him. "I always wondered."

It was one of the strangest moments of the day, watching her father acquire knowledge of this small technicality. He looked like a boy, bewildered and a bit hurt.

"It was a car accident on Christmas Eve. They were driving to their parents' house for brunch, and there had been ice the night before—she slid on a patch and went right off the bridge over the creek a mile from their house. It wasn't a far fall, but she hit in such a way that she was killed on impact. She shouldn't have died." Gary's eyes had taken on a glazed quality—they were old eyes again—and Jill kept hers glued to his. He didn't look at her, but stared beyond the fire. She grew chilly again, letting his words sink in. Lily's life was a classic tragedy, and Jill could see her clearly. She wanted to turn to her mom and comfort her, to wrap her arms around that neck she knew, inhale her perfume, and nestle into her arms to be a peace she had needed time and time again, but the vapor of Lily's memory blew quickly away. Why had he come here to tell her this?

"Who found her?"

He snapped back to present. "She was with Buck." There was a strange lilt to his voice.

"Did he not die?"

"He broke a wrist, that's all."

"Oh."

"As you can probably guess, it destroyed Lily. I'm sure you can tell from that letter to Rosa. Jodie was her best friend, really her only close relationship at that point, and she loved her sister more than she could have ever loved another person. Well, until you came along," he said, smiling slightly to himself. His face was painted with sadness. Jill was the only other love in Lily's life, not himself. The spectrum of emotion emanating from her father was foreign to her, his temporary verbosity. Someone entered the café, a little bell tinkled in announcement, and Jill looked toward the door.

"Lily left Italy that night, Christmas, to come home. She was a wreck. It's obvious why, but it was . . . devastating in more ways than one.

"Jill, your mom was in love with the man she'd met. She was deeply in love." He was looking at his hands. Jill looked at them too, her mind churning gears. "When you told me you'd met him, I couldn't believe it. I don't know why I thought it was impossible, but I did. Have you put this together with him?"

"I was supposed to go there tonight to say good-bye."

Gary nodded with the face of an afflicted man. "I truly think she would have stayed here. When I read the journal for the first time I thought how . . . funny it was the way she spoke about him. I don't think she realized she was in love until she came home."

"How do you know all this—when did you meet Mom?" Questions, questions she had asked before, hundreds of them, and suddenly he was ready to answer. The freezer door was open, the cold air escaping.

"I'll get there. Lily was back in Connecticut after the funeral. All of her passion and joy of being in Siena was gone, and she mourned." He shook his head, closing his eyes, and whispered, "God, it was agony. I've never seen a person so sad. Makes me sick thinking about it." He continued. "Your grandparents, your mom, Jodie's fiancé, Buck, were all, obviously, a mess. The funeral was on New Year's Day." His gaze drifted. "It was a painfully cold day. Windy, sleeting."

"Were you there?"

He nodded, took a long, deep breath, and with a tenderness she hadn't seen since she was a child, he looked her in the face. "Jillian, my sweet girl, this is the part that you haven't known. You know my full name is William Gary Dunn, and I've always gone by Gary. But there was one person who called me by another nickname—Buck." He paused. "Jodie was the only person who ever called me that. I was engaged to your Aunt Jodie when she died."

Jill recoiled, but stared into her father's face. His pleading expression, as if she stood over him, looking down. She raced to put pieces together, to make sense of the fragments, to sort through the things she knew, her memories, and picture Gary in another light, but the shock clouded her understanding. How had she never known? It felt as if she was meeting him for the first time, as if these two adults, strangers, were making each other's acquaintance over coffee and exchanging life stories. His manner, the truth, it was all brand new.

"We all mourned for a long time," he said once he'd determined her processing was sufficient. He spoke very slowly and quietly, but freely. His voice trembled, and Jill regarded him with a kind of curiosity.

"I stayed at her parents' house during most of the days that came after, didn't go to work much. I . . . died. Inside, when Jodie died. After we went off the road . . . I let her drive, I watched her . . ." He turned his hand in circles unconsciously. His weak wrist, the reason he wore a brace to play tennis. "We were two months away from getting married. March first."

She recalled a photograph she'd found once, hidden in the back of a drawer. It was of who she'd believed then to be her father and mother, but something about the woman had seemed foreign to her. Something about that woman had looked slightly different, but with the hair, some big sunglasses, the slightly blurred focus, she had written it off. Jodie and Lily had looked so much alike, they were often mistaken for twins. The image of that photograph was as clear as if she were looking through a window, and as she recalled it in memory, she realized the most conspicuous difference between the woman standing there and the mother she'd known was the joy on her face. That woman was Jodie, she knew now. He took a breath, seemed to gather his thoughts as if citing a tangible fact, his original wedding date, grounded him. This time he spoke faster, ploughing forward in the story relentlessly now, a pressured flood after the valve had been opened, though his voice still contained that dogged stoicism of his disposition.

"Lily and I got to know each other during those months after Christmas. She told me all about Italy and Amedeo—she was honest about it with me, I guess because I was safe, having been engaged to Jodie. Anyway, we just became great friends, and I think we helped each other mourn. Your mom had such anger toward their parents—I never even knew about Ronald until I read the journal and she was already gone. She needed someone else, and I was there and we just—grew to support one another."

He began to look exhausted, and Jill tried to rank her emotions and responses. The history shed new light on the relationship she had seen in action as a child, and on her father's somber and worn countenance. She wanted to weep over the nonexistence of a great love story that had led to Lily and Gary's wedding, though somewhere deep within her she found a well of comfort in the fact of their knowledge and care for one another. It was almost repulsive to think of the forces that had brought them together. She felt a new depth of sympathy for her father, a man who had lost two of the women he had undoubtedly loved.

"So you got married," Jill said. "Just to—have someone?"

"There's more," he said. "I couldn't have told you this before, Jill." The coffees were cold now, untouched, and the waiter came over to add another log to the fire. The drumbeat picked up again in her ears. What more could there be? Gary waited for the waiter to leave, then went on. "About four weeks after Christmas your mom realized she was pregnant. We had certainly never even come close to *that*, so she knew that the baby belonged to Amedeo."

Real nausea swept over Jill and she sat silent. After a moment, just above a whisper, "What happened to it? Did she miscarry? Abort?"

He stared at her, and they read each other in that moment more deeply than they ever had. He couldn't say it, but neither could she misunderstand.

Jill's vision blurred, and a throbbing silence filled the space between her father and herself, as the vibrating air after the thud of a gong. She felt she couldn't breathe. Closing her eyes, she bit the insides of her cheeks, and she clasped her hands together in her lap. Her face and neck grew hot. Staring at the darkness of her eyelids, she bit harder on her cheek and felt her foot begin to tap as the adrenaline washed over her as a tsunami. Pressing her eyes more tightly closed, she considered his words. This is why he had come. To deliver this news in person.

She stood suddenly. He rose, but she swatted him away. He sat obediently. Jill walked past the other tables of people, unable to hear anything except the inexplicable sound of the ocean, waves crashing on the sand. Standing outside the door of the café, she welcomed the cold through the fibers of her jeans and sweater. Swallowing over and over again, she tried to fit the information into her framework but could not. She was frantic, grasping for a ledge.

He was not her father. Start there. To cry would not be her body's first reaction, but she felt the rushing force of feeling exploding from within her chest, and she wanted to run as fast as she could forever. Jill began to walk away from the café. Faster and faster she sped down the sidewalk, removing her hands from the pockets of her jacket to feel the stinging cold. As the street turned uphill, she felt the burning sensation in her legs. All the way she replayed her memories through this new filter. He was not her dad. Amedeo was. Her nose was numb, but at her core she felt heat. A compass within her led Jill to streets she had tread in earlier days, wearing skirts and ballet flats, and eventually she looked up to discover that she stood at Porta Pispini, looking out over the first vista she had ever found in Siena, directed by Lily. It was silent but for the distant buzzing of a Vespa making sharp turns somewhere in the crooked roads of the city. The muffled quality of cold silence pressed around her, but the sun made her face bright. She leaned against the inside of the wall and anchored her hands on the stone to hold up the body that felt weak and flimsy.

Amedeo was her father.

Gary had accepted responsibility for her as a mercy, the fatherless child of the woman he had married as a consolation. Memories of their life together played back in her mind, and it made sense. Lily and Jillian were not the family he'd wanted, but they were the one he had endured. He was distant because he had lost everything.

39

After some time, she walked back to the café, but he was gone. She returned to the apartment. Gary was waiting, in the same seat as before, when Jill walked in. Lule stood in the kitchen.

"I give father warm tea," she said enthusiastically, and Jill thanked her as she flitted down the hall to her bedroom and slammed the door behind her.

Jill moved forward to where her father stood and sat down in the chair opposite his.

"I'm sorry," he said.

For what? she thought. "Is there anything else?" she asked numbly.

"Yeah," he said. He nodded, breathing in slowly. "Just a little bit."

Jill stared at him. He had to get it out.

"When your mom realized she was pregnant with you, she had to decide what to do. I tried to convince her to go back to Italy, tell him, and stay there with him . . . and you. She wouldn't though." He shook his head. "She refused to go back; I guess she felt like she had to stay. For her parents? For Jodie? I don't know why, but she wouldn't go back. She kept saying it would be better for him to be without her for some reason, but she didn't articulate her thoughts in this period very much. She was very isolated in her mind, if that makes sense. I got the impression she felt it wasn't as serious to him as it was to her, but she honestly barely spoke of Amedeo to me after that."

Ironic, knowing this man, Amedeo, better than her father did. How strange a twist. How funny the way of fate. *How merciful*, she thought at once.

"Around the end of January she approached me and asked me to marry her. We were very close at that point, joined by sadness and the whole experience, and also now by the beginning of the healing process, and she wanted to stay close to her family, but she wanted you to have a father. And I agreed, for better or for worse. I have questioned that decision a thousand times, wondered if she would have gone had I said no. But I said yes. I was lonely too, and it was a selfish, exhausted decision. Lily wrote to your birth father and told him she was pregnant with his child, but that she planned to stay in the US and marry me and take care of you. She only told me about the letter, I never read it, but we got married on February third in front of my folks and hers at a church in Connecticut. You were born five weeks early." He paused. "That's the whole story."

His expression was still now, less tortured, but his face was lined. He sipped the tea, and shook his head at some internal thought or notion. She watched him without looking in his eyes.

It was a few minutes before anyone said a word. Eventually it was Jill who spoke. "What happened to Mom?"

Her meaning was well understood. What happened to the Lily Jill had gotten to know over the past four months? Where did she go?

"Her heart was broken—she lost her sister and the love of her life." His words stung her, and she wondered if they stung him too.

"Did she ever love you?"

"Yes," he said. "I believe she did. And I loved her. But we were always in love with someone else too. Our love for each other was strong though. We were as happy as we could be, and we shared the pain of loss. We were support for each other, which is hard to understand, but it was a solid foundation for our marriage. We tried for a second child for a few years, but she couldn't get pregnant. Well, actually, it turned out I couldn't get her pregnant, but it was alright, I don't know that either of us wanted another child terribly. She was never the same after Jodie's death. She had left that happy heart here, in Siena, and there were only a few places I ever saw it. In her painting, and in the way she regarded you. Jillian, you were the joy of her life."

New tears beaded on her lower eyelashes, from a new source of feeling. They began to fall, and Gary scooted his chair around to her side, and placed his hand squarely on her shoulder blade. Lowering her head, she cried softly. Behind the blurred veil she revisited images stored in her memory. Watercolor paintings of cityscapes she now recognized in Siena, hills and vineyards, red roofs now familiar to her. A painting in this fashion hung, even now, above the fireplace in his house. She stopped crying, but her head stayed down as she thought. Raising her gaze, she looked at her father and for only the second time in her witness, he was crying. Staring at him, she was immobilized, regarding his collection of tears as beads of rain on the window, standard in a storm, only distinguished in their nearness. She could not touch him, or move.

He wasn't her father. Not her father by birth, anyway, and somehow she had known it. Ever there had existed between them an apartness that she could not have named before the moment of realizing his blood did not run through hers. He could have faked it a little better, she thought, but she had never really been his. Jill had been her mother's child, and perhaps, she saw now, it was the very thing that had caused him such a great deal of pain, the reason for which he had never had the courage to tell her the stories. Jill carried the blood that Lily had loved, not Gary's. Or Buck's, or whoever he was. And yet as she looked into his stricken face, she felt their woven bond more than she ever had, sharing the truth for the first time.

The sounds of the street outside carried up through the window. People laughing and shouting. The idling engine of a small utility car. A horn. Finally he spoke.

"Are you angry?"

"No."

He nodded thoughtfully.

"I'm just confused. And sad, I guess."

"I want you to know that to me, you've always been my daughter and I was never—sure. How to make you know, or when. I didn't ever want to tell you any of it. It would have been easier if he had left you and Mom, but he didn't. He also would have loved you, probably a lot better than I did."

She shook her head, but considered this. Picturing herself as a child with Amedeo, living in the apartment in Ram Valley, replacing Dovio there, layering Lily's cancer, her death, into that alternate history. Would Lily have even had the cancer? Could this other life have inoculated her against death and dying?

Pulling an envelope from the inside pocket of his coat, he nodded and said, "This is your birth certificate. The original, before we had it changed to say I was your father."

Sliding her index finger underneath the folded flap, she pulled it back, tearing the top of the yellow envelope. She pulled

out the single sheet of paper, watermarked and folded, then flat-
tened once more, and read the name printed on the line beside
the name of her mother.

Amedeo Perlo.

40

Frieda sits with her feet propped on the edge of the coffee table. She is wearing the low peep-toe wedges I was drooling over last weekend at Nordstrom. She is always wearing something I would buy. I mention the shoes. She asks me about how the semester is going. I ask her about her new house on the river—she bought it to restore with her new husband. She says she's too old to have kids at this point. She is my oldest friend. It's kind of pathetic to think of her as a friend, since we've paid her God knows how much money to talk to me for the past twelve years, but I do get the feeling she actually cares about me.

How's it been being home?

I mean, I wish I was in Mexico. I laugh. She nods in agreement. *No, I mean it's fine. I've seen some friends, caught up on sleep, you know. Lazy spring break.*

How is it with Gary?

Fine. It is fine. It's not great; it's not terrible. It has been largely unremarkable. We haven't fought; we've gone out to dinner a few times. *I mean, he's not off this week. He's at work most of the time.*

Is it good to be with him?

I look at the painting of the beach behind her desk. I love this painting—the way the movement of the waves is captured using pinks and oranges. The sunset, the small people right at the edge of the frame. She incorporated it a few years ago—

it's an original by a lady from Switzerland. It had to have cost her a fortune. I'm glad she's using the money she makes off of me to buy good art. I try to think through what the answer is. She has taught me to think before speaking, and I find it's helped me in more ways than just these meetings.

I feel sad around him. I don't know if I get sad, or if he's sad and I sense that. I don't feel angry at all anymore really. He annoys me, and it annoys me that we don't really talk, but I think at this point that's my fault as much as his. It's comfortable to be home, but it's like . . .

What is it like? It's like realizing what *The Giving Tree* was always about. It's like returning to the fairgrounds when the tents have been packed. It's like palettes of blue and purple without any yellow.

It's been melancholy for so long, and it takes being away to see it for what it is.

Frieda shifts, and I can't tell what's in her eyes behind the reflection off her glasses.

━

They waited in front of the door, and Jill fingered the locket mindlessly. She knocked once more, and a woman's voice came from somewhere inside, above.

Sophia pulled the door open and smiled affectionately. "Jill! Buona sera. Who is this?"

"This is my dad. Gary. Dad, Sophia." They shook hands.

"Va bene," she said, and Jill searched her face for knowledge. "Come in."

She led them up the staircase in the courtyard to the top-most floor. Pounding on his door, she said, "Brother! You have company."

In that moment, when there was still time, she felt the urge to run. She looked at her dad—his face was set to the door, wait-ing. Amedeo appeared.

"Jillian, I am—" his words fell off the edge of the cliff, and he stared at Gary. "Buona sera, stranger."

"I'm not a stranger, Amedeo." The men nodded at one another in a symbol of agreement of understanding.

Watching the ribbons linking their eyes, Jill didn't breathe or move. It was one of the rare instants when the timing of things from far corners of life converge in a single point, pulsat-ing with the marrow and meaning of the time. She was vaguely aware of Sophia's warm body behind her.

"Indeed not." Amedeo's eyes grew glassy, and he looked down to the tiles on the floor. He shifted his stance toward Jill.

"My darling," he said. He stared at her with feeling that seemed to drown him, placing his hands on her cheeks, lifting her chin as if she was a child. "I did not ever think I would know my daughter. And one day I am walking through the city where I have always lived, a city full of memories that have brought me both joy and sadness. You are standing there, lost," he laughed, "pick-pocketed! And I think I see Lily, only taller and with skin not so fair. I thought my mind was tricking me—do you remember?"

She nodded.

"And I think for weeks that it is a joke from heaven—until you tell me about your mother, that day on the porch. It couldn't be, and yet, so it was." His words were like a scalding pen, writing into her skin. He turned toward Gary. "Thank you."

Gary nodded, smiling slightly with a corner of his mouth, his expression inscrutable.

"Will you come inside?" Amedeo asked. "We have many things that need to be said."

Following him into the apartment, they walked toward the sitting room. Jill and Gary sat on opposite ends of a sofa, and Amedeo sat in a chair facing them. Sophia brought out a bottle of red wine and three glasses, gave them to her brother, and exited, kissing Jill on the head on her way out.

"I should tell you, Amedeo," Gary began, "that I've told her everything I know. Many of the details she read firsthand from Lily's journal, but only this evening we put all the pieces together. I had no idea Jill had met you here."

Nodding, Amedeo poured the wine and passed glasses to his guests. "Jillian, look at me."

She obeyed.

"Forgive me. I have only two regrets, one is in not raising you. I am sorry. I want to explain some things. Listen to me." He dove into the story with the same fervor Gary had, unleashing a deluge of information about the months he spent getting to know Lily.

"We fell in love. You have read of this in the journal, I suppose." She nodded. "The days I spent with Lily were the best of my life, and from the time we first went for dinner I begged her to stay with me, here, forever. She considered it, I know, but Jodie was very important for her. She felt it was her responsibility to take care of her sister, although I always thought it was probably the other way around. She also knew it was expected for me to marry Gabriella, and when my mother saw me falling in love with your mother, she was furious. Lily was not Catholic, not Italian, not Sienese, not many things my mother thought to be important, though I did not. When she met you, just a few months ago, she knew at once who you were. You are the image of Lily."

As he spoke, he looked at Jill, at Gary, cast his eyes around the room, as if looking for the presence of Lily herself. It was as if he were electrified. His audience was still, silent.

"I explained it once to Lily because she knew my mother acted cold, and this affected her. I think she felt as if she was a problem in the family—causing pain for my mother, for Gabriella. I sensed these things plagued her mind. I tried to say it wasn't the truth." He shook his head, wrought. Jill was fascinated, mesmerized by the story of the two men who had claimed to be her father, swimming in the ocean of meaning between them, strangely calm, soaring like a pelican just over the top of the water.

"The last time I ever saw her was Christmas Eve, the evening before she received the news that you had been in the accident." He flicked his head to Gary. "I remember this night very clearly. She had spent the day in Verona. We walked all over the city and counted the number of white lights over the streets. I begged her to marry me, and finally she agreed. I believed that night that she had to stay—she could not have left me for anything." He paused, sipping the wine. The story Amedeo was spinning wrapped her in a bind. He drained his reservoir as her father had done, after a burden that had been building for years.

"It is the way I will always remember her," he whispered. "I was at the vineyard on Christmas Day. That night, I came to her apartment with her gift and rang, but she was already gone. Her roommates told me what happened. I tried to call, to write. I thought of flying there, but decided to give it time. This is my second regret, one of an old man, greater than a hundred regrets of another," he said, almost to himself. "I did not go, I waited, and in a few weeks I got the letter she wrote. She told me she did not think she could return, that she was getting married. And she told me about you." He was crying; Jill knew from the two streaks that ran the length of his cheeks, though his voice didn't waver and the story did not slow.

"Why wouldn't you come?" Her throat felt dry when she spoke. She shook her head. "I don't understand why you never came."

He sat forward in his chair, he wanted to touch her, but they were seated too far apart. In his eyes was a darkness of apology. She felt her eyes filling with tears. "I don't . . ." he swallowed. Put his forehead in his hands, pressed his fingers into his thick, gray hair. His knuckles were the color of potatoes. He looked up again, but his head stayed low. "I thought it was better. For her, for you. In her letter this is what she wanted—to marry Gary and stay. I was undone; I could not believe I would have a child. I wrote to her and asked her to reconsider; I told her I would always love her. She never responded to me. I was young. I thought it was best for her, though I know now the error. This is a common mistake of youth—making some decision, and believing one's convictions must be a stake in the ground. From a place of arrogance, mislaid confidence, it is erroneous to believe our self-proclaimed verdicts cannot be revisited, evaluated again. And when I was finally able to look back and admit I was wrong, it was too late. She may have been dead by then."

He looked to Gary, who was still. It was a strange, palpable presence in the room—the presence of truth, the weight of a affliction released. "She sent me a photo of the three of you about a year after. You had moved to Washington. That was the last communication I received. In time I married Gabriella; she was a good woman, and I grew to love her. We have Dovio, my life, and when Gabriella was gone, I realized how I had come to love her more than I ever thought I could. But always I have loved Lily. I have prayed every day since I opened her letter that one day I would meet you."

Amedeo stood and walked to a desk in the corner of the room. Jill watched as he pulled a small drawer open and removed a wooden picture frame. He brought it to her. There were two picture openings. In one side was a picture of Lily, Gary, and a dark-haired infant. Jill. On the other side, a blurry black and white photograph of a young Lily standing under the arm of an Amedeo who looked much the same.

"Did you know she had died?" Jill said.

"When I met you, like I said before, you look so much like her. You told me then that you had lost your mother. When you said that to me, I think I knew. That night, as I could not let go of the image of you in the market, it was as if some spirit was whispering the truth. It was when you said her name to me later that I knew the woman I had loved was dead.

"But you—having you here was like finding this lost piece of myself. Sophia said, when you came for dinner, how you looked like someone she knew. I have already mourned, long ago, for my lost Lily." He turned to Gary now, who had been silent. "We have many things in common."

He nodded.

"So all the truth is in the light now," Amedeo said with finality.

There was silence, and Jill didn't know where to look.

"You should know," Gary said, surprising Jill with the sound of his voice. When she looked at him, he was looking at Amedeo. "She loved you. She always loved you." Then he turned to his daughter. "I'm so sorry. We didn't know what to do back then; we were kids. It's not an excuse, it's just what it was."

She looked at him for a long moment, fearless and directly into his calculating eyes. Then to Amedeo, whose face was open and easy like the hills outside the stone walls. Her fathers. So different in quality, and yet so tragically identical.

Suddenly an emotion overwhelmed her, abrupt and clear, and she gasped, sucking in a kind of sob.

"Okay."

She looked between them, back and forth, absorbing all the fear and age displayed in their faces. The triangle of space between them of fathomless depth lay dark.

"I have a charcoal for you," she said, facing Amedeo. "Of the dinner outside—the first time I ate with you."

He laughed, the familiar one she loved to hear. "I have one already. The one you named Lost Lily. Since it didn't win any prizes, I can keep it. If you'll let me."

On Christmas they went to mass in a small, grand, tucked away cathedral. Above Jill's pew was a painting of the Virgin Mary holding her son, a young mother looking fondly into the face of the miraculous infant God. Jill imagined Lily observing them with that same tenderness, looking down into the church, at her family seated in a line, refined into something else entirely by the very fact of her leaving them. With a lifetime separating them, in the same, mysterious city under the wide open sky, the stone hearts of a mother and daughter had softened to flesh.

Acknowledgements

Thanks are due to a litany of friends and colleagues: to Jessamyn Kirkwood and Joan Mitchell for editing the entire text with the precision and frankness required to make the story just right, and for their extraordinary grace and patience so I didn't lose heart. To early readers, Emily Disney, Allison Raney, Jean Waugh, Hannah Adams. To Kristen Freeman, for capturing the beauty of Siena in watercolor for the cover, and to Kelly Whitener for a painstaking attention to detail and perfection, assuring the cover design was perfect and true to the heart of the story. To Jody Shaw for printing draft after draft and hardly charging me a penny. To Ned Erickson for guiding me through the brambles of self-publication. To Lisa Parnell, for excellent formatting, and to Karen Cole for meticulous copyediting. To Teri Brennan, Inman Majors and Joan Frederick, who taught me to be a reader first, instructed the teachable parts of the craft of writing, and infused me with the courage I needed to keep at it. To my family for believing me to be a writer. To my dear, old friend, Kaili Emmrich, for being my tireless, courageous and loving travel companion in our own time in the walled city. And lastly, to my husband Mark, for giving me the writing desk as a wedding gift, for putting up with the endless number of hours I spend typing away at it, and for loving the quirkiest parts of me which allow me to see the world in words, sentences and stories. This book is for all of you, and I thank you.

Made in the USA
Middletown, DE
18 August 2015